The Mammoth Book of
SHORT EROTIC NOVELS

The Mammoth Book of

SHORT EROTIC NOVELS

Edited by
Maxim Jakubowski and
Michael Hemmingson

CARROLL & GRAF PUBLISHERS, INC.
New York

Carroll & Graf Publishers, Inc.
19 West 21st Street
New York
NY 10010-6805

First published in the UK by Robinson Publishing 2000

First Carroll & Graf edition 2000

ISBN 0-7394-0872-0

Printed and bound in the USA

CONTENTS

ACKNOWLEDGMENTS

NIGHT MOVES by Michael Perkins, copyright © 2000 by Michael Perkins. Printed by permission of the author.

HOTEL ROOM FUCK by Maxim Jakubowski, copyright © 2000 by Maxim Jakubowski. Printed by permission of the author.

SPANKING THE MAID by Robert Coover, copyright © 1982 by Robert Coover. Reprinted by permission of Grove/Atlantic and the author's agent, George Borchardt, Inc.

LAIR OF THE RED WITCH by O'Neil De Noux, copyright © 2000 by O'Neil De Noux. Printed by permission of the author.

DE SADE'S LAST STAND by William T. Vollmann, copyright © 1992 by William T. Vollmann. Reprinted by permission of the author and Grove/Atlantic. Originally appeared in *Esquire*, an abbreviated version of 'More Benadryl, Whined the Journalist' from *The Butterfly Stories*.

SPEAKING PARTS by M. Christian, copyright © 2000 by M. Christian. Printed by permission of the author.

INTRODUCTION

The short novel, the novella, the long story – call it what you will – is a tricky art form, especially for writers who write for publication, rather than self-esteem. While this literary form is considered (especially in mainland Europe) just that – an art form to be mastered – the situation in Britain and America, where commercial considerations dictate much of what is published, is more problematic.

Not long enough for solo book publication, too long for inclusion in magazines or anthologies: these are some of the obstacles the novella finds in its way.

However, the short novel is also the perfect form for literary erotica, allowing writers to develop their characters to greater depth beyond the gymnastics or hydraulics of the sexual act in all its myriad varieties. Both the editors of this anthology modestly claim to have, in the past, written some of their best erotic work at such length and this has been recognized by critics. We proudly refer you to MJ's "The Map of the Pain" or "The State of Montana" or MH's "The Naughty Yard" or "The Dress", as satisfying examples (available in previous Mammoth Books of Erotica anthologies or in single volumes).

The contributions we have had from some of the best writers of erotica currently practising the art, which we include in the present volume, prove the point: the reader isn't faced with a whole book of sensual forays, yet the reader also stays around longer, gets more involved, than they would with just a few pages of titillating prose and a "tableau vivant" in the form of a story.

We are confident that, once again in this series, you will be aroused, piqued, fascinated – hypnotized, even – by the halls of sexual mirrors our writers have conjured here. Some stories sound disturbingly autobiographical; others are fantastical; some are meditative; others full of action.

Putting this anthology together, with e-mail messages spanning the globe, was a joy and, at times, a pain, as so few writers could be included without fear of turning this mammoth into an unwieldy and too heavy and expensive volume, and many a good story could not be used. It's all part of the process. But, at the end of the day, this is a damn good book of erotic literature – there's definitely some sexy, thoughtful, funny and sad stuff going on in these pages: all the complexities and wonders of human sexuality. So, buy copies for friends, give them out as gifts, slip them mysteriously under the bed or on the bookshelves of those you are feeling rather amorous about . . .

Maxim Jakubowski & Michael Hemmingson,
London & San Diego, 1999

NIGHT MOVES

Michael Perkins

"Swing: to shift or fluctuate from one condition, form, position, or object of attention or favor to another."
Webster's New Collegiate Dictionary

Midnight in the Garden

Bruise on her breast,
   not my fingertips,
Gloss on her lips,
   not licked from me.
Hair a tangled halo
   I hadn't mussed,
Eyes swollen and wanton,
   not turned my way,
Her smell of lust
   stronger than
     sharpest memory;
I could not swallow,
   I could barely see.
This was what it meant:
   This was being free.

Part One

East Hampton, 1976

ONE

Mora and I had been in East Hampton for two days waiting for the sun to come out when we ran into Charles and Vy. It was July, the Bicentennial Summer, and we were on our first vacation as man and wife. We'd accepted a friend's invitation to spend a few days at his beach house, but the afternoon we arrived the rains came, and lasted through the following day. We were grumpy stuck inside. We wanted to lie naked in the sun.

The next morning, the sun made its appearance, and it was windy when we walked to the beach. We had the ocean to ourselves, but it was too rough to go in. Empty blue sky, empty white beach, empty green ocean. The freckled, lively children further down the beach who were our only neighbors had to be content with building sandcastles. Mora read a novel and wrote in her journal, frowning and chewing her lip. It was her way of arguing with me without saying anything, and also of arguing with herself instead of with me. I shrugged at her silence and went for a long run on the wet hard sand, where high rolling breakers left thick clumps of seaweed, but I couldn't outrace my frustration.

By evening, we were speaking only when spoken to and being scrupulously polite with each other. We brooded in marital silence over cold gin at Peaches, a restaurant in Bridgehampton where summer people went that year for a hamburger or a salad before rushing off to the parties that seem to run around the clock, summer weekends on the South Fork. When there was a breeze from the ocean, the leaves of the giant maples on the sidewalk outside scratched softly at the window screens. On each small round table a slender mirrored vase held a single rose. It should have been romantic; couples all around us thought it was.

I reached for her hand and she put it quickly in her lap.

"What the hell is wrong with us?"

She sighed and I knew she was grateful that I'd spoken first. The answer was sitting on her tongue. "It's marriage. Holy Wedlock."

"You want to expand on that?"

"I don't have to. We both know it's that – why it's that."

So we did. Jealousy. Possessiveness. Insecurity. Fights, screaming, threats, feeling trapped. And keeping score – that was the worst. That computerized reference file constantly added to of insult and injury, a never-to-be-erased tape of gritty misery.

"OK. What do we do now? Throw in the towel because the honeymoon isn't working out?"

"I don't know, Richard. I just think being unhappy is a waste of time."

"Agreed."

We stared at each other. Neither of us really *wanted* to be married. Not really. We were romantics, we weren't interested in snug harbors – when we spoke of love, we meant passion. Rub us together and you got fire.

From the time I first saw Mora I was under a spell. I know some magic was involved, because I was on the defensive after the break-up of a relationship I'd taken more seriously than I should have. The home truths I'd learned about my needs were so lacerating, I vowed eternal celibacy.

For six months I'd been living like a monk in a basement sublet in Brooklyn Heights. It had a single bed I used and a kitchen I didn't, and little else except for a color television set and a well-equipped darkroom. No pictures on the walls, no plants to be watered, no cats to wrap themselves around my ankles when I came back late from my studio on West 17th Street.

It was a low, unhappy period in my life. I told myself I'd snap out of my funk any day, but the truth was I was drifting, getting by in a low key. I had let being in love become a way of defining myself. Alone, I didn't know who I was.

Mora came along just when I was beginning to spend so much time in Village bars that the bartenders knew my name, occupation, and marital status. One of them was an actor I had used as a model. He knew a woman who needed some pictures.

"She comes in here all the time. Lives just around the block. She's real intense."

"You don't understand. I take pictures of products, not egos. I don't do portfolio glossies and I don't want to meet any women."

It was noisy in the bar, right before dinner. Maybe he didn't hear me.

"She's a lot of fun. Just let me tell her you'll do it."

A few days later she showed up at my studio. I was fussing with lights around an ornate, old-fashioned bathtub with claw feet. Later in the day, the agency that had had it delivered to me would come to fill it with towels – I did catalogs, too.

I earn a living with a 35 millimeter camera because when I was a boy I picked up a Brownie for the first time and discovered my third eye. I have a gift for seeing with the camera lens what the naked eye misses, moments when formlessness becomes form. When Mora walked through the door, it was one of those moments.

I stared. She stared back. She was so small I could have

fitted her in a large camera bag. The top of her head came to the middle of my chest. Her curly hair was short but not mannishly cut, a chestnut brown that smelled like oranges.

Her white skirt showed off her slender legs, and she had thrown a linen jacket over her thin shoulders. She wore a *figa* – a small, fist-shaped Brazilian good luck charm – on a gold chain around her throat, but no earrings, no bracelets: only a trace of lip gloss. Her tan was so deep, she looked like she'd just stepped off a plane from someplace south.

I looked away first, after seeing the mischief in her calm green eyes. "Ever modeled before?"

She shook her head. "Only for my boyfriend's Polaroid, but the pictures always came out blurry – you know how those things go. He found it hard to concentrate." She suppressed a smirk.

"You don't say."

We were grinning at each other. Hers was impish, provocative. "Have you acted before?"

"Never, if you don't count Gilbert and Sullivan in grade school. But I've tried everything else and all my friends are in theater this year, so I thought, why not?"

Her self-confidence was dazzling. It came out in the standard portrait shots I did of her. Her dark features were wonderfully mobile, and she kept that glint in her eye. After the shooting, I cancelled my appointment with the bath towel people and took Mora to dinner.

And so we met. And we made love. She was just as bold in bed as she was before the camera, very passionate and open; her energy was astonishing. A month later, I left Brooklyn and moved into her second floor apartment on Cornelia Street. Things happened fast around Mora.

We lived together for a year, more happily than I'd thought possible. Business went so well in the studio, I hired a part-time assistant; Mora didn't have to work because her father owned a shopping mall and sent her a monthly allowance. When she decided she had no acting talent, she got into politics for a while, and then she just started spending all her time at home cooking exotic meals; she told her friends she was too happy to concentrate on anything more.

What happened was that we got cocky. All the traditional signals had gone off at the right times, and we started thinking we were different, that we could nail our feelings to the wall where they would never change. One thing led to another and, before we knew it, we were standing in City Hall, saying our vows. Afterwards, we threw a party for our friends, and then when the shock wore off and we realized what we'd done, we stayed drunk for two days and had a terrific fight so we could squeeze the last ounce of passion out of making up.

Why did we do it? Talk to anyone: marriage is like getting a diploma in living as an adult. The license certifies a certain wilful madness for, as we found out, everyone lies about marriage, especially its kinkier aspects: the manacles of words at each wrist and ankle, the eager vows that become expectations. The endless expectations.

We were on our third round of drinks and Mora was snapping her foot back and forth restlessly and staring off into space. I looked around for a waiter so we could order dinner, when I saw Charles Venturi sit down at a table near us. He was the last person I expected to see. He'd been off in Europe for years – since the early seventies, when we had served time together on the same slick magazines. We were never close, but I had sought him out and spent time with him because he fascinated me.

Sitting across from him was a tall blonde woman in her late twenties who had lovely cheekbones, hollow cheeks, and long delicate wrists, the supple carriage of a dancer, the long neck and waist of a model. She was beautiful in the wiredrawn way that well-bred New England daughters who sing Bach on Sundays can be.

"Look over there," I said to Mora. "That's Charles Venturi."

"They're a handsome couple," she admitted. "They look interesting."

She followed me over to their table.

"Charles! How long have you been back?"

We shook hands and I introduced Mora. The woman with him was Vy Cameron. In the years I'd known Charles, I hadn't seen him with a woman who looked so capable of keeping up. I liked the determination I saw in her pale gray-blue eyes, and the demure way she shook my hand, fingers wrapped lightly around fingers. A lady, with an agenda.

The two of us exchanged the usual inane comments that pass for casual conversation in the Hamptons, but we kept our eyes on our mates. Mora and Charles were hitting it off. While he talked, she was giving him what I think of as the Treatment. The Treatment consists of her undivided attention, of long, smouldering looks, and sudden, surprising smiles that promise a lot more than understanding. It's flattering, and nearly always effective.

After a while, I interrupted them. I saw a chance to change the weather between Mora and I, the possibility of sun behind the clouds.

"Let's get together. Where are you staying?"

"With the man Vy lives with, Maurice."

I raised my eyebrows, and he looked unexpectedly sheepish for a minute.

"It's a long story. I'll save it for later." He winked.

He suggested that we meet on the beach next day. We talked about time and place – he knew a beach where it was possible to go without bathing suits – and returned to our table.

In bed later, Mora asked me to tell her more about him. I was suspicious of her interest and reluctant at first, but she cuddled up to me and I starting stroking her and talking. In the dark, her emerald eyes glowed like a cat's. A cat in heat.

TWO

When it comes to women, Charles has a gift. He hears what they're saying between the lines. They find him inordinately seductive, although there isn't much about his appearance other than his provocative black eyes that would suggest such powers of attraction. But he's solid and dark and intense.

His restless energy is the source of his charisma. His hunger for the varieties of experience. He grew up fast on the Italian Catholic streets of East Harlem, where he learned to see the world as a stage, and his part in it as an infinitely adaptable player. He was attracted to both the smell of incense and the smell of sex, the sharp aroma of men and the secret fragrance of women. By the age of forty his resume read like eight lives had been crammed into one. He'd been a translator, a student of Gurdjieffian teachings, a psychotherapist, a librarian, an editor of men's magazines – even a novice with shaved head in a Zen monastery. His appetite for biography was prodigious.

All this time, he was writing furiously; when he published the books that established his reputation, his radical ideas about sexuality were treated respectfully by slick national magazines, a few maverick critics, and even one incautious Nobel Laureate. It didn't hurt that he was called a pornographer by a few midwestern district attorneys who had no idea what he was talking about.

He became a cult figure in the sexual underground. When he stepped out of the shadows into the spotlight, he represented the forces of eros to the media. There was applause. He titillated people. Amused them. Sometimes even succeeded in outraging them. Then, one week, he was on the cover of *Life* magazine wearing eye shadow and mascara and grinning about the confusion of sex roles he embodied. It seems improbable, but it was the sixties. The pot boiled, and he was there to take his turn stirring it, along with student radicals, Black Panthers, Yippies, Weather People, and self-destructive rock stars. The seventies were a let-down for him. I think he went off to Europe primarily because he was bored and he wanted to see if he'd been missing anything there.

When we met him on the beach, next day, the sky was cobalt blue, and the ocean was calm as bathwater. Mora smiled at the sun. She was happy again. We found Charles sitting cross-legged on an orange beach towel at the foot of a golden dune, brown arms on his knees, gazing out over the rippling water. A lone sail boat patrolled the line of the horizon. I was disappointed when I didn't see Vy.

"Thank God for the sun," I said.

"That's a big ocean. I'm glad to be on this side of it."

I unfurled our blue chintz beach spread and Mora helped me to anchor it with our sandals. We took off our jeans and sprawled next to Charles. Mora began rubbing lotion into her legs.

"Where's Vy?"

"She had to play hostess for a while."

"For Maurice?"

He nodded. "She won't be long."

"You share her with him?"

He shrugged. "That's how it is."

"How do you feel about that?"

"He loves her in his own way, I guess." A faint smile played on his lips as he studied Mora. Her tight smooth flesh overwhelmed the white terrycloth bikini she wore.

"You're so casual," she said. "Have you known her long?"

"I met her when I got back from Europe. Some friends threw a welcome home party, and she was there. As soon as I saw her, I knew I was in trouble."

"Trouble?"

"I was turned on, and I knew we wouldn't be any good for each other – but I had to have her. I met my match."

"I want to hear more. All about her," Mora said. Erotic style fascinated her, and any woman who could live with two men deserved a great deal of study.

"What does she do?"

"She's a dancer. But she has many talents."

"You can tell us more than that."

"Well, you can ask her yourself," Charles said, pointing to a tall, erect figure walking down the beach toward us. Vy wore a Japanese kimono and clogs, and her blonde hair was piled on top of her head. We could hear her singing in a high, lilting voice when she got closer, but the words were lost in the muffled slap of the surf on the beach.

Her first words were breathless, almost hoarse. "I'm so fucking dry I'm going to have to do a little deep throat to get my voice in the right register. I'm a tenor in the heat." She patted her chest. Her palpitating heart.

Mora and I looked at each other. What heat?

"It's my coloring," Vy said. "I'm more susceptible than most people. I don't like the sun. It causes cancer and it dries up the skin."

"I worship the sun," Mora said.

"Well, nothing could have seduced me down to this beach but the thought of you three doing something delicious without me." She was overwhelming, regal. In supplication I opened the bottle of cold Retsina we'd brought, filled four paper cups, and handed one to her. Charles lit a joint and passed it around.

She settled herself on our blue spread. Mora watched her with narrowed, admiring eyes. "Now tell me what I've missed. Have you been talking about me? I hope so – it would make me feel so good. All Maurice talks about any more is deals. Buy that, sell this. Sometimes when he refers to me it's in the same tone of voice, and I feel like a jewel he's tucked into his safety deposit box."

She leaned back on her elbows, her gaze fixed on my face, the slender joint stuck in the corner of her mouth.

"I don't own a safety deposit box," Charles said.

"I don't own a bathing suit," she purred in a cool, milky voice, removing her kimono with ladylike panache. Her plump, berry-tipped breasts, flat white belly and wide hips were exquisite. Her skin blushed that faint pinkish hue found in the center of certain roses. In the cool salt breeze, she trembled almost imperceptibly, like a rabbit in a field of shotgun fire. I felt a sudden stabbing urge to take her in the crook of my arm and press my fingers gently in the wet hollows of her throat, her elbows, her knees; my groin was beating like a second heart.

Mora wasn't to be upstaged. She untied her bikini top with what was meant to be a casual gesture, but I knew that she was tense. Her normally puffy copper nipples were tight and hopeful.

Charles grinned happily at the women. "We are fortunate

men, Richard." Then he told us a story that set the mood for what happened later as much as the hot sun or the empty beach.

"I was walking on the beach this morning. I didn't know where I was going, just walking and thinking and looking for driftwood. There were no people around, so I took off my trunks. It was about ten o'clock when I realized I was walking through a gay beach. I almost stepped on a man who was lying in the surf, masturbating. Something in his face made me stop – whether it was pleasure or invitation, I don't know. I went down on him, and for five minutes, maybe ten – it seemed like hours – we were as close as any two bodies can get. Such an absolute passion – and it happened with a total stranger! Afterwards we didn't say anything, but neither of us were looking for romance."

"I *love* it," Mora exclaimed excitedly, clapping her hands. Her cat eyes flashed. "Anonymous sex, no attachments. It's too bad heterosexuals can't be so honest. I see so many people I'm turned on to, yet I don't want to talk to them. I want to *take* them. Just make love. Between men, it's better. You both know what you want, without any illusions . . ." She was breathless.

Vy crossed her arms and cupped her hands over her breasts protectively, as if guarding her heart. She closed her eyes and sat quite straight and still. "All there is is romance. The rest is technique," she said, without opening her eyes. "I've had expert lovers who couldn't get me wet because they didn't know any of the magic words."

She opened her eyes and focused on Charles. He stretched out casually next to her, propped on his elbows, looking out to sea. Something seemed to draw him: he started crawling crab-like on his belly out to the water, leaving a broad, wrinkled trail in the tawny sand.

We all stared after him. Mora sighed wistfully. "I should have been a man. You just don't know how much I fantasize about certain . . . situations."

"Well, my dear," Vy said coldly. "We all have to learn the hard way."

"I guess it's something I want to learn," Mora replied, unwilling to give Vy the last word. "Anyway, Charles says you're a part of the world I want to learn about."

The sharks might have envied Vy's smile. "I keep myself entertained."

The static between them made me decide to follow Charles into the surf. I crawled for a bit, felt silly, and walked the rest of the way. He was lying on his back, letting the sudsy foam wash over his body, decorating his hirsute chest and legs with green seaweed and fragments of sea shells. Looking at him lying there, I thought of the man in his story.

"Let the two of them work it out," he said. "We're just in the way."

"I'm grateful that Mora's found someone to talk to. She's been in a funk."

"Tell me about her."

"What you see is Mora. She hides nothing. She's an all-or-nothing type. Black or white, no grays."

"Get out of her way when she decides what she wants."

"Exactly. She wants my soul. She gets jealous if I talk with a bank clerk too long. I try to tell her that I'm not interested in anyone but her, but she sees what she wants to see. Marriage has done us in, I think."

He shook his head sympathetically. "But before you got married – how were things?"

"God was in his heaven and all was right with the world . . . You know what it's like."

"So why did you do it?"

"Get married? I guess I'd have to plead insanity. I knew better, and I did it anyway."

He snorted in recognition. "I'm sorry, but I think you're taking it all too seriously, Richard. Loosen up."

"How do I do that?"

"Stop arguing. Stop anticipating."

"Is that what you learned in Europe?"

He laughed this time. His eyes lit up with mirth. There was a patch of wet sand on his cheek. "What do you know about me, Richard?"

"Not much. But I always thought you knew about women."

"Then let me tell you something: Mora wants more than marriage can offer her right now. She wants to play, it's as simple as that."

"Simple?" I couldn't swallow that.

"Look, you're on vacation. Try something different."

He winked amiably, walked into the water to clean the sand off, and sprinted up the beach. I knew what he meant because the idea had been lurking in the back of my mind since we'd met at Peaches; but I knew that I didn't want anyone but me making love to Mora.

I knew she'd had lovers in the past, but they were shadows framed by shadows. Charles was sharp and immediate. Yet I had to admit to myself that the image of the four of us together on a bed heated my imagination – that perhaps my curiosity was stronger than my apprehension.

I wanted Vy, but I tried to shake my head clear of her as I walked back up the beach to our blue chintz island in the sand. Sleeping with other people when you're married leads to trouble, I told myself.

I should have listened, but of course I didn't.

Indelible image: Charles was standing in a half crouch, swimming briefs kicked aside, feet planted heavily in the sand, calves bulging, body glistening, while Vy's blonde head bobbed vigorously between his thighs. Mora was leaning back, breasts free, snapping pictures with my Pentax. In her hands it was almost a sexual instrument. I threw up my hands in surprise and she swung around to take my picture. Far down the empty beach, a boy was throwing rocks into the surf, but he was a speck in the distance.

Snap. There are glimpses, in a late afternoon sun, of the future. They come unbidden, and they enter the heart and lodge there. The dark fuzz on Charles's thighs; the shuddering in Vy's back as she pulled him into her; Mora's obvious arousal as she clicked the shutter. There was an excitement in the air – of people about to experiment with their lives – that wasn't to be dissipated by the salt breeze.

"It feels right," Mora said brightly when she handed me the camera.

"Does it?" I was doubtful. I had fists at the ends of my arms, fingers closed tightly into my palms. My tongue fluttered helplessly, like the tail of an animal I'd gotten stuck in my throat.

Vy leaned back from Charles, licked her lips delicately, and lighted a black Sobranie cigarette. She winked at me. Charles sat in the sand, looking seductive. I thought I could hear the wheels turning in his head.

"Why don't we have dinner together? We can whip up something easy at Maurice's, and let the evening take care of itself."

THREE

Vy drove off in a blue Mercedes. She blew a kiss through the window and scrunched gravel as she left the beach parking lot. The gesture seemed to enlarge her: fingertips to her lips, the wide unexpected smile, the pressure of her foot on the gas pedal. We followed in Charles's Clunker Deluxe. " 'The station car'," he joked. "That's what they call vintage Detroit iron out here. It's what I can afford. Maurice watches that Mercedes like a hawk. I think he has the soul of a chauffeur."

I shrugged. "Shoulders were made for burdens."

I sat on the outside and Mora was squeezed between us. We dripped sand on the floor of the car and the hot vinyl seats stuck to our thighs. Despite the heat, Mora's skin was cool and moist.

"You're a Scorpio sandwich," Charles said to her, reminding me that we shared our birthdays. Then he touched her.

We were heading down the Montauk Highway and had slowed on the outskirts of Amagansett, where a train had derailed. The road swarmed with police, gawkers, and dazed passengers. Charles lifted his hand from the steering wheel and pressed the back of it against Mora's breasts. Lightly. It was the simplest, most casual of gestures, so natural I felt like I was stealing something from them because I stared. I looked quickly out the window, feeling embarrassed – and angry at myself for feeling that way.

Mora giggled and clapped a hand over her mouth. She put her left hand on Charles's knee and her right hand on my thigh and stroked us both. Her face was red, even through her tan.

I don't know how to explain it, but I was as shocked as if Charles had stroked *my* nipples. Those weren't *his* breasts, they were mine. Mine. But I could tell by the way Mora was breathing that she didn't agree that marriage had made me a man of property.

We passed dunes tufted with islands of waving sword grass, rows of beach cottages, the potato fields of July, and then I saw the windmill in East Hampton. We drove through the town's sparkling center. In the late afternoon light it was still, unreal, a postcard.

"An extraordinary afternoon," I said in the silence. There was more I wanted to say, but I couldn't find the words. Mora's fingers were having the desired effect on me.

I was confused by the male complicity I felt with Charles. When he touched Mora, she became a strange woman we'd picked up together. From then on, two plus one equaled more than three.

FOUR

However shocking or perhaps just plain perverse it may seem, when I saw Mora naked with Charles and Vy it wasn't jealousy that I felt. It was lust that grew in my belly, like a sapling putting down roots. I knew the voyeur's stunned delight in achieving erotic perspective. Our nakedness created the illusion that we had entered another dimension, a counter world of the id, where our apprehensions were removed with our clothes and past and future ceased to exist.

Vy's bedroom was white, but by no means chaste. White walls, white sheepskin rugs on the parquet floor, huge antique mirrors, white vases filled with daisies, and a platform bed on which the three of them sat as if on a tongue sticking out of fluffy clouds, for the silk spread was white, but the sheets underneath were crimson. Satin.

I sauntered around the room, determined to be casual, sipping my brandy and looking at things, conscious of the cool night air on my bare skin. I studied four large framed photographs of Vy on one gleaming white wall, two of them by young fashion photographers I knew. In the portraits, she was elegant and stylish, with formidable cheekbones and a frosty gaze; I didn't see in them the woman I'd watched kneeling before Charles on the beach.

When I walked over to the bed, Mora and Vy were lying on each side of Charles like houris, watching him stroke himself. His tongue moistened his dry lips, and his strong hands moved slowly from his knees up his firm thighs to his rounded belly. His breath came in shallow gasps. His chest swelled and his nipples pointed. I shivered. We would play a game, a sexual Simon says.

We drew matches and Charles won. He asked that Vy and Mora stretch out between his thighs and handed me the Polaroid. I was happy to hide behind it because I felt flushed and my ears were ringing.

It was the first time I'd seen Mora hesitant about love-making; her touch was tentative at first and she followed Vy's lead. Charles's swollen flesh glowed wetly in the soft light of a bedside candle. From my new perspective as voyeur, I saw that what was exciting about oral sex was not the mechanics of one person satisfying another, but the selfless art of it, the submission of ego to pleasure. The women's tongues and fingers worked gently and assiduously; Charles groaned. The phrases that broke from his lips were the mutterings of gratified desire. I waited until they had forgotten the camera before I snapped a picture.

They all blinked and looked around dazedly when the flash went off. Once again; and then it was time to draw matches. Mora's turn. I was surprised when she moved toward Vy instead of Charles, but when she touched Vy's breasts, Vy turned her long body to the side.

"Not yet," she said huskily. "Let me warm up, first."

Mora smiled as if she'd expected the rebuff, and crawled to Charles, climbing atop him, swivelling her hips to claim his hardness. The two of them flowed into each other.

For a moment then, it hurt like hell. I remembered every time Mora and I had made love, the heat and wetness, our nerves rushing to release, our ragged romantic promises, the closeness of sex during times when we couldn't even speak to each other. I was drawn to her; I handed Vy the camera and knelt beside them, kissing Mora and stroking her taut breasts, placing my fingertips on her pubic mound to feel the movement of Charles's flesh inside her, beneath the soft maidenhair.

The room melted, contracting so that only the bed existed. My hands moved over their bodies, urging them together, teaching Charles about Mora's responses, sculpting them. When the flashbulb went off, we blinked like animals in the dark.

It was Vy's turn. "*Whoo*, boy," she exclaimed. "This is most extraordinary. Hot, hot, hot."

"Tell us what you want, before things get out of hand."

"I want to take Richard into the next room."

"No pictures?"

"Just the two of us, no silly cameras."

I was more than a little frightened of Vy. Shyness, I suppose, and the fact that I was attracted to her. The room she took me to was obviously a guest room. Rattan furniture in the shadows, a colorful hand-sewn quilt on a large brass bed, moonlight making patterns on a faded Chinese rug.

We didn't make it to the bed. I reached for her but she slipped away, onto her knees, and took my flesh into her warm mouth. I thought my knees would fold, and my hands went to her shoulders for support while fire raced up and down my spine. It was over before I could take a deep breath, while my fingers were still caressing her silky hair and finding the secret places of her delicate skull.

I was shaking all over. "*Whew!*" I breathed after a moment spent looking for my head, which had shot like a rocket to the ceiling. "That was too fast."

She chuckled, licking her lips like a cat over a saucer of milk. She rose gracefully and shrugged her square shoulders into her caftan. "That calls for a drink," she said, going into the next room for the brandy.

I was aware of a steady, rhythmic thumping through the wall and wondered for a minute if she'd return. I lighted a hurricane lamp next to the bed and waited. She reappeared with the bottle and two glasses, looking younger and more vulnerable in the flickering light.

"So the doors of marriage creak open," she said.

"I think you oiled the hinges with that one."

"Well, I'm good at what I do. I enjoy the power of doing that. It wasn't until I saw men from that perspective – on my knees, in absolute control of them – that I realized they weren't omnipotent."

She was too glib; it had bothered me since our first conversation. She sensed my skepticism. Not about what she'd said, but about her sophistication in regard to swinging.

"I was born this way. No illusions. I look at things in black and white. It's like not having eyelids."

I wanted to hold her, to press my body against hers, to feel the length of her thighs on mine, but she sat away from me, smoking one of her cigarettes. Her sharp profile cut through the aromatic blue haze.

"I wish I didn't love Charles so much, that I could turn it on and off."

I lifted my glass. "Here's to marriage."

She sniffled. She was squinting and her eyes were wet, but that might have been the smoke.

"Marriage? That's for victims. I don't intend to be a victim ever again. That's why I stay with Maurice, even though I know it drives Charles crazy."

"What have you got against marriage?"

She pouted mock-dramatically.

"His name is James Lee Tait. My used-to-be. Three years of holy wedlock made a sorrowful woman of me. He promised everything – he had the gift of promise, you know? – but in the end it was the same old song and dance."

"So you divorced him."

"Not without a lot of turmoil. A woman gets attached to you creatures, and a divorce is like losing . . . your past, maybe your future."

I wanted to understand. "Do you hate him?"

"No, not really. Let's just say I envy his get-up-and-gall. I suffered over that. He's a singer, and I waited in the wings of his career and let mine slide; I had my own ambitions."

"You make marriage sound like a minefield."

"It's no picnic. It's the most dangerous relationship you can have. A contract made in hell."

"And Charles? How does he fit in?"

"He doesn't believe in marriage, and he lets me do what I want to do. We have a pact: no apologies. Jimmy was the kind of man who was always saying 'I'm sorry' while he was stepping on my feet – but I could have twisted his balls into a daisy chain. Charles, on the other hand, makes no bones about being exactly who he is, and he never apologizes. I don't expect anything from him, so I'm never disappointed."

I stretched out in the bed, thinking about marriage, and Mora and Charles in the next room.

"Sorry. I'm rattling on, and I know you're thinking about Mora. She's so restless."

I told her about my first wife, wishing that the scars were visible so I could show her. I tried to explain about Mora. "Sometimes I feel like she's only mine on loan, that nothing will ever satisfy her."

"She's vibrating like a spinning top. Nothing will slow her down; she's like a natural force. Take it from another woman."

"I love her. You love Charles. We're crazy."

"Charles says two plus two equals twelve."

"Charles is crazy."

"I know."

"But you'd rather be with him right now, wouldn't you?"

"Well? Wouldn't you rather be with Mora?"

"That's not what's happening."

"You're evading the question. I mean, what if Charles fucks her better than you ever did? He's very good."

Check. I couldn't bear any more conversation. I wanted to make love to Vy. It was the only answer I had.

"I can't," she protested when I touched her. I put my hand through the opening in her caftan onto her cool stomach. "I absolutely cannot, I'm sorry."

"I don't understand."

"Charles and I made love while you were off looking for Mora before dinner. He's big, and I'm sore. It's my background," she sighed theatrically. "Fair-skinned mothers. Delicate skin. Look here, I'll show you."

She opened the caftan and spread her white thighs. "You see the blood?"

The lips of her vulva were irritated and swollen, and there was a tiny drop of blood on her clitoris. Imagine the center of a rose with a drop of blood on a petal . . .

I found cotton and peroxide in a bathroom medicine cabinet and brought them back without looking in on Charles and Mora. I heard them talking through the closed door and I wanted to eavesdrop, but I wanted to make love to Vy more.

"Your hands are so gentle," she told me when I wiped away the drop of blood and covered her soreness with vaseline. The glistening petals of her sex opened beneath my fingers.

"I'll stop. I promise you. If it hurts, I'll stop."

She squirmed evasively when I penetrated her. I stopped, moving again only when she opened to receive me. She whispered hotly in my ear while she licked it with the point of her tongue. "I trust you. No reason, but I do. I know you'll stop – but *please* don't stop now."

I cupped the plump weight of her buttocks in my palms and let myself be swallowed by her. We got lost in the dialogue of bodies, questioning and answering, alone on a gently rolling sea in the blackest night.

She pulled a yellow popper out of the darkness and crushed it between her fingers, holding the amyl nitrate to my nose and then to her own. We both inhaled deeply and felt our hearts rush to where our genitals were, riding on the cloudy, pungent chemical high like surfers on a wave.

"*Oooo!*" she cried out, as if in a dream. I heard someone

wailing, without realizing it was me. Each wave that took us was bigger than the last, and we were no longer rocking gently but struggling together to stay afloat.

I heard tapping on the floor and looked down to see my fingers doing a fast dance on the wide boards. I was half off the bed and sweat was pouring from me. Vy's body was arched, a dying swan. There was a roaring in my ears like the ocean at the same time I heard knocking on the door, and then I hit the last, biggest wave and was dragged head over heels into shore. Vy's whole body clenched and she followed me, digging her nails into the backs of my arms. A high thin noise came from her throat.

When I opened my eyes, Charles was standing over us, naked, grinning, scratching his chest. "Birds would give up a winter's feed to hit that note," he said, while Vy shuddered and I navigated the re-entry to consciousness.

"What time is it?"

"Half past four. You two make a lot of noise."

Mora moved from the shadows to stand beside him, her hand on his shoulder. Her hair was matted and wet and she was ragged around the edges. They looked like weasels who'd been in the chicken coop. There should have been feathers hanging from their swollen satisfied mouths.

"I won't be able to explain this away tomorrow morning," Charles said. "I won't believe it. It was so incredibly high at times. So intense."

"I guess we did it after all." Mora smiled tiredly, shaking her head in happy disbelief.

"I don't know what could be bad about this," I said.

Vy sat up and stretched, pulling Charles's hand to her breast. "It was divine, and I love you all, and I don't know what to say, except that we've been very wicked."

Charles yawned and rubbed his eyes sleepily. Mora came to sit next to me on the rumpled bed that smelled of sex and poppers and cigarettes. We kissed Charles and Vy goodnight with the gentle exhaustion of sated lovers, and Mora and I curled up spoon-fashion on the bed. She was mine again, for a few hours.

Part Two

New York City, 1977

FIVE

In the pictures I developed of the four of us on the beach, our faces are aglow with anticipation and pleasure. Our shyness is not fear of each other, but of the unknown. There are no shadows under our eyes, no tightness around our mouths; no hint of desperation clouds our sunny expressions. Our discovery of adultery was almost painless – and the timing was right.

"I thought I had it figured out," Mora said when we looked at the wet proofs in my darkroom. "Love and sex and relationship. Marriage – the idea that if you want this, you can't have that – that was what was wrong with us. Then what happens? We go and break all the rules. We find out that marriage has got corners and angles we didn't know existed."

Turn around. We were friends again. The bad habits we had fallen into disappeared overnight, as quickly as rubbing condensation from a window. We were able to treat each other lovingly again. Trust reappeared. Freedom was exhilarating.

Predictably, the few friends – married couples – we told about Charles and Vy thought we'd gone off the deep end. A relationship with one other person was difficult enough, they scoffed. Three was arrogance, asking for it on the chin. None of them raised moral objections and they didn't ask how we felt: and since we knew their marriages and their reasons for being cynical, we paid no attention to them.

Months after returning from East Hampton, we received a note from Vy. She was in London.

> "Richard and Mora loves –
> Still don't know what magic you worked.
> Let's get together when I get back
> so we can find out. Kisses, Vy Cameron"

Curious, Mora called Charles – not without some trepidation, but the phone was her instrument, not mine. I got on the extension.

"Maurice took her over to meet some of his friends," Charles explained. He sounded lonely by himself in Maurice's big house, and resentful that Vy had gone off without him. "I guess there's a party circuit for septuagenarians in the countryside around London. Discreet scenes in the stately homes of England."

"That lady gets around. I wish I had her style."

"Come out and see me. We'll go for walks on the beach, and spend a lot of time in bed. Just us chickens."

"It's the middle of the week, Charles. Richard can't get away; he has shootings lined up."

"I didn't invite Richard."

She paused and looked at me. "We're a team, you know that. I wouldn't go anywhere without him."

I threw her a kiss, my hand over the receiver.

"Look, the words wedlock and hammerlock are not synonymous. They don't add up to virtue. Besides, you're not just a 'twosome', you're half of a 'foursome' – silly words, it sounds like we're talking about golf . . ."

"I'm sorry –"

"Maybe if you did some homework, since I'm not around to keep things stirred up."

"What? What kind of homework?"

"*Now* I've got your interest piqued. I'll mail you your next lesson." I heard a dry chuckle on the other end.

I broke in. "Come and see us."

"Oh. There you are, Richard. You should breathe more heavily when you're spying on people."

"Mora knew I was on the extension. I trust her, but not you. Why don't *you* come visit us?"

"No, I don't think so. I'm going to hole up out here and try to get some work done. Fasting and abstinence and hard work, that's the prescription. I'll be a different man, the next time you see me."

"Like?"

"Lean and hungry, I suppose, and head over heels in love."

"You mean because absence makes the heart grow fonder?"

He chuckled again. "Love is what I feel when I want to get laid. Abstinence, that's what makes the heart grow fonder."

He wasn't kidding about our homework. The clipping arrived in the mail two days later. He had cut it from the classified section of a sex tabloid.

The advertisement was for a private club called Plato's Retreat that had recently opened on lower Fifth Avenue.

"The first on-premise club which meets in Manhattan – which means the party's right there . . ." It mentioned facilities like whirlpool baths, disco floor, swing rooms, and free bar and buffet.

It made me think of restaurant ads for Thanksgiving and Christmas and New Year's – a meal, some hats, streamers and horns. I imagined people as lonely as forgotten uncles and single people with nowhere else to go buying some holiday companionship for a package price.

We looked at each other.

"We could go and just see what's going on," Mora said, barely concealing the excitement in her voice.

"Somehow I don't think swinging is a spectator sport, love."

"Please, Richard: let's go take a look. I'm really curious."

"I don't know if I can handle it."

"We'll stick together, I promise. Besides, there'll be a woman for every man there. What if *you* meet someone?"

"I don't know. What if I do?"

"Well, you won't turn her down, will you?"

When we called the number in the ad for information, a woman told us that Plato's Retreat was open from ten until five in the morning, and directed us to an older loft building below Madison Square Park. We stood on the broad, empty avenue opposite the building, sharing a joint and getting our nerve up. It was Saturday night, after eleven. People were arriving in taxis and entering the building. A limousine hugged the curb.

Stoned, we took a small, rattling elevator to the fifth floor and stepped off into a spartan reception area crowded with a desk and three pretty, businesslike young women wearing black Plato's Retreat T-shirts. I handed over twenty-five dollars to the one who winked at me, and we received orange membership cards with the club name on one side and a list of rules on the other.

1. Only couples or unescorted females allowed in the club.
2. No single male will be admitted without an escort.
3. If female of couple leaves the club, the male escort must accompany her.
4. No drugs or drug abuse on the premises.
5. Neither part of the couple is prostituting themselves.

Stepping through black curtains sewn with sequins, we found ourselves at the head of a long, dark corridor where shadowy half-dressed figures stood about passing joints, plastic glasses in their hands. They gave us slow, appraising looks as we brushed past them, and past the voyeurs who crowded the doorways of the swing rooms. By peering over shoulders, I could see a few people rolling about athletically on mattresses. I was surprised by how passionless both participants and onlookers seemed.

In the main room at the end of the corridor, sixty or seventy fully dressed people crowded around a tiny dance area, watching two women wearing white towels move listlessly with the loud disco music. Others sat on giant inflatable cushions in a mirrored alcove next to a postage stamp-sized bar, where drinks were being dispensed by a moon-faced black woman in a low-cut silver blouse. The crystal ball revolving slowly above the room threw long shadows across the expectant, anxious faces of the middle class waiting to be set free of their inhibitions.

"My high school dances were livelier," I told Mora.

"It's still early. They'll loosen up, you'll see."

"What makes you so sure?"

"Because it's my night, and that's what I want to happen."

"See anyone you like?"

I pointed out a few couples, but she dismissed the men. I was puzzled. I realized that I didn't know what attracted her to certain men and not to others.

"How can you know what they're like if you don't talk to them?"

"It's what they do with their eyes. And their hands. Body language."

The men she was attracted to had to radiate a certain energy, an indefinable electricity that was invisible to me. I went to get drinks for us and when I got back to her she had her eye on a tall, lean man with curly hair, a bump on his nose and a prominent adam's apple. He was in the middle of a graceful dance with a heavy-breasted brunette whose blissful, lascivious grin betrayed no awareness that the towel she wore was slipping off her hips. His eyes were closed and his mouth was set in a severe pout. He looked like Huntz Hall, lantern-jawed Satch from the Bowery Boys' movies.

"Him?" I asked doubtfully.

"What's wrong with him?"

"I'm . . . surprised, that's all."

"Look at the way he dances. The man has energy in his back pockets to spare."

"Uh huh."

When the music stopped, he stood there wiping the perspiration from his face with a handkerchief. Mora saw her chance. She squeezed my hand, whispered, "Be back in a minute," and walked up to him. I watched him lean forward to talk with her over the noise, look in my direction, nod a few times, and then she was back.

"That's a smirk on your face," I said.

"He turns me on. He says we should go to the locker room and get undressed."

"That's friendly of him. Which one is the woman he came with? The brunette?"

"He works here."

"Oh."

"He says once you've got your clothes off, you won't have any trouble picking someone up."

She didn't get it.

In the locker room, he was waiting for us, talking with a dumpy woman in a Plato's T-shirt who was in charge of towels and padlocks. We undressed and he introduced himself, blinking myopically. His hand was large and wet.

"Richard, my name is Stanley. Mora says this is your first time here."

"That's right."

"I could tell when you walked in."

"How's that?"

"You're not lookin' at the women like you're here for the same thing they're here for, if you know what I mean."

Mora was standing between us, adjusting her towel to cover her breasts. He took her arm, winked at me, and started to leave.

"How long will you be? I mean, where will we meet?"

"Don't wait around," Stanley advised over his shoulder. "Just say hello. Just be friendly."

I was stunned. The dumpy woman looked at me like she

knew what I was thinking and handed me a towel to wrap around my waist. "He's smooth, isn't he?" she said. The son-of-a-bitch.

I made my way slowly through the crowd back to the bar, feeling self-conscious about my nakedness, feet avoiding people with shoes on, my chest brushing against fabric, fingers hooked in the towel so it wouldn't come unknotted. I got another drink at the bar and sat down on a nearby couch.

I tried to remember what it was like to pick up a woman, how it was done in the movies and on television. I hadn't tried to pick up anyone since high school. As I remembered, it was no fun.

If Vy had walked in the room right then, I would have climbed all over her.

After a while, I found myself staring at a Puerto Rican woman in a clinging black dress who was sitting on the other end of the couch. She had a nice, shy smile and a diamond ring on her finger, and she was watching her husband – a muscular man with more cleavage showing than most of the women in the room – flirt with a blonde dancing in front of him. The blonde was attracting an audience of still-clothed men who stood around, whispering their admiration, but she was playing to the Puerto Rican hunk. She wore a black lace camisole and one thin strap kept falling off her shoulder, baring a small, firm round breast; as she whirled, she flipped up the front of her undergarment, revealing plump boyish buttocks and pale straw pubic hair shaved in the form of a heart.

Seeing her husband so transfixed, the Puerto Rican woman moved toward me on the couch. I smiled cautiously and looked into eyes as round and bright as new black buttons. Thinking that no one was looking, that her husband was preoccupied with the blonde, I put my hand on her knee. She looked pleased but nervous.

I was wrong about her husband. The next thing I knew, he was angrily knocking my hand away and hissing at me. Spitting words of warning. I'm sure I blushed. I muttered my apologies and turned my head back to the dance floor.

Mora had predicted that people would loosen up as it got later, and they did. Those who'd come to gawk were leaving, clothes were disappearing, and towels were slipping provocatively. I didn't see Mora anywhere. The Bee Gees' "Stayin' Alive" bounced around the room like a badminton ball on moving jets of water. The smoothness of disco music, its continuous, creamy beat, its plaintive voices echoing forever the rhythmic invitation to dance, pulled me to my feet.

Mora wasn't in the swing rooms, so I went to the steamy, wet room where three whirlpool baths churned in semi-darkness. Couples cavorted in the bubbly water. I saw Mora and started to join her. A man next to me came to life.

"Couples only," he growled, pointing to a sign above the door that the rising steam had obscured. I noted his thick biceps and stepped back, but a small boy inside me jumped up and down in protest.

"But I'm half of a couple. The other half is in there, and I want to say hello to her."

"Maybe she don't want to see you right now. Wait till she comes out. Be a gentleman."

I took a deep breath and nodded. There was nothing to do but wait for her at the bar. All that mattered was that one of us was having a good time, I told myself. The booze made the lie somewhat more palatable.

I tried to strike up conversations with various women at the bar, but they could smell my desperation, the way dogs smell fear. Mora emerged at last, wrapped in a white towel. She glowed. Her pupils were bright, and her damp skin was red from the heat of the whirlpool. Her small hands were water-wrinkled.

"*Whew!* I am wiped out, Richard."

She put her arms around my waist and nuzzled her damp forehead into my shoulder like a puppy.

"I saw you in there – you were very busy."

"I don't have the words to express it . . . You know how, when you're a kid, you don't think you belong anywhere?"

"I do, sure."

"Richard, I felt like I *belonged*, like there was a secret society of people like me . . ."

I was upset. "Like a stamp club?"

She stepped back. "Oh, shit, Richard. If you don't understand, I don't know who will."

"I've been feeling like an outcast from that secret society of yours."

"I'm really sorry I was gone so long. Why didn't you join us?"

I told her about the bouncer and she frowned.

"Come on, we'll go back in. We'll stay together."

Our bare feet squished on the wet carpeting of the whirlpool room. I blinked my eyes to adjust to the darkness. She dropped her towel and lowered herself into the swirling water slowly, until she was covered up to the neck. Hazy amber lights set into the side of the tub made her look silver, like a mermaid shimmering in the warm water. I settled next to her, my genitals floating free. We were alone, although small groups of people nearby were groaning and splashing about enthusiastically.

She beamed like a kid at Christmas and fondled me, her hand making waves in the water. We kissed long and slowly, and didn't come up for air until we heard splashing in the water near us.

"I think we've got company," Mora whispered in my ear, the point of her tongue playing warmly in its whorls.

When I looked up, I saw the blonde from the dance floor sitting between Stanley's legs. He grinned at me like a benevolent pasha and winked at Mora. I stared at the blonde's long slender legs and the heart-shaped pubic hair between them, and she smiled back at me with curiosity in her eyes.

"People are talking about you two," Stanley said.

"Who?" I was skeptical.

"The regulars. People in the scene."

"Maybe they're talking about Mora, but I've been batting zero."

"Shyness turns women on. Tracey noticed you."

Bullshit she'd noticed me, but I didn't care – for some reason, Stanley had brought her along, she was sitting not four feet away, and all I had to do was figure out some clever way of crossing the ocean between us.

She made it easy by speaking first, in a squeaky voice that managed to make Brooklyn sound sexy. "I saw your mustache, and I just adore mustaches, and Stanley said you were probably a really nice guy, so when he asked me to come in here with him for just a minute I decided to forget that it was two in the morning because I like nice people more than I like going home in a cab by myself – don't you think Plato's is really neat? I feel right at home . . ."

Mora and I looked at each other in disbelief, and then turned to study Tracey from top to bottom. It was true: she was indeed one of the most beautiful women either of us had seen outside of the pages of *Playboy*. The important details were all in place: her firm breasts and plump buttocks belonged in a centerfold, her skin was smooth and soft, and she was without wrinkles or scars. She even wrinkled her nose like a cheerleader.

I looked her straight in the eyes, all at once sure where I had hesitated before.

"Tracey," I said. "You are a goddess. I say that without a doubt in my mind."

She cooed. "I *knew* you were going to be a sweety! I can always pick them out – and nice equals sexy."

I felt buoyant. Maybe it was the water, but I think it was relief. I reached for her ankle and she let me hold it while Stanley floated through the water to Mora. Then she took my hand and placed it on her belly. "I want to feel you in my belly, filling me up."

I couldn't believe my luck. Like a kid about to raid the cookie jar, I looked around to see if anyone was watching. Mora was riding Stanley in the water, holding on to his shoulders with her fingertips and looking into his eyes. I touched Tracey's breasts and felt electricity course through my palm and wrist and up my arm. I thought I heard her purring when I kissed her inner thighs, and then she folded herself into me, hands braced against the edge of the tub, and we became deep sea divers, carrying on like estrous dolphins.

It seemed like hours later that we surfaced, only to hear the announcement over the sound system that the club was about to close. Sex had stretched time like a rubber band.

Close? Tracey and I held on to each other like exhausted boxers against the ropes. Mora and Stanley were out of the water, drying themselves off. I hadn't had enough – I didn't care what time it was, I had only just discovered the delights of Plato's, and I wasn't ready to go home. Another ten minutes . . .

I was also water-logged; every cell squished. Tracey gave me a huge grin as she climbed out of the whirlpool, and I managed to plant a kiss on her firm left buttock.

"It's four o'clock in the morning, lover," she said. "Time to go home."

I stood up. "Here's a towel, Richard," Mora said.

I took it reluctantly, looking around like a man who's been rudely awakened from a glorious wet dream. I heard Stanley's laughter in the background.

Mora put her arm around me and whispered in my ear, "You see what it's like now. You see how you can get lost in it. Can you blame me for doing what I can?"

"Not any more. Not now." I was sure that I could promise her that understanding.

Out on the street, we blinked at the dawn light like sleepy moles and walked down Fifth Avenue with our arms around each other. The early morning city was like an open bedroom; we scrutinized the people we passed on the sidewalk as if they were hurrying naked through Plato's. The world was sexualized.

"I told you that you would meet someone," Mora said.

"If it hadn't been for you . . ."

"Stanley gave me his telephone number. He made a big deal of it."

"Do they live together?"

"I think so. Do you want to do it again?"

"It's not fair to ask me now," I told her. "It's Christmas morning."

She squeezed me. "You know what? I'm happy. I think we make a good team."

"Sweet Jesus, take pity on our lust."

SIX

Mora was sitting up to her neck in a tub of hot water and I was scrubbing her back. Her skin was turning red from the water and my fingernails, and the rising steam was curling the yellow wallpaper. Her slippery soft body was light as cork under my hands, the delicate bones of her arms and legs like wires holding her in the water.

We were talking about Plato's. She said her mother had always told her that in marriage you can't eat your cake and have it too. She referred to her mother when she was uncertain; it helped her make up her mind, usually the other way.

"You can't have it both ways."

I wondered. Most of the people at Plato's were married, and I supposed they lived tolerable lives together, no different from ours except that they shared a recreational interest – they went to bed with strangers. Sex to them was an end in itself, its own perfect justification.

"Your mother also said marriage was forever."

"Only bachelors, loose women and divorced people fucked around."

"But swingers don't have to get divorced – they divorce sex from love. The advantages are obvious."

She chuckled. "They don't have to say they're working late."

"Or rent motel rooms."

"And they can still file joint returns."

I lifted the damp hair from the back of her neck and kissed the hollow there – it always gave her goose pimples. "They don't have to tell lies, but they must get jealous sometimes, like everyone else," I whispered.

"That tickles!"

We messed around until everything got slippery. A little later, the phone rang in the bedroom. It was Stanley, inviting us to a private party at his place in New Jersey. Mora was tentative when she talked with him, but I knew she wanted to go. So did I.

Stanley lived in one of those high rise towers on the bluffs in New Jersey, ten minutes by taxi on the other side of the Lincoln Tunnel. It was an evening in late November, and there was a promise of snow in the air. A uniformed doorman checked off our names against a typed guest list. He was businesslike, but his eyes lingered on Mora's breasts. *He* knew what we were up to.

Tracey opened the door and squealed happily at the sight of us. Her black silk blouse gaped open and, when she kissed me on the cheek, my hand slipped inside of its own accord.

"Stanley, come see who's here," she called over her shoulder. "I'm really happy you decided to come. Stanley wasn't sure . . .."

He appeared behind Tracey and moved to kiss Mora. It was the first time I'd seen him dressed – patent leather loafers, loud green slacks, loose patterned shirt open four buttons. He looked better in a towel.

When he kissed Mora's neck, he looked up at me from under her ear, blowing her hair away, his stiff palms moving down her back to cup the soft weight of her ass.

"My queen for the evening," he smiled.

Tracey frowned at this and took my hand from her breast, leading me into the apartment.

She showed me where I could hang our coats, playing the hostess. "I bet he says that to all the girls," I said.

She smiled brightly and excused herself. There were more people at the door, and Stanley and Mora were holding up traffic. "I don't know where we're going to put them all. If people don't start moving into the bedrooms, this is going to turn into a cocktail party – you know what I mean?"

People were sitting on couches and chairs and on the

carpeted floor, passing around joints and talking about lawn
care, good gas mileage, swingers' clubs – and relationships.

Relationships. It might have been a party of middle-aged
people anywhere in America – except they weren't talking
about business because, for swingers, it's not status that's
important – what you *do* – but what you look like, and what
turns you on. They were talking about the arrangements men
and women make in order to balance desire with duty. The
structures of love. Marital balance sheets.

I listened because it was an opportunity to hear how
serious swingers – the people who pursued this life week
after week, year after year – dealt with the problems Mora
and I had encountered since we stepped outside the closed
circle of marriage.

As a group, they were no more nor less attractive than the
crowd you'd find on a Saturday night in a disco in Fort Lee,
New Jersey. No matter what shape their bodies were in, they
dressed in tight, light clothing; they wore gold chains and
digital watches, and the men tended to show more chest than
their women showed cleavage. They smoked a lot of cigarettes but they didn't drink much.

At first, their faces were hard to distinguish, because the
only light in the large living room came from recessed spots
set behind greenery that grew on one wall, over a bubbling
fountain constructed of plaster made to look like stone.
Another wall was decorated with paintings of bull fights
and crossed swords on wooden plaques, but the opposite two
walls were glass, to take advantage of a magnificent view of
the Manhattan skyline at night. I was sitting on the floor, in a
line with the Empire State Building, and when I stood up I
could see the twinkling lights of the city reflected in the inky
blackness of the Hudson. Some people were looking through
a telescope set on a tripod in the corner of the room.

You could tell the party hadn't really gotten underway by
the lack of people in the bedrooms. We strolled in and out of
four of them, and saw a few people having serious conversations or simply petting, before I noticed a brunette lying on a
bed masturbating. Her skirt was thrown up around her waist

and her ankles were locked together. She had both hands between her legs, her back was arched, and the sweat poured from her forehead. Her eyes were shut tight.

A man wearing a white turtleneck and blue blazer – a man in his mid-fifties with a gray toothbrush mustache – was kneeling on the bed next to her, with the intent expression of a man helping his wife give birth by breathing with her. He didn't notice us.

Both their faces were bright red and she was babbling when he put his hand on her thigh.

Her eyes snapped open and she brought her hands up to hold out to him. He clasped them and kissed her fingers, one by one.

"Can I get you a drink, darling?" he asked solicitously. He had an English accent.

"You're not getting me drunk tonight."

"No, of course not. That's not my intention. But I do want you to have a good time. I want you to mix with people and be gay."

He treated her like she might explode, like someone who's just been released from a mental hospital. I was fascinated. She jerked her skirt down when she noticed us standing there in the darkness.

"I wasn't putting on a show," she growled.

"Didn't mean to intrude, but it was getting crowded in the living room," I explained hastily.

"Oh, hello," the Englishman said, stepping around the bed and holding out his hand. "Peter's my name. This is Johanna."

He and Mora smiled at each other.

Johanna looked coldly at me. "You're a voyeur," she accused.

"Look, if you wanted to play with yourself in private, you could have stayed home and drawn the blinds."

I was glad she hadn't; she was ravishing, with long dark hair loose about her shoulders and breasts heaving beneath her sweater. She had delicate nostrils and a thin, painted mouth and her eyes burned with frustration.

"Wait a minute, darling," Peter said. "No reason to get upset. We'll go get some drinks and give you a chance to get yourself together." He pushed us out and closed the door.

"The first attractive woman besides you I've seen, and she's crazy," I whispered to Mora.

"She's off, tonight," Peter said. "But Johanna is as changeable as New England weather. You just have to be patient. When she's good she's very, very good, but when she's bad . . ." He sighed, and shook his head. Then he looked at me and brightened. "But maybe your meeting was fortuitous. I've known her to start out an evening hating someone, and then surprise me. She likes the unexpected move."

"It must be exhausting to deal with her," Mora said.

"I know she's much too young for me. She's on her own trip, as you say here. She says I can accompany her on it, if I want to, but I'm not allowed to complain."

We refilled our glasses and he went back to collect Johanna. While we'd been gone, the crowd in the living room had thinned out.

Then I heard a familiar voice. Stanley led Vy and Charles into the room, feathers of snow in their hair. They looked glamorous and happy and the talk in the room stopped for a minute to register their presence. Stanley made an attempt to introduce them, but Vy stopped him.

"Surely I haven't been gone that long, Stanley – that people have forgotten. This is like a family reunion. Hello, Peter. Is that Johanna in the corner, over there?"

"Hello, Vy," I said.

"I was hoping you'd be here. Baby, it's *so* good to see you! Did you know they'd be here, Charles?"

Our reunion was a four-way hug in the middle of the living room; for the moment we were a closed circle, oblivious of everyone around us.

"I hear you liked Plato's," Charles said. He smirked.

"You know we did," Mora told him.

Vy examined us both with a look of mock severity. "So while the cat's away, the mice played? You let the Devil tempt you – you couldn't wait for me?"

She exchanged greetings with the other people in the room – apparently she knew them all – and sat down on the rug to pull off her tight velvet trousers. Like a restless hen on a nest, she squirmed provocatively until her long white legs were bare. The dark blonde tuft of hair at the bottom of her belly gleamed like wheat. She reached for her big leather bag and pulled out a long madras skirt to wrap around her waist.

"No more underwear, thank God. For some reason, Maurice insisted on lingerie in London. He said that his friends would be shocked if I didn't have any, but I think he had a kinkier motive."

She hadn't lost her ability to grab the center of attention. Every eye in the room watched her get into her skirt. What was it that made me think she was changed – or had my perception of her altered? The circles under her eyes were darker, she'd braided her hair, her fingernails were bitten – but it wasn't the details that made me see her fresh; it was an aura, as if she'd learned something about herself in England and the knowledge was spreading in circles from the center of her being.

Peter handed her a drink, and Stanley asked her about England. She was gracious, a queen with her court. Maybe that was what I noticed about her: a new authority that enabled her to hold the floor with ease.

"I met more submissives in England than I could shake a stick at," she chuckled drily. "And more lords this-and-that with beautiful soft eyes and eccentric tastes . . . They all have old names and large country places with butlers, and their great soft eyes get wickedly moist when you flick a riding crop. Leather is very popular, very chic with Maurice's friends." S&M was unexplored territory for us.

Mora and I looked quizzically at each other. We had only the vaguest notion of what she meant, but I could see that everyone else knew what Vy was talking about and that she was a star.

Charles walked into the kitchen to get himself a drink – I think he was probably feeling neglected – and I followed him, hoping that he could enlighten me.

"What is a 'submissive'?" I asked.

"Stop putting me on, Richard. You're being ingenuous."

I held up my hands. "I ask in all innocence. I really don't know what she's talking about. She's changed – hasn't she?"

He stared at me, his lower lip dropped in thought. "You really have some catching up to do . . ."

Peter had been pouring himself a straight vodka without ice at the counter next to where we were standing. He broke in. "Excuse me, I couldn't help overhearing what you said, Richard. About Vy, I mean. I've been a fan of hers since we met – I'd call it an encounter, because it was very dramatic, but she may have forgotten – at a party at the UN Plaza last winter. Do you remember how grand she was, Charles? Some of us were in awe."

"Tell him what a submissive is, Peter."

"I'd rather talk about Vy. She's much more fun to talk about than my Johanna. Vy is a queen, but Johanna has become a pumpkin. Vy understands what a terrible responsibility she has. There isn't enough of her to go around."

"You lost me," I admitted. "I thought I knew something about Vy, but I guess I don't."

"There's a lot people don't know about Vy. She shows everyone a slightly different angle – it's definitely one of her charms."

Having said this, he drifted off in search of Johanna.

"I'm still in the dark," I said to Charles.

"The English don't know how to get to the point. Vy says sex with them is like a Japanese Tea Ceremony."

"I have the feeling that I'm going to have to ask Vy to explain – you're being just as vague as Peter."

"And you're being dense. One trip to Plato's and you end up in the inner circle of the sex world on the East Coast, and yet you won't see what's right in front of your eyes. Vy is a dominatrix – that's why Maurice took her to England. Do you know what she carries in that big leather bag? Whips. Leather cuffs. Nipple clamps. Dildoes. Rush . . ."

I shook my head. "You could have told me."

"For Christ's sake, Richard. You fell in love with her, didn't you?"

The living room was almost empty. I wandered down the hall toward the bedrooms, wondering what scenes I'd find Mora and Vy and Charles in the middle of, hoping that Tracey would be sitting somewhere by herself.

The first bedroom I walked into was occupied by people I didn't know. I stood and watched them for a while, feeling curiously lust-less. Mora was in the next room, on a couch with Charles and Stanley and Tracey. It was a four-way connection: Stanley knelt behind Mora, who had Charles in her mouth while Tracey knelt above Charles's lips. Stanley wore a bottle of Rush on a chain around his neck and I watched him lean over Mora's back to hold the bottle to her nostrils before bringing it back to his own nose. They looked like a team of acrobats, totally absorbed in a difficult maneuver they hadn't rehearsed for.

In the third bedroom, Vy was sitting in an easy chair, next to a queen-sized bed two couples were romping about on. Peter was kneeling before her, caressing and kissing her feet. She was idly untwisting her braids, looking bored.

"I'm glad you're back," I said, touching her hair.

"I thought about you over there, Richard. Maybe more than I thought about Charles – isn't that strange?"

"Charles just told me how naive I am."

"Naive?"

"About you. And what you carry in your bag."

She blushed. "I hope he told you good things."

"You're a star."

"I do what turns me on when I'm in the mood. Are you shocked?"

"Why should I be? It was just something I didn't know about. Now I know."

"Does it make any difference?"

"I don't think so."

She reached for my hand and pressed it to her cheek and

we remained like that for a while, staring and not saying anything.

Peter stood up, realizing that he'd lost Vy's attention. "Have you seen Johanna, old man?"

"She's in the living room."

"Oh, God. I'd better go rescue her. She'll be getting drunk, and then she's impossible to deal with."

"Poor Peter. He can't handle that woman at any time. He's an old teddy bear."

"I want to make love to you."

"I would like that very much."

She stood up and I pulled her into my arms, pressing her long body into mine so that I could feel her knees and pelvic bones and breasts. She shuddered, and I felt it go down her body.

"If Charles and Mora saw us right now, I don't think they'd understand," she whispered in my ear.

I knew what she meant – that fucking was all right, but a long embrace was a sign that something serious was going on.

"Can't leave you two alone for a minute," Charles said, from behind us. Mora was with him and they were both naked. A streak of semen glistened on Mora's left thigh and her hair was matted. Her eyes looked like she'd been on a long trip.

"Enjoying yourself, lover?" Vy asked, stepping away from me.

"It's like a geriatrics convention here. Mora and I are ready to play, and everyone is sitting around talking about relationships and the etiquette of a good swing. Can you imagine?"

I kissed Mora and she snuggled into my chest.

"How are you doing?"

"I'm throbbing from my toes up. I could go on all night, but Charles is right – there's nobody left to party with."

"We could always go to Plato's."

Charles and Vy didn't like the idea. I wasn't crazy about it, myself, but I wanted more time with Vy. I knew that Charles was getting restless and, if he went home, Vy would go with him.

"If you feel like being adventuresome," Vy suggested, "there's a new place called Night Moves we could try. Maurice told me about it."

"I'm game," Charles said, "as long as it's not the same *old* faces."

"It's on-premise, like Plato's. Very hip, Maurice said."

"How do we get there?" Mora asked. "It's too late for a bus."

"We'll grab a cab, or maybe we can find a ride," Vy said.

"Let's do it," I agreed.

"Who has a car?"

"I have an idea," Vy volunteered. "I'll talk to Peter."

We all groaned in unison. Not Peter.

"Have faith, children. Don't forget that I carry special powers in my bag. Let me deal with this."

Charles and Mora dressed while Vy went off to talk with Peter. Ten minutes later, she came to get the three of us and she had her coat on. Obviously she had conquered.

"Johanna is going to drive us in Peter's Cadillac. He'll get a ride with someone."

"How did you manage that?"

"He wants a private session with me. And Johanna wants to party. She's weird, and she's getting drunk, but I approve of her nuttiness."

"Just a bunch of old farts," Johanna said when we left, jingling the keys of the Cadillac in her hand. When Peter had tried to kiss her goodbye she'd turned her head so that he was presented with her ear.

Mora and I sat in the front seat with her. We had to hang on to each other when she took the corners, but she was a good driver. She steered the big beast with one hand, swinging wide around taxis and surprised pedestrians. She glided over the dark slick streets, wet with the melting snow, like a skate on ice.

SEVEN

Night Moves was discreetly planted in the middle of a block of factory buildings and warehouses. Noisy with hand carts, trucks and honking traffic during the day, at midnight it was a closed drawer. The only signs of life on the empty street were the colored lights of the firehouse across from the club. I could see firemen inside polishing a giant red engine.

The light snow had stopped and a thin layer of white slush covered the sidewalks. Vy strode regally in front, head back, heels tapping impatiently.

"Pinch me," Mora said when we stopped at the glass front of the club to wait for Johanna to park her car. The sign said NIGHT MOVES, but otherwise it looked like the wholesale soda and beer distributor next door, blank and black and anonymous.

I knew what Mora meant, so I kissed her instead.

"Yes, it's true. We're doing *this* again."

"Just like we know what the hell we're doing."

"Well, at least we all share the same fantasy. We have that in common." I was excited but apprehensive.

The five of us were a crowd in the pocket-sized reception area. There was a cigarette machine, a pay phone, a few hand-lettered posters too small to read in the dark (one announced a wet T-shirt contest), and – standing behind a counter next to the curtained entrance – a thin young black man with tack-sharp smartass eyes. He recognized Vy and made a small fuss over her while he checked our coats.

"And I thought this was going to be a slow night," he drawled, looking Mora and Johanna over.

Just as Charles and I were digging in our wallets for the twenty-dollar membership fee a sign on the counter asked for, a man who was obviously in charge stepped from behind the curtain and waved us in. Vy introduced him as Bob, the manager. He wore a thick mustache and a three piece suit.

"I'm president of this lady's fan club," he told us proudly, taking her hand and pressing it to his heart.

Inside, we stood around chatting for a while, blinking in

the darkness. Clever track lighting and plenty of candles illuminated an intimate stage set. To our right, a gleaming oak bar was tended by female bartenders in T-shirts and satin shorts. Across from it and on a higher level was a carpeted lounge that led to a small mirrored disco floor. A young, lively-looking crowd filled the moulded plastic booths.

I saw two Lacoste shirts, I swear it. The men who wore them had long blow-dried blond hair and they glowed with sun and good health. Tourists. Sitting with them were two of the most luscious-looking college girls I'd ever had the pleasure of ogling from afar.

I nudged Charles, to point them out, but he was focused on Johanna. He couldn't take his eyes off the way she wiggled her behind on the bar stool, alternately flirting and scowling and sipping scotch. Vy and Mora stood on the other side of her at the end of the bar, foreheads pressed together as they compared notes on the people they saw.

"She's a heartbreaker," he sighed.

"She's drunk, too. But look over there – it's the flesh God promised us. In our adolescent fantasies."

He studied them skeptically.

"I grant you that they are flowers of young American womanhood, but they're also tourists. They'll sit and watch and look decorative and, after they've gotten excited, they'll go home with the guys they came with. Mark my words – they won't even leave a trail of smoke behind them."

"I'm going to talk to them a little later."

"God bless. They'll write in their diaries about you."

We were in the way of incoming traffic. A dozen attractive couples passed the bar, conscious of being on display. There was a lot of eye contact and body movement, but I didn't see anybody as good-looking as the college girls. I sipped my drink and thought about them, trying out and discarding various introductory lines in my mind, telling myself to be bold, that I had nothing to lose and everything to gain by approaching one of them.

A man who was probably telling himself the same thing

walked up to Vy and Mora and got brushed off, but he didn't even pause to acknowledge defeat before moving on to Johanna, who practically jumped into his arms. As he led her off towards the back room, she turned and winked at Charles.

"Perfidious bitch," Charles muttered after her.

"Let's go talk to Mora and Vy. We'll all go into the back room."

But they wanted to dance.

We moved onto the dance floor, and let a Rod Stewart song lead us around the polyurethaned oak floorboards beneath the silk parachute canopy. The floor-to-ceiling mirrors multiplied our images as we shook our bodies and whirled about.

Dancing loosened me up. When the music stopped, I sat on a carpeted step, aware that the college girls were right above me. I wasn't surprised when Mora danced Charles off the floor and through the curtains into the back room.

Vy joined me on the step, sitting with her elbows on her knees.

"I'm tired. Maybe it's just jet-lag, but I can't boogie the way I used to."

"Dancing is a warm-up exercise for the real thing."

I put my arm around her shoulders and she looked down at my hand for a long moment before covering my fingers with hers.

"And how do you like Night Moves?"

"It's not a circus, like Plato's. It's just the right size."

"This is the first time I've dared to bring Charles here. He's been funny since I got back, anyway."

"Funny?"

"Different. He didn't want me to go to England – almost as if he's jealous and can't talk about it. I think he wants to punish me, but he doesn't know how to go about it."

I thought about her relationship with Maurice, her reputation as a dominatrix, and said something I immediately regretted.

"You could teach him about punishment, couldn't you?"

She was stung. "Don't be a son-of-a-bitch, Richard."

"I can't help thinking about that bag of yours. And Maurice."

She pushed my arm from her shoulder and stood up. Her eyes were cold. "I thought . . . Well, never mind what I thought. I don't have to explain myself to anyone. Not even you, Richard."

Before I could say anything – and if I could have grabbed my words from her ears and crushed them underfoot, I would have – she squared her shoulders and strode across the dance floor, straight into the back room.

I sighed and stood up, just as one of the college girls passed me, trailed by the blandly smiling Lacoste shirts. The three of them started to jiggle and strut and I decided, what the hell, and approached the remaining college girl. I bent over to whisper in her pink, shell-like ear, blowing aside wisps of soft gold hair.

"I like the way you look. You are so special, it takes my breath away. I would love to . . ."

I have to give her credit for a classy brush-off. Without looking up, she shook her head slightly and said, "It's not me you're looking for."

I was surprised – and relieved – to find Charles back at the bar. His expression was cloudy. Disappointed.

"I didn't expect to find you here," I said, ordering another glass of wine.

"I'm surprised myself. Mora's hard to hold on to."

"So what happened?" As if I couldn't guess.

"The manager, Bob. He saw her and came over to collect on the entrance fee. She went off without a whimper."

"She's a woman with a strong sense of duty." We drank to her.

"I ran into Johanna – actually it was more of a tripping motion – and stopped to say hello."

"Had she changed her mind about you?"

"She hissed at me like a wet cat."

"Maybe she's serious."

"You know I'm persistent, Richard. I can't help myself for

trying, but I go ahead and try. Know what I said to her? 'You look best on your knees, giving head.' "

"The direct approach. I see."

He looked around. "I don't see the college girls."

"It wasn't me they were looking for," I admitted.

"Lord, what makes women so contrary? So . . . ungrateful for our efforts, so closed of heart."

We might have sung the Chasing Male Blues right there, in the middle of a sexual game park, but Mora interrupted in time to remind us of our opportunities. She slid in between us.

"Why are you sitting out here?"

"Just taking a break, you know."

"Well, there are a lot of women in the back."

"What's Vy up to?" Charles asked. "It must be like old Home Week."

"Last time I saw her, she was talking to Johanna."

Charles did a quick double-take at the news. I watched his mind turning over the possibilities, like a hungry raccoon turning stones over in a creekbed. When his curiosity was tickled, he rumpled his hair from back to front, raising a crest above his forehead. His eyes turned heavenward for a sign.

"I wonder what *that's* all about . . ."

"Well, let's go find out," Mora said, taking our arms as if we were brothers out courting the same young maid, and pointing us to the back room.

Stepping into the back room at Night Moves was like walking into the Arabian Nights. The plush sprawling orgy room seemed fur-lined. We walked across mattresses and around huge pillows on which people lay in every position making love, inhaling the mixed odors of warm flesh, marijuana and tobacco smoke, amyl nitrate and perspiration, perfume and incense. Above the low, throbbing music rose the sounds of orgasm and of bodies moving together in the dark; the whispered, urgent imprecations of those close to the edge, and the quick, breath-snatching sobs of those who'd gone over it.

I remembered what Mora had said about a secret society of people who liked to make love as much as she did, and I wasn't surprised when a black hand reached out to circle her ankle. The kid with the smartass eyes who worked the door showed white teeth. Mora smiled, shrugged helplessly at us – *noblesse oblige* – and allowed herself to be pulled down into the darkness next to him.

We found Vy at the center of a circle of naked onlookers. She was kneeling beside Johanna, who lay on her side, also naked, her wrists tied behind her with a black silk scarf. There were beads of perspiration on her upper lip and between her heaving breasts, and her pupils were dilated.

"I'm not going to . . ." she sputtered, but Vy put her hand over her mouth, and she stopped.

"There you are, dear. And Richard, too. Johanna has been asking for you. I warned her that you might be busy."

Johanna shot Charles the fierce look of a victim who is determined that the sacrifice will be conducted according to her own fantasies.

"What made her change her mind?"

"She didn't. You were always the object of her fancy."

"Of her hostility, you mean."

"The more of that, the better."

I saw then that he recognized what Johanna wanted, what Vy meant, and the wicked anticipation in his eyes made me feel sick with fear and disgust for a minute. I didn't understand; why wasn't making love enough?

Did the people watching understand? – or were they, too, just curious about a need greater than theirs?

"You don't like that, do you?" Vy asked me when we moved to a space of our own, between two massive pillows.

"I don't understand it. Why isn't fucking enough?"

I waited for an answer, but she was suddenly impatient with my earnest innocence. I saw pity and scorn mix in her eyes, and – just as suddenly as she'd entered it – she left my life. I was stunned. I expected the floor to open and swallow me. I knew her well enough to know it was a definitive exit.

Looking around at the moving shadows, I wondered

wearily why I was there among them. I was overcome by a feeling of lostness. Vacancy. Sitting there in the middle of the orgy, I argued with myself: marriage and freedom. Life sexualized. The sweet power of lust. The evils of jealousy.

Let it be over, I thought. I just wanted to escape, to take Mora home and lock the door. I needed her – and she was my wife. My wife.

I found her with her legs over the black guy's shoulders, split open for him as he drove deep into her, spanking her ass with each powerful thrust. I knelt beside them and whispered in her ear, "It's time to go home."

EIGHT

I hit her, and she sneezed, but I hit her again, and her head bounced against the metal cyclone fence. It was just before dawn on Ninth Avenue. Bleak, so bleak. There was an excavation behind the fence and I wondered if I had the insane strength to pick her up and throw her into it – and if there was enough loose dirt to bury her with. I hated her with the white-hot intensity of a jealousy freed at last from civilized constraints.

"*You mother-fucker-bastard-son-of-a-bitch*!" she screamed, wailing like an outraged child, rubbing her knuckles over her bruised cheek.

"You had to fuck so much, you couldn't come with me even at five in the morning?" I shouted, hitting her again.

"Just because *you* couldn't get laid in a whorehouse doesn't mean *I* have to stop!"

She grabbed my jaw in her strong small hands and twisted my head toward her. "*Look at me, Richard*! Just look at me! My nose is bleeding and there's snot . . ."

I pulled out my handkerchief to give to her – like a good husband – and she knocked it to the ground.

"Did you have to yell that I was crazy to the whole club, just because I wanted you to come home with me?" I was so hurt that I thought I would vomit right there at her feet. Self-disgust choked me.

"Fuck you! You bastard, to hit me, *fuck* you and your feelings! I don't *care* how you feel any more!"

She came at me with her fists and feet, pummeling me in the belly and on the chest, kicking my shins.

"All I wanted was for you to come home with me," I pleaded, holding up both hands to protect myself.

"I was coming, God damn it!"

My eyes filled with hot tears. "But what about us? You love me and I love you, and that should mean *something*."

"This is my life, and this is how I want to live it, Richard."

The morning sun struck her wet face. I couldn't hit her, and I couldn't hold her. She wasn't mine.

"Come home?"

"I can't stop now. I can't."

HOTEL ROOM FUCK

Maxim Jakubowski

How they first met is unimportant.

Or, at any rate, another story altogether.

A different one.

Here, they both arrive at Kennedy Airport on different flights from Europe, barely one hour and two terminals apart. Initially the flight she had suggested taking was bound for Newark and cheaper, but he had been unable to coordinate his own travel arrangements to match hers.

After retrieving his case from the luggage delivery area and verifying her flight details, he kills time wandering through the busy, rundown hallways and alleyways of the building cluttered with passengers in various forms of transit. Idly wondering what she might actually look like. Checks out the stroke magazines in the news concession. There's a new one he's never come across before, called *Barely Legal*. He nervously glances aside as he leafs through it. Time passes slowly. A double cheeseburger and fries and a large coke take up another ten minutes.

He finally makes his way toward the terminal where the Sabena flights disembark, dragging his own case behind him on its dodgy wheels. A screen announces the arrival of her plane. She must now be queuing at passport control.

He finds a seat to the right of the luggage pick-up area, from which vantage point he will see all the passengers come out of the corridor from immigration. He holds his breath one moment. Suddenly, the whole thing doesn't sound so wise after all. What if, what if?

The Brussels flight crowd stream through the corridor. So many of them: the plane must have been quite full. They all saunter down the short flight of stairs towards the luggage carousels.

She is among the last to emerge. A dozen times already he has convinced himself she wasn't on the plane. Had been playing a game with him all the time. Had missed the flight by barely a minute or so back in Europe. Had been discovered by her masters and held back in captivity. Had come to her senses and realized this whole New York thing was quite pointless after all.

Finally, a slip of a girl with luminous features makes her way past the security guard posted at the top of the short flight of stairs and tiptoes her way down, concertina'd almost by two burly six-footed businessmen in charcoal-coloured suits and matching attache-cases. Her dark blue skirt is short, swirls around her knees. Her T-shirt is white, its thin material clinging to her skin. Even from where he sits, he can see the outline of her nipples through it, or is it the rings?

Jesus, she is so young!

But he knew that already, didn't he?

As she reaches the bottom of the stairs and her involuntary escorts scatter into different directions, she looks around the luggage enclosure, seeking him.

Her eyes alight on him. The sketch of a smile spreads across her lips.

He stands up. Smiles back at her.

His heart skips a beat or two or three.

She stands there motionless, as the arriving crowds mill all around her, a statue of perfection at the centre of the hurly-burly of the airport.

She slips her rucksack from her shoulders. He moves toward her, feeling all around him freeze, like a slow motion scene in a movie with the soft rock soundtrack missing and replaced by a cacophony of disruptive languages in a cocktail of voices.

Inches apart.

The heat from her body reaches toward him, a hint of spearmint on her breath.

"Hello, Thalie."

"*Bonjour.*"

She leans over, kisses him on the right cheek.

He briefly imagines she's telling herself he's so much older than she thought, fatter, less than handsome.

"For a moment, I thought you weren't coming," he says as, behind her, the luggage begins to accumulate on the conveyor belt.

"I said I would come," she answers. "Why should I not?"

"I'm just rather insecure," he says.

"I'm a lot of things," she smiles. "But not that."

"So, no regrets?" he asks her.

"Not yet," she tells him. "You asked me to come. Here I am."

"Good," is all he can summon as an answer. Then, "What does your case look like? We'll look out for it."

"I haven't one," she says, pointing at the rucksack at her feet. "This is all I've brought. Some changes of underwear. For my first time in New York, I thought it would be nice to buy some new clothes while I'm here."

He smiles. "We can buy them together. That would be nice."

"Sure."

"They must have been surprised when you checked in back in Brussels, no? Travelling so light?"

"I just said I was a student."

"I see," he says.

She bends to retrieve her rucksack. "Shall we?" she asks.

"Yes." He picks up his case. "Let's go and find a cab."

The driver must be from Haiti, he reckons. His radio is tuned to a station full of static, reggae and rap and French patois.

She sits close to him on the back seat. He tries to recognise the perfume she is wearing.

JFK Boulevard. Van Wyck Expressway. Jamaica. Queens. Past La Guardia and the mortal remains of some long past exhibition by a dirty lake. The car is held up for fifteen minutes on the approach to the Midtown Tunnel. The driver puts a hand through the partition requesting toll money. He still has a pocketful of coins from his last trip to America.

In the darkness of the tunnel, she places her hand on his. Since meeting up at the airport, they have barely spoken. Mostly about the weather: here; back in London; back in Belgium. How their respective flights had gone. Had she managed to sleep, and how he had spent the time reading. The in-flight movies and meals.

Small talk at its most banal.

They finally drive out of the tunnel into the canyons of Manhattan and he breathes a sigh of relief. In the hotel room, he knows, he will be more eloquent, less shy and tongue-tied.

The traffic in the cross streets slows them down further as they navigate the traffic lights up to midtown.

They finally reach the hotel he has booked them into. Not the usual one where most staff in reception know him already, but one close by. He pays the cab driver. A porter rushes forward to assist with the luggage. There is only his case, propped in the cab boot against a worn spare tyre. She carries her rucksack by its strap, and straightens her blue skirt as she steps out of the yellow vehicle.

He catches the porter's glance. Feels suddenly like a guilty, dirty old man, with this young girl at his side. Twenty-five years' age difference. I am a cliché, he thinks. Damn it, he's not going to feel guilt now, is he?

At reception they make a big fuss of him. Ten years since he has stayed here last, according to the computer.

The elevator. The long corridor festooned by Andy War-
hol prints. He inserts the electronic card key into the slot, the
door flashes green and opens.

"Welcome to New York, Thalie," he says as a wave of
infinite tenderness washes over his heart.

There is little for him to unpack as she uses the bathroom to
freshen up from the journey. He listens to the water splash
behind the door as he hangs his shirts and jackets in the
cupboard. It's only mid-afternoon.

She emerges. Smiling sweetly. Now she looks even younger. Wonderfully slim, her loose dark hair falling over her
shoulders, reaching midway down her back. Her waist looks
as if he could hold it within his two outstretched hands. Her
breasts jut against the thin material of her white cotton T-
shirt, and his eyes can't avert the hypnotic shapes that strain
the alignment of the whiteness. He guesses at the strap of a
bra over her shoulders, but the cups must be soft and barely
disguise the ever-aroused state of their contents.

"Are you hungry?" he asks her.

"Not really," she answers. "I snacked on the plane. But it
wasn't very nice, I must say."

"It never is," he remarks. "Because of the time difference
with Europe, I always find it better to have a meal when I get
here, as late as possible. Puts one's body clock on New York
time. Otherwise, we'll end up waking in the middle of the
night and we'll feel even more tired."

"If you wish," Thalie says. "Is it what they call jet-lag?"

He nods. Gazes at her.

Her eyes are pale brown, a delicate colour variation he
would give heaven and hell to be able to define. The knot in
his stomach grows ever more painful with every passing
minute. Eventually, he knows, he will have to get to grips
fully with this crazy situation he has somehow engineered.

"Shall we go out? Maybe down to the Village. Have a walk.
I'll show you around. Maybe see some shops for you. Have a
bite to eat."

"Whatever."

It's spring. The sun is out. Everything feels unreal.

They walk. It feels like miles, but neither of them are tired. They browse. He can't help visiting a few bookstores. She gets a top at Urban Outfitters, but will not let him pay. He introduces her to the dark chocolate with dark chocolate Häagen-Dazs bar which is not available in Europe. They have an early dinner, around seven, in a Ukrainian restaurant on 2nd Avenue, near the corner of St Mark's Place. Night falls. They are about to catch a cab back to their hotel when a pea-coloured chenille sweater catches her attention in the dimly-lit window of a thrift store. This time, he insists on paying. As they exit the shop, she pulls her purchase out of its paper bag and slips it on.

"It's suddenly grown colder, hasn't it?" she remarks.

"Yes," he agrees.

There is sea of yellow cabs cruising down the Avenue, all with their lights on. He extends his arm to hail one. The driver is from Lithuania, and insists on practising his English on them when he discovers that his passenger hails from England. He has relatives in Swindon, and is surprised to learn his passenger has never come across them.

There is a new porter on duty at the hotel door. To avoid judgment on their apparent age difference or the risk of being told he cannot bring young ladies into the hotel – a thought that has dominated his mind throughout the cab ride up from the East Village – he exaggeratedly holds his card key aloft as they walk into the hotel. Possibly guessing his embarrass-ment, Thalie holds his hand in hers, whether to compound his self-consciousness or reassure him, he is unsure.

Green light.

The door opens.

The room is not overly large. The sparse furniture pur-ports to be antique, a Picasso face is spread across the left wall, the narrow double bed – by no stretch of the imagina-tion anywhere near king-size – dominates the landscape that is going to be theirs for the next four days. Heavy brocade curtains are drawn. It's a quiet room; he is not sure whether the window gives on to 44th Street or not.

She drops her rucksack to the floor, kicks off her flat shoes and approaches the bed. Tests its firmness with her hand and then sits on its edge as he watches her. She pulls the new sweater over her head. Looks him in the eyes.

He remains silent.

Attempting to put off the inevitable, maybe?

"So," he finally ventures, "am I what you expected?"

The wrong age, the wrong middle-age spread, the wrong short-sighted eyes, the wrong kind of clothes, the wrong size cock, the wrong man?

"I don't know," she replies. "You tell me." Then, as an afterthought, "But I do like your voice."

"Is it the voice of a master, or the voice of a slave?" he asks her.

"Do you really want me to answer that question now?" Thalie says.

"You're right. I don't. Maybe you can tell me at the end of the week."

"Exactly. I've agreed to come here with you, but I can only be myself, you know that already . . ."

"Yes," he quickly interrupts her. "And, as we talked before, back then, I respect your nature. I shall not attempt to change it. You are what you are: I accept that fully."

"Good. I'm not seeking to be rescued . . ."

"I understand."

"I am yours for this week we shall spend together in this room. Totally. Do to me what you will. Use me. Beat me. Humiliate me. My only pleasure is in giving myself. For you, I will be no different than I have been for others, with others. My holes are yours. All I am is a body, with holes made to be filled, used . . ."

Hearing her say it like this hurts even more than when she had initially written it.

But he tries to show no sign of the torment spiralling across his heart.

"I understand," he repeats.

As she rises to her feet, she utters the last words he would hear from her until the following morning, "I know there will be tenderness, but please, oh please, do not fall in love with me." Thereafter, there were sounds. In abundance. But no more words. Only moans, sighs, cries, the whole orchestral palette of sex.

She approaches him. Closer than they have ever been.

Her lips move toward his.

They kiss.

She tastes of Ukrainian tea.

He takes her into his arms. Holds her tight as their kiss continues. Tongue. Teeth. Breath held back. His hands now linger all over her, feeling her softness, exploring her warmth, he feels her eager responsiveness as tremors of lust race through his body. He takes a step back, interrupting their feverish embrace. Recalls all she has revealed of her subservient nature.

"Undress," he orders her.

Her eyes look up towards the light fixture.

"One item at a time," he continues. "I want to examine your body."

She lowers her eyes and proceeds to pull the white T-shirt off, twisting its folds over her head, mussing her long brown hair which falls back down on her shoulders. Her skin is porcelain white. His heart tightens as sudden memories of another woman with the same pale skin flood back through his mind. Small flowery patterns crisscross the flimsy flesh-coloured bra she is wearing. It has no under-wiring. Her small, pert breasts visibly don't require any. Her hands move to her back and she unhooks the bra and her chest is fully revealed. There is a dark mole an inch or so below her left nipple. Discreet dots of pigmentation are scattered across the approach to her modest cleavage, too pale even to merit the epithet of freckles.

The golden rings hang from her nipples, catching a fleeting reflection of the light from the hotel room's ceiling fixture and its three low-wattage bulbs. They are thin, half the diameter of a wedding ring. She watches his eyes alight on them. She straightens her back, offering her ringed breasts to him. He extends a hand, touches the metal adornments. They feel light. Carefully he twists one of the rings and observes the way the darker, puckered flesh of her nipple follows the movement of the ring between his fingers. Her gaze is unflinching. He twists further, and with a finger of his other hand begins to manipulate the other ring in similar fashion. He watches as the pierced nipples harden and lengthen imperceptibly as he continues to manipulate the gold rings and her nipples. He pulls on one of them and he sees her flinch. But she says nothing.

Finally, he lets go and allows his now free hands to roam over her shoulders, caress her back. He plunges his fingers into her loose hair, pulls her head back and kisses her again, his tongue delving as deep as he can manage toward her throat. He can feel the rhythmic beat of her heart.

Her sharp nails begin to scratch his own back.

He keeps his eyes open as he kisses her. Notices the faint pale pink scar on her upper lip. Almost shaped like the letter B. Remembers its origin: Anne-Louise B. and the male friend also called B. were drunk and had heated up a paper clip in the flame of a lighter until it glowed red and tried to brand her with their joint initial.

He pushes Thalie gently away.

"Suck me," he tells her.

Naked to the waist, like a fragile doll in her blue, now billowing skirt, she lowers herself to her knees, face in alignment with his crotch and unclips his belt, unbuttons the top of his trousers and pulls them down to his knees. He is already partly hard and his cock is straining against his dark grey boxer shorts, an obscene bump of maleness.

She inserts a finger under the elastic and releases the cock.

He realises momentarily that he probably smells down there: the eight hours' flight and sweat, the long afternoon walk, the sweat, the heat. He should have washed first.

Her mouth approaches. Her tongue licks his shaft, slowly, tantalizingly; a hand cups his heavy, dark balls and her lips close in on the glans as she takes him into her mouth. The heat is wonderful. She allows him all the way in, his tip bumping against the back of her throat. She doesn't gag as she impales her mouth over him. No woman has taken him in so far without choking. She has, he knows, been mercilessly trained by previous users under dire threat of punishment or violence. His cock grows inside her mouth.

Her tongue surrounds his hardness, dancing lightly around his captured stem, teasing, licking, caressing. Her lips hold him in a soft but firm vice, slip sliding over his engorged flesh, welcoming his invasion, wordlessly inviting him to thrust ever deeper into her.

His eyes wander across the horizon of the room. The Picasso head is watching them as the young girl studiously keeps on sucking his middle-aged cock.

At this rate, he knows, he won't last much longer. He does not wish to come so soon, inside her mouth. He retreats, withdraws from her mouth. She looks up at him, puzzled, thinking maybe she hasn't performed well enough and is due for punishment.

He attempts a smile of kindness to reassure her.

"Undress," he asks her. "Take the rest off now."

She obeys.

Stands up and unzips the blue skirt. It slips to the hotel room carpet. The shape of her body is the nearest he has come to witnessing perfection, outside of no doubt doctored photographs in magazines. At the age of twenty, neither gravity nor the ravages of time have yet taken hold and begun their seditious work.

Her knickers are modest, thick white cotton, practical, sexless.

She bends over slightly to pull them down.

He knows what to expect. From what she had written.

He also knows it's the first thing that initially attracted him to her, and convinced him he had to see her one day. A prurient curiosity that betrays the filth in him.

The bunched-up piece of white underwear now lies in a small heap on the carpet. She straightens up. His eyes move up her smooth legs. Slowly. Almost hesitantly.

It's as he knew it would be.

His turn to move to his knees and approach his face to her

genital area.

Quite hairless, both above and around her cunt. Like the crotch of a doll or a pre-pubescent girl.

Not a wisp of hair, not even a darker shadow of hairs past. The same milky white shade that characterizes her whole body.

And the rings.

Gold.

Each one a thin band, like a cheap wedding ring.

Eight of them.

Four hanging from each labia, in perfect alignment, pulling both outer lips out of the central gash, the darker, redder skin like meaty folds on a butcher's stall, raw, almost bloody, as if the necessary piercings had only been done recently.

He gasps.

Incongruously wonders whether there is enough metal here to set off airport alarms.

Each set of labial rings is held together by a thin contraption of stainless steel, like a nurse's large safety pin with three branches. The middle one is threaded through all the rings while the two outer ones squeeze the pin tight and the whole is kept closed by a minuscule padlock.

He approaches his fingers, gingerly touches the chastity device protecting her entrance; his hand feels the intense heat emanating from the invisible depths of her cunt.

The rings effectively seal her tight. There is not even space to insert a finger. As she had warned him. Even during her period, she is unable to use a tampon and has to rely on sanitary towels.

"It's awesome," he whispers in the now hushed silence of the room. "It's . . . beautiful." And barbaric, he thinks, but he is so turned on.

He can't take his eyes off her locked cunt.

She remains quite silent.

Observing him.

Judging him?

This older man, with his thinning hair, his cock jutting out as if on military parade, his love handles, the sombre bags under his eyes, his trousers bunched around his ankles.

He finally takes off the rest of his clothes and asks Thalie to lay down on the bed, on her back and indicates she should open her legs wide.

He kneels, forces the angle between her thighs even wider and examines her like a doctor, mentally storing every detail of her adornments, her mutilation, as he gazes across the brazen display of the wonder of her jewelled portals.

He moves his face against her cunt, feels her inner warmth vibrate toward his cheeks, tries to slip his tongue between the minute gaps between the rings, but there is no access. She is utterly sealed.

Thalie extends a hand, musses his hair, sensing his obvious frustration.

He is on his knees at the foot of the bed, his head at the apex of her thighs, inhaling deeply, trying to seize the ineffable smell of her.

The sheer hardness of his cock weighs against his stomach.

He thinks of investing her mouth again, but Thalie shifts on her side and repositions herself on all fours on the bed, her rump raised toward him. A perfect, pale sphere, punctured by the darker heart of her anus; both her hands move back to either side and stretch her globes apart, inviting him. He wets his cock and thrusts himself into her arse in one swift movement. His head punctures the tight sphincter and his whole cock is quickly embedded inside her. She shifts to accommodate him better.

He digs inside her and for the next ten minutes, an eternity, he fucks her arse, watching the skin around her aperture distend with every in-and-out movement of his thick cock. He moans. She moans. He sweats. The perspiration drops from his forehead to his chin and then onto her back, where it pools slowly, a small transparent pond of humidity vibrating intensely to the accompaniment of every tremor that crosses her body as he tries to force himself ever deeper into her bowels. His lips are dry. She bites hers, out of pleasure or pain. His heart beats a light fantastic. Picasso is on the wall. The clandestine sounds of the hotel bathe them in ominous silence. Their fuck is an island of motion cut off from the rest of the world. He holds back as long as he can manage. Below the dark piston of his cock and its mechanical assault of her innards, the rings shine, wetness from above and inside her bathing them in an unmistakable sheen of lust. His frenzied eyes mirror his soul, flitting from arsehole to ring-bedecked cunt and his hardness just refuses to fade away.

Her sounds of sex are silent. Gentle cries, repressed gasps, deep breaths. She adjusts the position of her body to accommodate his movements, to accept him even deeper, her sphincter muscles tightening rhythmically around him before releasing his penis again, then tightening again, capturing every renewed attack. His tip is deep inside her bowels. Where it burns. And feels good.

Finally, he can hold out no longer. Thalie's whole body is just made for sex, a finely-honed machine for the benefit of his pleasure. He comes. He roars. Her name. A profanity. Feels his come burst out of him and bathe her insides, like a river of sin, a torrent out of control. He rests his hands on the bed, bent over her, the beat of his breath returning to normality. Silence continues. She says nothing either. At last, he feels his hardness begin to recede and pulls back, withdrawing his still pulsating cock from her. It emerges, bathed in come and inner juices. Her hole is shockingly dilated, red raw at the edges, like a small dark bottomless crevice. Never has he witnessed a sight so pornographic and, at the same time, so shockingly beautiful. The temporary scar his raging cock has left on her.

But he also knows she did not come.

They lay down together, moist body against pale body.

"Tired?" he asks her.

He pulls the covers over their bare bodies.

She nods, her eyes half-closed.

"It's the jet-lag catching up," he says. It's only ten at night in Manhattan.

He wakes at two in the morning, still nine p.m. European time, with a hard on, his mind and body in tumult. She is on her side, her back to him. He pulls her sleeping body toward him and the contact of her flesh only accentuates his desire. He pushes a finger into her arsehole. She is still dripping, leaking his earlier come. He slips his cock into her and begins fucking her again. It takes him ages to orgasm as he rages against her with every movement, angrily seeking release. At one stage, he surprises himself and finds his hands beginning to tighten around her thin neck as his thrusts take a vengeful rhythm. He quickly releases the pressure of his fingers there. He doesn't know whether she is awake or still sleeping. But her whole body accepts him.

He awakes again; there is a thin sliver of light peering through the heavy curtains. Early morning. This time Thalie is no longer sleeping, busy sucking on his cock with greedy appetite. Her eyes stay closed, he sees, as she does this.

When he is fully erect, she squats above him, stretches her rump cheeks open and plants herself on his cock, once again taking him deep into her arse. When he finally comes, the feeling is so strong, he thinks he is going to pass out.

"So, do I please you?" she asks, her first words since the previous evening.

"Yes, Thalie, you do," he answers.

Q & A

"*How did you first meet Anne-Louise?*"

"*She was my gymnastics professor.*"

"*How old were you?*"

"*Sixteen.*"

"*Tell me about it, her and you? How it happened?*"

"*I was born in a well-off, heavily Catholic family. We weren't rich, but life was easy and I was spoilt as a child. I have a sister, but she is sixteen years older than me. I've always believed she was very unhappy about my arrival at such a late stage.*"

"*Is she aware of what you have become?*"

"*Yes.*"

"*And she did nothing about it? You must hate her.*"

"*No, I don't. I love her, feel very close to her.*"

"*She knows Anne-Louise?*"

"*Yes.*"

"*You met through her?*"

"*Not quite. I was a good pupil at school, but I excelled in sports. I particularly enjoyed gymnastics; I was told I had talent. For my sixteenth birthday, I asked for private lessons in one of the city's better clubs. My parents agreed to it, and I was signed in for lessons two evenings a week and following school on Wednesday afternoons. Anne-Louise was my professor. She was already a friend of the family, and I remembered her often mocking me when I was younger, because of my lack of feminine opulence. 'The Plank' when I was thirteen, later 'No Bum' when I reached fourteen. My body developed late.*"

"*She seduced you?*"

"*Not quite. She was very pleasant to me during the course of the early lessons. She recognized my innate talent and the suppleness of my body. Initially, I attended the lessons wearing shorts and a T-shirt, but soon she asked me to wear a dancer's leotard so that she might be able to supervise and see how all my muscles worked. She taught me a lot, often correcting my stance or the use of the wrong muscles with a small wooden cane.*"

"*She beat you?*"

"*Lesson after lesson, her instructions became more and more difficult to follow and she would strike me harder. Surprisingly, I began to look forward to her striking me, even though it was sometimes painful. To this day, I still hanker to submit to her; she was so beautiful. So tall and blonde. And her severity struck an unusually responsive chord inside me as I took instruction. I think I had basically been submissive in spirit ever since my early childhood.*"

"*How come?*"

"*Even as a child, I recall never wishing to be a Princess when we played games with my sisters or friends. I preferred to imagine myself as a servant.*"

"*How did the relationship progress to you becoming, so to speak, her slave?*"

"*Soon, she began to realize, I think, that I was sometimes making deliberate mistakes and she began striking me for no* reason at all, and noted that I did not object. One day, for the first time, she struck me badly with her long, thin cane before our lesson even began. Told me it was to encourage me. She had guessed my masochist nature. That day, following the lesson, I deliberately followed her into the shower and confessed how attractive I found her and that I was in love with her. She surprised me by replying that she had lusted after me ever since I had been younger, and her earlier taunts had just been indications of her disguised desire for me. We kissed."

"And?"

"She warned me of her dominant character and that, in any form of relationship, I would have to submit to her will. I readily agreed. She made love with me there and then under the shower. It was heavenly. She knew every spot to touch, as if by magic."

"Had you been with boys before?"

"Somehow, I had never been attracted to men much. I'd kissed one or two boys, even allowed one to fondle my breasts under my shirt, but I hadn't ventured further."

"You were still only sixteen?"

"Yes. From the next day onward, I began following Anne-Louise's instructions. I wanted only to please her. She said I should no longer wear jeans, dress like a tomboy. I must always wear dresses or skirts, no pantyhose, only stockings. Every day after school, I would go to her house on the other side of town and wait for her to return from her lessons or the stadium where she worked on a part-time basis. She would often leave instructions for me on small pieces of paper on the kitchen table. I had to follow these most precisely. One day, she left an apron for me to wear, alongside the note. I was to become her servant."

"What was the sex like?"

"In bed, she was brutal and authoritarian. She enjoyed ordering me around, loved to humiliate me, sometimes inflicted much pain. But I enjoyed it more than I had enjoyed anything in my life before."

"I don't want to sound like a dime-store psychiatrist, but had you previously felt unloved, unwanted at home?"

"Not at all. It's just the way I am. I don't think anything will ever change my nature."

"How did things develop, then, with Anne-Louise?"

"After three months of living like this, rushing to her place every day straight from school, all feverish, anxious for more of her harsh love and punishment, desperately trying to get away from home over the week-ends to spend more time with her, I decided to leave school and put myself completely at Anne-Louise's service."

"What did your parents have to say about it?"

"There was nothing they could say. I was a lesbian and a masochist; they disinherited me. To this day, they only refer to me as 'the young whore'."

"So, you began living with Anne-Louise?"

"I was her maid during the day and her toy at night. She became even harder on me now, would not accept a word of disobedience, insisted on the highest standards only of house-work, cleaning and cooking. Whenever I failed, or forgot an instruction, the beating was most severe. The worse it became, the happier I was."

"Tell me how?"

"For Valentine's day, she bought a whip and a pair of handcuffs for me. The whip was to be used on me, of course. Thereafter, most days she handcuffed me before leaving for her work. Thus constricted, she said I would have more time to think of her all day. Naturally, my work around the house suffered badly. Which gave her even more opportunities to use the whip on me. But sex with her after every whipping was better than ever. I could wish for no other fate. Very soon, she began to use the whip on my body for no other reason than arousing me further sexually. Now she no longer even needed a reason to beat me, mark me."

"And you enjoyed this?"

"I was deliriously happy. This was what I was born to be. Later, she would take me to Brussels on special shopping trips to a store in a large Galerie that specialised in fetish and S&M apparel. She bought increasingly sophisticated devices and clothing for me. She would make me wear elaborate black leather outfits that made me look like a whore at a sadomaso-chists' convention. She had me play with toys in front of the assistants in the store as she exercised her power. Would have me

gagged, plugged, displayed. Force me to wear underwear she had deliberately dirtied before. Back at her home, I had to serve her completely, in every detail. It soon became my task to lick her clean after she had been to the toilet. She loved me and I loved her. I thought this bliss would last forever."

Mid-morning in the Manhattan hotel room. He calls out for bagels from Mom's Bagels, two streets away. For him, a garlic bialy with Nova Scotia lox and cream cheese and a plain bagel with cream cheese and jelly for her.

They devour the food in bed, close to each other. He feels comfortable with her, their bare bodies touch as they shift, neither draws back from the contact. He loves the fact that, like him, she is a creature of silences, doesn't find it necessary to make small talk and fill every precious moment of silence with needless words. A thin dollop of red jelly drops onto her left breast. He bends over and licks her clean, his furtive tongue nibbling on her ring, stretching the tender skin beneath. A warm feeling suffuses his lower stomach. Blood is already coursing back towards his tired cock.

Aware he is probably in no condition to perform again yet, he draws back and takes the kiss to her lips.

She smiles.

They have opened the curtains. Sunlight floods the room, the bed, their uncovered bodies.

He tells her about the last time he had stayed here. For two nights in a row, a couple in the room next door had practised particularly noisy sex, the sounds of which could just not be avoided through the thin hotel wall, keeping him awake and arousing his own lust. The woman had proven especially vocal, every thrust inside her provoking further moans, gasps or profane vocabulary in her lexicon of pleasure. The man, on the other hand, appeared to copulate in silence, leaving all aural accompaniment up to his partner: but must have had incredible staying power, as the sounds of their frantic love-making reverberated through to his room for almost two hours. On and on the sounds of nearby sex continued and he had begun to wonder what this shrill, enthusiastic woman might actually look like. The following night, the carnival occurred again in the adjoining room. On the third day, as he was leaving his room for his morning appointments, he finally caught a glimpse of a woman closing the door to the next room. To his disappointment and amazement – by now, he had visions in his mind of Greek goddesses or hardcore stars of the pornographic screen – she was a stocky, matronly Chinese woman with an old-fashioned fur coat draped across her shoulders, wearing sensible shoes and with a chignon in her hair. Anything but his dreams.

Thalie laughs at his story.

"Well, I don't think we bothered the neighbours much," she remarks. "We're both wordless fornicators, I noticed."

He smiles back at her, preferring not to tell her his other story of a hotel room fuck. In Paris, window opening onto a sea of Latin Quarter roofs. Where the sounds of the adjoining room had in fact been more muted but still caught his attention. Aroused, he had taken a glass from the bathroom and stuck it against the separating wall, cupped his ear against it and listened to the couple frolicking a few inches away and masturbated to the sound of their fucking.

Finally, they get up.

In the light of day, he finds her more beautiful than ever. And younger. Less than half his age.

"Who gets to use the bathroom first?" he asks her.

"You go," she answers. "I feel wonderfully lazy this morning."

He shaves. Christ, does he look tired! The new razor blade revives his skin. He washes the foam away and cleans his teeth. He tests the heat of the water bursting from out of the shower head, finds the right balance of hot and cold and steps into the shower area. He is soaping his cock, washing away their combined juices, when he hears her knock on the bathroom door.

"Yes?"

"Can I come in?" she asks him.

"Of course," he replies. There is no need for false modesty now.

She tiptoes in, walks across the damp tiles and sits herself on the toilet bowl. Facing him, legs wide apart and proceeds to pee as he stands under the pouring water just a few feet away. He notices the eight rings hanging loosely from her labia as the thick stream of urine jets out of her and realises the safety pin and the padlock are no longer in place. His first glance at the pinkness inside her cunt as her leaves separate, gape, to make way for the release of her warm stream.

She looks up towards him, with a wry smile on her lips.

His eyes interrogate her silently.

"You never asked," she says, as the last drops of pee keep on dribbling out of her. "A real master always does: he orders."

"I didn't realize . . ." he mumbles.

"I was allowed to bring the padlock key with me," she confirms.

"I see," is all he can feebly say. Feeling as if he has failed the first test.

"Can I join you under the shower?" Thalie asks.

"Of course," he says.

Her body shines under the pounding water. They embrace. Kiss. Separate. Their hair soaking wet now. United by the cleansing spurts of hot water. They soap each other with all the delicacy they can each muster. Kiss again. They both step out of the shower. He turns to switch the water off and, when he turns again to face her, she delicately takes his cock in her wet fingers.

"There was still some soap," she says.

She squeezes it. Hard.

He takes her hand away.

"Stay like that," he says.

She remains immobile, water still dripping down the expanse of her body. He takes hold of a towel and dries her, enveloping her body in its softness. He glides his finger through her hair.

"Oh, Thalie," he says.

"Yes?" she asks.

"I want to make love to you properly now," he answers.

He bends and picks her up in his arms. She is so light, he notices; and they make their way from steamy bathroom to the bed in the hotel room now blinded with light.

He pulls a curtain half-closed. There is still enough light for him to see all of her.

He installs her on the bed. She remains inert. Her opening gapes, as if alive, breathing like an invitation to pleasure. He delicately spread-eagles her limbs in a semblance of cruci-fixion across the crumpled sheets and buries his face in her cunt. He opens her up at long last and spies the infinite shades of nacreous pearl of her inner walls. Parting her, rings to each side he plunges his tongue inside her and a tremor flashes through her whole body. She still tastes of soap but her juices are soon abundantly flowing, pungent, aromatic, overflowing, bathing his chin as he labours away now, play-ing with her engorged clit. He has reached his destination, her portals of paradise. The velvet pearl pulses strongly against the tip of his tongue. Thalie moans. Widens the angle between her legs further in acceptance of his adoration. His face retreats. He looks up at her. Her face and the whole area leading to her breasts are flushed a deep hue of pink. Her eyes are closed.

He inserts a finger, then two, inside her cunt. She is like a furnace inside. He moves his other free hand towards her rear and sticks a finger inside her arsehole, where she is still gooey from their earlier exertions. Thalie gasps as both her holes are invaded.

Through the incandescent body heat, he feels the pulse of her heart beat against his probing fingers. He bends. With-draws the digits and takes her now protuberant clit between his teeth and nibbles away at it. He feels her close to coming, for the first time since they have been together. His mouth takes leave of her copiously flowing juices and he climbs over her and inserts his cock inside her.

A wordless sound passes her lips.

Tenderness sweeps across his heart as he begins moving inside her. The fit is exquisite. The gold rings on either side of her cunt lips slide effortlessly against his shaft, enhancing the sensations without overpowering them. As he thrusts in and out of her, the thought occurs to him that if he were her master, he would have her pierced yet again, a ring or a stud in her clitoris, just to enhance the friction against his glans as it labours and retreats against her opening time and again. Yes, a nice thought. And a big if.

He closes his eyes in turn and surrenders to their first moment of love.

Q & A

"*How did things begin to change in your relationship?*"

"*She liked to show me off to others. Demonstrate the extent of her power over me.*"

"*Men? Women?*"

"*She would invite friends to our home and play at humiliating me in front of them.*"

"*How?*"

"*By having me wear the outfits she had bought for me. Playing games she knew I was bound to lose, and then punishing me for my missteps. I would have to strip in front of her guests and have my rear caned or whipped. If there were other women, she would make me lick her sex in their presence: sometimes had me lie on the floor while they peed over me. I would have to serve food naked but for a dog collar and was forbidden to react while they pinched me, touched my intimate parts, sometimes tried to trip me to cause further punishment.*"

"*But were there men?*"

"*Initially, only one. A close friend of hers. His name was B. He's a lawyer from the city.*"

"*Was he her lover?*"

"*No. Anne-Louise hates men, sexually. But she was close to B. She liked exposing me to him, making me bend over so that he could peer inside me, even touch, which she knew I hated. The more ill at ease I was in these situations, the more it excited her and the crueller she became with him as witness to my degrada-tion.*"

"*What sort of things would she do for him?*"

"*She liked to demonstrate my absolute obedience. One day, I was made to lie on my back on the floor as she inserted a series of ever-larger objects inside my vagina, which I had to hold wide open for them. First a dildo, then a bottle, then a cucumber. All the time, I could see the bump inside his trousers swell as she teased him that wouldn't he like it to be him in that nice virgin cunt."*

"You were still a virgin?"

"Technically, yes. I hadn't yet been penetrated by a man. By Anne-Louise and objects only."

"How did it happen, the first time?"

"With B. One morning, Anne-Louise summoned me and instructed me that I should take a taxi to his apartment and do every single thing he would ask me to do. When I protested, she whipped me badly. Said I did not understand what true love was. I argued that I did. But she owed B. some debt, and he wanted me and that was that. Anyway, she told me, it would be good for my training, I had to be broken in. I went to him. Hated every moment. Later, there were other men she loaned me to."

"Did she ever want to watch you being fucked by them?"

"No. If she was there, she would move to another room."

"But did she ever ask you about what happened with the men?"

"Curiously, no. Although I was avid to tell her all, to demonstrate the extent of my affection for her by describing the pain they had inflicted on me, how they had used me, violated all my holes, made me choke on their filthy penises and forced me to swallow their ejaculate, played with me, beat me too. I wanted to tell her, 'Anne-Louise, I have accepted all this for the sake of you.' But she never asked. And if there were marks, cuts, bruises on my body, she would whip me in response, as if it were all my fault."

"Sounds very much like one-way traffic to me."

"She said that the coming of my seventeenth birthday would mark a significant point in our relationship. That I had satisfied her so far and she would show me her gratitude on this occasion."

"What did she do?"

"We drove to Brussels on a Saturday morning. I thought she

would be getting me new outfits at the shop in the Galerie, but this was not the case. It was a large building in the suburbs, a doctor she knew well. I would come across him again at the special parties. He used electrolysis to depilate my pubic area. I'm told it will never grow back again. Then, he pierced my breasts and fitted the rings I still have now. I was in heaven. I was Anne-Louise's slave, in both body and spirit."

"What are those special parties you mentioned?"

"They occurred later. I will tell you."

"OK."

Their second full day in Manhattan. The spring weather is clement. They walk. Catch cabs. Shop. Snack. Battery Park. The Cloisters. Central Park, watching the squirrels hop along the scarce vegetation.

They talk.

"Are you happy?" he asks her. "It's such fun showing you this city, all these places I have known and liked for years. I try and imagine what it feels for you to see them for the first time."

"It's nice," she answers. "But you're too soft with me. I don't deserve this, you know. If I were in your place, I would be crueller, much harder. Somehow I think you're too sensitive. Almost like a girl . . ."

His face clouds over. "If you were in charge and I was a girl, would you fuck me?" he quietly inquires.

"I would," Thalie says. "I would stretch you, hurt you until you plead for mercy, but I wouldn't give you any. I have been taught well. Switching is no problem."

"I see."

"Would you prove your devotion to me by letting me treat you like that?" Thalie asks him as they cross toward the Plaza Hotel.

He doesn't hesitate. "I would," he replies.

"OK," she says.

They catch a cab which takes them to a dark side street near the Port Authority Terminal. In a sex shop manned by Pakistani assistants, they buy a strap-on dildo. Flesh-coloured, veined, awesomely realistic and life-size. And handcuffs. So that he doesn't change his mind, she says.

He is in no hurry to return to their hotel room.

He reminds her she wanted to go to Macy's.

She wanders indifferently through the designer label departments.

"I want to buy you something nice," he insists.

"Why?" she queries. "How do you want me to dress? Like a whore or a princess?"

"As a young woman."

She agrees to stockings, a silk cream-coloured see-through blouse and a flowing skirt in rainbow colours.

They arrive back at the hotel mid-afternoon. The room has been made, and the smells of sex have faded.

"Undress," she orders him, herself stripping from the waist downwards and fitting the strap-on belt around her waist. He notices she has reattached the safety pin and the padlock.

He silently sheds his clothes, takes a step towards the bathroom, planning to wash the sweat away from his body.

"Don't," she forbids him. "I want you dirty. I want to smell your vileness as I fuck you."

He knows he shouldn't protest; his face reddens as his arse crack feels all clammy, and his feet sticky.

"On your knees. NOW!"

He gets down on all fours.

"Raise your head."

He does. His eyes are parallel with her labial rings. He notices she is seeping there. She is excited. She thrusts the artificial cock toward his mouth.

"Suck me," she intimates.

The rubbery material fills his mouth; the taste is unpleasant. She only lets him suck the dildo for a minute or two then withdraws it and places herself behind him. All she wanted was for him to wet it.

She places the strap-on head against the outer ring of his sphincter and begins pushing it in.

It enters him with surprising ease. Initially, there is little pain and he is almost disappointed.

The feeling doesn't last and soon he is biting his lips to repress heartfelt sounds of anguish as Thalie goes to war on him, viciously twisting the implement of torture within his gut as she endlessly adjusts her stance to increase its depth, the angle of attack and the unremitting pressure on his protesting bowels. He knows she is enjoying this. But he reasons, beyond the valley of pain, that she deserves at least this; that this is his own particular way of experiencing some of the humiliation that has been lavished on her by so many others. He communes with her as she keeps on fucking his arse, until the skin inside and outside is raw from the friction. His heart beats wildly; bile pools at the back of his throat; he has difficulty breathing. There is no longer any pleasure in the act for him.

Then, as suddenly as she entered him, she pulls it out in one swift movement and he momentarily feels as if his whole insides are being suctioned out.

He collapses, stomach first, onto the hotel room floor.

"There," she says. "I think you would make a better slave than a master. Very docile. You take your suffering in silence; that's a good sign," she remarks.

For a moment, a germ of an idea settles in his mind. An image of the two of them as slaves, collared together, made to perform for the benefit of others.

At last, he rises, as his breath returns. Thalie now sits on the bed, watching him. The strap is now detached from her; her hands shield her jewelled pubes.

"I hurt you, didn't I?" she asks, watching him rub his hole with the back of his hand. There is some blood.

"You did," he says.

"Then I must be punished," she says. "That is the way."

As he washes the traces of the fuck away some minutes later, he realizes she is now testing him. It's scary: could he ever become her master? Keep her?

He dresses.

The crease of his boxer shorts rubs painfully against his bruised flesh as he walks back into the room. Thalie is watching a game show on the TV set.

"I'm taking you out," he tells her, switching the pro-
gramme off.

"Where to?"

"Never you mind."

Somehow, he always knew it would come to this.

She understands.

Asks: "How should I dress?"

"Like a whore. Wear that blouse and no bra, and stockings. And your shortest skirt. No underwear."

She nods.

Night falls as their cab rushes down Fifth toward SoHo.
He instructs her. At all times, she will sit with her legs open;
there is to be no false modesty. She is his property for tonight
and the following day and he will brook no disobedience. She
will only talk when spoken to.

She indicates her assent to his terms.

"You will take no pleasure from what is done to you,
because I won't, either . . ."

"A master would take pleasure in displaying me," she
interrupts him.

He slaps her cheek, as punishment for her uncalled verbal
response.

"Quiet, now."

Her cheek reddens from the blow. She lowers her eyes.
The driver looks inquiringly into his rear mirror at the older
man and the young woman. Even though the light outside is
dimming, he clearly saw her nipples through the shimmering blouse as she entered his cab, and he tries to get a better
look.

A jazz club. Grimy walls, cigarette smoke, dissonant
melodies running like waves across the ceiling over the sparse
audience. He has her drink vodka and orange, although he
knows she dislikes the concoction. Men at the bar glance in
their direction. Her skirt is hitched up to mid-thigh. He
fingers her under the table. She squirms.

Her rings are wet with her secretions.

He informs her of the fact. Presents a finger to her.

"Lick me clean."

She does, just as the waitress approaches their table, inquiring after another round.

"Touching," the waitress mumbles, visibly disapproving and mistaking Thalie's appetite for a gesture of love.

"Isn't it?" he responds with a wry smile.

The tension is palpable, as he summons his courage.

She senses it and remains damningly silent and expressionless.

Finally.

"Anything?"

"Yes," Thalie replies. "Anything: it is my nature to be a slave."

He rises from his seat as the band on stage finish their set in a flourish of drum rolls and reverb, takes hold of her hand and they make their way to the toilets. He briefly holds his breath and then enters the men's, followed by her. There is a harsh smell of antiseptic lingering in the air; the ceiling is low, the surroundings claustrophobic. There is no one there. Just a yellowing row of urinals, a creaking fan circling like a low-flying aircraft close to the peeling, concrete ceiling, a sink with a dripping tap, a dirty towel and, behind a wooden door painted jet-black, the lone toilet seat. He opens the cubicle and orders Thalie to sit. He pulls her blue skirt up to her waist, unveiling her rings, and opens the buttons of her blouse so that her breasts are also on display.

"Like that. Yes."

She doesn't answer.

"The first man to come in," he says.

She nods silently.

They wait. Each passing second extends to eternity.

Finally, the door to the men's toilets swings open and a tall black guy walks in, hands already unzipping his flies. He heads towards the urinal, his back to Thalie in the cubicle.

"Hi." He recognizes the guy, who played bass in the gang, a lanky man in denim.

"Hi, man. How ya doin'?"

"Listen. I have something for you . . ."

The musician starts peeing. "Nah, man, I have my own supplier. Thanks anyway."

"It's not drugs."

The black guy shrugs. "Yeah? What then?"

"I have a woman here. She'll suck you dry for free. Interested?"

The man looks over his shoulder at him, weighing the seriousness of the offer. Notices the open cubicle and Thalie sitting there, splayed open, all her gold rings on display.

He catches his breath. "What's in it for you?" he asks, turning round and zipping his jeans up. His eyes are now fixed on the obscene spectacle of the young woman, her white flesh like a beacon in the sordid surroundings. "Wow," he whispers to himself.

"I watch. That's all."

"You serious?"

"Absolutely."

"I'd always heard you limeys got your kicks in weird fashion," he says, a grin spreading over his dark features.

He approaches the cubicle and its immobile prisoner. He unzips and pulls out his cock. It's long, thick, uncut. Offers it to her, hesitantly as if all this is about to disappear in a puff of smoke and is but a crazy mirage, a drug-fuelled dream. Thalie bends her face forward to take the cock.

"Sweet gal," says the musician as her lips first graze his stem, before she takes him all in. "Will she swallow?" he asks.

"Yes," he answers.

And watches the spectacle.

Black against white.

Black inside white.

To the bitter end.

After it is over, he allows her to adjust her apparel and cups his hands together to allow her to drink the tap water and wash her mouth.

Relief floods over him that no other man entered the bathroom while the three of them were there. He's not sure he could have controlled the situation any further.

Still, she says nothing.

They finish their drinks and listen to the first quarter of an hour of the band's second set. He hails a cab and they return to the hotel.

This is the first night in Manhattan they do not make love.

Q & A

"*Did things happen that you particularly disliked?*"

"*Many. What I still found most difficult was when she invited friends around to demonstrate her power over me and my subservience, and took great pleasure humiliating me in their presence. The sex I didn't mind. But I did feel shame. More so, when we left the house to go to parties and she had me walk out onto the street wearing accessories and clothing which were so explicit as to provide little doubt as to my status as her personal slave. A dog collar, a skimpy maid's outfit, sometimes even a thin metal chain that connected to the handcuffs she made me wear for the short walk to the car park.*"

"*You were afraid that people might recognize you?*"

"*Not really. I did not like the fact that my slavery might be recognized by others.*"

"*I'm not sure I understand. You are proud of what you are.*"

"*I know. The worst time was when she invited my sister along for tea to the house, one evening. I hadn't seen her for nearly a year. I had to wear the maid's outfit with the apron and serve them in silence. My sister's smile nauseated me. When asked if the tea and biscuits I had baked were to her liking, my sister, no doubt previously prompted by Anne-Louise, expressed reservations and I was told the only recourse was for me to be flogged in her presence. Which Anne-Louise did with unusual ferocity. I was made to bend across a chair a few inches away from where my sister sat, my dress was pulled up above my waist and my knickers pulled down to my knees, and I still remember every blow against my bare skin, even now. When Anne-Louise had completed the punishment, she actually invited my sister to beat me likewise. Which she agreed to do, the damn traitor. I couldn't sit for days after that beating.*"

"*You were going to tell me about the parties?*"

"*There were two sorts. Once or twice a month, Anne-Louise would have friends over: mostly other women, sometimes couples for drinks in the evening. I would be made to serve. Often I would have to give evidence of my servility and accept a flogging or the caress of the whip. The guests would seldom become involved. This was more a demonstration of Anne-Louise's power over me. At most, I would have to display my body for their after-drinks recreation, allow them to touch and twist my breast rings, provide evidence of my absolute docility and obedience.*"

"*What sort of people were these friends of Anne-Louise's?*"

"*Professional, middle-class, middle-aged. The women were lesbian or bisexual but she would never loan me to them. Their fun with me was restricted to the games with me on that particular evening.*"

"*The other parties?*"

"*They were more extreme. Infrequent, also. I think I only attended five. Usually took place on Saturday nights and ran through the night. Never at Anne-Louise's place: usually at plush residences somewhere in Brussels or in nearby towns. I never knew where exactly we were, as I was blindfolded by Anne-Louise as we neared the locations.*"

"*Sounds frightening.*"

"*It was. Anne-Louise said I now had to prove that I was fully trained as a sub and these parties would be my final test. I was eager to prove her confidence in me was well placed and swore I would do everything I was told. It wasn't easy, but then I had little choice.*"

"*What sort of people attended these parties?*"

"*People like Anne-Louise. Genuine, experienced masters. They were here to show off their slaves, male as well as female. We all wore collars and were forbidden to talk to each other as we were cuffed together awaiting our fate for the evening. Whatever happened to any of us, we were made to watch, and looking away would result in further punishment.*"

"*What happened to you?*"

"*Even now, I can't talk about many of the things that were done to me, or I was made to do to others.*"

"*What can you reveal?*"

"Often the masters would play games, make bets on us, pick cards for the humiliations that would be inflicted on us. A party night would seldom pass by without my not having been used in all holes by all the masters present, male as well as female. On my first such party, my anal virginity was auctioned. I was blindfolded and made to kneel and suck every cock in the room, including the male slaves who were present. Unbeknown to me, the first one who managed to make me gag would be designated to be the first to bugger me. I had successfully sucked three of the men and swallowed them when I felt another place himself ahead of my mouth and heard sniggers across the room. I knew something was wrong right there and then. A voice behind me remarked that I might require some help, and my hair was brutally pulled back and my head pushed forward onto the expectant cock. He was so heavily hung that the pressure applied to the back of my head forced me to swallow him and he was shoved all the way into my throat. I couldn't breathe. My lips were stretched to their fullest around its thickness and no air could pass from my lungs to my mouth. I couldn't help gagging. It had been a set-up. He was one of the young slaves and his penis had elephantine proportions. At the next party, I was told he measured twelve inches or more."

"Jesus!"

"I had no choice. I was installed at the centre of the room as all watched and the young boy sodomized me. It hurt badly. I even fainted halfway through and had to be revived with smelling salts. They had no pity on me. When it was over and I stumbled back to the far wall, where the other slaves were grouped, I noticed Anne-Louise had not remained in the room for the ceremony. One of the other girls – she was a tall, red-haired beauty with ever such pale skin – whispered to me that she had gone through the same ordeal. They always chose the pimply young slave boy with the enormous cock for a female slave's first experience of sodomy. Something about stretching us for further use. A master saw her talking to me, chided her and announced this was one transgression too far. Could she not manage to keep her mouth closed long enough? Next time, she would be the one to be punished. She went paler than pale and

tried to refrain her tears from flowing. I saw that she was terrorized. In the meantime, the young boy who had hurt me so much was now still the centre of attraction and being made to suck his own master to hardness before he was made to kneel on all fours himself and his master buggered him in turn."

"How could you accept such things, Thalie?"

"Because Anne-Louise ordered me to and I was in love with her."

"The things we do for love . . ."

"While you were being used by others at these parties, what did Anne-Louise do?"

"She liked to whip and torture the other masters' female slaves. I once had to watch her fist another girl. She had never, until then, done that to me. The poor kid screamed but Anne-Louise didn't stop."

"You must have been scared by that?"

"Yes, but not so much as the day I had to watch the tall red-haired girl being punished. She had accumulated too many faults, according to her master, and had to be made an example of. And all of us other slaves present were warned that if we even looked away one single second, a similar fate would befall us. It was awful."

"What did they do to her?"

"She fought against them but she didn't stand a chance. It took four masters to hold her down, while another brought it in . . ."

"What . . . ?"

"They placed her in the right position, kicked her legs apart and it happened. Even now, I still have nightmares thinking of what I saw. Scratched deep lines of blood across her back once it was over."

"God!"

"That very moment, I swore I'd commit suicide if I ever allowed something like that to happen to me."

"I can imagine."

"Later, as the others played with the rest of us slaves, I saw her sobbing against the wall. They had connected her collar to the dog's leash and she sat there motionless while the come still

oozed out of her. I never saw her again. She was never brought to the other parties I attended, even though her erstwhile master was present. Now, he had another woman."

"What can I say, Thalie? And you were still only seventeen?"

"After that night, I think Anne-Louise began to sense my unease about the sexual escalation in the relationship. A couple of days later, she stuck a Polaroid next to my bedside table. She had taken it when the red-haired girl was being violated. This was clearly a warning to me not to doubt her resolve and dare any form of disobedience to her will. But we only attended two more special Saturday night parties during the course of the following six months and nothing more untoward than sex and whippings occurred, as if the group knew they had crossed a dangerous borderline. At the final party Anne-Louise took me to, I could somehow feel her distancing herself from me already, but I did not wish to acknowledge that a page was about to be turned. That night, the tall pimply young slave boy with the uncommon endowment came up for punishment and I was fitted with a strap-on and made to fuck him. I had never realized before I could switch from sub to becoming a most ferocious, vengeful dom. I plundered him with a vengeance. I eventually had to be pulled away, out of him by Anne-Louise. She had of course used a strap-on on me, on many occasions, but we had never switched; she was not into penetration."

"You said things were changing?"

"For some time, Anne-Louise had hinted that the present she was planning for my eighteenth birthday would be unforgettable. Two months prior to the event, she took me again to the doctor in Brussels and my lips were pierced and the eight rings installed. I was told it would take some weeks to heal. Anne-Louise seldom used me in the weeks between my labial piercings, and often only returned home late with no word of explanation."

"So what did she actually give you for your eighteenth birthday?"

"There was not even a greetings card in the morning. I slaved away in the kitchen all day and she came home around seven. She asked me to follow her to the bathroom, ordered me to undress, examined my rings and the now fully-healed piercings. I was told

to close my eyes and felt her fit something across the rings. It was a special kind of safety pin which fits through both sets of four rings and closes with a miniature padlock, totally sealing the entrance to my vagina. There was a kind of beauty to it, this chastity device whose usefulness I couldn't quite understand. Later, she explained to me that she had tired of me, wished to install a new friend in the house. By fitting me with the padlock, she would still control me from a distance. I was to leave her house the following day! I was dumbstruck. I cried for hours."

They spend their final day in Manhattan together, as normal lovers do.

They linger in bed, have breakfast sent up, touch, kiss, caress, talk about the weather.

He plans their day. They will lunch at a small Japanese sushi bar on the corner of 13th Street and 6th. She tells him she has never eaten raw fish before.

"You'll see," he reassures her. "It's nice."

They will catch a movie at the Angelika, trawl Tower Records for the obscure country and western CDs still missing from his extensive collection, explore the quaint streets of Alphabet City and end up with a final meal in a Cajun joint close to the Flatiron Building. Oysters, gumbo and whatever main entrée catches her fancy.

"Fattening me up, eh?" Thalie remarks.

"Exactly. You're all bones and rings, my dear . . ."

He's not sure if she appreciates the joke.

"I'm off to shave."

"OK."

When he returns from the bathroom, her face is flushed. Her eyes shift when he looks at her; she appears guilty.

"What is it?" he asks her.

"I've been bad."

"How?"

"While you were washing, I touched myself."

"So?"

"You didn't use me, yesterday night. I needed relief."

"It's not a problem, Thalie."

"It's wrong for a slave to seek her own pleasure, without the consent of her master. You must punish me."

His heart sinks.

So this is the way it is.

He handcuffs her hands to the bed post and arranges her nude body in the shape of an X across the soft green bed cover. She is not wearing the safety pin. As he widens the angle between her legs, her cunt gapes.

He hangs the "Don't Disturb" sign outside the door and leaves her in the room, captive, laid out like an offering. Although not for the maid!

He loiters around the reception area until he finds a suitable male. A German tourist, wealthy-looking but with no taste in clothes. At first, the man does not take him seriously, but he insists. They share a coffee in the breakfast room. He explains. They do the deal. He gives the German the card key to their room.

He has no wish to watch.

"You have two hours," he says. "Be out of the room by then. She is handcuffed. I have the keys with me. She will not speak, or cry, or scream."

"And I . . . ?" asks the German, begging for confirmation of his wildest dreams.

"She is totally yours. Anything you want."

They are two of the slowest hours of his life. He walks four blocks North, then five blocks South. Peruses every window without even noting their varied contents. When he finally returns, Thalie is still handcuffed to the bedpost, the taste of another man still leaking from her, dotting her stomach, her face, her breasts.

She smiles at him.

His slave.

That night, he sleeps badly, his mind in tumult.

Sunrise comes early, with a blanket of low clouds waltzing over the top of the highest skyscrapers.

He tells her about the dream.

In it, he has failed abysmally at becoming a master and the only alternative is to become a slave himself. To stay with

Thalie, he sends a begging letter to Anne-Louise, offering himself in exchange for further time with her. His pitiful demeanour makes her laugh but, as a game, she accepts.

Initially, she puts him on a diet, having no need of an overweight slave. Then, when he becomes suitable, she shaves his pubic hair and brands him, a large B carved into his buttocks. He is allowed to sleep in the same room as Anne-Louise and Thalie, but on the floor, at the foot of their bed, where he is forced to listen to their lovemaking and Thalie's severe beatings. He is beaten, too, made to wear an apron and serve their food; if ever he is caught with an erection, he is whipped until he bleeds. But he is happy now, just living under the same room as his companion of slavery. Eventually, he is allowed to attend the special parties where his role is to suck all the men to hardness before they fuck Thalie, then to lick them clean after they have withdrawn from her orifices. In turn, she is to prepare the men who bugger him. He is no longer allowed to touch her, only to watch the increasing stations of her degradation. But the punishments get worse and worse, as he finds it impossible to repress his excitement as his cock invariably reacts shamelessly every time another man penetrates her.

Finally, the circle of masters decree the ultimate punishment at the next party he is to be brought to.

Which is when he awoke.

"A companion in slavery," Thalie remarks. "Yes, I think that would be quite appropriate for you . . ."

"Would I?"

"But it's all a dream, you know. Anne-Louise hates men; she would never want you as her slave. If you had a wife to offer in exchange for time with me, maybe then she might entertain your proposal. Dream on."

"I will," he says.

Q & A
"What did you do when Anne-Louise threw you out?"
"I pleaded, made a fool of myself, threw myself at her feet.

Even begged to be retained, if only as a servant, so that I may look after her and her new, young mistress."

"Did you meet her, this new girl?"

"Yes, some months later. Tall, blonde: everything I wasn't. New. Virgin territory for Anne-Louise's cruel whims."

"But she didn't allow you to stay on?"

"No. I was desperate. I knew my parents would never have me back. I had given up my studies without obtaining any diplomas or qualifications. How could I find a job, somewhere to live? During the two years I had spent with Anne-Louise, I had deliberately lost the few friends I had before our encounter. I had nothing. I never even had any more normal clothes to wear. Anne-Louise had once mentioned, almost as a joke, a couple who had on two occasions visited her soirées and been witness to my servility and asked where they could find a similar maid. Maybe I could go and place myself in their service. The idea didn't appeal to me. Become a servant to people I had already privately served as a slave. But I had no other alternative. Anne-Louise phoned them and a deal was agreed."

"And that's where you are now?"

"I've now worked here two years almost. They leave for work – they are both senior managers for a large insurance company in a nearby town – early in the morning and my duties are to keep the house clean, wash, iron, dust, prepare the food. I am not allowed any mail or telephone calls. I play on the Internet. Watch TV. They are hard on me. The woman has custody of the padlock key, but she is capricious and often declines to set the rings free, particularly when I'm having my periods. It amuses her. Most of the time, I am just their servant, but sometimes they remember my nature and my past, usually when they have drunk heavily. He fucks me while she watches, then has me lick her. Christmas last, I was seemingly too enthusiastic while he used me extensively and the next day, out of jealousy, she beat me badly."

"Do you still hear from Anne-Louise?"

"Not often. She keeps in touch, though."

"Do you still love her?"

"Yes, as much as ever."

"Will she ever have you back?"

"I live in that hope, but I realise how unlikely it is. I'm realistic."

"Are you happy?"

"Yes, in my own way. But living with my owners is boring. The house is in the middle of nowhere. The only contact I have with other human beings is when they take me on holiday with them. Spain in the summer; a house in the mountains in France near Easter. In Spain, I am allowed to wear shorts and bikinis. The padlock is taken off and I am allowed to be naughty. I fuck boys; with rubber protection, of course. They don't mind, as long as I'm not late back at their villa to cook the meals."

"Can you see your life remaining the same for years to come, Thalie? A leading question, I know."

"I'm only twenty. I am a sub . . . But I do harbour hopes of convincing Anne-Louise of giving me to B."

"But he's the man who tried to brand you?"

"I know, but I think he would be a good master for me."

"It's your life."

"It is."

"And I'm no knight in shining armour, Thalie. I have no mission in life to change your nature. You touch me, though. I feel much tenderness for you."

"Do you think you could be my new master, then?"

"I'm not sure. Willing to give it my best shot (hear my smile between these lines) . . ."

"If you were a true dom, you would know already. I don't think you are, somehow."

"I'm sadly aware of the fact. But I still want to see you. Badly. Can you find a way to get away for a few days? Meet me somewhere? Anywhere? There must be some pretext you can use, a white lie. That aunt in Paris who's left you the deeds of the apartments she owns and rents out, for instance. You could invent a reason to go there, to sign legal papers . . . Please, Thalie."

"Maybe. Let me think."

He packs.

He had asked the day before whether they should purchase a case for the clothes they had bought together, but she declined. She came with nothing and insists she should return to her owners similarly. It would be suspicious otherwise and, unlike Anne-Louise's, she does not appreciate their beatings. He realizes he had never even asked her what alibi, what lie she had used to justify her trip.

He watches as she stuffs the barely-worn chenille jumper, the rainbow skirt, the cream see-through blouse, the stockings and sundry knick-knacks into the hotel room's wicker waste basket. He's packed the cuffs and the strap-on in his own case, although he's thinking of disposing them in a washroom at the airport. It would be too embarrassing to be searched at customs.

They take the lift in heavy silence. He settles the bill with his credit card and the doorman hails a cab.

"Newark."

It's early morning, ahead of the commuter traffic. The journey barely takes half an hour. Throughout, he holds her hand in his.

Way down his throat, there are a million words he wishes to say, but they break up like flotsam against the rampart of his lips. He knows he hasn't the eloquence to change her life. Or his.

Her flight is a whole hour earlier than his.

Her thin, fragile silhouette disappears down the neon-lit corridor that leads to her departure lounge. He has checked: her plane is on time. They haven't even said goodbye. Before the bend, she turns, smiles and blows him a kiss.

He knows he will never see her again. The letters will continue for a short time; then they will slow down and a day will come when she just disappears, the property of a new master, who will forbid all contact with her former life. And his mind will imagine the worst. Violation. Torture. Death. Because the life she has chosen is a one-way street.

And his heart doesn't own the right passport.

SPANKING THE MAID

Robert Coover

She enters, deliberately, gravely, without affectation, circumspect in her motions (as she's been taught), not stamping too loud, nor dragging her legs after her, but advancing sedately, discreetly, glancing briefly at the empty rumpled bed, the cast-off nightclothes. She hesitates. No. Again. She enters. Deliberately and gravely, without affectation, not stamping too loud, nor dragging her legs after her, not marching as if leading a dance, nor keeping time with her head and hands, nor staring or turning her head either one way or the other, but advancing sedately and discreetly through the door, across the polished floor, past the empty rumpled bed and cast-off nightclothes (not glancing, that's better), to the tall curtains along the far wall. As she's been taught. Now, with a humble yet authoritative gesture, she draws the curtains open: Ah! the morning sunlight comes flooding in over the gleaming tiles as though (she thinks) flung from a bucket. She opens wide the glass doors behind the curtains (there is such a song of birds all about!) and gazes for a moment into the garden, quite prepared to let the sweet breath of morning blow in and excite her to the most generous and efficient accomplishments, but her mind is still locked on that image, at first pleasing, now troubling, of the light as it spilled into the room: as from a bucket . . . She sighs. She enters. With a bucket. She sets the bucket down, deliberately, gravely, and walks (circumspectly) across the room, over the polished tiles, past the empty rumpled bed (she doesn't glance at it), to draw open the tall curtains at the far wall. Buckets of light come flooding in (she is not thinking about this now) and the room, as she opens the glass doors wide, is sweetened by the fresh morning air blowing in from the garden. The sun is fully risen and the pink clouds of dawn are all gone out of the sky (the time lost: this is what she is thinking about), but the dew is still on every plant in the garden, and everything looks clean and bright. As will his room when she is done with it.

He awakes from a dream (something about utility, or futility, and a teacher he once had who, when he whipped his students, called it his "civil service"), still wrapped in darkness and hugged close to the sweet breast of the night, but with the new day already hard upon him, just beyond the curtains (he knows, even without looking), waiting for him out there like a brother: to love him or to kill him. He pushes the bedcovers back and sits up groggily to meet its challenge (or promise), pushes his feet into slippers, rubs his face, stretches, wonders what new blunders the maid (where is she?) will commit today. Well. I should at least give her a chance, he admonishes himself with a gaping yawn.

Oh, she knows her business well: to scrub and wax the floors, polish the furniture, make the master's bed soft and easy, lay up his nightclothes, wash, starch, and mend the bedlinens as necessary, air the blankets and clean the bathroom, making certain of ample supplies of fresh towels and washcloths, soap, toilet paper, razor blades and toothpaste – in short, to see that nothing be wanting which he desires or requires to be done, being always diligent in endeavoring to please him, silent when he is angry except to beg his pardon, and ever faithful, honest, submissive, and of good disposition. The trivial round, the common task, she knows as she sets about her morning's duties, will furnish all she needs to ask, room to deny herself, a road (speaking loosely) to bring her daily nearer God. But on that road, on the floor of the bathroom, she finds a damp towel and some pajama bottoms, all puddled together like a cast-off mop-head. Mop-head? She turns and gazes in dismay at the empty bucket by the outer door. Why, she wants to know, tears springing to the corners of her eyes, can't it be easier than this? And so she enters, sets her bucket down with a firm deliberation, leans her mop gravely against the wall. Also a broom, brushes, some old rags, counting things off on her fingers as she deposits them. The curtains have been drawn open and the room is already (as though impatiently) awash with morning sunlight. She crosses the room, past the (no glances) empty rumpled bed, and opens wide the glass doors leading out into the garden, letting in the sweet breath of morning, which she hardly notices. She has resolved this morning – as every morning – to be cheerful and good-natured, such that if any accident should happen to test that resolution, she should not suffer it to put her out of temper with everything besides, but such resolutions are more easily sworn than obeyed. Things are already in such a state! Yet: virtue is made for difficulties, she reminds herself, and grows stronger and brighter for such trials. *"Oh, teach me, my God and King, in all things thee to see, and what I do in any thing, to do it as for thee!"* she sings out to the garden and to the room, feeling her heart lift like a sponge in a bucket. *"A servant with this clause makes drudgery divine: who sweeps a room, as for thy laws, makes that and th'action fine!"* And yes, she can still recover the lost time. She has everything now, the mop and bucket, broom, rags and brushes, her apron pockets are full of polishes, dust-cloths and cleaning powders, the cupboards are well stocked with fresh linens, all she really needs now is to keep – but ah! is there, she wonders anxiously, spinning abruptly on her heels as she hears the master relieving himself noisily in the bathroom, any *water* in the bucket –?!

He awakes, squints at his watch in the darkness, grunts (she's late, but just as well, time for a shower) and, with only a moment's hesitation, tosses the blankets back, tearing himself free: I'm so old, he thinks, and still every morning is a bloody new birth. Somehow it should be easier than this. He sits up painfully (that divine government!), rubs his face, pushes his feet into slippers, stands, stretches, then strides to the windows at the far wall and throws open the tall curtains, letting the sun in. The room seems almost to explode with the blast of light: he resists, then surrenders to, finally welcomes its amicable violence. He opens wide the glass doors that lead out into the garden and stands there in the sunshine, sucking in deeply the fresh morning air and trying to recall the dream he's just had. Something about a teacher who had once lectured him on humility. Severely. Only now, in the dream, he was himself the teacher and the student was a woman he knew, or thought he knew, and in his lecture "humility" kept getting mixed up somehow with "humor", such that, in effect, he was trying, in all severity, to teach her how to laugh. He's standing there in the sunlight in his slippers and pajama bottoms, remembering the curious strained expression on the woman's face as she tried – desperately, it seemed – to laugh, and wondering why this provoked (in the dream) such a fury in him, when the maid comes in. She gazes impassively a moment (yet humbly, circumspectly) at the gaping fly of his pajamas, then turns away, sets her bucket down against the wall. Her apron strings are loose, there's a hole in one of her black stockings, and she's forgotten her mop again. I'd be a happier man, he acknowledges to himself with a wry sigh, if I could somehow fail to notice these things. "I'll start in the bathroom," she says discreetly. "Sir," he reminds her. "Sir," she says.

And she enters. Deliberately and gravely, as though once and for all, without affectation, somewhat encumbered by the vital paraphernalia of her office, yet radiant with that clear-browed self-assurance achieved only by long and generous devotion to duty. She plants her bucket and brushes beside the door, leans the mop and broom against the wall, then crosses the room to fling open (humbly, authoritatively) the curtains and the garden doors: the fragrant air and sunlight come flooding in, a flood she now feels able to appreciate. The sun is already high in the sky, but the garden is still bejeweled with morning dew and (she remembers to notice) there is such a song of birds all about! What inspiration! She enjoys this part of her work: flushing out the stale darkness of the dead night with such grand (yet circumspect) gestures – it's almost an act of magic! Of course, she takes pleasure in *all* her appointed tasks (she reminds herself), whether it be scrubbing floors or polishing furniture or even scouring out the tub or toilet, for she knows that only in giving herself (as he has told her) can she find herself: true service (he doesn't have to tell her!) is perfect freedom. And so, excited by the song of the birds, the sweet breath of morning, and her own natural eagerness to please, she turns with a glad heart to her favorite task of all: the making of the bed. Indeed, all the rest of her work is embraced by it, for the opening up and airing of the bed is the first of her tasks, the making of it her last. Today, however, when she tosses the covers back, she finds, coiled like a dark snake near the foot, a bloodstained leather belt. She starts back. The sheets, too, are flecked with blood. Shadows seem to creep across the room and the birds fall silent. Perhaps, she thinks, her heart sinking, I'd better go out and come in again . . .

At least, he cautions himself while taking a shower, give her a chance. Her forgetfulness, her clumsiness, her endless comings and goings and stupid mistakes are a trial, of course, and he feels sometimes like he's been living with them forever, but she means well and, with patience, instruction, discipline, she can still learn. Indeed, to the extent that she fails, it could be said, *he* has failed. He knows he must be firm, yet understanding, severe if need be, but caring and protective. He vows to treat her today with the civility and kindness due to an inferior, and not to lose his temper, even should she resist. Our passions (he reminds himself) are our infirmities.

A sort of fever of the mind, which ever leaves us weaker than it found us. But when he turns off the taps and reaches for the towel, he finds it damp. Again! He can feel the rage rising in him, turning his gentler intentions to ash with its uncontrollable heat. Has she forgotten to change them yet again, he wonders furiously, standing there in a puddle with the cold wet towels clutched in his fists – or has she not even come yet?

She enters once and for all, encumbered with her paraphernalia which she deposits by the wall near the door, thinking: it should be easier than this. Indeed, why bother at all when it always seems to turn out the same? Yet she cannot do otherwise. She is driven by a sense of duty and a profound appetite for hope never quite stifled by even the harshest punishments: this time, today, perhaps it will be perfect . . . So, deliberately and gravely, not staring or turning her head either one way or the other, she crosses the room to the far wall and, with a determined flourish, draws open the tall curtains, flooding the room with buckets of sunlight, but her mind is clouded with an old obscurity: when, she wants to know as she opens wide the glass doors to let the sweet breath of morning in (there are birds, too, such a song, she doesn't hear it), did all this really begin? When she entered? Before that? Long ago? Not yet? Or just now as, bracing herself as though for some awful trial, she turns upon the bed and flings the covers back, her morning's tasks begun.

"Oh!" she cries. "I beg your pardon, sir!"

He stares groggily down at the erection poking up out of the fly of his pajama pants, like (she thinks) some kind of luxuriant but dangerous dew-bejeweled blossom: a monster in the garden. "I was having a dream," he announces sleepily, yet gravely. "Something about tumidity. But it kept getting mixed up somehow with –"

But she is no longer listening. Watching his knobby plant waggle puckishly in the morning breeze, then dip slowly, wilting toward the shadows like a closing morning glory, a solution of sorts has occurred to her to that riddle of genesis that has been troubling her mind: to wit, that a condition *has* no beginning. Only *change* can begin or end.

She enters, dressed crisply in her black uniform with its starched white apron and lace cap, leans her mop against the wall like a standard, and strides across the gleaming tile floor to fling open the garden doors as though (he thinks) calling forth the morning. What's left of it. Watching her from behind the bathroom door, he is moved by her transparent earnestness, her uncomplicated enthusiasm, her easy self-assurance. What more, really, does he want of her? Never mind that she's forgotten her broom again, or that her shoe's unbuckled and her cap on crooked, or that in her exuberance she nearly broke the glass doors (and sooner or later will), what is wonderful is the quickening of her spirits as she enters, the light that seems to dawn on her face as she opens the room, the way she makes a maid's oppressive routine seem like a sudden invention of love. See now how she tosses back the blankets and strips off the sheets as though, in childish excitement, unwrapping a gift! How in fluffing up the pillows she seems almost to bring them to life! She calls it: "doing the will of God from the heart!" "*Teach me, my God and King, in all things thee to see*," she sings, "*and what I do in any thing, to do it as for thee!*" Ah well, he envies her: would that he had it so easy! All life is a service, he knows that. To live in the full sense of the word is not to exist or subsist merely, but to make oneself over, to *give* oneself: to some high purpose, to others, to some social end, to life itself beyond the shell of ego. But he, lacking superiors, must devote himself to abstractions, never knowing when he has succeeded, when he has failed, or even if he has the abstractions right, whereas she, needing no others, has him. He would like to explain this to her, to ease the pain of her routine, of her chastisement – what he calls his disciplinary interventions – but he knows that it is he, not she, who is forever in need of such explanations. Her mop fairly flies over the tiles (today she has remembered the mop), making them gleam like mirrors, her face radiant with their reflected light. He checks himself in the bathroom mirror, flicks lint off one shoulder, smoothes the ends of his moustache. If only she could somehow understand how difficult it is for me, he thinks as he steps out to receive her greeting: "Good morning, sir."

"Good morning," he replies crisply, glancing around the room. He means to give her some encouragement, to reward her zeal with praise or gratitude or at least a smile to match her own, but instead he finds himself flinging his dirty towels at her feet and snapping: "These towels are damp! See to it that they are replaced!"

"Yes, sir!"

"Moreover, your apron strings are dangling untidily and there are flyspecks on the mirror!"

"Sir."

"And another thing!" He strides over to the bed and tears it apart. "Isn't it about time these sheets were changed? Or am I supposed to wear them through before they are taken to be washed?"

"But, sir, I just put new –!"

"What? *WHAT* –?!" he storms. "Answering back to a reproof? Have you forgotten all I've taught you?"

"I – I'm sorry, sir!"

"Never answer back if your master takes occasion to reprove you, except –?"

"Except it be to acknowledge my fault, sir, and that I am sorry for having committed it, promising to amend for the time to come, and to . . . to . . ."

"Am I being unfair?" he insists, unbuckling his belt.

"No, sir," she says, her eyes downcast, shoulders trembling, her arms pressed tight to her sides.

He is strict but not unkindly. He pays her well, is grateful for her services, treats her respectfully: she doesn't dislike him or even fear him. Nor does she have to work very hard: he is essentially a tidy man, picks up after himself, comes and goes without disturbing things much. A bit of dusting and polishing now and then, fold his pajamas, change the towels, clean the bathroom, scrub the floor, make his bed: really, there's nothing to complain about. Yet, vaguely, even as she opens up the garden doors, letting the late morning sunshine and freshness in, she feels unhappy. Not because of what she must do – no, she truly serves with gladness. When she straightens a room, polishes a floor, bleaches a sheet or scrubs a tub, always doing the very best she can, she becomes, she knows, a part of what is good in the world, creating a kind of beauty, revealing a kind of truth. About herself, about life, the things she touches. It's just that, somehow, something is missing. Some response, some enrichment, some direction . . . it's, well, it's too repetitive. Something like that. That's part of the problem anyway. The other part is what she keeps finding in his bed. Things that oughtn't to be there, like old razor blades, broken bottles, banana skins, bloody pessaries, crumbs and ants, leather thongs, mirrors, empty books, old toys, dark stains. Once, even, a frog jumped out at her. No matter how much sunlight and fresh air she lets in, there's always this dark little pocket of lingering night which she has to uncover. It can ruin everything, all her careful preparations. This morning, however, all she finds is a pair of flannelette drawers. Ah: she recognizes them. She glances about guiltily, pulls them on hastily. Lucky the master's in the bathroom, she thinks, patting down her skirt and apron, or there'd be the devil to pay.

Something about scouring, or scourging, he can't remember, and a teacher he once had who called his lectures "lechers".

The maid is standing over him, staring down in some astonishment at his erection. "Oh! I beg your pardon, sir!"

"I was having a dream . . ." he explains, trying to bring it back. "Something about a woman . . ." But by then he is alone again. He hears her in the bathroom, running water, singing, whipping the wet towels off the racks and tossing them out the door. Ah well, it's easy for her, she can come and go. He sits up, squinting in the bright light, watching his erection dip back inside his pajamas like a sleeper pulling the blankets over his head (oh yes! to return there!), then duti-fully shoves his feet into slippers, stretches, staggers to the open garden doors. The air is fragrant and there's a morning racket of birds and insects, vaguely threatening. Sometimes, as now, scratching himself idly and dragging himself still from the stupor of sleep, he wonders about his calling, how it came to be his, and when it all began: on his coming here? on *her* coming here? before that, in some ancient time beyond recall? And has he chosen it? or has he, like that woman in his dream, showing him something that for some reason enraged him, been "born with it, sir, for your very utility"?

She strives, understanding the futility of it, for perfection. To arrive properly equipped, to cross the room deliberately, circumspectly, without affectation (as he has taught her), to fling open the garden doors and let the sweet breath of morning flow in and chase the night away, to strip and air the bed and, after all her common tasks, her trivial round, to remake it smooth and tight, all the sheets and blankets tucked in neatly at the sides and bottom, the upper sheet and blankets turned down at the head just so far that their fold covers only half the pillows, all topped with the spread, laid to hang evenly at all sides. And today – perhaps at last! She straightens up, wipes her brow, looks around: yes! he'll be so surprised! Everything perfect! Her heart is pounding as the master, dressed for the day, steps out of the bathroom, marches directly over to the bed, hauls back the covers, picks up a pillow, and hits her in the face with it. Now what did he do that for? "And another thing!" he says.

He awakes, feeling sorry for himself (he's not sure why, something he's been dreaming perhaps, or merely the need to wake just by itself: come, day, do your damage!), tears himself painfully from the bed's embrace, sits up, pushes his feet into slippers. He grunts, squinting in the dimness at his watch: she's late. Just as well. He can shower before she gets here. He staggers into the bathroom and drops his pajamas, struggling to recall his dream. Something about a woman in the civil service, which in her ignorance or cupidity, she insisted on calling the "sibyl service". He is relieving himself noisily when the maid comes in.

"Oh! I beg your pardon, sir!"

"Good morning," he replies crisply, and pulls his pajamas up, but she is gone. He can hear her outside the door, walking quickly back and forth, flinging open the curtains and garden doors, singing to herself as though lifted by the tasks before her. Sometimes he envies her, having him. Her footsteps carry her to the bed and he hears the rush and flutter of sheets and blankets being thrown back. Hears her scream.

He's not unkind, demands no more than is his right, pays her well, and teaches her things like, "All life is a service, a consecration to some high end," and, "If domestic service is to be tolerable, there must be an attitude of habitual deference on the one side and one of sympathetic protection on the other." "Every state and condition of life has its particular duties," he has taught her. "The duty of a servant is to be obedient, diligent, sober, just, honest, frugal, orderly in her behavior, submissive and respectful toward her master. She must be contented in her station, because it is necessary that some should be above others in this world, and it was the will of the Almighty to place you in a state of servitude." Her soul, in short, is his invention, and she is grateful to him for it. "*Whatever thy hand findeth to do,*" he has admonished, "*do it with all thy might!*" Nevertheless, looking over her shoulder at her striped sit-me-down in the wardrobe mirror, she wishes he might be a little less literal in applying his own maxims: *he's drawn blood!*

He awakes, mumbling something about a dream, a teacher he once had, some woman, infirmities. "A sort of fever of the mind," he explains, his throat phlegmy with sleep.

"Yes, sir," she says, and flings open the curtains and the garden doors, letting light and air into the stale bedroom.

She takes pleasure in all her appointed tasks, but enjoys this one most of all, more so when the master is already out of bed, for he seems to resent her waking him like this. Just as he resents her arriving late, after he's risen. Either way, sooner or later, she'll have to pay for it.

"It's a beautiful day," she remarks hopefully.

He sits up with an ambiguous grunt, rubs his eyes, yawns, shudders. "You may speak when spoken to," he grumbles, tucking his closing morning glory back inside his pajamas (behind her, bees are humming in the garden and there's a crackly pulsing of insects, but the birds have fallen silent: she had thought today might be perfect, but already it is slipping away from her), "unless it be to deliver a message or ask a necessary question."

"Yes, sir."

He shoves his feet into slippers and staggers off to the bathroom, leaving her to face (she expects the worst) – shadows have invaded the room – the rumpled bed alone.

It's not just the damp towels. It's also the streaked floor, the careless banging of the garden doors, her bedraggled uniform, the wrinkled sheets, the confusion of her mind. He lectures her patiently on the proper way to make a bed, the airing of the blankets, turning of the mattress, changing of the sheets, the importance of a smooth surface. "Like a blank sheet of crisp new paper," he tells her. He shows her how to make the correct diagonal creases at the corners, how to fold the top edge of the upper sheet back over the blankets, how to carry the spread under and then over the pillows. Oh, not for his benefit and advantage – he could sleep anywhere or, for that matter (in extremity) could make his own bed – but for hers. How else would she ever be able to realize what is best in herself?

"A little arrangement and thought will give you method and habit," he explains (it is his "two fairies" lecture), but though she seems willing enough, is polite and deferential, even eager to please, she can never seem to get it just right. Is it a weakness on her part, he wonders as he watches her place the pillows on the bed upside down, then tug so hard on the bottom blanket that it comes out at the foot, or some perversity? Is she testing him? She refits the bottom blanket, tucks it in again, but he knows the sheet beneath is now wrinkled. He sighs, removes his belt. Perfection is elusive, but what else is there worth striving for? "Am I being unfair?" he insists.

He's standing there in the sunlight in his slippers and pajama bottoms, cracking his palm with a leather strap, when she enters (once and for all) with all her paraphernalia. She plants the bucket and brushes beside the door, leans the mop and broom against the wall, stacks the fresh linens and towels on a chair. She is late – the curtains and doors are open, her circumspect crossing of the room no longer required – but she remains hopeful. Running his maxims over in her head, she checks off her rags and brushes, her polishes, cleaning powders, razor blades, toilet paper, dustpans – oh, no . . . ! Her heart sinks like soap in a bucket. The soap she has forgotten to bring. She sighs, then deliberately and gravely, without affectation, not stamping too loud, nor dragging her legs after her, not marching as if leading a dance, nor keeping time with her head and hands, nor staring or turning her head either one way or the other, she advances sedately and discreetly across the gleaming tiles to the bed and, tucking up her dress and apron, pulling down her flannelette drawers, bends over the foot of it, exposing her soul's ingress to the sweet breath of morning, blowing in from the garden. "I wonder if you can appreciate," he says, picking a bit of lint off his target before applying his corrective measures to it, "how difficult this is for me?"

He awakes, vaguely frightened by something he's dreamt (it was about order or odor and a changed condition – but how did it begin . . . ?), wound up in damp sheets and unable at first even to move, defenseless against the day already hard upon him. Its glare blinds him, but he can hear the maid moving about the room, sweeping the floor, changing the towels, running water, pushing furniture around.

"Good morning, sir," she says.

"Come here a moment," he replies gruffly, then clears his throat.

"Sir?"

"Look under the bed. Tell me what you see." He expects the worst: blood, a decapitated head, a bottomless hole . . .

"I'm – I'm sorry, sir," she says, tucking up her skirt and apron, lowering her drawers, "I thought I *had* swept it . . ."

No matter how much fresh air and sunlight she lets in, there is always this little pocket of lingering night which she has to uncover. Once she found a dried bull's pizzle in there, another time a dead mouse in a trap. Even the nice things she finds in the bed are somehow horrible: the toys broken, the food moldy, the clothing torn and bloody. She knows she must always be circumspect and self-effacing, never letting her countenance betray the least dislike toward any task, however trivial or distasteful, and she resolves every morning to be cheerful and good-natured, letting nothing she finds there put her out of temper with everything besides, but sometimes she cannot help herself. "Oh, teach me, my God and King, in all things thee to see, and what I do in any thing, to do it as for thee," she tells herself, seeking courage, and flings back the sheets and blankets. She screams. But it's only money, a little pile of gold coins, agleam with promise. Or challenge: is he testing her?

Oh, well, he envies her, even as that seat chosen by Mother Nature for such interventions quivers and reddens under the whistling strokes of the birch rod in his hand. "Again!"

"Be . . . be diligent in endeavoring to please your master – be faithful and . . . and . . ." Swish-*SNAP!* "Oh, sir!"

"Honest!"

"Yes, sir!"

She, after all, is free to come and go, her correction finitely inscribed by time and the manuals, but he . . . He sighs unhappily. How did it all begin, he wonders. Was it destiny, choice, generosity? If she would only get it right for once, he reasons, bringing his stout engine of duty down with a sharp report on her brightly striped but seemingly unimpressionable hinder parts, he might at least have time for a stroll in the garden. Does she – *CRACK!* – think he enjoys this? "Well?"

"Be . . . be faithful, honest and submissive to him, sir, and –" Whish-*SLASH!* "And – *gasp!* – do not incline to be slothful! Or –" *THWOCK!* "Ow! Please, sir! " Hiss-*WHAP!*

She groans, quivers, starts. The two raised hemispheres upon which the blows from the birch rod have fallen begin (predictably) to make involuntary motions both vertically and horizontally, the constrictor muscle being hard at work, the thighs also participating in the general vibrations, all in all a dismal spectacle. And for nothing? So it would seem . . .

"Or?"

"Or lie long in bed, sir, but rise . . . rise early in a morning!"

The weals criss-cross each other on her enflamed posteriors like branches against the pink clouds of dawn, which for some reason saddens him.

"Am I being unfair?"

"No – no, s –" Whisp-*CRACK!*

She shows no tears, but her face pressed against the bedding is flushed, her lips trembling, and she breathes heavily as though she's been running, confirming the quality of the rod which is his own construction.

"Sir," he reminds her, turning away.

"Sir," she replies faintly. "Thank you, sir."

She enters, once and for all, radiant and clear-browed (a long devotion to duty), with all her paraphernalia, her mop and bucket, brooms, rags, soaps, polishes, sets them all down, counting them off on her fingers, then crosses the room deliberately and circumspectly, not glancing at the rumpled bed, and flings open the curtains and the garden doors to call forth the morning, what's left of it. There is such a song of insects all about (the preying birds are silent) – what inspiration! "Lord, keep me in my place!" The master is in the shower: she hears the water. "Let me be diligent in performing whatever my master commands me," she prays, "neat and clean in my habit, modest in my carriage, silent when he is angry, willing to please, quick and neat-handed about what I do, and always of an humble and good disposition!" Then, excited to the most generous and efficient accomplishments, she turns with a palpitating heart (she is thinking about perfect service and freedom and the unpleasant things she has found) to the opening up and airing of the bed. She braces herself, expecting the worst, but finds only a wilted flower from the garden: ah! today then! she thinks hopefully – perhaps at last! But then she hears the master turn the taps off, step out of the shower. Oh no . . . ! She lowers her drawers to her knees, lifts her dress, and bends over the unmade bed.

"*These towels are damp!*" he blusters, storming out of the bathroom, wielding the fearsome rod, that stout engine of duty, still wet from the shower.

Sometimes he uses a rod, sometimes his hand, his belt, sometimes a whip, a cane, a cat-o'-nine-tails, a bull's pizzle, a hickory switch, a martinet, ruler, slipper, a leather strap, a hairbrush. There are manuals for this. Different preparations and positions to be assumed, the number and severity of the strokes generally prescribed to fit the offense: he has explained it all to her, though it is not what is important to her. She knows he is just, could not be otherwise if he tried, even if the relative seriousness of the various infractions seems somewhat obscure to her at times. No, what matters to her is the idea behind the regulations that her daily tasks, however trivial, are perfectible. Not absolutely perhaps, but at least in terms of the manuals. This idea, which is almost tangible – made manifest, as it were, in the weals on her behind – is what the punishment is for, she assumes. She does not enjoy it certainly, nor (she believes – and it wouldn't matter if he did) does he. Rather, it is a road (speaking loosely), the rod, to bring her daily nearer God – and what's more, it seems that she's succeeding at last! Today everything has been perfect: her entry, all her vital paraphernalia, her circumspect crossing of the room and opening of the garden doors, her scrubbing and waxing and dusting and polishing, her opening up and airing and making of the master's bed – everything!

True service, she knows (he has taught her!), is perfect freedom, and today she feels it: almost like a breeze – the sweet breath of success – lifting her! But then the master emerges from the bathroom, his hair wild, fumbles through the clothes hanging in the wardrobe, pokes through the dresser drawers, whips back the covers of her perfectly made bed.

"What's this doing here –?!" he demands, holding up his comb.

"I – I'm sorry, sir! It wasn't there when I – " "What? *What –?!*" He seizes her by the elbow, drags her to the foot of the bed, forces her to bend over it. "I have been very indulgent to you, up to now, but now I am going to punish you severely, to cure you of your insolent clumsiness once and for all! So pull up your skirt – come! pull it up! you know well enough that the least show of resistance means ten extra cuts of the – *what's this?!*" She peers round her shoulder at her elevated sit-me-down, so sad and pale above her stockings. "I – I don't understand, sir! I had them on when I came in –!"

Perhaps he's been pushing her too hard, he muses, soaping himself in the shower and trying to recall the dream he was having when she woke him up (something about ledgers and manual positions, a woman, and the merciless invention of souls which was a sort of fever of the mind), perhaps he's been expecting too much too soon, making her overanxious, for in some particulars now she is almost too efficient, clattering in with her paraphernalia like a soldier, blinding him with a sudden brutal flood of sunlight from the garden, hauling the sheets out from under him while he's still trying to stuff his feet into his slippers. Perhaps he should back off a bit, give her a chance to recover some of her ease and spontaneity, even at the expense of a few undisciplined errors. Perhaps . . . yet he knows he could never let up, even if he tried. Not that he enjoys all this punishment, any more (he assumes, but it doesn't matter) than she does. No, he would rather do just about anything else – crawl back into bed, read his manuals, even take a stroll in the garden – but he is committed to a higher end, his life a mission of sorts, a consecration, and so punish her he must, for to the extent that she fails, he fails. As he turns off the taps and steps out of the shower, reaching for the towel, the maid rushes in.

"Oh, I beg your pardon, sir!"

He grabs a towel and wraps it around him, but she snatches it away again: "That one's damp, sir!" She dashes out to fetch him a fresh one and he is moved by her transparent enthusiasm, her eagerness to please, her seemingly un-quenchable appetite for hope: perhaps today . . . ! But he has already noticed that she has forgotten her lace cap, there's a dark stain on the bib of her apron, and her garters are dangling. He sighs, reaches for the leather strap. Somehow (is there to be no end to this? he wonders ruefully) it should be easier than this.

She does not enjoy the discipline of the rod, nor does he – or so he believes, though what would it matter if he did? Rather, they are both dedicated to the fundamental proposition (she winces at the painful but unintended pun, while peering over her shoulder at herself in the wardrobe mirror, tracing the weals with her fingertips) that her daily tasks, however trivial, are perfectible, her punishments serving her as a road, loosely speaking, to bring her daily nearer God, at least in terms of the manuals. Tenderly, she lifts her drawers up over her blistered sit-me-down, smoothes down her black alpaca dress and white lace apron, wipes the tears from her eyes, and turns once more to the unmade bed. Outside, the bees humming in the noonday sun remind her of all the time she's lost. At least, she consoles herself, the worst is past. But the master is pacing the room impatiently and she's fearful his restlessness will confuse her again.

"Why don't you go for a stroll in the garden, sir?" she suggests deferentially.

"You may speak when spoken to!" he reminds her, jabbing a finger at her sharply.

"I – I'm sorry, sir!"

"You must be careful not only to do your work quietly, but to keep out of sight as much as possible, and never begin to speak to your master, unless –?"

"Unless it be to deliver a message, sir, or ask a necessary question!"

"And then to do it in as few words as possible," he adds, getting down his riding whip. "Am I being unfair?"

"But, sir! you've already –!"

"What? *What?!* Answering back to a reproof?"

"But –!"

"*Enough!*" he rages, seizing her by the arm and dragging her over to the bed.

"*Please!*"

But he pulls her down over his left knee, pushes her head down on the stripped mattress, locking her legs in place with his right leg, clamps her right wrist in the small of her back, throws her skirts back and jerks her drawers down.

"*Oh, sir!*" she pleads, what is now her highest part still radiant and throbbing from the previous lesson.

"SILENCE!" he roars, lifting the whip high above his head, a curious strained expression on his face. She can hear the whip sing as he brings it down, her cheeks pinch together involuntarily, her heart leaps: "*He'll draw blood!*"

Where does she come from? Where does she go? He doesn't know. All he knows is that every day she comes here, dressed in her uniform and carrying all her paraphernalia with her, which she sets down by the door; then she crosses the room, opens up the curtains and garden doors, makes his bed soft and easy, first airing the bedding, turning the mattress, and changing the linens, scrubs and waxes the tiled floor, cleans the bathroom, polishes the furniture and all the mirrors, replenishes all supplies, and somewhere along the way commits some fundamental blunder, obliging him to administer the proper correction. Every day the same. Why does he persist? It's not so much that he shares her appetite for hope (though sometimes, late in the day, he does), but that he could not do otherwise should he wish. To live in the full sense of the word, he knows, is not merely to exist, but to give oneself to some mission, surrender to a higher purpose, but in truth he often wonders, watching that broad part destined by Mother Nature for such solemnities quiver and redden under his hand (he thinks of it as a blank ledger on which to write), whether it is he who has given himself to a higher end, or that end which has chosen and in effect captured him?

Perhaps, she thinks, I'd better go out and come in again . . . And so she enters. As though once and for all, though she's aware she can never be sure of this. She sets down beside the door all the vital paraphernalia of her office, checking off each item on her fingers, then crosses the room (circumspectly etc.) and flings open the curtains and garden doors to the midday sun. Such a silence all about? She tries to take heart from it, but it is not so inspiring as the song of birds, and even the bees seem to have ceased their humming. Though she has resolved, as always, to be cheerful and good-natured, truly serving with gladness as she does, she nevertheless finds her will flagging, her mind clouded with old obscurities: somehow, something is missing. "Teach me, my God and King, in all things thee to see," she recites dutifully, but the words seem meaningless to her and go nowhere. And now, once again, the hard part. She holds back, trembling – but what can she do about it? For she knows her place and is contented with her station, as he has taught her. She takes a deep breath of the clean warm air blowing in from the garden and, fearing the worst, turns upon the bed, hurls the covers back, and screams. But it is only the master. "Oh! I beg your pardon, sir!"

"A . . . a dream," he explains huskily, as his erection withdraws into his pajamas like a worm caught out in the sun, burrowing for shade. "Something about a lecture on civil severity, what's left of it, and an inventory of soaps . . . or hopes . . ."

He's often like that as he struggles (never very willingly, it seems to her) out of sleep. She leaves him there, sitting on the edge of the bed, squinting in the bright light, yawning and scratching himself and muttering something depressing about being born again, and goes to the bathroom to change the towels, check the toothpaste and toilet paper, wipe the mirror and toilet seat, and put fresh soap in the shower tray, doing the will of God and the manuals, endeavoring to please. As he shuffles groggily in, already reaching inside his fly, she slips out, careful not to speak as she's not been spoken to, and returns to the rumpled bed. She tosses back the blankets afresh (nothing new, thank you, sir), strips away the soiled linens, turns and brushes the mattress (else it might imbibe an unhealthy kind of dampness and become unpleasant), shakes the feather pillows and sets everything out to air. While the master showers, she dusts the furniture, polishes the mirrors, and mops the floor, then remakes the bed, smooth and tight, all the sheets and blankets tucked in neatly at the sides and bottom, the top sheet turned down at the head, over the blankets, the spread carried under, then over the pillows, and hanging equally low at both sides and the foot: ah! it's almost an act of magic! But are those flyspecks on the mirror? She rubs the mirror and, seeing herself reflected there, thinks to check that her apron strings are tied and her stocking seams are straight. Peering over her shoulder at herself, her eye falls on the mirrored bed: one of the sheets is dangling at the foot, peeking out from under the spread as though exposing itself rudely. She hurries over, tucks it in, being careful to make the proper diagonal fold, but now the spread seems to be hanging lower on one side than the other. She whips it back, dragging the top sheet and blankets part way with it. The taps have been turned off; the master is drying himself. Carefully, she remakes the bed, tucking in all the sheets and blankets properly, fluffing the pillows up once more, covering it all with the spread, hung evenly. All this bedmaking has raised a lot of dust: she can see her own tracks on the floor. Hurriedly she wipes the furniture again and sweeps the tiles. Has she bumped the bed somehow? The spread is askew once again like a gift coming unwrapped. She tugs it to one side, sees ripples appear on top. She tries to smooth them down, but apparently the blankets are wrinkled underneath. She hasn't pushed the dresser back against the wall. The wardrobe door is open, reflecting the master standing in the doorway to the bath-room, slapping his palm with a bull's pizzle. She stands there, downcast, shoulders trembling, her arms pressed to her sides, unable to move. It's like some kind of failure of communication, she thinks, her diligent endeavors to please him forever thwarted by her irremediable clumsiness.

"Come, come! A little arrangement and thought will give you method and habit," he reminds her gravely. "Two fairies that will make the work disappear before a ready pair of hands!"

In her mind, she doesn't quite believe it, but her heart is ever hopeful, her hands readier than he knows. She takes the bed apart once more and remakes it from the beginning, tucking everything in correctly, fluffing the pillows, laying the spread evenly: all tight and smooth it looks. Yes! She pushes the dresser (once he horsed her there: she shudders to recall it, a flush of dread racing through her) back against the wall, collects the wet towels he has thrown on the floor, closes the wardrobe door. In the mirror, she sees the bed. The spread and blankets have been thrown back, the sheets pulled out. In the bathroom doorway, the master taps his palm with the stretched-out bull's pizzle, testing its firmness and elas-ticity, which she knows to be terrifying in its perfection. She remakes the bed tight and smooth, not knowing what else to do, vaguely aware as she finishes of an unpleasant odor. Under the bed? Also her apron is missing and she seems to have a sheet left over. Shadows creep across the room, silent now but for the rhythmic tapping of the pizzle in the master's hand and the pounding of her own palpitating heart.

Sometimes he stretches her across his lap. Sometimes she must bend over a chair or the bed, or lie flat out on it, or be horsed over the pillows, the dresser or a stool, there are manuals for this. Likewise her drawers: whether they are to be drawn tight over her buttocks like a second skin or lowered, and if lowered, by which of them, how far, and so on. Her responses are assumed in the texts (the writhing, sobbing, convulsive quivering, blushing, moaning, etc.), but not specified, except insofar as they determine his own further reactions – to resistance, for example, or premature acquiescence, fainting, improper language, an unclean bottom, and the like. Thus, once again, her relative freedom: her striped buttocks tremble and dance spontaneously under the whip which his hand must bring whistling down on them according to canon – ah well, it's not so much that he envies her (her small freedoms cost her something, he knows that), but that he is saddened by her inability to understand how difficult it is for him, and without that understanding it's as though something is always missing, no matter how faithfully he adheres to the regulations.

"And –?"

"And be neat and clean in your –" whisp-*CRACK!* "– *OW! habit! Oh! and wash yourself all over once a day to avoid bad smells and –*" hiss-*SNAP!* "– and – *gasp!* – wear strong decent underclothing!"

The whip sings a final time, smacks its broad target with a loud report, and little drops of blood appear like punctuation, gratitude, morning dew.

"That will do, then. See that you don't forget to wear them again!"

"Yes, sir." She lowers her black alpaca skirt gingerly over the glowing crimson flesh as though hooding a lamp, wincing at each touch. "Thank you, sir."

For a long time she struggled to perform her tasks in such a way as to avoid the thrashings. But now, with time, she has come to understand that the tasks, truly common, are only peripheral details in some larger scheme of things which includes her punishment – indeed, perhaps depends upon it. Of course she still performs her duties *as though* they were perfectible and her punishment could be avoided, ever diligent in endeavoring to please him who guides her, but though each day the pain surprises her afresh, the singing of the descending instrument does not. That God has ordained bodily punishment (and Mother Nature designed the proper place of martyrdom) is beyond doubt – every animal is governed by it, understands and fears it, and the fear of it keeps every creature in its own sphere, forever preventing (as he has taught her) that natural confusion and disorder that would instantly arise without it. Every state and condition of life has its particular duties, and each is subject to the divine government of pain, nothing could be more obvious, and looked on this way, his chastisements are not merely necessary, they might even be beautiful. Or so she consoles herself, trying to take heart, calm her rising panic, as she crosses the room under his stern implacable gaze, lowers her drawers as far as her knees, tucks her skirt up, and bends over the back of a chair, hands on the seat, thighs taut and pressed closely together, what is now her highest part tensing involuntarily as though to reduce the area of pain, if not the severity. "It's . . . it's a beautiful day, sir," she says hopefully.

"What? *WHAT?!*"

Relieving himself noisily in the bathroom, the maid's daily recitals in the next room (such a blast of light out there – even in here he keeps his eyes half closed) thus drowned out, he wonders if there's any point in going on. She is late, has left half her paraphernalia behind, is improperly dressed, and he knows, even without looking, that the towels are damp. Maybe it's some kind of failure of communication. A mutual failure. Is that possible? A loss of syntax between stroke and weal? No, no, even if possible, it is unthinkable. He turns on the shower taps and lets fall his pajama pants, just as the maid comes in with a dead fetus and drops it down the toilet, flushes it.

"I found it in your bed, sir," she explains gratuitously (is she testing him?), snatching up the damp towels, but failing to replace them with fresh ones. At least she's remembered her drawers today: she's wearing them around her ankles. He sighs as she shuffles out. Maybe he should simply forget it, go for a stroll in the garden or something, crawl back into bed (a dream, he recalls now: something about lectures or ledgers – an inventory perhaps – and a bottomless hole, glass breaking, a woman doing what she called "the hard part" . . . or did she say "heart part"?), but of course he cannot, even if he truly wished to. He is not a free man, his life is consecrated, for though he is *her* master, her failures are inescapably *his*. He turns off the shower taps, pulls up his pajama pants, takes down the six-thonged martinet.

"I have been very indulgent to you, up to now," he announces, stepping out of the bathroom, "but now I am going to punish you severely, so pull up your skirt, come! pull it up!"

But, alas, it is already up. She is bent over the foot of the bed, her pale hinder parts already exposed for his ministrations, an act of insolence not precisely covered by his manuals. Well, he reasons wryly, making the martinet sing whole chords, if improvisation is denied him, interpretation is not.

"Ow, sir! Please! *You'll draw blood, sir!*"

"Neat and clean in habit, modest –" *WHACK!* "– in . . . in carriage, silent when –" Whisp-*SNAP!* "OW!!"

"Be careful! If you move, the earlier blow won't count!"

"I – I'm sorry, sir!"

Her soul, she knows, is his invention, and she is grateful to him for it, but exposed like this to the whining slashes of the cane and the sweet breath of mid-afternoon which should cool his righteous ardor but doesn't (once a bee flew in and stung him on the hand: what did it mean? nothing: she got it on her sit-me-down once, too, and he took the swelling for a target), her thighs shackled by flannelette drawers and blood rushing to her head, she can never remember (for all the times he has explained it to her) why it is that Mother Nature has chosen that particular part of her for such solemnities: it seems more like a place for lettings things out than putting things in.

"Well? Silent when –?"

"Silent when he is angry, willing to please, quick and –" swish-*CRACK!* "– and of good disposition!"

"Sir," he reminds her: *THWOCK!*

"SIR!" she cries.

"Very well, but you must learn to take more pleasure in your appointed tasks, however trivial or unpleasant, and when you are ordered to do anything, do not grumble or let your countenance betray any dislike thereunto, but do it cheerfully and readily!"

"Yes, sir! Thank you, sir!"

She is all hot behind, and peering over her shoulder at herself in the wardrobe mirror after the master has gone to shower, she can see through her tears that it's like on fire, flaming crimson it is, with large blistery welts rising and throbbing like things alive: he's drawn blood! She dabs at it with her drawers, recalling a dream he once related to her about a teacher he'd had who called his chastisements "scripture lessons", and she understands now what he's always meant by demanding "a clean sheet of paper."

Well, certainly it has always been clean, neat and clean as he's taught her, that's one thing she's never got wrong, always washing it well every day in three hot lathers, letting the last lather be made thin of the soap, then not rinsing it or toweling it, but drying it over brimstone, keeping it as much from the air as possible, for that, she knows, will spoil it if it comes to it. She finishes drying it by slapping it together in her hands, then holding it before a good fire until it be thoroughly hot, then clapping it and rubbing it between her hands from the fire, occasionally adding to its fairness by giving it a final wash in a liquor made of rosemary flowers boiled in white wine. Now, she reasons, lifting her drawers up gingerly over the hot tender flesh, which is still twitching convulsively, if she could just apply those same two fairies, method and habit, to the rest of her appointed tasks, she might yet find in them that pleasure he insists she take, according to the manuals. Well, anyway, the worst is past. Or so she consoles herself, as smoothing down her black skirt and white lace apron, she turns to the bed. "*Oh, teach me, my*

God and King, in all things thee to . . ." What –? There's something under there! *And it's moving . . . !*

"Thank you, sir."

"I know that perfection is elusive," he explains, putting away his stout engine of duty, while she staggers over, her knees bound by her drawers, to examine her backside in the wardrobe mirror (it is well cut, he knows, and so aglow one might cook little birds over it or roast chestnuts, as the manuals suggest), "but what else is there worth striving for?"

"Yes, sir." She shows no tears, but her face is flushed, her lips are trembling, and she breathes as though she has been running.

He goes to gaze out into the garden, vaguely dissatisfied. The room is clean, the bed stripped and made, the maid whipped, why isn't that enough? Is there something missing in the manuals? No, more likely, he has failed somehow to read them rightly. Yet again. Outside in the sleepy afternoon heat of the garden, the bees are humming, insects chattering, gentler sounds to be sure than the hiss of a birch rod, the sharp report as it smacks firm resonant flesh, yet strangely alien to him, sounds of natural confusion and disorder from a world without precept or invention. He sighs. Though he was thinking "invention", what he has heard in his inner ear was "intention", and now he's not sure which it was he truly meant. Perhaps he should back off a bit – or even let her off altogether for a few days. A kind of holiday from the divine government of pain. Certainly he does not enjoy it, nor (presumably) does she. If he could ever believe in her as she believes in him, he might even change places with her for a while, just to ease his own burden and let her understand how difficult it is for him. A preposterous idea of course, pernicious in fact, an unthinkable betrayal . . . yet sometimes, late in the day, something almost like a kind of fever of the mind (speaking loosely) steals over – enough! *enough!* no shrinking!

"And another thing!" he shouts, turning on the bed (she is at the door, gathering up her paraphernalia) and throwing back the covers: at the foot on the clean crisp sheets there is a little pile of wriggling worms, still coated with dirt from the garden. "WHAT DOES THIS MEAN?!" he screams.

"I – I'm sorry, sir! I'll clean it up right away, sir!"

Is she testing him? Taunting him? It's almost an act of madness! "Am I being unfair?"

"But, sir, you've already –!"

"What? *WHAT?!* Is there to be no *end* to this?!"

He holds her over his left knee, her legs locked between his, wrist clamped in the small of her back, her skirt up and her drawers down, and slaps her with his bare hand, first one buttock, reddening it smartly in contrast to the dazzling alabaster (remembering the manuals) of the other, then attacking its companion with equal alacrity.

"Ow! Please, sir!"

"Come, come, you know that the least show of resistance means ten extra cuts of the rod!" he admonishes her, doubling her over a chair. "When you are ordered to do anything, do not grumble or let your countenance betray any dislike thereunto, but do it cheerfully and generously!"

"Yes, sir, but –"

"What? *WHAT?!*" Whish-*CRACK!*

"OW!" *SLASH!*

Her crimson bottom, hugged close to the pillows, bobs and dances under the whistling cane.

"When anyone finds fault with you, do not answer rudely!" Whirr-*SMACK!*

"NO, SIR!"

Each stroke, surprising her afresh, makes her jerk with pain and wrings a little cry from her (as anticipated by the manuals, when the bull's pizzle is employed), which she attempts to stifle by burying her face in the horsehair cushion. "Be respectful –?"

"Be respectful and obedient, sir, to those –" swish-*THWOCK!* "– placed – OW! – placed OVER you – AARGH!" Whizz-*SWACK!*

"With fear and trembling –" *SMASH!* "– and in singleness of your heart!" he reminds her gravely as she groans, starts, quivers under his patient instruction.

"Ouch! Yes, sir!"

The leather strap whistles down to land with a loud crack across the center of her glowing buttocks, seeming almost to explode, and making what lilies there are left into roses. *SMACK!* Ker-*WHACK!* He's working well now.

"Am I being unfair?"

"N-no, sir!" *WHAP! SLAP!*

Horsed over the dresser, her limbs launch out helplessly with each blow. *"Kneel down!"*

She falls humbly to her hands and knees, her head bowed between his slippered feet, that broad part destined by Mother Nature for such devotions elevated but pointed away from him toward the wardrobe mirror (as though trying, flushed and puffed up, to cry out to itself), giving him full and immediate access to that large division referred to in the texts as the Paphian grove.

"And resolve every morning –?"

"Resolve – *gasp!* – resolve every morning to be cheerful and –"

He raises the whip, snaps it three times around his head, and brings it down with a crash on her hinder parts, driving her head forward between his legs. "And – *YOW!* – and good-natured that . . . that day, and if any . . . if any accident – *groan!* – should happen to –" swish-*WHACK!* "– to break that resolution, suffer it . . . suffer it not –" *SLASH!* "Oh, sir!" *SWOCK!*

He's pushing himself, too hard perhaps, but he can't –

"Please, sir! *PLEASE!*" She is clinging to his knee, sobbing into his pajama pants, the two raised hemispheres upon which the strokes have fallen making involuntary motions both vertically and horizontally as though sending a message of distress, all the skin wrinkling like the surface of a lake rippled by the wind.

"What are you doing?! *WHAT DOES THIS MEAN?!*"

He spanks her with a hairbrush, lashes her with a cat-o'-nine-tails, flagellates her with nettles, not shrinking from the hard service to be done, this divine drudgery, clear-browed in his devotion to duty. Perhaps today . . . !

"SIR!"

He pauses, breathing heavily. His arm hurts. There is a curious strained expression on her face, flushed like her behind and wet with tears. "Sir, if you . . . if you don't stop –"

"What? *WHAT?!*"

"You – you won't know what to do *next!*"

"Ah." He has just been smacking her with a wet towel, and the damp rush and pop, still echoing in his inner ear, reminds him dimly of a dream, perhaps the one she interrupted when she arrived. In it there was something about humidity, but it kept getting mixed up somehow with hymnody, such that every time she opened her mouth (there was a woman in the dream) damp chords flowed out and stained his ledgers, bleached white as clean sheets.

"I'm so old," he says, letting his arm drop, "and still each day . . ."

"Sir?"

"Nothing. A dream . . ." Where was he? It doesn't matter.

"Why don't you go for a stroll in the garden, sir? It's a beautiful day."

Such impudence: he ignores it. "It's all right," he says, draping the blood-flecked towel over his shoulder, scratching himself idly. He yawns. "The worst is past."

Has he devoted himself to a higher end, he wonders, standing there in the afternoon sunlight in his slippers and pajama bottoms, flexing a cane, testing it, snapping it against his palm, or has he been taken captive by it? Is choice itself an illusion? Or an act of magic? And *is* the worst over, or has it not yet begun? He shudders, yawns, stretches. And the manuals . . . ? He is afraid even to ask, takes a few practise strokes with the cane against a horsehair cushion instead. When the riddles and paradoxes of his calling overtake him, wrapping him in momentary darkness, he takes refuge in the purity of technique. The proper stretching of a bull's pizzle, for example, this can occupy him for hours. Or the fabrication of whipping chairs, the index of duties and offenses, the synonymy associated with corporal discipline and with that broad part destined by Mother Nature for such services. And a cane is not simply any cane, but preferably one made like this one of brown Malacca – the stem of an East Indian rattan palm – about two and a half feet long (give or take an inch and a half) and a quarter of an inch thick. Whing-*SNAP!* listen to it! Or take the birch rod, not a mere random handful of birchen twigs, as often supposed, but an instrument of precise and elaborate construction. First, the twigs must be meticulously selected for strength and elasticity, each about two feet long, full of snap and taken from a young tree, the tips sharp as needles. Then carefully combining the thick with the thin and slender, they must be bound together for half their length, tightly enough that they might enjoy long service, yet not too tightly or else the rod will be like a stick and the twigs have no play. The rod must fit conveniently to the hand, have reach and swing so as to sing in the air, the larger part of all punishment being the anticipation of course, not the pain, and must immediately raise welts and blisters, surprising the chastised flesh afresh with each stroke.

To be sure, it is easier to construct a birch rod than to employ it correctly – that's always the hard part, he doesn't enjoy it, nor does she surely, but the art of the rod is incomplete without its perfect application. And though elusive, what else is there worth striving for? Indeed, he knows he has been too indulgent toward her up till now, treating her with the civility and kindness due to an inferior, but forgetting the forging of her soul by way of those "vivid lessons," as a teacher he once had used to put it, "in holy scripture, hotly writ."

So when she arrives, staggering in late with all her paraphernalia, her bucket empty and her bib hanging down, he orders her straight to the foot of the bed.

"But, sir, I haven't even –"

"Come, come, no dallying! The least show of resistance

will double the punishment! Up with your skirt, up, up! for I intend to – WHAT?! IS THERE TO BE NO END TO THIS?!"

"I – I'm sorry! I was wearing them when I came – I must have left them somewhere . . . !"

Maybe it's some kind of communication problem, he thinks, staring gloomily at her soul's ingress which confronts him like blank paper, laundered tiffany, a perversely empty ledger. The warm afternoon sun blows in through the garden doors, sapping his brave resolve. He feels himself drifting, yawning, must literally shake himself to bring the manuals back to mind, his duties, his devotion . . . "Sir," she reminds him.

"Sir," he sighs.

It never ends. Making the bed, she scatters dust and feathers afresh or tips over the mop bucket. Cleaning up the floor, she somehow disturbs the bed. Or something does. It's almost as if it were alive. Blankets wrinkle, sheets peek perversely out from under the spread, pillows seem to sag or puff up all by themselves if she turns her back, and if she doesn't, then flyspecks break out on the mirror behind her like pimples, towels start to drip, stains appear on her apron. If she hasn't forgotten it. She sighs, turns once more on the perfidious bed. Though always of an humble and good disposition (as she's been taught), diligent in endeavoring to please him, and grateful for the opportunity to do the will of God from the heart by serving him (true service, perfect freedom, she knows all about that), sometimes, late in the day like this (shadows are creeping across the room and in the garden the birds are beginning to sing again), she finds herself wishing she could make the bed once and for all: glue down the sheets, sew on the pillows, stiffen the blankets as hard as boards and nail them into place. But then what? She cannot imagine. Something frightening. No, no, better this trivial round, these common tasks, and a few welts on her humble sit-me-down, she reasons, tucking the top sheet and blankets in neatly at the sides and bottom, turning them down at the head just so far that their fold covers half the pillows, than be overtaken by confusion and disorder.

"Teach me, my God and King," she sings out hopefully, floating the spread out over the bed, allowing it to fall evenly on all sides, *"in all things thee to –"* But then, as the master steps out of the bathroom behind her, she sees the blatant handprints on the wardrobe mirror, the streamers of her lace cap peeking out from under the dresser, standing askew.

"I'm sorry, sir," she says, bending over the foot of the bed, presenting to him that broad part destined by Mother Nature for the arduous invention of souls. But he ignores it. Instead he tears open the freshly made bed, crawls into it fully dressed, kicking her in the face through the blankets with his shoes, pulls the sheets over his head, and commences to snore. Perhaps, she thinks, her heart sinking, I'd better go out and come in again . . .

Perhaps I should go for a stroll in the garden, he muses, dutifully reddening one resonant cheek with a firm volley of slaps, then the other, according to the manuals. I'm so old, and still . . . He sighs ruefully, recalling a dream he was having when the maid arrived (when was that?), something about a woman, bloody morning glories (or perhaps in the dream they were "mourning" glories: there was also something about a Paphian grave), and a bee that flew in and stung him on his tumor, which kept getting mixed up somehow with his humor, such that, swollen with pain, he was laughing like a dead man . . .

"Sir?"

"What? *WHAT?!*" he cries, starting up. "Ah . . ." His hand is resting idly on her flushed behind as though he meant to leave it there. "I . . . I was just testing the heat," he explains gruffly, taking up the birch rod, testing it for strength and elasticity to wake his fingers up. "When I'm finished, you'll be able to cook little birds over it or roast chestnuts!" He raises the rod, swings it three times round his head, and brings it down with a whirr and a slash, reciting to himself from the manuals to keep his mind, clouded with old

obscurities, on the task before him: "Sometimes the operation is begun a little above the garter –" whish-*SNAP!*
"– and ascending the pearly inverted cones –" hiss-
WHACK! "– is carried by degrees to the dimpled promon-
tories –" *THWOCK!* "– which are vulgarly called the
buttocks!" *SMASH!*

"Ow, sir! PLEASE!" She twists about on his knee, biting
her lip, her highest part flexing and quivering with each
blow, her knees scissoring frantically between his legs. "Oh,
teach me," she cries out, trying to stifle the sobs, "my God
and –" whizz-*CRACK!* "– King, thee – *gasp!* – to –"
WHAP! "– SEE!"

Sometimes, especially late in the day like this, watching the
weals emerge from the blank page of her soul's ingress like
secret writing, he finds himself searching it for something, he
doesn't know what exactly, a message of sorts, the revelation
of a mystery in the spreading flush, in the pout and quiver of
her cheeks, the repressed stutter of the little explosions of
wind, the – whush-*SMACK!* – dew-bejeweled hieroglyphs
of crosshatched stripes. But no, the futility of his labors,
that's all there is to read there. Birdsong, no longer threatening, floats in on the warm afternoon breeze while he works.

There *was* a bee once, he remembers, that part of his dream
was true. Only it stung him on his hand, as though to remind
him of the painful burden of his office. For a long time after
that he kept the garden doors closed altogether, until he
realized one day, spanking the maid for failing to air the
bedding properly, that he was in some wise interfering with
the manuals.

And what has she done wrong today? he wonders, tracing
the bloody welts with his fingertips. He has forgotten. It
doesn't matter. He can lecture her on those two fairies,
confusion and disorder. Method and habit, rather . . .

"Sir . . . ?"

"Yes, yes, in a minute . . ." He leans against the bedpost.
To live in the full sense of the word, he reminds himself, is
not to exist or subsist merely, but to . . . to . . . He yawns. He
doesn't remember.

While examining the dismal spectacle of her throbbing sit-me-down in the wardrobe mirror (at least the worst is past, she consoles herself, only half believing it), a solution of sorts to that problem of genesis that's been troubling her occurs to her: to wit, that change (she is thinking about change now, and conditions) is eternal, has no beginning – only conditions can begin or end. Who knows, perhaps he has even taught her that. He has taught her so many things, she can't be sure any more. Everything from habitual deference and the washing of tiffany to pillow fluffing, true service and perfect freedom, the two fairies that make the work (speaking loosely) disappear, proper carriage, sheet folding, and the divine government of pain.

Sometimes, late in the day, or on being awakened, he even tells her about his dreams, which seem to be mostly about lechers and ordure and tumors and bottomless holes (once he said "souls"). In a way it's the worst part of her job (that and the things she finds in the bed: today it was broken glass).

Once he told her of a dream about a bird with blood in its beak. She asked him, in all deference, if he was afraid of the garden, whereupon he ripped her drawers down, horsed her over a stool, and flogged her so mercilessly she couldn't stand up after, much less sit down. Now she merely says, "Yes, sir," but that doesn't always temper the vigor of his disciplinary interventions, as he likes to call them. Such a one for words and all that!

Tracing the radiant weals on that broad part of her so destined with her fingertips, she wishes that just once she might hear something more like, "Well done, thou good and faithful servant, depart in peace!"

But then what? When she returned, could it ever be the same? Would he even want her back? No, no, she thinks with a faint shudder, lifting her flannelette drawers up gingerly over soul's well-ruptured ingress (she hopes more has got in than is leaking out), the sweet breath of late afternoon blowing in to remind her of the time lost, the work yet to be done: no, far better her appointed tasks, her trivial round and daily act of contrition, no matter how pitiless the master's interpretation, than consequences so utterly unimaginable. So, inspirited by her unquenchable appetite for hope and clear-browed devotion to duty, and running his maxims over in her head, she sets about doing the will of God from the heart, scouring the toilet, scrubbing the tiled floor, polishing the furniture and mirrors, checking supplies, changing the towels. All that remains finally is the making of the bed. But how can she do that, she worries, standing there in the afternoon sunlight with stacks of crisp clean sheets in her arms like empty ledgers, her virtuous resolve sapped by a gathering sense of dread as penetrating and aseptic as ammonia, if the master won't get out of it?

She enters, encumbered with her paraphernalia, which she deposits by the wall near the door, crosses the room (circumspectly, precipitately, etc.), and flings open the garden doors, smashing the glass, as though once and for all. "Teach me, my God and King," she remarks ruefully (such a sweet breath of amicable violence all about!), "in all things thee to – oh! I beg your pardon, sir!"

"A . . . a dream," he stammers, squinting in the glare. He is bound tightly in the damp sheets, can barely move. "Something about blood and a . . . a . . . I'm so old, and still each day –"

"Sir . . . ?"

He clears his throat. "Would you look under the bed, please, and tell me what you see?"

"I – I'm sorry, sir," she replies, kneeling down to look, a curious strained expression on her face. With a scream, she disappears.

He awakes, his heart pounding. The maid is staring down at his erection as though frightened of his righteous ardor: "Oh, I beg your pardon, sir!"

"It's nothing . . . a dream," he explains, rising like the pink clouds of dawn. "Something about . . ." But he can no longer remember, his mind is a blank sheet. Anyway, she is no longer listening. He can hear her moving busily about the room, dusting furniture, sweeping the floor, changing the towels, taking a shower. He's standing there abandoned to the afternoon sunlight in his slippers and pajama bottoms, which seem to have imbibed an unhealthy kind of dampness, when a bird comes in and perches on his erection, what's left of it. "Ah –!"

"Oh, I beg your pardon, sir!"

"It's – it's nothing," he replies hoarsely, blinking up at her, gripped still by claws as fine as waxed threads. "A dream . . ."

But she has left him, gone off singing to her God and King. He tries to pull the blanket back over his head (the bird, its beak opening and closing involuntarily like spanked thighs, was brown as a chestnut, he recalls, and still smoldering), but she returns and snatches it away, the sheets too. Sometimes she can be too efficient. Maybe he has been pushing her too hard, expecting too much too soon. He sits up, feeling rudely exposed (his erection dips back into his pajamas like a frog diving for cover – indeed, it has a greenish cast to it in the half-light of the curtained room: what? isn't she here yet?), and lowers his feet over the side, shuffling dutifully for his slippers. But he can't find them. He can't even find the floor! He jerks back, his skin wrinkling in involuntary panic, but feels the bottom sheet slide out from under him – "What? *WHAT?!*"

"Oh, I beg your pardon, sir!"

"Ah . . . it's nothing," he gasps, struggling to awaken, his heart pounding still (it should be easier than this!), as, screaming, she tucks up her skirt. "A dream . . ."

She enters, as though once and for all, circumspectly deposits her vital paraphernalia beside the door, then crosses the room to fling open (humbly yet authoritatively) the curtains and the garden doors: there is such a song of birds all about! Excited by that, and by the sweet breath of late afternoon, her own eagerness to serve, and faith in the perfectibility of her tasks, she turns with a glad heart and tosses back the bed-covers: "Oh! I beg your pardon, sir!"

"A . . . a dream," he mutters gruffly, his erection slipping back inside his pajamas like an abandoned moral. "Something about glory and a pizzle – or puzzle – and a fundamental position in the civil service . . ."

But she is no longer listening, busy now at her common round, dusting furniture and sweeping the floor: so much to do! When (not very willingly, she observes) he leaves the bed at last, she strips the sheets and blankets off, shaking the dead bees into the garden, fluffs and airs the pillows, turns the mattress. She hears the master relieving himself noisily in the bathroom: yes, there's water in the bucket, soap too, a sponge, she's remembered everything! Today then, perhaps at last . . . ! Quickly she polishes the mirror, mops the floor, snaps open the fresh sheets and makes the bed. Before she has the spread down, however, he comes out of the bathroom, staggers across the room muttering something about "a bloody new birth", and crawls back into it.

"But, sir –!"

"What, what?" he yawns, and rolls over on his side, pulling the blanket over his head. She snatches it away. He sits up, blinking, a curious strained expression on his face.

"I – I'm sorry, sir," she says, and, pushing her drawers down to her knees, tucking her skirt up and bending over, she presents to him that broad part preferred by him and Mother Nature for the invention of souls.

He retrieves the blanket and disappears under it, all but his feet, which stick out at the bottom, still slippered. She stuffs her drawers hastily behind her apron bib, knocks over the mop bucket, smears the mirror, throws the fresh towels in the toilet, and jerks the blanket away again.

"I – I'm sorry, sir," she insists, bending over and lifting her skirt: "I'm sure I had them on when I came in . . ."

What? Is he snoring? She peers at him past what is now her highest part, that part invaded suddenly by a dread as chilling as his chastisements are, when true to his manuals, enflaming, and realizes with a faint shudder (she cannot hold back the little explosions of wind) that change and condition are coeval and everlasting: a truth as hollow as the absence of birdsong (but they are singing!) . . .

So she stands there in the open doorway, the glass doors having long since been flung open (when was that? she cannot remember), her thighs taut and pressed closely together, her face buried in his cast-off pajamas. She can feel against her cheeks, her lips, the soft consoling warmth of them, so recently relinquished, can smell in them the terror – no, the painful sadness, the divine drudgery (sweet, like crushed flowers, dead birds) – of his dreams, Mother Nature having provided, she knows all too well, the proper place for what God has ordained. But there is another odor in them too, musty, faintly sour, like that of truth or freedom, the fear of which governs every animal, thereby preventing natural confusion and disorder. Or so he has taught her. Now, her face buried in this pungent warmth and her heart sinking, the comforting whirr and smack of his rod no more than a distant echo, disappearing now into the desolate throb of late afternoon birdsong, she wonders about the manuals, his service to them and hers to him, or to that beyond him which he has not quite named. Whence such an appetite? – she shudders, groans, chewing helplessly on the pajamas – so little relief?

Distantly blows are falling, something about freedom and government, but he is strolling in the garden with a teacher he once had, discussing the condition of humanity, which keeps getting mixed up somehow with homonymity, such that each time his teacher issues a new lament it comes out like slapped laughter. He is about to remark on the generous swish and snap of a morning glory that has sprung up in their path as though inspired ("Paradox, too, has its techniques," his teacher is saying, "and so on . . ."), when it turns out to be a woman he once knew on the civil surface.

"What? *WHAT?!*" But she only wants him to change his position, or perhaps his condition ("You see!" remarks his teacher sagely, unbuckling his belt, "it's like a kind of callipygomancy, speaking loosely – am I being unfair?"), he's not sure, but anyway it doesn't matter, for what she really wants is to get him out of the sheets he's wrapped in, turn him over (he seems to have imbibed an unhealthy kind of dampness), and give him a lecture (she says "elixir") on method and fairies, two dew-bejeweled habits you can roast chestnuts over. What more, really, does he want of her? (Perhaps his teacher asks him this, buzzing in and out of his ear like the sweet breath of solemnity: whirr-*SMACK!*) His arm is rising and falling through great elastic spaces as though striving for something fundamental like a forgotten dream or lost drawers.

"I – I'm sorry, sir!" Is she testing him, perched there on his stout engine of duty like a cooked bird with the lingering bucket of night in her beak (see how it opens, closes, opens), or is it only a dimpled fever of the mind? He doesn't know, is almost afraid to ask.

"Something about a higher end," he explains hoarsely, taking rueful refuge, "or hired end perhaps, and boiled flowers, hard parts – and another thing, what's left of it . . ." She screams. The garden groans, quivers, starts, its groves radiant and throbbing. His teacher, no longer threatening, has withdrawn discreetly to a far corner with diagonal creases, where he is turning what lilacs remain into roses with his rumpled bull's pizzle: it's almost an act of magic! Still his arm rises and falls, rises and falls, that broad part of Mother Nature destined for such inventions dancing and bobbing soft and easy under the indulgent sun: "It's a beautiful day!"

"What? *WHAT?!* An answering back to a reproof?" he inquires gratefully, taunting her with that civility and kindness due to an inferior, as – hiss-*WHAP!* – flicking lint off one shoulder and smoothing the ends of his moustache with involuntary vertical and horizontal motions, he floats helplessly backwards ("Thank you, sir!"), twitching amicably yet authoritatively like a damp towel, down a bottomless hole, relieving himself noisily: "*Perhaps today then . . . at last!*"

LAIR OF THE RED WITCH

O'Neil De Noux

It's always a good day when the client shows up.

On this bright, New Orleans autumn morning, my newest client opens the smoky-glass door of my office, peeks in and says, "Are you Mr Caye?"

"Come in." I stand and wave her forward. Leaning my hands on my desk, I watch Mrs Truly Fortenberry cautiously step in. A big woman, Truly has mousy brown hair worn under one of those turban hats, the kind Ann Sheridan made popular during the war. She wears a full brown skirt with a matching vest over a white blouse.

A typical-looking 1948 housewife, Truly glances around my office, at my tired sofa, at the hardwood floor in need of waxing, at the high ceiling with its water marks. She looks at the row of windows facing Barracks Street. With the Venetian blinds open, the oaks and magnolias of Cabrini Playground give this section of the lower French Quarter a country feel in the middle of town.

Truly clears her throat, takes another step in and says, "I took the liberty of bringing a friend." Turning, she waves at the shadow I see through the smoky-glass. "Uh," Truly says, stepping aside, "this is Diane Redfearn. My friend and neighbor."

As the second woman steps in, Truly adds, "She wants to hire you, too."

Diane Redfearn moves around Truly, stops and bats a pair of large brown eyes at me. Her blonde hair up in a bun, she wears a powder blue suit dress with sloping shoulders and a curving waistline. I had ogled a model in that same outfit, an upcoming '49 fashion. It was a D.H. Holmes ad in yesterday afternoon's *Item*. I like ogling fashion models. So sue me.

Diane, a long, cool blonde, makes the model in the paper look like a chubby, over-fed boy. She follows Truly across my wide office to the matching wing chairs in front of my desk (I bought the chairs at a furniture auction on Magazine Street. When was that, three years ago?). Diane slinks into the chair on the left and crosses her legs.

Truly sits in the other chair, filling the seat with her broad hips. I sit in my high-back captain's chair.

"Any problem finding the place?" I ask as I notice the bevy of diamonds, two rubies and an emerald dotting their fingers.

"Oh no. Your directions were perfect." Truly blinks her deep set eyes at me and leans forward. "I told Diane how nice you were on the phone, Mr Caye. And since she's in a similar position, I convinced her to come along."

Diane bats her eyes at me.

"Lucien," I tell them. "My first name's Lucien."

"Oh." Truly leans back and digs something out of her oversized purse. She places a five-by-seven-inch photo on my desk. "This is my husband."

I have to stand to reach the picture.

Diane opens her purse and pulls out a photo and leans forward, uncrossing her legs. Her breasts push nicely against the front of her dress. I smile and take the picture. She leans back and recrosses her legs.

I catch a whiff of expensive perfume. Nice. Very nice.

Sitting back, I look at Truly's picture first. It's a studio shot with Truly standing next to a mohair chair where a man sits.

His hands in his lap and his legs crossed, the man has a Boston Blackie pencil-thin moustache and a goofy look on his wide face. His dark hair lies thick and curly on an oversized head.

We had a guy like that in our outfit back in Italy. Head too big for his helmet, so he never wore it. Never got hurt either. Just a big jolly fella: he even came to see me in the hospital after that damn German sniper winged me back in '44. Monte Cassino. But that's another story.

Diane Redfearn's husband is another sort completely. He's alone in his photo, posing as he looks to his right, a cigarette in his raised right hand. He looks like Ronald Coleman, without the moustache, a distinguished-looking gentleman wearing a cravat and what has to be a silk shirt. I hate cravats.

I put the photos down and pick up my fountain pen, holding my hand over my note pad. "So, what can I do for you ladies?"

Truly clears her throat and says, "Our husbands have left us. Mine two weeks ago. Diane's last week."

God, I hate domestic cases. But with the state of my bank account, I can't afford to be choosy.

Truly looks at me as if I'm supposed to say something. Diane's brown eyes remind me of a sad puppy dog.

"So, Mrs Redfearn. What can you tell me about your husband, besides he's blind?"

The women look at one another momentarily before Diane tells me her husband isn't blind.

Lord help me.

Truly clears her throat again and says, "They left us after visiting the red witch."

It's my turn to clear my throat.

"The red what?"

"The red witch." Truly points to my windows. "You can see her place from here. She's your neighbor."

I look out the windows for a moment before reaching over to turn on the small, black revolving fan that sits on the corner of my desk. The air feels good on my freshly shaved face.

"Um," I say as intelligently as I can.

They both speak.

"She always wears red," Truly says.

"She's not really a witch," Diane says.

Truly turns to her friend. "We don't know that. She calls herself a witch."

They both look at me and Truly says, "We want to hire you to . . ."

"Investigate this woman." Diane completes the sentence and brushes a loose strand of hair away from her eyes. She blows at it when it falls back, her lips pursed in a nice red kiss. I try not to stare, but she's hard to look away from. Thin and buxomy and married . . . my kinda woman.

"We tried talking to the police," Truly says. "My uncle knows someone downtown."

I nod as I pull my gaze from Diane's lips.

"They sent someone to talk to the red witch's neighbors," Truly adds.

"But no one seems to know much about her," Diane says.

"Except cats and dogs have disappeared."

"Cats and dogs?" I put my pen down.

Both women nod. The strand of hair falls across Diane's eyes again. If I could only reach it.

I pick up my pen and ask, "When do your husbands visit her?"

"Oh," Truly bounces in her seat. "They don't any more. My husband's in Cleveland."

I look at Diane, who tells me her husband is in Mexico.

"They moved out *after* visiting the red witch," Diane explains.

"We want you to find out what she told them," Truly says.

Diane looks down at her lap. "We want to know what happened . . ."

"When they visited this . . . sorceress."

I stand and move to the windows and open one. A nice breeze floats in, bringing the scent of freshly cut grass. I spot a city worker pushing a mower across Cabrini Playground. Shiftless, his brown skin shimmers with sweat under the bright sun.

"Where does she live?"

Truly clamors over and points up Barracks Street across the corner of the playground to a row of buildings on the lake side of Burgundy Street. Her elbow brushing mine, her perfume isn't the scent I'd caught earlier.

"See that second cottage from the end? The one painted yellow?"

I nod.

"That's the place. Her cauldron."

Cauldron? Isn't that some sort of kettle? I don't ask. I turn around and Diane is standing.

Truly notices and hurries back to pick up her purse. I move back to my desk.

"There's nothing more we can add," Truly says as she pulls a white envelope out of her purse and hands it to me. "If you need more money, just let me know."

I place the envelope on the desk and shake Truly's hand. It's sweaty. Diane's hand quivers when we touch and she smiles softly before pulling it back.

She brushes the loose strand of hair from her eyes again. "You'll let us know as soon as you can?"

"Absolutely." I reach for my pen and paper. "I have your number, Mrs Fortenberry, but . . ."

"Both numbers are in the envelope," Truly says as both women move quickly to the door and leave without looking back. The door closes and I stretch and yawn, then pick up the envelope. Inside, an ivory-colored sheet of paper is wrapped around a C-note. Ben Franklin never looked as good. On the paper are their names, and phone numbers: Fortenberry *Chestnut-0719*; Redfearn *Chestnut-0729*. Cozy.

The electric wall clock reads ten-fifteen.

The red witch should be up, even on a Saturday.

I reach into my desk drawer and pull out my snub-nosed .38 Smith & Wesson, slipping it into its tan leather holster on my right hip. I pick up Fortenberry's and Redfearn's pictures, my pen and pad and tuck them into my tan suit coat, which I don on my way out.

Stepping into the morning sunshine, I wait for my eyes to adjust. I never wear hats. They mess up my hair.

The warm autumn breeze feels almost cool, flowing through my damp hair. It's wavy brown and in dire need of a haircut. I'm thirty, six feet tall and have standard-issue Mediterranean brown eyes. I'm half-French and half-Spanish – old blood, pre-American occupation blood. No aristocracy, however. Both sides of my family have been laborers forever, even after emigrating to Louisiana long before Washington and Jefferson started their little revolution.

Moving under the shade of the balcony, I stop next to one of the black, wrought iron railings that support the second story balcony running the length of the building – I rent the apartment above my office – I check my pre-war 1940 DeSoto parked against the kerb. A trail of cat prints dot the hood, reminding me the car needs a good washing. Gray, the DeSoto provides good cover on surveillances and hides most of the dirt, until a cat strolls across it.

I cross Barracks Street and walk next to the low brick wall, with its own black wrought iron railing, that surrounds the playground. The lower French Quarter has certainly seen better days, before everyone around here started speaking harsh Yankee English.

Abutting the sidewalk, the houses across the street are connected by party walls. Masonry plastered over brick and cypress, and painted in muted pastels, the buildings look tired and time-worn.

Rounding the corner, I look at the row of Creole cottages lining Burgundy Street. The second one, painted yellow, is a typical one-story brick cottage with a roofed dormer. In red, the numbers 1233 are prominent on the left cypress post that supports the gingerbread overhang above the small front gallery.

I take the three brick steps up to the small gallery and spot another sign, this one hand painted in black letters next to the bright red door. SORCERESS EROS, the sign reads. LOVE SOR-CERESS.

"Yeah." I chuckle as I ring the doorbell. "Right."

I ring it a second time and the door opens.

She puts a hand up on the door frame and says, "Yes?"

Her light green eyes stare at me so directly, it's almost startling. Women don't usually stare like that, unless they're a different sort. And she's clearly not.

In her early twenties, she has a perfectly symmetrical face with a small, pointed chin and cupie-doll lips, painted a deep red. Her straight hair is long and dark brown, parted in the center. She's a looker, all right, even if she wasn't wearing a tight, blood red dress and matching heels.

"Yes?" She repeats as I look back up at her big eyes.

I realize I have no game plan, so I opt for the direct approach. I pull a card from my pocket and hand it to her. As she looks at it, I tell her I'm a neighbor, pointing over my shoulder toward Barracks Street.

She takes a step back and, still looking at the card, asks me in. She closes the door.

Dark, the front room is stuffy with the strong scents of incense and scented candles – vanilla, cinnamon, lilac maybe. A line of candles sits atop a chest of drawers to my right; two more are on the coffee table. Incense smolders in an urn on an end table next to the maroon sofa, reminding me of high mass. I cough.

"Oh," she says, "it's cooler in back." She leads me through the front room, down a narrow hall, past two bedrooms on the right, to a brightly lit kitchen. The rear door is open to a small patio filled with banana trees.

She moves to a window and flips on a window fan, then pulls the chain on the ceiling fan above the small, Formica table. She slips my card in a breast pocket and asks if I'd like some coffee.

"Sure." I watch her nice, round hips move away. She's about five-three and slim, but not skinny. Shapely slim. My kinda woman.

She turns to the stove and lights a burner beneath a white porcelain coffee pot. Turning back, she smiles, moves up and says, "Give me your coat. You look hot."

I pull off my jacket and she takes it and drapes it over the back of a chair next to the table. She points to another chair and says, "Sit down, Mr Caye."

She sits across from me. The fan-driven breeze feels good, especially on the perspiration collecting around my temples. Her creamy, white skin looks paler in the bright light. She's very pretty. I notice she isn't sweating at all.

"So," she says, "what can I do for you?" Her gaze is penetrating, almost invasive.

"I never noticed your sign before. You're new to the neighborhood, aren't you?"

She nods. "Moved in last month."

I loosen my navy blue tie and unbutton the top button of my white shirt. Then I smile and ask, "What does a sorceress do, these days?"

"Help people."

"So a love sorceress must help people with love problems?"

"Sometimes." She stands and moves to a cabinet next to the sink, where she digs out two cups and saucers. "Cream or sugar?"

"Black."

She fills our cups, puts them on the table and sits again.

I wait. It's an old police trick. People will automatically restart a conversation if you just wait.

"You have a love problem?" Her right eyebrow rises.

I look into those light eyes, which seem suddenly different. She looks at me in an innocent, child-like way, the kind of look you'd see on a grade-school girl. The atmosphere seems intoxicating again, thick, even with the air blowing over me.

Slowly, almost imperceptibly, her head nods. She takes a sip of coffee and says, "You're here about someone else's problem. Why don't you just come out and ask?"

I take a sip of the strong coffee and chicory.

"Two actually." I put the cup down. "Fortenberry and Redfearn. Sounds a little like a British law firm."

"Actually Mr Fortenberry is an architect and Mr Redfearn, an industrial engineer. But I can tell you little else about them."

"Why not?"

"It's confidential."

I grin. "As I recall, the law recognizes doctor–patient, priest–penitent, lawyer–client confidentialities. I don't remember anything about sorceress–confessor?"

She takes another sip of coffee.

"How long were you a police officer?" She smiles again. She's bright. I like that.

"Seven years." I want to ask her how old she is, but down south we just don't do that. She can't be much over twenty. So I ask, "How long have you been a sorceress?"

"Professionally? Two years."

I take another sip. "You from around here?"

"Born and raised. Went to Sacred Heart. Where'd you go to school?"

I should have known. When someone doesn't have a recognizable accent, they're usually from where you're from.

"Holy Cross," I tell her. Like dogs, we've just sniffed each other. Sacred Heart – she's an uptowner – upper class. Holy Cross – I'm from the lower part of town – working class.

She pulls her hair away from her face with both hands. I like watching women do that.

"So how did you become a sorceress? They teach it at Sacred Heart?"

She laughs lightly, then her face turns serious. She looks at the window fan and says, "I was born a sorceress." She turns to me with ovaled eyes. "I have a gift, Mr Caye. I can sense feelings in people."

And it occurs to me – I don't know her name, but I don't ask. I wait for her to continue her train of thought. She doesn't disappoint me.

"I can sense things about people. Sometimes before they do."

She finishes her coffee and asks if I'd like another cup. I shake my head and finish mine.

"We're not talking about witchcraft here, are we?"

"Hardly." She unbuttons the top button of her dress, reaches in and pulls out a gold chain and crucifix. "I'm still a practicing Catholic."

"Then you don't sacrifice cats and dogs." I watch her face carefully and the surprise there turns into a wide smile.

"No. I love animals."

"Then you don't know why so many cats and dogs are missing in the neighborhood?"

She picks up our cups and saucers and moves to the sink. She wipes her hands on a red checkered dishcloth. Turning, she rests one hand along the kitchen counter and lifts her hair off her nape with her other hand to let the fan cool her neck. Her eyes stare at me. I almost smile, because she's waiting now – for me to restart the conversation.

"So what do you do, exactly?"

"People come to me with problems." Her voice is deeper. "Sometimes, I'm able to help them."

"So you have the power to make people happy?"

"Sometimes I can point them in the right direction. It's up to them."

I wait a second before saying, "Mrs Fortenberry and Mrs Redfearn think you seduced their husbands. Caused them to leave their wives."

Her eyes still look innocent as she shakes her head. She lets her hair fall.

The doorbell rings.

"Sounds like my eleven o'clock appointment is early."

She starts for the door and I scoop up my coat and follow her back through the house, back into the insufferable front room. When she turns back to me and looks up with those soft eyes, I apologize.

"I put you on the spot and you didn't throw me out. Thanks."

She turns to open the door and I have another question. "What's your name?"

"Maggie. Maggie LeRoux."

Nice French name.

She opens the door to a young man with wavy brown hair and glasses. He wears a tweed suit and looks soft, almost effeminate as he stands there awkwardly.

"Come in, Thomas," Maggie says with a warm smile.

Thomas extends a hand for me to shake and says, "And you are?"

I tell him my name as we shake hands. His hand is clammy and limp.

I resist wiping my hand on my pants after he pulls his hand away.

"And what do you do?" Thomas asks, his eyes suddenly intense.

"Detective."

"Oh, my." He smiles and there's something familiar about his face. "I'm a playwright." He turns to Maggie and says he's ready. She ushers him in.

I step out, toss my coat over my shoulder and walk away.

I don't go home. I turn right and walk up Burgundy, past more Creole cottages and multistory townhouses, passing beneath more lacework balconies.

An early lunch at the Napoleon House sounds like a good idea to me.

Starting my canvass at the corner of Governor Nicholls and Burgundy, I find no one in the first few houses who know anything of the woman in the yellow house down the block.

Four doors from Maggie's cottage, the door is open on another cottage, this one painted a pale blue. I knock on the screen door and a woman's voice answers, "Hello?"

I knock again.

A slim woman with her hair in a bun steps into the front room. She wears a casual off-white dress and has a mop in her hand.

"I'm not buying anything today," she tells me.

"I'm not selling anything."

She huffs and leans on the mop handle. "Then what do you want?"

"I'm a detective. I'd like to ask you a couple of questions."

She moves forward and I see she's not a bad looking woman at all. No make-up on her face and a little perspired from housework, she's not bad at all.

"It's not about that woman again, is it?"

I turn toward Maggie's house and smile slightly. "Wo-man?"

"The red witch."

"Actually, it is."

"Well, come on in."

We talk in her living room. Me on a green easy chair. She on the matching sofa. The room smells of old cigarette smoke. The ashtray on the end table next to me has a gray line of ashes still in it. Her name is Agnes English and no, her husband hasn't left her. He's at work at Hibernia Bank. No, she's never even seen Maggie, but her cat's been missing for two weeks.

"A yellow tabby. Maybe you've seen her. Name is Judy and she's such a love."

"Just disappeared?"

Agnes nods and tears well in her eyes.

A half hour later, I'm knocking on another screen door, this one on the house next to Maggie's. Another woman with a mop moves into the front room, squints at me and asks what I want.

As soon as I tell her I'm a detective, she shushes me and moves quickly to the screen door.

"Keep your voice down," she says as she unlatches the door and lets me in.

In a light-weight sky blue blouse and short white shorts, she's a sight with her long strawberry-blonde hair pinned with two barrettes. She leads me through the front room, which smells faintly of pine oil, back to a bright kitchen. I can make out her visible panty line along her ass as she moves in front of me. I like that in a woman.

"Coffee, officer?" she asks. Her eyes are the same color as her blouse.

"Sure."

I watch her bend over for the grounds and flutter back to the sink to fill the percolator.

"I'm Lola Kinks." She plugs in the percolator. She's suddenly self-conscious, standing with the strong sunlight behind her and the way I'm leering at the front of her shorts and the dark patch between her legs.

She moves to the small wooden table, sits and crosses her legs.

I sit across from her as the blush slowly fades from her pretty face.

As soon as Lola tells me she's a widow, something inside stirs, something down south. I readjust myself as I sit.

When she mentions Okinawa, the stirring fades.

"My husband was killed in the last day of battle. Sniper."

She's a war widow. Dammit. I hate moving in on war widows. Like most surviving veterans, I feel a little guilty that I lived. It just seems slimy to ease in on a war widow, even three years after Hiroshima.

As the coffee perks, Lola tells me how she'd married her high school sweetheart, spent a whirlwind honeymoon in Mexico, then sent him off to the Pacific. He fought at Eniwetok and Saipan before Okinawa.

Damn, he'd seen some of the heaviest action.

When the coffee's ready, she fixes us some and I try not to leer at her, although I do steal another peek at her ass as she's pouring cream in her cup.

"Didn't mean to get off the subject," she says as we start in on our coffee. "I guess you're here about the red witch again, aren't you?"

"Why do you call her that?"

"Ever see her? She's spooky and with that sorceress sign. Who knows what she's up to next door."

I take out my note book. "Ever see anything unusual?"

"All the time."

Lola tells me about moaning and wild laughter, about boogie-woogie music, about strange smells, about hearing incantations and voices whispering harshly late at night.

"Smells?"

"Not cooking smells. But like in church. Incense and other strange odors." She goes on but tells me nothing new.

I remind myself how good detective work is done in details, not broad strokes. But these details are redundant. I close my note book and thank the widow Kinks.

As she leads me out I ask if she's heard of any missing animals.

"My dog ran away the same week the witch moved in. Dug a hole under the fence and I haven't seen him since."

A black lab, he answers to the name Nigger.

Jesus, lady!

She shakes my hand and gives my hand a gentle squeeze. And there's something there, for a moment, in those sky blue eyes. But she blinks and looks away and it's gone.

"She's a flirt, you know."

"Really?" I act surprised.

"She flirts with my fiancé."

Fiancé? Did she say fiancé?

"In the backyard last Saturday. I saw her smiling at him and her in a silk robe with God knows what underneath."

A war widow with a fiancé. If there's one thing a man like me knows, a woman with a fiancé is as approachable as a nun. Women with fiancés are newly in love. Bored housewives are more my style.

It takes a few more minutes, but I manage to escape from the widow Kinks' house and those pretty blue eyes.

The electric clock on my bedroom wall shows it's almost midnight.

I sit in my easy chair, just inside my balcony's French doors, as a light rain wets the Quarter. A cool breeze floats in through the partially opened doors. With the porch light on outside Maggie's, I can see the red door clearly. I raise my glass of Johnnie Walker Red and compliment whoever laid out Cabrini Playground. The trees are interspersed perfectly to give me a clear view of Maggie's.

A dull light flickers in her front room. Candles, probably, but I haven't seen the red witch since I got back – unless I close my eyes.

Maybe it's the smoky scotch or maybe she put a spell on me, but when I close my eyes, I see those hips moving lithely, like a cat, beneath that tight dress. I see those ovaled, green eyes staring back at me. The cupie-doll lips, pursed as they come in close for a kiss, touch my lips and . . .

I down the scotch and yawn.

Tomorrow, I tell myself. I think it's time I become a client of the red witch. What have I got to lose?

That night I dream, but not about Maggie's lips. I'm back in Italy, crouched on a dusty hill, a German machine gun strafing around me. The rat-tat-tat of the automatic rifle burps and the ground shakes and I stand up. No. Yes! I stand up, take careful aim at the German helmet behind the machine gun and squeeze the trigger of my M-1.

A stream of banana pudding gushes from my rifle and I know if I can cover the bastard with enough banana pudding, he'll drown. Only I run out of banana pudding. So I race down to the Italian fruit peddler at the bottom of the hill and ask him to hurry with the bananas.

I point up the hill and tell him the Germans are dug in and need to be drowned. He shakes his head and tells me not to worry. He points overhead at a formation of heavy bombers.

We move to the side of the hill and watch the bombers destroy the Sixth Century Benedictine Monastery atop Monte Cassino. Germans were using the monastery to spot for their field artillery. The bombers reduce the ancient citadel to rubble, which only provides better cover for the crack troops of the First Panzer Division who've kept us at bay for weeks.

I try to explain to the fruit peddler that the Germans up our small hill have machine guns and we need banana pudding right away. He calls me *pazzo Americano* – crazy American. I run off in search of another fruit peddler.

Only, when I turn around I'm back at Anzio beach where hellfire rains down on us from long range German artillery. You know, the guns of Krupp. A dogface next to me in the foxhole turns and shouts, "Pray! Pray to God for help!"

I start praying and he grabs my arm.

"But tell him not to send Jesus. This is no place for kids!"

A shell blows up next to us and I wake up.

Rain slams against the balcony doors. I roll over and try to force myself to dream of the cupie-doll lips.

Thankfully, I don't dream at all.

Maggie answers the door wearing a flowered sarong skirt and a red blouse with black piping. She's barefoot, a coffee cup in her hand. I raise the brown bag in my hand. She smiles and her lips are candy-apple red this morning.

"Beignets," I tell her. "From Morning Call."

She leads me back through the house, through the smoldering incense and candles to the kitchen where both fans are already blowing. As she pours me a cup, I pile the half dozen beignets on a saucer and place them in the center of the Formica table.

In a short sleeved white shirt and dungarees, I'm casual today. I even wear tennis shoes.

She sits across from me, picks up a beignet and takes a dainty bite of the French pastry – powdered sugar sprinkled on square donuts without holes. I pick up a beignet and tell her, "I came as a customer today."

She smiles. "I figured that would be your next move."

"I have problems," I tell her. Only I can't help the wicked grin from crossing my lips.

"I know," she says seriously.

A half hour and two cups of coffee later, I'm in the living room, reclined on the maroon sofa with candles burning around me and incense smoking up the place. Maggie moves next to me and rubs a potion on my forehead and the back of my hands. It's cool and smells like overripe bananas.

She moves to the chest-of-drawers and lights two large green candles, then comes back and sits on the coffee table, crossing her legs, closing the sarong that gave me a quick look at her pale thighs.

"Close your eyes," she says softly.

I go along. The air becomes stuffier and I smell something else. The green candles. Musty, they smell like mud. No, they smell like an old shoe left out in the rain.

"Tell me your most pressing problem." Her voice sounds distant, but I open my eye and she hasn't moved.

"I dream about the war a lot." My eyelids close by themselves. I try to force them open, but they're too heavy. I drift.

I can hear her breathing close to me now. Her breath brushes my cheek.

"That isn't your problem," she says and I feel her rub lotion on my forehead again. She takes my hands in hers and rubs my knuckles. It takes a moment for me to realize she's humming softly. A sweet tune, her voice is soothing. And I drift again, further and further. I'm carried on her voice and feel as if I'm floating.

"So," she says when I open my eyes. "Feel better?"

I sit up and stretch. I feel much better, rested, as if I've slept for hours. I look at my watch and it's been less than an hour. Sitting up, I realize I've a raging hard-on. Glad my pants are baggy.

She stands and moves to the green candles and blows them out.

"Come back to the kitchen," she says. I follow the easy movement of her hips beneath the sarong to the well-lit kitchen where she pours us each a fresh cup of java.

As I take a sip, she says, "Your dreaming about the war is your way of working it out. Your dreams will become less violent. They have already, over the last year, haven't they?"

The rich coffee and chicory warms me. I'm cold and can't understand why.

"The war isn't your problem."

"What is?" I ask, half jokingly.

"Sex."

The big eyes look innocently at me.

Sex, huh? I gotta admit, she knows how to keep it interesting.

"You want sex."

"What, now?" I laugh.

"Always." She's serious.

I take another sip and lean back in the chair.

"What red blooded American boy doesn't want sex all the time? I'm an ex-cop, and ex-GI. I'm French and Spanish. I've got hormones coming out of my ears."

She shakes her head, pulls her hair back with one hand as she takes a drink of coffee. She puts the cup down and I smell her perfume for the first time. Less sweet than Diane Redfearn's, it's nice and subtle.

"I've never met a man with as powerful a sex drive as you." She says it so seriously, I can't laugh, although I want to.

"You want sex now with me and you want sex with your clients." She props her elbows up on the table. "You want sex with just about every woman you see. The attractive ones, anyway."

"What's abnormal about that?"

"Your sex drive is super-potent. Insatiable. You want mind-numbing sex." She says it matter-of-factly, as if she just told me I wanted to be a fireman when I grow up.

I laugh aloud. And I wonder where she's going with this. She's right about one thing. I'd love to screw her – right now. On the kitchen table. Jesus! Maybe I am insatiable. I shake the thought away.

"Your sex drive is quite similar to a male cat's."

She catches me with my cup to my lips. I cough and spill coffee on the table. She reaches back, pulls a towel off the counter and tosses it to me. I shake my head as I wipe up the spill.

Me – a tom cat?

"That's right," I tell her. "You're good with animals, too. You tell this stuff to the tom cats in the neighborhood?"

She takes a drink of coffee.

"What'd you do, liberate all the cats and dogs in the neighborhood?" I say, facetiously as I raise my cup again.

"I freed them. I felt their desires, the inner dreams and set them free. They ran away. Just like your clients' husbands." She gives me that big-eyed, innocent look again.

I put the cup down. "Wait." I raise an index finger. "Let me get this straight. Fortenberry and Redfearn went through what I just went through and you told them their secret desires and they left their wives?"

She nods and finishes her coffee.

"It took several sessions," she says as she stands and puts her cup in the sink.

"What did you tell them? What are they looking for? Other women?"

She puts her hands on the table and leans toward me. "That's confidential."

The doorbell rings.

"I have an appointment. Thanks for the beignets." She shakes her head. "And the interesting walk through your psyche."

I'm dismissed, I guess. She leaves and I follow her down the hall. She turns into a bedroom. I stop outside just as she comes out brushing her long hair.

"How much do I owe you?"

"Five dollars."

I pull a fin out and follow her into the front room. She moves to the door and lets in a middle-aged woman in a cardigan suit. No I don't want to immediately fuck her new client! Although, I must admit, the woman has a nice, shy smile and her full lips look . . .

A picture of Thomas the playwright in the afternoon's *Item* catches my attention as I wait in my office for my clients.

No wonder his face was familiar. He's Tennessee Williams, author of *A Streetcar Named Desire*, the play that's got Broadway sizzling. Seems he just won the Pulitzer Prize. Maggie's got some clientele.

My office door opens and Truly Fortenberry leads the way in. In another full dress, green this time, she wears a floppy hat with a pink carnation. Diane Redfearn wears a slim-fitting, yellow dress. Her hair in a bun, she wears no hat. They sit in the same chairs, Diane crossing her long legs.

Freshly shaved, I have on my best blue suit, a starched white shirt and powder blue tie. Women have told me blue goes well with my dark complexion. With the windows open and the ceiling fans on high, the room feels almost cool.

"I'm not sure what to make of this," I start. "So I'll just tell you straight. The red witch is more like a hypnotist. She claims to be able to discover people's inner desires and frees them."

"Frees them?" Truly leans forward.

"She claims that's why all the cats and dogs have left the neighborhood. She freed them."

Truly bats her confused eyes at me. Diane looks down at the purse in her lap.

"I don't think she had sex with your husbands."

Truly looks even more confused. Diane lets out a long sigh.

"Mrs Redfearn, what did your husband tell you when he left?"

She looks up and shakes her head.

"Did he tell you he was going to sail around the world or something like that?"

She shakes her head again and looks at the windows. Her chest rises as she takes in a deep breath. "He said he was going to Mexico to find a lost city and that he wants a divorce."

I turn to Truly who clears her throat and digs a handkerchief from her purse.

"Mine told me he was tired of living with me, tired of being married and wants to live in Cleveland." Her eyes glisten and she has that look on her face. I've seen it before, the look of desertion, the look of betrayal, the look of an abandoned lover. It's not a pretty sight, especially on Truly Fortenberry's puffy face.

"Why?" she moans. "Why would he leave me for . . . Cleveland?"

Diane stands and wraps an arm around her friend.

I wait as Truly cries. What the hell can I tell her? Who, in his right mind, would leave New Orleans for Cleveland? The obvious answer was whoever was married to Truly. I don't say that, but I can't help thinking it. And I wonder if she thinks it too. It's an unwritten law of nature. Unattractive people know they're unattractive.

God, I feel terrible. Really. I know I'm superficial when it comes to women, but I wish there was something I could do for Truly Fortenberry. But I'm no wizard. And I'm sure, if she visited the red witch, Maggie would discover Truly's inner desire was to be married to Mr Fortenberry.

I look out the window as a mockingbird lands on the wrought iron part of the playground fence across the street. Immediately it goes through its long litany of calls – bouncing, ruffling its gray and white feathers. A male probably, advertising its voice to passing females.

Finally, Truly stops crying and fixes her face. She stands and thanks me. I tell them I'll try to find out more about the red witch, if I can. Diane says it won't be necessary as I shake her soft hand. For a moment there's some eye contact between us, but I can't read it.

They leave me with a good whiff of Diane's strong perfume.

As I said – nice. Very nice.

The rain started an hour ago; and as I sit in the easy chair behind my closed balcony doors, windblown rain washes across the balcony in waves. It's so dark outside, it looks as if the rain has put out the yellow electric streetlights.

The bathroom light is still on behind me, so I know the electricity hasn't gone out. Leaning back in the chair with my tie loosened and an untouched glass of scotch in my left hand, I watch the rain. The nearly full bottle of Johnnie Walker Red lies next to my foot. In case I need a quick refill.

The persistent drum of the shower has me drowsy. Leaning back, I close my eyes and envision the cupie-doll lips in candy apple red, pursed in a sweet kiss. I see those hips moving away from me, lithely, in a smooth feline movement. I see her legs crossed in the sarong. I watch her uncross them slowly. The sarong falls open and the front of her sheer white panties comes into view. I see the dark mat of her pubic hair through the panties.

I hear her humming again, her voice echoing in my mind. The tune fades, then rises again. I try to open my eyes, but my eyelids are so heavy, I can only crack them. I try harder. Then I feel her fingers on my chin. Softly, she traces her fingertips down my throat, then back up to my chin.

I'm on her sofa and strain to open my eyes. I think I see her face above me but it fades and her fingers leave my throat. The humming is to my right, hovering above me. Turning my head, I try to look, but everything's hazy.

I feel myself fall into a deep well.

It's so hot I can barely breathe.

I have to open my eyes. Concentrating, focusing all my strength, I pull myself back.

The humming returns, still above me and to my right.

I force my eyelids to open but no matter how hard I try, I only manage to crack them. The darkness fades slowly and I see her, swaying next to me, her hands clasped behind her head. Her eyes are still closed.

Her hands move down the back of her neck and around to her throat. And slowly she unbuttons her blouse, pulls it out of the top of her sarong and drops it on the coffee table behind her.

She reaches back and unfastens her white brassiere and I strain to focus my eyes on her round breasts. Her pink nipples are pointed as she continues swaying. She reaches to the knot on the side of her sarong. She drops the sarong atop her blouse and bra.

I crane my neck more to the right. Her white panties are sheer enough to reveal her dark triangle of pubic hair. She turns her back to me, her hips still moving slowly to her humming. She pulls off her panties, her nice round ass not three feet from my face.

She turns back and continues her rhythmic gyrations. I stare at this naked vision, my gaze roaming from her pubic hair up to her breasts up to her lovely face. She leans forward, her breasts falling toward me. Moving from side to side, she rocks her breasts above me like a pendulum.

I want to touch them but my hands won't move.

Her eyes open now, she pulls back and steps closer to the sofa. Still swaying, she presses her bush forward and her silky pubic hair brushes the side of my face, back and forth, back and forth, ever so lightly.

She takes a step back and goes down on her knees. Her face moves forward and her lips touch my cheek. It takes a few moments to realize she's kissing me. Her lips move to mine. Her kiss is so soft I can barely feel it. But she presses harder and I try to kiss her back, but my lips won't respond. Her tongue slips into my mouth and she kisses me deeply.

Pulling back, she stands and I feel my hand rising. She's lifting it. She rubs my open palm along the side of her leg, then around to her ass. I feel her crack but can't get my hand to squeeze in response.

Maggie moves my hand around to her bush. She opens her feet and slips my hand between her legs. She rubs my fingers along her inner thighs, then turns my hand palm up. My fingers press against her pussy and she moves her hips back and forth on my hand. My middle finger slips into the folds of her pussy, into the hot wetness.

The humming is replaced by heavy breathing. Holding my arm with her left hand, maneuvering my hand with her right, she fucks herself with my finger. My thumb massages her clit as my middle finger works inside. Am I moving my fingers or is she?

Maggie gasps. Her gyrations increase, the weight of her body pressing harder against my hand. Waves of pleasure cross her face. She throws her head back and cries out and I feel her climax on my hand in deep spasms.

Gasping, Maggie collapses next to me. I see her reach up and close my eyelids. She speaks in a distant voice.

She tells me I will remember nothing.

And I fall into that well again.

There's something else, something suddenly cool on my hand, the hand that fucked Maggie. It's a face rag. She's wiping my hand before she wakes me.

My eyes snap open as a rush of wind and rain rattles the French doors.

Jesus! What a dream.

Wait. It didn't feel like a dream. It felt more like a

memory. In that hour I was on Maggie's sofa, is this what happened? Did that little woman take advantage of me? Use me?

I reach down to straighten my swollen dick. Leaning forward, I look at the darkness of Cabrini Playground. She's so close I can almost feel her.

Maybe, when the rain lets up, I'll creep over, like an alley cat.

Maybe, just maybe, she wants me to slink over to her.

Telling me all that about my sex drive. Maybe that's what she wants. At thirty, I should know women by now; but the older I get the less I seem to know.

My doorbell rings and I almost kick over the scotch bottle.

I swallow my drink in one gulp. It burns my throat and warms my belly. I put the empty glass on the coffee table on my way through the living room. The doorbell rings again as I step out the door to the landing. I look down the stairs and see a shadow outside the building's pebbled-glass front door, which is locked at night.

As I descend the stairs the shadow moves slightly; and I see it's a woman. I hurry to pull open the door. It takes me a second to recognize her with her long hair dripping wet around her pretty face. Her hair looks darker wet.

Diane Redfearn pulls her hair back with both hands, steps into the doorway and cranes her neck to the side. Her lips pursed, she leans toward mine and we kiss in the doorway. Softly, she presses her rain-washed lips against mine. Her lips part and her tongue probes for mine.

We French kiss in the doorway, my arms pulling her close, her drenched coat soaking me. The heat of our kiss and the cool water against my skin is electrifying. I feel her arms around me.

A rush of wind and rain blows over us and Diane pulls her mouth away, takes my hand and leads me up the stairs and into the open door of my apartment.

"I'd noticed," she says softly, "your name next to apartment number 202 on the ringer outside the first time we came. I almost rang it, but Truly said your office was downstairs."

I close the door and she turns and pulls off her dark blue coat, dropping it next to the sofa.

She wears the same yellow dress. It clings to her damp body. She reaches back and unbuttons it, pulling it off her shoulders. Her lacy white bra is sheer, revealing nice, round nipples. I pull off my tie and unbutton my shirt.

Her velvet brown eyes watch my eyes carefully as she steps out of her dress and drops her half-slip.

My shirt tossed aside, I drop my pants and step forward as she starts to unfasten her stockings.

"Let me," I say as I go down on my knees in front of her. I unhook her right stocking from her garter belt and work the stocking down her long, cool leg. Tracing my fingers up her left leg, I unhook the second stocking, my fingers following it down her leg. She drops her bra on my head.

My face is inches from the front of her panties. I reach up and unfasten her garter belt, dropping it next to the stockings. My fingers rise along the back of her legs, across her ass to the top of her panties. I pull them down slowly, my gaze never leaving her crotch. Her mat of dark blonde pubic hair is damp. I lean forward and kiss it.

She gasps as she reaches down and pulls me up by the ears. Her bra falls off my head.

It's her turn now. She goes to her knees and runs her fingernails along the back of my legs. She pulls my shorts off and kisses the tip of my swollen dick. She kisses her way down my dick to my balls and kisses her way back up.

Her tongue flicks the tip of my dick, which throbs in response. Her mouth opens and slides over my dick. She sucks for a second and then works her head up and down, her tongue rubbing my dick.

I pull her up, shove my tongue into her mouth and feel the length of her hot body against mine. I scoop her up in my arms and carry her into the bedroom, without losing a stroke of our French kiss.

I lay her on the bed and stand over her. God, she's gorgeous naked. Unbefuckinlievable! Her breasts, even as she lies on her back, rise firm and full. Her round nipples are erect. She opens her legs and I climb atop this beautiful woman. I kiss my way down from her lips to her breasts, sucking each nipple, nibbling each before kissing my way to her flat stomach and down past her bush to her soft, inner thighs.

She raises her knees, her legs wide and her gorgeous, pink pussy is open in front of my face. I kiss each side and kiss her soft, silky pubic hair. My tongue flicks across her clit. She lets out a little cry. I press my tongue against her clit and rub it up and down and up and down and up and down.

She grinds her hips against my tongue. I reach around her legs and grab her breasts. I knead them as I continue tonguing her clit. She moans and gasps and cries out. She shoves her hips against me and bounces and grinds and I keep on licking until, with a jolt, her hips lift from the bed and she comes in a deep climax, her thighs squeezing against my ears until they ache.

I keep licking.

I lick as she gyrates, as her hips dig for the pleasure. I lick until her legs fall open and she pulls me up to her eager mouth. I feel her hand reach down to guide my dick into her wet pussy. It takes my thick dick a few seconds to work its way in. She gasps and puffs as she tries to catch her breath.

I moan as I start grinding my dick in her hot pussy. The muscles in her pussy pull in response. Jesus! And I fuck her in long, deep strokes, in and out and in and out, back and forth, riding her until I feel it coming. I stop. She pulls at me, works her pussy around my dick, but I hold still. When it subsides, I go back to the screwing. I keep this up for as long as I can, holding it back at the last moment, until I can hold it no more and I gush in her in long, deep spurts.

Rolling off, I scoop her in my arm and she kisses my face and snuggles against me. It takes a while for my breathing to return to normal. Pressed against me, she raises a hand and gently rubs my belly. Her fingers eventually work their way to my pubic hair.

"You sure your husband isn't blind?"

Smiling now, she tickles my dick with her fingernails.

"Then he's just stupid, right?"

She strokes my dick. I'm not ready, but my dick, which has a mind of its own, gets hard between her fingers. She climbs on me, straddles me and rubs her pussy against my dick.

I reach up and grab her breasts, squeeze them and crane my neck up to suck each nipple, to nibble each, as she rubs her pussy up and down the length of my hardening dick. She reaches down and guides the tip of my dick into her and rides me like I'm a fuckin' horse.

"Come on," she gasps. "Fuck me. *Fuck* me! *Fuck me!*"

I want to tell her that's what the fuck I'm doing, but why spoil the mood? Instead I watch this gorgeous blonde bounce on my dick.

The second time always takes longer and I savor the good fuck.

She comes again, bucking against me, just before I come. Her pretty face reaches for the pleasure. Man, there's nothing to compare to this – fucking a beautiful woman and seeing all the pleasure I'm giving her.

Diane rolls off me and lies panting on her back.

I get up immediately and crack open the French doors, using the bottle of scotch to keep it from opening too far. The rush of cool air is invigorating. I climb back into bed and lie on my belly next to Diane.

Her eyes closed, she breathes softly and I begin to drift.

Later, she rolls over and wakes me. I go to the bathroom and on my way back, I fetch my glass from the living room. I refill the glass, reposition the scotch bottle against the French doors. The rain has stopped.

The lair of the red witch is completely dark and looks ghostly, its yellow paint pale beneath the amber streetlights. Sipping the scotch, I stare at the house for a while, then turn to watch Diane sleep. On her back, her legs open, she's a vision in the soft light.

Finishing my drink, I go back out into the living room to make sure my front door's locked. When I turn around, Diane's in the bedroom doorway, her hands high on the door frame as if she's blocking me from going back in the bedroom with a naked body from a school boy's wet dream. With her arms raised, her full breasts look even fuller.

My dick stirs.

She smiles wickedly and moves to me. I meet her halfway and she pushes me back on the sofa.

"No, sit up," she tells me as she kneels in front of me. She opens my knees and kisses her way up to my semi-hard dick. She licks it, kisses it, brushes it with her teeth, sucks it. Her head rising and falling, she sucks until I'm nice and stiff.

Standing, she climbs on me, her hands on my shoulders, those luscious breasts in my face. Her pussy rubs against my dick and Diane slowly positions herself until she impales herself on my dick. She sinks on me and I feel those pussy muscles grab my dick.

She starts a slow, grinding fuck. I cradle her ass in my hands. My mouth moves again from nipple to nipple, sucking each as this woman fucks me, rides me, bucks me. It is so delicious, so hot and wet and I finally come after such a long time, I feel I'm about to pass out.

By the time we get to fifths, I'm shooting blanks, but it's just as good.

Frying eggs and bacon the next morning, I make sure the bacon doesn't splatter. I'm still naked. My sofa is dotted with wet spots and my bed's a wreck and Diane is long gone.

She didn't even leave a note, the hussy.

My kinda woman.

I pour myself a thick cup of coffee and chicory and take a deep sip. Hot and strong – I need it. I'm wasted. I feel like I've been on Anzio beach for a week, until I move and my balls remind me of all the pleasure and I smile.

An hour later, after a shave and a long shower, I walk out of my building into the bright sunshine. I pull on a pair of aviator's sunglasses and yawn. The warm air smells musty as it always does in the old quarter after a long rain. The ancient mortar and bricks and cypress absorb the rain and seems to remain perpetually damp.

I wear a blue shirt today and dress gray pants with my new

black Florsheims. No hat, of course. Moving up Barracks I cross over to the playground side and make my way up to Burgundy to the red door of Maggie, the Love Sorceress.

To my surprise, it's open.

I knock and peek in. The sofa's missing and a chest-of-drawers and an end table are against the far side of the room. No lit candles, the room is bright with the curtains open.

"Good," Maggie calls out from a back room. "You made good time."

She steps into the front room, blinks at me and giggles. "I thought you were the movers."

In a pink T-shirt and red shorts, her hair in a pony tail, she looks like a high schooler – a damn good looking high schooler. The cupie-doll lips are a deep scarlet today.

I hold up the palms of my hands and ask what's going on.

"I never stay more than a month or two in one place." She folds her arms across her chest and looks around me, not at me.

"What?"

"I'm moving to Mid-City. I'll send you the address, although you don't need me any more. Even when you get horny again." She says it matter-of-factly, without feeling, as if I'm not there. She taps her fingers on her arms.

"I don't understand."

"I like moving to new places," she says quickly, takes in a deep breath, then stops tapping her fingers. She looks right at me and says, "Diane Redfearn came to you last night, didn't she?"

My mouth opens, but I say nothing.

"I thought she might."

And it comes to me. "She came to see you."

Maggie nods.

"You sent her to me?"

"She sent herself."

"Her deepest desire?"

She looks down and shrugs.

"Wait. You mean to tell me she came to me for 'mind-numbing sex' at your suggestion?"

Maggie takes in a deep breath and looks up, focusing those large green eyes at me.

"You have a right to know, I suppose."

"Yeah."

"She didn't go to you for 'mind-numbing sex'."

"Then what for?"

"A child," she says.

And I can hear my heart beating as I stand in the doorway. It sounds like thunder.

THE BANISHING

Mark Ramsden

ONE

"Good-looking wealthy couple, both bi, seek female slave to join happy open marriage on a trial basis. London House with dungeon, country cottage and regular first-class travel for successful applicant. Interests include all known forms of S&M, water sports, anal worship. Both partners switch and are willing to experiment. Limits always respected but candidates willing to push through pain barriers will be rewarded beyond their wildest dreams."

"Did we miss anything out?" said Amanda Wood, a Juno-esque brunette whose close-cropped hairstyle highlighted her beguiling green eyes and full lips.

"Not much," said John, who was anything but beautiful, with his craggy face and hair shaved almost to the bone. There were some intriguing scars marking his bullet-shaped head but it was his cold blue eyes which most people remembered, sometimes before shaking their heads to banish the memory. He seemed to have seen too much for his own peace of mind and that was often as much as people needed to know.

"You make us sound like a couple of perverts, if you ask me," he said, almost smiling for once. "And it doesn't really say what we look like."

"Don't want to frighten anyone off," said Amanda. "Do we?"

John looked at his long-standing partner, the person he sometimes called the love of his life and sometimes called all the names under the sun. He scowled and narrowed his eyes but she had known him too long to be troubled by his fierce expression. She poked the tip of her tongue out of her mouth and smiled. His face didn't soften but he was nonetheless thankful that he could still feel his cold heart melt.

From the erotic journal of John and Amanda:
What Amanda Wood thinks John Palmer looks like

It doesn't matter. Standard bloke, I suppose, but taller than most. He has all his hair but shaves it brutally anyway. His face is full of character – piercing eyes and full lips that always seem ready to twitch into a sardonic smile. The point of him is power. Life force. Zest. Vigour. A certain devil-may-care insouciance. And humour, although he is so deadpan you can hardly tell when he's joking. Always that steely glint in his eye. Who cares if he's no pin-up? Attraction is all about chemicals and the way you think their personality might complement yours. And knowing that he looks after himself and that he could look after me, if necessary. I don't want a hurt little boy looking for reassurance, I want a man. And I've got one.

I wanted him to fuck me, the first time I saw him in action in the gym. He was obviously more interested in getting fit than preening himself in front of the mirror. He had solid muscle but he wasn't ripped or cut like the bum-boys who usually feature in any magazine article about fitness centres.

It doesn't take very long for any S&M enthusiast to talk about bums and we might as well discuss John's as it's just about perfect. It's tight and taut, no hair. His face is rugged, to put it mildly, but I prefer that to your average olive-skinned Adonis.

He trains to win, whether it's running, chess or tiddlywinks. There's a cruel streak in there, too, but that's fine by me. I don't want a house-trained moggy with fleas and no claws. I want a lion. Someone who is going to scratch. And yet someone secure enough to submit to me without turning into one of the dickless wonders who crawl round the floor at fetish clubs. There are times I want to push him past his limits and for that I want a strong man. A real man. Which is what I've got.

What John Palmer thinks Amanda Wood looks like

Gorgeous. But wounded, too. Haunted eyes that betray the same nervy intelligence that Gillian Anderson has used to captivate most of the planet's male occupants. (Although I can never sit through the increasingly inane and implausible X-Files.) Now Amanda is going to rip my heart out and eat it in front of me because I have transgressed the first commandment. Thou shalt not mention any women other than me. Thou shalt also not even acknowledge or be aware of their existence. And if thou dost, there shall not be enough flowers and triple-goo ice cream in the whole world to make up for it. But she need have no fear of any mortal woman. To look at Amanda is to be captivated by her green eyes, which seem to hint at some Asiatic ancestors – pulp novelists usually refer to "almond-shaped eyes" at this point, and I don't seem to come up with anything better, so it will have to stand.

It is one of life's little ironies that she has breasts large enough to make the average doltish male deliriously happy but my own obsession is with bottoms. While I never tire of rubbing my face into her soft, bouncing breasts and teasing her nipples with my tongue, my attention will probably be more fixed on her bottom and its globes of endlessly squeezable and kissable flesh. Our lovemaking often starts with one of my hands stroking her moist vulva while I gratefully kiss and nibble at the deep, majestic divide of her bottom. Perhaps I haven't said much about what Amanda looks like but the only thing that needs to be known is that her eyes seem endlessly deep, endlessly understanding. She doesn't like her snub nose or the cute gap in her front teeth but it's hard to find anyone who actually likes what they look like these days. I was certainly never interested in the brain-dead model types that are on the cover of every men's magazine. I don't like football, expensive cars or fighting either; I sometimes wonder if I am really a man at all, by the current media definition. Anyway, Amanda certainly needs to have no fear from any of the women we occasionally invite to join us, but open marriages are hard work – perhaps even harder to sustain than the conventional model.

And here Amanda has scrawled, "Tell me about it."

By the time their advert was published they had just returned from a late summer holiday in Syracuse, Sicily, where they had taken a house near the sea. They had planned to spend the sparkling, starry nights invoking Pan, the god of sex and wine. They could recover on the beach the next day; watching the fishing boats bobbing up and down on the warm Mediterranean. But it had been anything but idyllic. They had spent most of their time arguing, while teenage psychopaths screeched around the tiny streets on their mopeds. It was even a relief to return to the grey skies of London and their house in Hampstead. From here they could at least look down on the people trapped in the centre of the city while they poured themselves another glass of something expensive and planned their next elegant debauch.

It was that hour of the day where they really had to decide to do something or they were lost, but they were still idling over a late breakfast on the terrace. There had been more tension between them ever since they had arranged to meet one of the women who had replied to their advert.

"Have you noticed that couples in pornography never argue?" said Amanda, leafing through the contact mag where they had placed their ad.

John almost smiled. He was still angry, for reasons that are rarely mentioned in fantasy fiction of any kind; close proximity to a long-standing partner, the personal habits and little behavioural tics that tend to grate as you enter your second decade of cohabitation.

"That's because erotic fiction describes an ideal world that doesn't exist," said John, trying not to sound too wistful. After all, he had been lucky to find a woman like Amanda. She was beautiful, infinitely wise, even capable of sustaining an open marriage with a minimum of plate-throwing and screaming. Although their relationship was presently mired in something best not analysed too closely, at least they both still thought they were better off together than apart.

"Never mind," said Amanda. "I'm sure this new plaything of yours will be the answer to our problems. And you won't go falling in love with her. Will you?"

These comments were dripping with so much irony that John judged it safer to stay silent for the moment. Adding new partners to an established relationship was indeed a dangerous remedy; sometimes the patient didn't survive. And it was always hard to judge when infatuation with the new-found object of desire became love. Even when it did, how could this be allowed to flourish? For there was too much invested in their own partnership to risk getting in too deep with anyone new.

Amanda obviously thought that John had spent too much time contemplating Victoria Lambert's letter and photograph. She did indeed have a flawless body, a beautiful face and, according to her, an undying thirst for sensual exploration. It seemed too good to be true. Particularly as she reminded John of a lost love he had never told Amanda about.

He couldn't quite make up his mind whether to ring her or not, not because she was unattractive – far from it – but he was worried about upsetting the delicate balance of their relationship, which had to continue long after whatever happened with Victoria. Like an alcoholic seated before a foaming beer that remained undrunk, trembling on the brink, John spent many furtive moments staring at the photo of a shyly smiling young blonde woman. She seemed eager to embody a type of unquestioning acquiescence that exists more often in the minds of men than in reality. Amanda was unimpressed, as well she might be.

"She's just what you need," she said scornfully. "A younger, dumber blonde version of me. A docile little blonde slave you can tutor in the ways of righteousness."

John kept his face absolutely rigid but there may have been a flicker of something in his eyes, for she smiled knowingly. "I knew you would fancy that," she said. She liked showing just how well she knew him. Precisely because it rubbed him up the wrong way.

"I like the *Withnail and I* quote," he said.

"Hmm," she murmured, not at all convinced and not shy about letting him know it. "Anyway. Are you sure she's right for us? She might be a bit *too* dumb."

John raised an eyebrow as he awaited an expert demolition of Victoria's tastes, dreams and aspirations. "She's a dancer, apparently," said Amanda, her tone lightly ironic. "She was in West End Musicals."

She looked at him as if she had just furnished proof that Victoria had just served ten years for the especially brutal murder of a bald man called John, the first in a series of ingeniously cruel slayings of blokes called John, particularly those who placed contact ads in sex magazines.

When he didn't rise to the bait, Amanda waved the letter in the air and started again, her eyes just that little bit wider and her voice just that little bit louder. "She can't resist telling us she was in *Cats*. Or was, until she injured herself."

John nodded, ignoring her corrosive tone, thinking back to when he had been foolish enough to invest in the theatre. Dancing was a hell of a life and yet young girls still flocked to prove themselves in this most exacting and cruel of professions. All for a pittance and the chance to dance to some of the worst music ever written, in front of tourists and coach parties. These young women did of course have very finely shaped legs and bottoms, an inexhaustible wellspring of excess energy and a certain desire for applause and recognition that made them almost pathetically eager to please. But this was hardly the sort of insight he wanted to share with Amanda.

"It means she will be very fit," said John, who was trying

not to sound too smitten. "And also determined to get what she wants. A hard worker. And . . . at least she can spell. And write in English."

They exchanged a glance. Considering the state of some of the mail they had got, perhaps Amanda had been wrong to condescend to her just because she was a dancer.

"Let's audition her, then," said Amanda. "You obviously won't be happy until you've fucked her."

"What was that about *Cats*?" said John, making a feline, yowling sound and scratching at the air between them.

"Don't make me scratch you," said Amanda. Their eyes locked as they came to a decision. An experimental kiss sharpened their hunger for each other. And soon they were making as much noise as the average feline couple in the throes of some rooftop tryst.

It was a night shortly after a full moon when Victoria knocked on their door. Her blonde hair shone; her clear blue eyes seemed innocent of any guile or deceit. It was altogether ridiculous that such a stunning woman should have to answer an advert in a contact magazine. But then where else could she safely seek to explore the dark desires within her? Hanging around in squalid, noisy clubs was hardly a sensible solution, as John and Amanda knew to their cost. The dull repetitive music was often painfully loud to those not using ecstasy and most of those dancing were merely sensation-seekers who thought it was a big thrill to wear tight-fitting lycra in a night club.

Standards of club etiquette often left a great deal to be desired, with predatory males often trying to join in on personal scenes uninvited. Some dungeon areas were often so small there was rarely room to swing a cat – or any other implement which could cause erogenous zones to smart and tingle. Clubs were the reason why John and Amanda now selected their partners from personal ads.

Vicki had dressed all in white: a clingy silk shirt and tight white jeans and high heels. Her cascade of blonde ringlets must have cost a lot of time and money. Her complexion was flawless and her glistening lipstick and big blue eyes seemed likely to bewitch any man who looked in her general direction. More to the point – what John would see – was the sort of helpless, gullible, fifties starlet vulnerability that men loved so much and modern women detested. Were men still this stupid to fall for such an obvious package? Ask a silly question.

Victoria was not especially tall, for a dancer, which was a relief to Amanda, but she was conscious that she couldn't compete with Victoria's flawless pink skin, her wide open smile and her air of shy but knowing exuberance. All in all, she was enough to make builders fall off their ladders, and it was amusing for Amanda to watch John go all grave and courteous as he tried to stop his desire showing.

After the wine had been poured and the traffic criticized, Amanda showed Vicki a new cat o'nine tails. The gleaming black handle smelt divinely of fresh leather and the tails could easily be used gently enough to caress whoever was lucky enough to submit to her. While Amanda addressed Vicki, she ran her fingers through the strands of the cat.

"With us, once a slave is accepted – broken in, as it were – there will be times when we use this crop for punitive purposes, as opposed to mere erotic gratification. We will be in charge; the slave's own personal agenda comes second."

Amanda arched an eyebrow at Vicki, who seemed unable to reply, struggling with some unresolved inner tension.

"Yeah, that's what really gets me going," she said finally. "It's knowing I've earned it. Not, you know, just playing."

John closed his eyes. It was better than he could have hoped for. He repeated her words silently, committing them to memory. He knew they would resound for the next few days, if not for the rest of his life.

"After the first few sessions, we like to live in our chosen roles twenty-four hours a day," said Amanda, who seemed taller all of a sudden. Had she taken Vicki's statement as a challenge? "I hate play-acting. I get awfully bored with following a prearranged script, don't you? It has to be real, for me."

John watched them size each other up. Vicki was looking at a taller, richer, better educated, more worldly-wise woman. But, as Amanda was well aware, Vicki was younger, cunning and, above all, blonde. She was used to watching men fall apart as soon as she batted her eyelashes at them. She must have known John was already besotted.

"Something is troubling you," said Amanda. "Speak."

"You hate me because I'm younger than you," said Vicki. "It's not my fault."

She looked at John, as if he would intercede in her favour, but John was working very hard at maintaining an unreadable, neutral face.

"I should put you straight over my knee for that," snapped Amanda, who seemed genuinely annoyed. "Wait there while I decide upon your punishment." John watched Vicki's face flush with excitement and felt his own body respond. Amanda looked outwardly in control but John suspected that she, too, was starting to feel the pulse of insistent desire. She seated herself at the table where their journal lay open and started to scribble in its pages, while John contented himself with pleasant anticipation of what was to come.

Not much later, they moved into their cellar and changed into the clothes appropriate for play. Amanda wore knee-length shiny black boots, black stockings, a very small leather skirt and a gleaming red corset which pushed her breasts up and outwards. Vicki wore panties which were transparent enough to reveal that she shaved her pubic hair. She had a small coiled whip etched on her left buttock, a detail which was all the more powerful for being her only tattoo. He was glad she hadn't gone overboard with the body art. Some of their recent applicants had all sorts of junk scrawled all over them, as if their skin was of no greater value than the average municipal convenience wall.

John wore his leather trousers and waistcoat. He had been training hard to maintain his muscle tone for their new partner, even though he knew it was often only of interest to himself just how well-defined his pectorals and biceps were. More importantly, he had to appear calm, which was difficult with Vicki looking so luscious. But, despite his poker face, Amanda could tell his pulse rate had risen. The beast inside him was ready to prowl. He would have to ask her permission before the feast, of course, but she could hardly say no without being accused of jealousy. While John was pouring Victoria a dry white wine spritzer, Amanda was quizzing Victoria about her recent experiences with contact ads.

"I was two years with Master George," she said, intoning this ludicrous name as if either John or Amanda should have heard of it. "You don't know him? He's been on Channel 5 a lot. He's well known on the scene."

John had indeed heard of Master George, an egregious figure whose hatred of women shone out of a fat face which resembled nothing more than the sort of potato which quality-conscious supermarkets would no longer sell.

By the time they had heard Victoria say the words Master George often enough to dread their repetition, John had a sudden inspiration. "Perhaps your initiation could be a banishing of your previous partner," said John. "Then you could be free to start again."

Amanda picked up on this quickly, always eager to intensify the ritual element of their sex life. It was her usual way of dragging John into her occult dabblings, without him being too aware of what was happening. "Yes," she said. "We could work a ceremony that would help you start a new life. You would be born again."

The atmosphere in the room was distinctly heavier, now that they were closer to the moment of truth. Amanda dimmed the lights until there were only flickering candles to provide illumination. They scanned each other's faces for clues as to what might happen next.

Vicki looked apprehensive, perhaps at the sound of the words "initiation", "ceremony" and "born again". John offered her a reassuring smile and refilled her glass, to help her make the transition between the world of polite conversation and the hidden depths of their shared desires.

He lit some sandalwood incense, which some thought was an aphrodisiac although, since Vicki's arrival, such overrated herbal essences were hardly essential. Plainsong played softly on the stereo as Amanda took up her position in the centre of the room. She looked the picture of the stark and severe dominant woman as she let the tails of the cat trail through her gloved fingers. Almost as soon as she had established this persona, she stepped out of the role by smiling at Vicki and letting the cat's tails trail over their guest's hardened nipples. It was important to establish trust before they took her on a journey through her deepest desires.

"I think you need to get rid of this 'Master George'," said John. "You need to banish him. Or, more accurately, you will do the hard work. We will merely set the appropriate atmosphere."

Vicki looked uncertain. Perhaps she liked being in thrall to the man who had dominated her for so long.

"The moon is waning," said Amanda. "It's a perfect time to get rid of old baggage." She somehow managed to make it sound like an unmissable opportunity, the occult equivalent of the January sales.

"Like an exorcism?" said Victoria, her voice hushed, her eyes wide.

"Nothing so dramatic," said John, with a half-smile. "But we will get rid of 'Master George' for you, if you truly wish it."

"Anyone calling themselves 'Master George' sounds like a prat," said Amanda. John watched Vicki's face fall and felt a twinge of sympathy for her.

"Could you not have used a more elegant phrase, my dear?" he said to Amanda, and then wished he hadn't as he watched her eyes flicker. It was risky to continue in this vein, but he felt that Vicki needed defending. "If 'Master George' had managed to captivate Vicki for so long, he cannot have been entirely devoid of merit."

Amanda made no reply but swished her crop through the air. It wasn't entirely clear who she would like to use it on presently. John was also undecided as to who should submit to whom. The longer he looked at Vicki, the more he could feel some force inside himself telling him to fall to his knees.

Time stood still as they listened to the chanting of the monks and of the ageless voices inside them. Suddenly, John knelt down in front of Vicki, without losing eye contact. "I would consider it an honour if I could massage your feet," he said. He watched Vicki's reaction carefully. She looked flattered but was obviously uneasy as to how to proceed.

"Don't know what to say," said Vicki. "I'm used to people telling me what to do."

"I wouldn't look a gift horse in the mouth," said Amanda, walking behind John and swishing the tails of the cat lightly across his buttocks. "Particularly not when this one has such fine flanks. He can be disobedient, but, if you train him well, he will take you where you need to go."

John heard the ominous undertone behind the deceptively sweet tone of Amanda's voice and found it unbearably exciting.

"Give him a foot to play with," ordered Amanda. "He won't go away until you do."

Shyly, Vicki proffered one of her small feet. She appeared uncomfortable with the situation, perhaps afraid that her battered and callused dancer's feet would be unacceptable. If only you knew, thought John, as he reverently dipped his head to kiss her toes, cupping her heel in his hand and stroking the underside of her feet in a slow firm motion. He was aiming to soothe her, making sure his touch was firm enough to avoid a tickling sensation. He sought in vain to remember snippets of wisdom from guides to massage and reflexology, but then it was easier to let Vicki's little satisfied moans and sighs tell him whether he was on the right track or not.

When he looked upwards, he was gratified to find that Vicki's eyes were closed and her head was thrown back. John rubbed and kneaded her feet, drawing moans of pleasure from her. For a while, she drifted off somewhere, unable to speak as she lost herself in a world of sensation. Her eyes stayed shut as she opened her mouth to speak.

"Ooh, it's so long since anyone's done that. I'd forgotten . . . aaah . . . how sensitive my toes were. Yes!"

John let his tongue explore the gap between each toe in turn, teasing out tastes and flavours that were reminiscent of a really subtle mozzarella, a comparison he knew he would be keeping to himself until he knew Vicki a great deal better than he did presently. As he worked away diligently, he tried not to think of the delights to come later, when he would run his tongue over her hot, lightly flogged bottom. But that was pure greed. It was better to concentrate on the humbling, repetitive nature of his present task. He worked hard at keeping up a slow rhythmic stroking motion, hoping to further intensify the mild trance the two of them were sharing.

"I hope I'm clean enough for you, master," said Vicki, as John continued to lick and nuzzle her toes.

"You don't have to call me 'master'," said John softly. Amanda raised an eyebrow and John had to suppress a smile. He felt anything but masterful, these days, although that had been his chosen role when he had first met Amanda.

"It's time you undressed, my dear," said Amanda, who was clearly irritated at the pampering this supposed "slave" was receiving.

Vicki opened her eyes and immediately looked from John to Amanda, as if deciding who to obey.

"Let him indulge himself," said Amanda. "But we have work to do."

As soon as Vicki was naked, Amanda cuffed her wrists to a flogging post and started to whip her, very gently, as John continued to kiss her feet and calves. As Amanda increased the pace and strength of the still gentle flogging of Vicki's round pink bottom, John was gradually working his way up from her small, badly-callused feet. He kissed and stroked each inch of her muscular calves, occasionally glancing up at her shaven vulva, which was now moist and glistening. As Amanda continued to flog Vicki lightly, the tails of the cat sometimes caught John's back and shoulders. He continued to explore the silky skin of Vicki's thighs with his eager fingers and tongue as she shifted her weight to cope with her mounting excitement. John could feel the tensile strength of her muscles moving underneath her silky skin.

"It is time we freed you from your so-called master," said Amanda, in the low insistent voice she sometimes used to hypnotize the unwary. "As each stroke is delivered, I want you to imagine that your master is yet further away from you and smaller in size. On the final stroke, we will banish him from your present life entirely. Are you ready?"

There was a pause before Vicki consented.

"Don't be frightened," said John. "Amanda is very careful not to damage the skin. This is more of a symbolic cleansing of your last life. Put yourself into her hands."

Vicki considered this for a moment, then closed her eyes. "Yes, beat him out of me. I want to be free."

"And so you shall," said Amanda, giving her cat a swish through the air. "Concentrate, and we will rid you of the ghost of 'Master George'."

Amanda used her implement with more strength now but the blows were still little more than caresses. With a long slow build-up, it was always possible for the submissive to absorb more.

"I'm going to strike harder, now," said Amanda. "Picture 'George' growing smaller and smaller in your mind's eye. Can you see him?"

Victoria moaned her assent. Amanda gently guided John to where he could kiss Vicki's wet sex. She kneaded each of Vicki's nipples in turn, watching her reaction carefully, then struck once more. After the slapping sound of the impact, Vicki gasped and moaned as the hot, intense impact spread through her bottom and around her whole body. She cried out after the second of these harder strokes, at which Amanda stroked her glowing skin.

"It's all right," breathed Vicki. "Do it harder!"

"Concentrate," said Amanda firmly. "Make George vanish! Watch him shrink, fade and die." With each of these words, she laid on another stroke.

The blows were still only enough to redden the surface of her flesh but Vicki was starting to move from side to side now, an enchanting little dance that inspired Amanda to dip her face down to kiss the lingering smarts better.

John was by now rubbing his erection into Vicki's legs as he buried his head in her soaking wet mound. He could hear his fevered blood thundering around his body as Vicki begged for Amanda to continue what she had started.

"Go on!" she whispered. "Don't stop."

"Very well," said Amanda, who was still rubbing the chubby red flesh of her bottom with her gloved hand. She could feel the heat from her lightly whipped flesh even through the velvet gloves. John was kissing and licking Vicki's thighs now, eager to discover more of her secrets.

"Don't be greedy, John," said Amanda rather sharply. She applied gentle pressure on the top of his head to move him back down Vicki's thighs. She gave him a sharp stroke of the crop to remind him who was boss, before uncuffing Vicki's right hand.

"Stroke yourself, dear. And see yourself standing tall. You don't need a 'master'." Amanda kissed her full on the lips as she guided Vicki's hand to where it would do the most good. As Vicki grunted and groaned, Amanda looked down at John and arched an eyebrow. It was as if she was saying, "See how close I am to her. Will you ever be as close as I am?"

John caught the look but had no idea whether she was trying to prove a point or even whether he was merely being paranoid. Besides, the heat and scent of Vicki was rather more important.

"Forget the past," breathed Amanda, directly into Vicki's ear. "Cherish yourself. You deserve to be worshipped," said Amanda. "John! Time to make yourself useful!" With that, she guided John behind Vicki.

He nuzzled Vicki's hot bottom gratefully, running his tongue over the soft, silken cheeks.

"Lick her!" commanded Amanda. "Right between the cheeks! Right up and down! That's it. Now, don't stop. Or else!"

As this was his heart's desire, he didn't exactly need to be told or to be spurred on by the cat o'nine tails. Amanda reddened his flesh for him anyway before using her gloved fingers to stimulate Vicki. They drifted together, onwards and upwards, until the trivial matter of who was dominating whom had ceased to be relevant.

TWO

The air in the cellar was heavy with incense. Candles at floor level provided an eerie, flickering light which barely illuminated the darkness in which Amanda and Vicki stood. They were close enough to kiss. Close enough to be aware of the scent of each other's bodies. Close enough to whisper into each other's ears. Every now and again, they would look over at John, who was kneeling in the corner, naked.

He spent a good deal of time clenching and unclenching his pectoral muscles, for he was conscious of his advancing years and wished to maintain some semblance of his former glory. These exercises also helped keep his mind off the ache in his legs: it was hard to kneel for so long. He was also wondering whether he was up to whatever they were planning for him. Or whether they would ignore him in order to play with each other, which would hurt a great deal more than any momentary discomfort suffered in the cause of pleasure.

A week had elapsed since their last session with Vicki. A whole week, in which John's thoughts had rarely been away from her. Amanda was also relishing the situation they were in. As his long-term partner, it amused her to train up a new dominatrix for him – particularly as Vicki had come to them as a slave. They were still arguing as to who should take the most credit for this transformation, during which John had heard a great deal about Amanda's theories about spirit possession and multiple personality.

"It's not as simple as being submissive or dominant," she had said. "Perhaps we are all at the mercy of the many different people inside us. And the spirits we invoke. Particularly any we fail to banish."

John knew better than to argue. If she wanted to deny personal responsibility and put her mood-swings down to the activities of long-dead mythical deities or stray poltergeists, that was up to her. What her theory seemed to boil down to, in practice, was that she was right all the time, whatever he had actually said or done. And it was quicker not to argue.

Even so, he had to take issue whenever Amanda teased him about how well he had adapted to the submissive role. He was keen to point out that this was a temporary measure. Perhaps too keen, for Amanda had smiled and murmured something about protesting too much. He couldn't say any more without digging himself in deeper, but he still wanted to keep some distance between himself and the soft white blob men you could see being led round the floor at fetish events. Where was the convenient label to fit his present sexuality? Masochist but not submissive? Occasionally acquiescent? Willing to say "Yes, mistress," in return for therapeutic chastisement?

As soon as Vicki had arrived for her second visit, such questions became only of academic interest. Whatever happened now was going to be all about her: her needs, her desires. Her smile seemed wider, her voice deeper. She seemed more confident; she didn't constantly seek reassurance. Her blonde hair was now much shorter and her heels were higher. She was wearing black and red; perhaps white had been discarded along with her former slave status. It was too early to say if they had cleansed her of the malign influence of her last partner, the idiot "Master George". But John couldn't wait to see her attempt a whole evening in her new role. Perhaps she would even have both her hosts kneeling down and licking her boots, before long. For the moment, it was Amanda who was strutting around the cellar, laying down the law as Vicki listened intently.

"The moon is still waning," said Amanda. "And autumn is the time when we harvest. When we separate the wheat from the chaff." She ran her hands over Vicki's body, stopping to stroke and caress wherever Vicki's soft sighs and moans indicated that she had found the right spot. They looked good together, entirely at ease in each other's arms. John was still kneeling, still trying to ignore the ache in his legs. If he didn't know any better, he would think that Vicki was about

to take Amanda away from him. Say what you like about
open marriages. They were never dull.

He watched them kiss, Vicki returning Amanda's initial
advance with more than enough enthusiasm to make his own
presence irrelevant. Any possible erotic excitement John
might have felt was deadened by the sickening feeling that
this experiment could go badly wrong. Over the past week, he
had seen the balance of power in their relationship shift
decisively in Amanda's favour. And to think he had been
concerned that his partner might feel left out! If anyone was
likely to be discarded, now Vicki had arrived, it was more
likely to be himself. As for Amanda's pontificating on the
subject of the change of the seasons . . . this particular autumn
seemed to be the time to honour the return of Miss Bossy
Boots, who would do well to remember that she used to be a
supply teacher before his money enabled her to pack it in. He
might even had said as much, this time last week; but, since
Vicki's transformation, everything had changed. In his new,
less exalted place in the household, it would not be appropriate
for him to make any supposedly amusing remarks.

He had to strain his ears to hear what they were saying, but
since Vicki was wearing gleaming boots and a thin pink
rubber bodice, through which her nipples protruded, it
hardly mattered. Her long legs and taut bottom were
sheathed in gleaming black rubber; it was almost worth
the ache in his legs to view her from this angle. The pain
triggered an incongruous memory of a supervised Buddhist
meditation session, where his spirit had floated off somewhere out into space, even as his legs had seized up in agony.

It was all about concentration, reaching a trance state. He
fixed his attention on Vicki's strong well-defined calves and
thighs and watched the muscles ripple gently beneath the
sheen of tight-fitting rubber as she shifted her weight from
one foot to another.

"Now then," said Amanda briskly. "Before I can let you
loose on John, you must be punished for whatever lewd
behaviour you have indulged in since last week. It's important that you know your place."

There was a brief battle of wills as their eyes locked. It wasn't long before Vicki was looking down at the floor and Amanda's eyes were shining triumphantly. She was still on top.

"Do you have something to tell me?" she asked Vicki. "Any improper conduct? Or have you merely been leading young men on? And then running off home to pleasure yourself in the privacy of your bedroom?"

Vicki seemed almost to smile but instead maintained her blank submissive pose, one she seemed very comfortable with. "Oh, please. I've been ever so good." She was pouting now, standing with her feet turned inwards. The pose pleased John and irritated Amanda. "I thought we agreed that I only got punished when I deserved it!"

"You can leave whenever you like," said Amanda, ice-cold all of a sudden. "John would probably be heartbroken. But he would soon find a replacement for you. There isn't exactly a shortage of young, dumb blondes."

Vicki stood up straight; her voice aged a couple of decades. "It's not my fault I'm younger than you," she said.

Amanda smiled faintly, then they stared at each other until Vicki looked away. "That's all right, dear. I just wanted to get you annoyed enough to give John the treatment he so richly deserves. Look at him! Obediently waiting for you. But first you have to submit to the lady of the house."

Without another word, Vicki bent over and remained absolutely still, hands flat on the floor. Amanda took a moment to savour her dominance, then softly smacked her, pausing to kiss where her hand had just landed before continuing the process. The impact of hand on rubber-clad bottom sounded a great deal more dramatic than the actual effects. Vicki was soon sighing with pleasure and waggling her hips to suggest that perhaps Amanda was erring on the side of leniency.

As each increasingly firm smack resounded, John was transfixed by a vision of Vicki using a whip on himself. He saw himself chained to the whipping post, hands secured above his head, most of his body encased in latex. He wanted

Vicki to put his tightest-fitting mask on. He wanted her to rub the insides of it with her most intimate scents. During the long confinement in sweetly aromatic darkness, he would be drifting into a trance which might even allow himself freedom from the confines of his body. This was a risky process, in that it was tempting to roam free and never return, but it was something he would love to do again – especially if guided by Vicki, his new obsession.

Instantly, he knew that Amanda would resent any such intimacy and that he would have to keep any such plans to himself. He had been careful never to mention Vicki's name in the week that had passed but Amanda had still been on edge – even though she was keen on Vicki herself. But then, no one had yet come up with a foolproof way of maintaining an open marriage without someone getting hurt, and it didn't look like they would be the first.

What was certain was that he was becoming more and more addicted to Vicki, his new drug of choice. He was well aware that her effects would soon wear off, but was hoping that they wouldn't see so much of her that they would become bored. As usual, this was a decision that Amanda was likely to take. Right now, she seemed happy enough, spanking Vicki harder and faster in response to her groans and whimpers.

Amanda carried on past the time when Vicki sounded distressed rather than delighted, judging that she could stand having her limits pushed a little. When Amanda eventually stopped, Vicki sighed in gratitude. Her eyes were sparkling as she stood up and it was some time before their fervent reconciliatory embrace came to an end.

John was still waiting patiently, trying not to look too ravenous for whatever was going to happen next. He knew if he looked too keen, Amanda might well decide to keep him waiting even longer.

"It's time you gave John what he needs," said Amanda. John was careful not to appear grateful. "And don't be too gentle. Go and do your worst."

"I can hardly wait to start on him," said Vicki, as Amanda

looked over at her partner. By the mischievous glint in her eyes, it was clear that she was in no hurry to pander to him.

"You *must* wait," said Amanda sharply. "Let him wait upon *our* pleasure for a change. It will teach him a valuable lesson."

Vicki stole a glance at John, who remained waiting, head bowed. He wanted to give her a reassuring smile but felt this was inappropriate. Amanda was in charge. His only responsibility was to obey her orders.

"It still feels weird," said Vicki. "I spent most of my life being dominated. But after last week . . . I don't know any more. Maybe the other stuff was just buried all this time."

Amanda let the words hang in the air for a moment, then nodded approval. "More people should see fetishism as a journey," she said. "Not just repeating the same things over and over again. So many people get stuck re-enacting the same childhood trauma over and over again. They never get past the initial wound. I think it's time for you to move on. If John was allowed to say anything today, he might even agree."

Here she nodded towards her partner, stepping out of character long enough to give him a skewed smile and a wink. "Besides, the more men we can make realize that there is nothing 'manly' about bossing women about, the better. Then they can assume their rightful place as the sexual playthings of women. They can stop wearing those nasty rough clothes and dress in the silk knickers they have always really wanted to wear. They wouldn't have to drink too much or fight each other all the time; they would be happy. But I mustn't be too harsh on them. They do have their uses, after all."

Amanda gave Vicki a playful pinch. Perhaps she was seeking to remind her of the happy hours they had spent tangled up in each other's bodies while John kissed and stroked them gently. Time had slowed down while they spent hours feasting upon each other, lapping happily at each other's clefts while John tried not to feel jealous at their obvious pleasure in each other. He didn't quite succeed, of course – indeed, not by a rather large margin – but managed instead to console himself with the thought that he would be able to store this memory away for future reference. He knew he would return often to this memory to trigger off afternoon bouts of solo play.

As to whether they could really have cleansed her of the memory of her former partner, John was more sceptical. Perhaps it wasn't possible to wipe out years of conditioning in one session. With a smile he remembered the strategy of expensive shrinks; what she obviously needed was more of their special therapy, a series of lengthy sessions in which the patient may not be cured but the therapists would certainly be enriched.

The women vanished for a moment. John could hear whispering and giggling and the occasional passionate kiss, but that was not enough to enable him to guess what might happen next.

"Close your eyes, John," ordered Amanda. "We are ready to start."

The first thing he heard was two pairs of high heels clicking over the stone floor of the cellar until they were close to him. He could sense perfume, body heat and the individual scent of their bodies. As Amanda put her gloved hand in his mouth, he nuzzled on the proffered fingers gratefully, groaning out loud as the moment of truth approached.

But he would have to wait. With an affectionate pat on his head and a softly whispered, "Down, boy," the fingers were removed. Amanda was still more concerned with Vicki.

"This is the last lesson in your training, my dear," Amanda said. "We have started to banish your last master. Rome was not built in a day but I hope you are learning to stand on your own two feet, free of the pernicious influence of you know who. 'Master George', indeed! You should be walking all over men, not taking orders from them. John! Look at Vicki's new toy."

John opened his eyes to see Amanda gently flicking the end of a strap-on phallus which Vicki was wearing. As the rubber dildo bobbed up and down, the women shared a conspiratorial smile. John felt edgy and anxious, but nothing worth having came without some effort or discomfort. He would just have to hope he was up to the coming ordeal.

"It's lovely," said Vicki, running her hand over the realistically sculpted veins on the hard rubber phallus. "But I want a bigger one."

"Don't we all, dear?" said John. He shared a smile with Vicki, then turned to look at Amanda.

"Who asked you?" she said. Her lips twitched briefly but she was not happy about John's unsolicited comment. They had often clashed about the importance of staying in their defined roles. In John's view, she should lighten up occasionally. And if his behaviour was really so unbearable, at least she had an excuse to invent some fiendish new torment they could both enjoy. He was already a little apprehensive of the size of the strap-on Vicki was wearing. It had only been used once: a memorable evening. He hoped that it wouldn't come into action until they had played for some considerable time, so he would be ready to relax enough to accommodate the dauntingly large black rubber phallus. Maybe it wouldn't come into play; perhaps she was just wearing it as a symbol of her dominance over him. And maybe Santa Claus brought presents every Christmas for children who had never been naughty . . .

"Warm him up, first," said Amanda, handing Vicki a well-worn tawse. "Then give it to him hard."

John looked up at Vicki, who seemed to be waiting for his permission to start. "My hide is as hard as my heart," he said. "Let yourself go."

Their eyes locked for a moment – which might have been a few seconds and which might have been forever.

Eventually she said, "Present yourself," stroking the tip of a crop slowly down his back before gently tapping his buttocks. He didn't need any further invitation; he turned and lowered his face to the floor. Soon he was being warmed by a pair of gloved hands and the tip of a crop. The blows started soft and slow and very gradually increased in pace and strength.

Every now and again, they would pause to kiss and fondle each other. John felt it was undignified to beg, but he was close to pleading as these clinches threatened to become the main event, rather than the exploration of his body. Soon the crop was back in action, spreading heat and light just where it was needed most, and Amanda had moved to one side to watch her protégeé in action.

"I like it when they wriggle," said Vicki, sounding very different from the shy ingenue of last week.

"Well, you'll have to hit harder than that, dear," said Amanda. "This one has been very well trained, though I say it myself."

Vicki worked on him for some time while Amanda cradled his head between her thighs, whispering to him what was most likely to inflame his senses. John snuffed up her scent eagerly, feeling privileged to be the plaything of two beautiful women.

"Now you're hot, you need cold cream," said Vicki, laying her crop aside. Her touch was divine and the anticipation of what was to come was sending him close to delirium. She rubbed the cream in thoroughly and then started to penetrate him gently with the tip of her fingers. He pushed back hard at her invading fingers, not wanting to leave her in any doubt that he needed what was to come.

"Steady now, Vicki. Don't spoil him." Amanda positioned her foot so John could lick and nuzzle her toes. "He likes it rough. And don't worry about safe words today, dear. This isn't some boring, candy-floss sex club for middle-class couples with 2.4 children. If you want to fuck him senseless with that thing, you may do so."

"This is just a game you are playing, right?" said Vicki, not at all comfortable with the edge in Amanda's voice.

Just do it, thought John, but he was not going to indulged just yet.

"If you say so," said Amanda. "If it is a game, the only rule is that you win. And he loses. And afterwards I will give you a big sloppy kiss. In the winner's enclosure. While he mixes the drinks. Sound nice?"

Vicki smiled. "Yeah. I thought you were going to be a lot harder on me."

"We might still be hard on you. Just wait till you have to write a ten page essay in our big black book. Something like, 'What Vicki thinks of her introduction to John and Amanda'. And you had better go into detail." Amanda swished a cat o'nine tails through the air, although any potential menace was easily dissipated by her hint of a smile. Vicki already knew that any punishment always came with some serious pampering afterwards.

"Unless you can write something hot, you will be really punished," said Amanda, in ringing tones of mock-severity. "No warm-up and each stroke will really count." She wagged a finger at Vicki whose eyes widened prettily. "Anyway, it's probably time for you to fuck him. He obviously can't wait much longer."

"No," giggled Vicki, giving John's engorged penis a fond squeeze.

"Careful, now," said Amanda. "Don't get him too excited. His heart might not stand it."

The contempt in her voice sounded a little too real for John's taste. All week Amanda had been trying her best to rile him, but it was hard to know just how much was for the purposes of roleplay and how much was because she was genuinely annoyed about his desire for Vicki.

"Now you can show just how much you want her," said Amanda, as she guided the dauntingly wide tip of the phallus to his anus. "Open up for Vicki, dear. You know you want it."

The tone was scathing but she held him tight and kissed him passionately before leaving Vicki to push the phallus against him. He found the blonde's struggles to guide her new toy almost unbearably cute: the way the tip of her tongue protruded as she concentrated, her frown and occasional soft curses. After a brief, rather undignified struggle, she was inside him and they were soon engrossed in a three-way exchange of passion. She was careful to be gentle and considerate, perhaps too much so, for after the initial thrill had faded John was soon aware that he would not reach orgasm by this method. He needed the merest touch of manual or oral stimulation but both women were studiously avoiding giving him the relief he needed.

After Vicki had withdrawn from him, Amanda scratched his bulging erection with one of her blood-red fingernails.

"He's very keen on you," said Amanda. Her tone was caustic, as grating as the very fine sandpaper they kept for their more extreme sessions. "Let's see just how keen he is. He likes champagne too. Let's see if he likes it enough to drink it second-hand."

There was a grateful moan from John. Soon he was looking up at the stark divide of Vicki's sex as she positioned herself over his face.

"What about the floor?" she said, still sounding a bit shocked by what was about to happen. But also excited, ready to do something new.

"Don't worry about that," said Amanda. "He'll lick that up. He likes that."

"I don't know if I can," said Vicki.

John almost smiled. Was she teasing him, just to make the experience more powerful when she did eventually relent and let her sour-sweet liquid gush all over him? Surely she was not yet so artful?

"More champagne, dear?" said Amanda, handing her a glass. "Go on, gulp it down. I want to see him thoroughly covered. It's time he learned his place in this house. Do you know, I think he might thrive on a diet of second-hand champagne. He certainly looks eager for you to start, doesn't he?"

Amanda touched the tip of John's erection briefly. He was on the brink of orgasm but knew Amanda would never allow him release until she had pushed him further than he had ever been before. This was the price to be paid for his infatuation with Vicki.

He was trying not to use the word love in this context, but the more he tried to ignore the possibility he was falling for Vicki, the stronger his feelings became. And, with this coming baptism, he was likely to become even more besotted.

"Have another glass, dear," said Amanda, kissing Vicki full on the lips. Her hands started to wonder around Vicki's body, pinching the flesh until she found the two most important openings to her body and eased a finger in each. There was nothing John could do except watch. And dream. Anything and everything might happen, in just a few short moments. If they could ever leave each other alone.

To think even as long ago as last week he had imagined betraying Amanda with Victoria. If anyone was likely to be left out of any new partnership, it was highly likely to be himself. The limits of his betrayal would only have been a few nights with Vicki, somewhere they could relax free from the scrutiny of Amanda's prying eyes and acid tongue. But he now knew this would never happen and, what's more, it never should happen. It was better this way.

"I shouldn't really drink any more," said Vicki, who was starting to giggle as the alcohol got through to her. "I feel light-headed."

You and me both, babe, thought John. He watched the full cheeks of her bottom wobbling slightly as she shifted her weight from foot to foot.

"Many persist in seeing water sports in the context of dominance and submission," said Amanda, who sometimes forgot that not everyone wanted to be lectured. "It doesn't have to be part of a humiliation scenario; it can be a joyful celebration of the partner's body," she continued.

Vicki was all ears but John could have done with less talk and more action. Just shut up and tell her to piss all over me, he thought, but his fervent attempts at telepathy were to little avail. As yet. Still, he could be content with letting the anticipation build.

"We should view this exchange as a liquid kiss," said Amanda. "There need be no shame in accepting a warm fluid coming straight from the centre of your partner's sexuality."

No shame indeed, thought John. Just get on with it!

"The communion service is descended from occult ceremonies in which bodily fluids would be placed in a chalice. The Holy Grail itself is undoubtedly a vessel meant to symbolise the vagina, a cup in which various fluids can be drunk."

Yes, yes. Just tell her to squat over my face. Let me gaze up at her lovely cleft and the rounded cheeks of her bottom. Let her relax enough to get used to the idea. Let it flow down over me. Let me drink it in and lick her afterwards.

"Fresh urine usually smells and tastes good, provided the partner is in good health and one is attracted to them in the first place," said Amanda.

Vicki was still wide-eyed, getting used to the idea of what she was about to do.

"You don't have to ask if he wants you to do it. Look at him! He is yearning for you. Won't do him any harm to let him wait. Drink more champagne. Make sure you have a full bladder before you anoint him. If you're really good, I'll let you drink mine."

"Is it . . ." Vicki couldn't complete her question because to do so would seem ungrateful. But you couldn't be too careful, these days. "Is it safe?" she said, in a very quiet voice.

Amanda smiled. "It's low risk, with regard to HIV transmission. Only a tiny amount of the HIV virus is contained in urine and saliva kills that off. As long as it is kept away from cuts and abrasions and the receiving partner's gums are not bleeding, this is safe sex."

Please, please, please. Just do it, thought John. It had been some time since he had prayed to anybody or anything, but he was getting close now. I need this, I want it, I must have it . . .

"It's coming!" said Vicki, sounding as exhilarated as John felt.

As the warm aromatic fluid coursed over his face and mouth, he gulped and swallowed, struggling to keep pace with the force of the flow. For one absurd moment, he recognised the taste of the chemical sweetener she had popped into her after-dinner coffee; then he was lost once more as Amanda used her most spiteful crop on him with more energy than was customary.

The combination of the smart of the crop with the tidal waves of briny fluid washing over and through him were enough to make his tired flesh sing and his soul sing with joy. It was almost as if there was still enough alcohol left in her champagne-tinged urine to make him drunk. They really must try her out on some of the vintage wines he had laid down in his cellar.

Amanda was mumbling something about banishing "Master George" but, while she did so, John could clearly see the stern humourless "master" he himself had once been dissolve. He closed his eyes, breathed deeply and began to see himself kneeling before Vicki, who was seated on a silver throne around which the sea swirled. She raised a wand with which she was lustily hitting him wherever she could, an impish knowing smile trained directly on him. He knew that they would never switch roles. Even with Amanda, they seemed to have permanently reversed polarity. She was in charge now. It seemed appropriate that she took him in hand to push him over the edge. As he lost control and felt the tides sweep him away he saw Amanda's face. "You belong to me," she was saying. "You always will."

And he moaned his agreement as she held him afterwards for what seemed like an eternity. But behind his closed eyelids, he was looking at Vicki's face as she smiled triumphantly. They untangled from each other slowly, each unwilling to return to the more mundane world they usually inhabited.

Champagne helped, of course, as did a brief ritual cleansing by Amanda. This may have sent any stray demons packing or it may have merely served as a useful cooling-off period before it was time to play at being normal again: John really didn't mind which, after an experience like that.

Then it was time for the women to retire upstairs to replenish their glasses while John swabbed the floor. As he joined them, it seemed that Vicki was drunk on something more potent than champagne.

"This feels so good, doesn't it?" said Vicki, with something approaching a wicked grin on her lovely face. "I think I want to be dominant all the time. I really think it's me."

"Glad we could be of service," drawled Amanda, but whatever irony was in her voice seemed to float over Vicki's head.

"Yeah, I'm ever so grateful. I mean, if you want me to do you, some time . . ."

Amanda declined the invitation gracefully with just a sideways shake of her head and a dry smile. "I'm going to be too busy training this one for a while," said Amanda, nodding over at John. "I think you've fused the part of him that used to be dominant. Taught him a lesson he might have needed for a long time."

It was open to question whether this statement was merely an affectionate little tease which went with the previous session, but John was finding it more exciting, and ultimately more satisfying, to take it as read. He felt a warm glow suffuse his body and soul at the thought of discarding all the stiff, humourless baggage that went with being dominant.

Let someone else worry about setting the agenda. He could just abandon himself to the moment. Besides, the submissive often got the best of the deal in these exchanges. Everything was focused on them, and their often notoriously picky desires. ("Up a bit, down. No, not there! Don't you know anything?") It was often hard to tell who was actually dominating whom, standing there listening to a torrent of orders coming from his theoretically submissive partner.

John felt drained but glowing with an inner fire he had not felt for some time – not since he had first met Amanda, in fact. He could hear the occasional waspish undertone in Amanda's voice as she replied to Vicki's breathless babble, but their guest was oblivious to anything except the surge of fire in her veins and the long trapped flow of power and dominance that had always been rightfully hers.

"You've given me wings. I'm ready to fly," she said, face flushed with an innocent joy that neither John nor Amanda could share right now. For the sake of appearances, they drank till dawn with their guest, then called a cab for her, remembering to send her flowers later that day. As soon as she had gone they had quickly agreed that it was too dangerous to see her again too soon. Then they fell asleep in each other's arms.

THREE

What Vicki wrote in John and Amanda's big black book

I learned so much! I can't believe it! I thought I knew all there was to know about pervy stuff till I met John and Amanda. They're really generous hosts. As for Amanda, who else would lend you their husband to practise being a mistress on? And John wasn't used to being submissive although he was a quick learner, I'll say that for him. You two are the greatest! Thanks ever so much!

John didn't need to look in their erotic diary any more. He had memorized Vicki's words, which was maybe just as well as they had agreed that they should wait a long time before seeing her again. Although Amanda had ritually banished the energy they had summoned with her, Vicki was still a constant presence. He had betrayed too much of his desire for her to Amanda. As a result, his own status in the house had been considerably diminished. It was also getting harder for him to cope with his growing addiction to Vicki, perhaps not to the real person but to some quality or value she represented.

He knew that there was nothing more pathetic than a man seeking out a younger partner every time his relationship was in crisis, or so the conventional wisdom had it. Mother Nature, the Goddess, the life force – however you wanted to put it – she seemed to think it was a very good idea indeed for him to seek out a new partner. In fact, this was whispered in his ear at every possible opportunity, by some malevolent sprite who had been around several millennia longer than whoever invented monogamy as an instrument of social control.

It was only ten a.m. and John had already poured himself two ounces of a very expensive single malt. Sipped carefully, this would last till lunch, and would hopefully take some of the edge off his hunger for Vicki. He inhaled the scent of the whisky warily, waiting five minutes before wetting his lips with the merest possible drop of the liquid. It was perhaps half an hour before he tasted the smoky fluid, time spent entirely in wrestling with his desire to call Vicki, something he had agreed with Amanda he would not do. The two ounces of dark smoky fragrance lasted until lunch, after which he went for a long walk on the Heath. After which he settled down to serious drinking, after which he called a number of drug dealers, after which it was prudent to stay out until he had recovered from the effect of their products. At no time did he ring Vicki but when he awoke the next day, suffering from three different types of withdrawal, he was beginning to wonder whether it was worth the cost.

John knew he was behaving like a teenager but that didn't alter the way he felt. He missed Vicki bitterly. And as the days grew darker and the nights colder, he started to yearn for her. It was infantile, it was selfish and it would lead nowhere. He was supposed to have grown out of this stuff. After all, any fool could fall in love. The hard bit was seeing whether it was real enough to last through decades of living together.

Weeks later, just as he was starting to forget her, a letter arrived. He wasn't even sure if he should open it. He was already in too deep. He decided to read it on Hampstead Heath, where at least he could digest the contents without Amanda's catty comments.

He walked for an hour or so, until the biting wind found its way through his winter clothes into his bones. There was a sheltered spot from where he could see the city centre, but today he drew no comfort from looking down at those trapped in the traffic. He toyed with the idea of burning the letter before he had read it but forced himself to open it. Would she accuse them of using her then casting her aside? Would it contain a plea to visit them again? Perhaps she needed help of some kind.

In the event, the contents were far less dramatic than he

had thought. It seemed that it was he alone who was suffering from the brief upheaval of Vicki's arrival.

Dear John and Amanda, I just wanted to say thank you! I'm going to be away for a while. I've met someone who is going to look after me. As long as I'm really mean to him! I don't know how to thank you. You two have freed me for the first time in my life. I never knew I could dominate men. And I really like it! I'll always have you to thank for that, John. I can be myself. I'll never be a slave, ever again.

If only I could say the same, thought John, rather wistfully. He had crossed that line which divides sex as pleasure and sex as an expression of love. He was old enough to know better but, try as he might, he couldn't quite dislodge the hooks Vicki had left in him. And this letter didn't help.

He stared into space for a while then realized that he should burn it. He was already in thrall to her memory. Making a fetish out of objects connected with her would only make matters worse. Perhaps he should try some of Amanda's hocus-pocus, create a ritual peace and then banish her.

He breathed deeply and slowly for a while, closing his eyes to intensify his concentration. He then repeated a banishing incantation he had once heard Amanda use as he burned the letter. He smiled as the flames singed his fingers. With any luck, the pain would add some force to his heartfelt plea to be free of her.

Seconds later, he knew it was no use. He might as well have cut out his own heart. He looked in the flames and saw Vicki's mischievous smile. There was no way of banishing that presence and there was probably no way of using new partners to tart up a relationship that had gone sour. And just splitting up with people didn't work, either. How often had he done that, just to spend years yearning after the rejected partner? They would have to stumble on somehow, even if a little ghost called Vicki was here to stay, lodged somewhere deep in his heart where other idealised spirits dwelt.

It was so stupid to compare a living woman like Amanda with a fantasy figure. It was even stupider to be a slave to someone who didn't exist. He looked at the leafless trees preparing to endure another long, hard wait for spring and tried not to empathize too much with these gnarled old survivors. Then he ground the remaining ashes of the letter into dust and went home to a real woman called Amanda.

DE SADE'S LAST STAND

William T. Vollmann

THAILAND

Once upon a time a journalist and a photographer set out to whore their way across Asia. They got a New York magazine to pay for it by claiming they were going to do a story about the Khmer Rouge.

They each armed themselves with a box of condoms. The photographer, who knew such essential Thai phrases as *very beautiful!*, *how much?*, *thank you*, and *I'm gonna knock you around!* (*topsa-lopsa-lei*), preferred the extrastrength lubricated, while the journalist selected the nonlubricated with special receptacle end. The journalist never tried the photographer's condoms (he didn't even use his own as much as he should have), but the photographer, who tried both, decided that the journalist had made the right decision from a standpoint of sensation; so that is the real moral of this story, and those who don't want anything but morals need read no further.

Now that we've gotten good and evil out of the way, let's spirit ourselves down to the two rakes' room at the Hotel

Metro, Bangkok, where the photographer always put on sandals before walking on the sodden blue carpet to avoid fungus. As for the journalist, he filtered the tap water (the photographer drank bottled water; they both got sick). There was a giant beetle on the dresser. The journalist asked the bellboy if beetles made good pets. Yes, he grinned. It was his answer to every question. Good thing for him he doesn't have a pussy, said the photographer, untying his black combat boots with a sigh, putting foot powder on. The journalist stretched out on his squeaking bed, waiting for the first bedbug. The room reminded him of the snow-filled, abandoned weather station where he'd once eked out a miserable couple of weeks at the north magnetic pole; everything had a more or less normal appearance but was deadly dangerous, the danger here being not cold but disease; that was how he thought, at least, on that first sweaty, supercautious night when he still expected to use rubbers. The photographer had already bought a young lady from Soi Cowboy. In the morning she lay on the bed with parted purple-painted lips; she put her legs up restlessly.

Last night *tuk-tuk* fifty baht, she said.

So you want some more money for the *tuk-tuk* ride, is that what you're trying to tell me? said the photographer in disgust. Man, I don't believe it. You know, she already got a thousand baht – that's why I had to get that five hundred from you.

The woman's teeth shone. She slapped her thigh, yawned, walked around staring with bright black eyes.

Where do you come from, sweetheart? asked the journalist, flossing his teeth.

Me Kambuja.

Cambodia?

Yes. Kambuja.

We go Kambuja, said the journalist. You come Kambuja?

No.

Why?

She grimaced in terror. Bang, bang! she whispered.

2

The journalist kept thinking of the hurt look in the Cambodian girl's eyes. What to do? Nothing to do.

3

There was a bar aching with loud American music, pulsing with phosphorescent bathing suits. He picked number fourteen in blue and asked her to come with him but she thought he wanted her to dance, so she got up laughing with the other girls and turned herself lazily, awkwardly, very sweetly; she was a little plump.

You come with me? he said when he'd tipped her.

She shook her head. I have accident, she said, pointing to her crotch.

She sat with him, nursing the drink he'd bought her; she snuggled against him very attentively, holding his hand. Whenever he looked into her face, she ducked and giggled.

You choose friend for me? he said. Anyone you want.

When you go Kambuja?

Three days.

She hesitated but finally called over another lady. This my friend Oy. My name Toy.

You come to hotel with me? he said to Oy.

She looked him up and down. You want all night or short time?

All night.

No all night me. Only short time.

Okay.

4

In the back of the taxi he whispered in her ear that he was shy, and she snuggled against him just as Toy had. She smelled like shampoo. She was very hot and gentle against him. Knowing already that if he ever glimpsed her soul it would be in just the same way that in the National Museum one can view the gold treasures only through a thick-barred cabinet, he tried to kiss her, and she turned away.

Please?

She smiled, embarrassed, and turned away.

No?

She shook her head quickly.

5

He reached over her to turn out the light, and she cuddled him. He rubbed her small breasts and she moaned. He kissed her belly and eased his hand in between her legs. She'd shaved her pubic hair into a narrow mohawk, probably so that she could dance in the bathing suit. He stuck his mouth into her like the midget in the show had, wondering if she'd push him away, but she let him.

When push came to shove, he didn't use a condom. She felt like a virgin. When he was only halfway in she got very tight and he could see that she was in pain. He did it as slowly and considerately as he could, trying not to put it in too far. Soon he was going faster and the pleasure was better and better; she was so sweet and clean and young. He stroked her hair and said: Thank you very much.

Thank you, she said dully.

He got up and put on his underwear. Then he turned on the light and brought her some toilet paper.

She was squatting on the floor in pain.

Look, she said.

Blood was coming out of her.

I'm sorry, he said. I'm really sorry.

No problem, she smiled.

I'm sorry!

Maybe I call doctor.

He got her some bandages and ointment. She prayed her hands together and said thank you.

He gave her a thousand baht. She hadn't asked for anything. Thank you, sir, she smiled.

Enough for doctor?

This for taxi. This for *tuk-tuk*.

He gave her another five hundred, and she prayed her hands together again and whispered: Thank you.

He gave her some ointment, and she turned away from him and rubbed it inside her. When they finished getting dressed she hugged him very tightly. She turned her face up to let him kiss her if he wanted. He kissed her forehead.

She hugged him again and again. When he'd shown her out to the *tuk-tuk*, she shook his hand.

Well, he said to himself, I certainly deserve to get AIDS.

6

I can't help but feel it's wrong, he said.

Well, we're giving 'em money, aren't we? said the photographer very reasonably. How else they gonna eat? That's their job. That's what they do. What's more, we're payin' 'em real well, a lot better than most guys would.

7

What did the journalist really want? No one thing, it seemed, would make him happy. He was life's dilettante. Whatever path he chose, he left, because he was lonely for other paths. No excuse, no excuse! When the photographer led him down the long, narrow tunnels of Klong Toey (they had to buy mosquito netting for Cambodia), he got bewildered by all the different means and ways, but everyone else seemed to know, whether they were carrying boxes on their shoulders or hunting down cans of condensed milk, dresses, teapots, toys; it was so crowded under the hot archways of girders that people rubbed against one another as they passed, babies crying, people talking low and calm, nothing stopping. How badly had he hurt Oy? He had to see her. Lost, the two loathsome johns wandered among framed portraits of the king, greasy little bloodred sausages, boiled corn, packets of fried green things, oil-roasted nuts that smelled like burned tires, hammerheads without the handles . . . But it was equally true that the johns felt on top of everything because they were screwing whores in an airconditioned hotel.

8

In the bar after the rain, the girl leaned brightly forward over her rum and Coke with a throaty giggle; everyone was watching the game board, smoking cigarettes while the TV said: Jesus Christ, where are you? and the girl said to the photographer: Tell me, when you birthday?

She said to the journalist: You smoke cigarette? so he bit down on his straw and pretended to smoke it, to make her laugh.

The girls leaned and lounged. The photographer's girl was named Joy. She kept saying: Hi, darling! Hi, darling! Her friend's name was Pukki.

Come here, darling, said Pukki. What you writing?

I wish I knew. Then I'd know how it would turn out, said the journalist.

He likes to write long letters to his mother, said the photographer.

You buy me out please, Pukki cried to the journalist.

I love Oy, he said. Tonight I buy Oy.

That's real good, said the photographer admiringly. That's the way to show 'em!

The photographer squeezed Joy's butt and Pukki's tits, and all the other girls cried in disgust real or feigned: You butterfly man! He bought Joy out, and Pukki screamed at the journalist: *Please*, you no buy me out, *whaiiiiieee?*

I'm sorry, he said. I promised Oy. I'm really sorry.

Why did he want Oy? Because he had hurt her?

He slipped her a hundred baht and she brightened.

9

So they went to Oy's bar, the photographer, the journalist, and Joy. The manager came and said: Oy? Which Oy? Evidently there were so many Oys.

The photographer went and looked (he was very good at picking people out), but he couldn't find her.

10

All night the TV went *aah!* and *oi!* to dubbed movies while the prostitute lay wide-eyed in the photographer's bed, bored and lonely, snuggling her sleeping meal ticket while the journalist, unable to sleep on account of the TV and therefore likewise bored and lonely, could not ask her to come even though the photographer had offered because he didn't feel right about it, the way she snuggled the photographer so affectionately (when he got to know her better he'd understand that she wouldn't have come anyway) and besides he was worried about the growing tenderness in his balls. Then he had to piss again – that was a bad sign; as soon as he pissed he felt the need to piss again.

11

When Joy left, she was dressed conservatively, smiled blandly; she shook each of their hands. Did she become that way in the morning, after the photographer fucked her up the ass, and she saw that he was like the others? Or was her affection just an act?

Probably she'd be dead in five years. Eighty per cent of the Patpong girls tested positive for AIDS that fall. The journalist's heart sank.

12

And what's *this* injection? the journalist asked.

The doctor's glasses glinted. Pure caffeine, he said enthusiastically.

If I wear a rubber from now on so that I don't infect the other girls, can I keep having sex, starting today?

I think it would not be good for you, said the doctor. You

see, the gonorrhea has already migrated far into the spermatic cord . . .

13

Receipt number 03125 (two soda waters, sixty baht) was already in the cup, and fever-sweat from the clap ran down his face. The journalist was working, and the girls sometimes gathered around to watch him write. Lifting his head from the bar, the photographer explained to them: My friend likes to write long letters to his balls.

They were in Oy's bar. The Western video was repeating and dinner had closed because it was 6:00 now, Oy's hour to come to work, as the photographer had kindly ascertained; and paunchy white guys grinned. The staff was getting ready for dance time.

The journalist's teeth chattered with fever. Man, I hope you make it, said the photographer, and there was worry and sarcasm in his voice.

I'm all right, the journalist said. Do you see Oy around?

At 7:00, Toy came. She said hi, smiling; she said no Oy today. There was something so sincere about her that the journalist almost said to hell with it and asked her to go with him, but she would only have said no. He wrote her a note for Oy, showing her each of the note's words in the English–Thai dictionary: *Oy, I worry you blood that night. Are you OK?*

Will Oy come today? he asked her again, just to be sure.

Toy patted his arm. Not today, she said.

You come hotel me, Toy?

No, sir.

You my friend?

OK friend OK.

Then Oy showed up from somewhere, smiling. Toy went off to dance.

He bought out Oy, saying: I just take you back. Just sleep watch TV no fucking just sleep you know OK?

OK, laughed Oy.

She seemed in perfect health. That annoyed him after all his anxiety. Oy? he said. Oy? I'm *sick* from you.

Oy hung her head, smiling.

The photographer went back to the other bar to buy Joy, and the four of them walked down the hot, narrow alley, the two girls in fancy evening wear, the two boys in faded clothes a little dirty; what a treat! Oy stopped in a store to buy condoms (and it never occurred to the journalist until much, much later that she might have been doing it for him); he said no need and she was happy. They got a taxi to the hotel. Joy rode in front with the driver. Oy pressed against him. He held her hand, gave her leg a feel; her dress was drenched with sweat. You hot? he said. She nodded; she'd always nod, no matter what he said.

He led Oy into the hotel while the photographer paid off the driver.

The journalist went grandly up to the desk. Two-ten, please.

All the Thais in the lobby watched silently. Oy hung back, ashamed. They began talking about her. She raised her head then and followed her owner into the humid heat and mildew smell of the stairwell. At the first landing, when she could no longer be seen, she took his hand and snuggled passionately against him.

He told her again that she'd gotten him sick but that it was OK.

I go doctor; doctor me in here! she giggled, pointing to her butt. Later, when he'd gotten her naked, he saw the giant bandage where she'd had some intramuscular injection.

The photographer came in. Same room? said Joy on his arm.

It's OK, the journalist told Oy. No sex. Don't worry.

That was truly his plan – just to lie there in the darkness with Oy, snuggling and watching Thai TV while the photographer and Joy did the same. Needless to say, once the photographer took a shower and came out wearing only a towel and cracking jokes about his dick, the journalist could see how it would actually be.

Oy crawled into bed with the journalist, snuggling him, and he slid a hand between her legs.

I go ten o'clock, she said. Toy birthday party. Toy my sister.

Whatever you say.

She let him kiss her a little but she didn't like it. Her body was slender, but her face looked rounder and older tonight; her voice was hoarser. She kept coughing. After a while she started playing with his penis, probably to get it over with. He had an erection, but no desire to use it; his grapefruit-swollen balls seemed to be cut off from the rest of his body. He still didn't plan to do it, but when he got up to go to the bathroom with just the shirt around him, the two whores sitting eating room service (the bellboy had carefully looked away when he brought it into the half-darkened room, the photographer and the journalist lounging like lords with their half-naked girls beside them), the head of his dick hung down below the shirt and they started laughing and then he started getting wild like the class clown. First he began tickling Oy. Then he started lifting her around and pulling the covers down to show her off naked; she laughed (prob-ably thinks you're a real pest! said the photographer, shaking his head); she kept rubbing against him to make him do something, and then she'd look at the clock . . .

Eventually she rubbed against him in just the right way, and then he knew he'd have to do it. What a chore! He squeezed K-Y into her and handed her the rubber. She said she didn't know how to put it on. Wasn't that *something*? She tried sincerely, but she just didn't understand it. He did it and then thrust into her. She pretended to come and he pretended to come; he didn't care. In the carpet of light from the half-open bathroom door the other two were doing it in the far bed; Oy lay watching them, and she clapped her hand to her mouth and snickered softly; meanwhile Joy suddenly noticed that Oy was on top of the journalist and rolled away from her trick and went into the bathroom and turned the shower on loud for a long time.

The journalist really enjoyed playing with Oy's body, lying

there relaxed and feverish, doing whatever he wanted while the TV went *ai-ai*. Light-headed and distant, he enjoyed snuggling up to her and smelling her, sucking her shaved armpits, pursuing with kisses her face, which sought to evade him; every now and then he'd catch her and kiss her lips and she'd laugh. Whenever he'd touch her between her legs she'd start going *um um* and begin swinging her hips as if in ecstasy, but she stayed dry and her face didn't change and her heart didn't pulse at all faster beneath his other hand. He lounged, played, stroked in a delightful fog of disease like the foggy sprawl of Bangkok he'd be leaving in four hours, soaring east over big gray squares of water going into grayness, riding the hot orange sky.

He said: Oy, you want go Kambuja?

No want! No want! Kambuja people is bad people! Thai people like this (she prayed); Kambuja people like *this!* (she saluted fiercely). The journalist saluted her in return, and she cowered back.

CAMBODIA

The plane sped through the morning, its shadow wafting over cooled patches of trees and rectangles of various greens and grays, all shining wet. Then they arrived in Cambodia, which seemed a no-nonsense country. There was a line of soldiers on the runway, each soldier directing the photographer and the journalist on to the next.

15

He went into the hotel lobby and took a few stacks of riels out of the paper bag. Help yourself to some money, he said to the concierge. He was hot, weak, and dizzy. Thanks to the caffeine injection, he hadn't slept for two nights. In the wide listless courtyard and porticoes of the Ministry of Foreign Affairs, which seemed almost empty like the rest of Phnom Penh (how many people had been killed off?), he and the photographer sat playing with their press passes, waiting for their fate to be decided. *In our country, at the moment, the militia plays more of a role than the army*, an official explained, and the journalist wrote it down carefully while the photographer yawned. They took a cyclo back to the hotel, and the photographer went outside to snap some land-mine beggars while the journalist lay down on the bed to rest.

16

The morning sky was a delicate gray. The journalist lay in bed, clutching his distended balls. It was warming up nicely. His underpants steamed against his ass. The hotel maid came in and cleaned. She made seven thousand riels a month. The Khmer Rouge had killed her father, grandfather, sister, and two brothers. She'd worked hard for the Khmer Rouge in the fields . . .

17

The English teacher wrote *sixteen* in standard and phonetic orthography on the blackboard while the children wrote *sixteen* in their notebooks, and the English teacher got ready to write *seventeen* but then the power went out and they sat in the darkness.

Your English is very good, said the journalist.

Yes, the teacher said.

Where did you learn it?

Yes.

What is your name?

Yes. No. Twenty-two.

Well, that's *real* good, said the photographer brightly. That's *real* nice. Do you know what the word *pussy* means?

18

How happy he was when on the third day of the antibiotics something popped like popcorn in his balls and he started feeling better! The tenderness was now in his lymph nodes, but it would surely go away from there too.

To celebrate, he showed all the hotel maids his press pass. You very handsome, they said.

19

They had an appointment with the English teacher who couldn't speak English. The small children were silhouetted in the dark, singing *A, B, C, D, E, F, G* . . . On the blackboard it said *The English alphabet*. The teacher pointed at this, and the children said: *Da iii-eee aa-phabet*.

Why does the alphabet only go up to *S*? asked the journalist.

Yes, the teacher replied.

The journalist pointed to a photograph that concentrated darkness like an icon. My father is die by Pol Pot regime, said the teacher simply. He go to Angkor Wat to hide Buddha. They die him by slow pain . . .

For a moment the journalist wanted to embrace him. Instead he stared down at the floor, and the sweat dripped from his nose and forehead. As soon as he wiped his face it was wet again.

20

In the hotel there were paintings of bare-breasted girls in butterfly-winged skirts standing waist-deep in the mist before science-fiction palaces. The night was so hot that the journalist's face felt as if it had peered into a steaming kettle. He went into the room, turned the air conditioning on (he and the photographer, being boys of high morals, always traveled first-class), and took a shower. He was standing naked in the cool water when the photographer came in with two whores.

21

The photographer found them in a disco. He always gushed when he made a novel score.

I was gonna take the tall one, he said, because I kept thinking how it would be, you know, with her legs around me, but as soon as we got into the street the short one took my hand, so that's that.

The girls went through all the pills and medicines first, sniffing the packets, going *nnnihh!*, giggling at the condoms, whispering and pointing like schoolgirls. The photographer's girl was already in the shower and out, halfway demure in her towel. The journalist's girl stayed dressed. She did not seem to like him very much, but then that didn't seem unusual to him because girls never liked him; was it his fat legs or his flabby soul? Look at 'em! shouted the photographer. They're as curious as fucking *monkeys*, man! With great effort they mouthed the Khmer words in the dictionary section of his guidebook; they opened the box of sugar cubes, which were swarming with ants, and ate one apiece. The journalist's girl had a beauty spot over one eye. When she opened and closed everything, her eyebrows slanted in elegant surprise. She wore a dark striped dress. There was something very lady-like about her. She intimidated him slightly. He lay sweatily on the bed watching them; when they'd completed their inspection they neatened everything up like good housewives, so that it took the journalist and the photographer days to find their possessions.

22

The photographer's girl got ready right away. But after half an hour the journalist's girl was still silent in the bathroom with the door closed. She stood staring at the back of her little mirror, which had a decal of a man and woman together.

23

He communicated with her mainly by signs. She liked to smell his cheeks and forehead in little snorts of breath, but not to kiss him; whenever he tried, she'd whirl her head away into the pillow, so he started Buddha-ing her in just the same way that

Oy had steepled her hands very quickly together for good luck when he'd bought her out, she probably hoping he wouldn't see, probably praying that he'd give her a lot of money; so he did this to the Cambodian girl; he'd seen the beggars do it; he'd do it to say please, then he'd touch his forefinger from his lips to hers, and she'd Buddha him back to say please no. Sometimes he did it anyway, and she'd jerk her head away, or let him do it only on her closed lips. Then sometimes he'd steeple his hands please and point from his lips to her cunt, and she'd wave her hand no, so he wouldn't do that; he'd pray to kiss her again, and she'd pray him no; so he'd pray and point from his crotch to hers, and she'd nod yes.

24

He smiled at her as affectionately as he could. He wanted her to like him. It just made things easier when the whore you were on top of liked you. No, that's how the photographer would have put it, but the journalist had a deeper thrust (if you know what I mean). The truth was, he really did like her. He traced a heart on her breast with his finger and smiled, but she looked back at him very seriously. Then suddenly she ran her fingernail lightly round his wrist and pointed to herself. What did she mean? So many prostitutes seemed to wear religious strings for bracelets; was that what she meant? Somehow he didn't think so . . .

25

Give 'em more Benadryl; come on, give 'em more Benadryl, the journalist whined as the photographer's girl turned on the light, giggling for the fourth or fifth time that night; he didn't know exactly what the hour was, since his watch had been stolen in Thailand, possibly by Oy. The photographer's girl loved to watch the journalist making love. Even when the photographer was screwing her she'd always be looking avidly into the other bed, hoping to see the journalist's buttocks pumping under the sheet; whenever she could she'd sneak up and pull the sheet away to see the journalist naked with a naked girl; then she'd shriek with glee. It was very funny but it got a little less funny each time. Fortunately they obediently swallowed whatever pills the journalist gave them; the photographer told them that the journalist was a doctor, and the journalist neither confirmed nor denied this report, which most likely they didn't understand anyway. So he gave them Benadryl – one for his girl, three for the other, who was hyperkinetic. Even so they both kept turning the lights on to see what time it was; they wanted to leave by the end of curfew.

26

Once they'd left, he told the photographer he didn't want to see her again. Why, she hadn't wanted to do *anything*! And she'd seemed so sorrowful he'd felt like a rapist. What did she expect anyway? But as soon as he'd conveyed these well-reasoned sentiments, his heart started to ache. He didn't tell the photographer, of course. They rarely talked about those things. Why her? he wondered. But he remembered how she'd hung his trousers neatly over the chair, how she'd ordered his money in neat piles without stealing any, how before leaving she'd taken each of his fingers and pulled it until it made a cracking noise, then bent it back; this was her way of pleasing him, taking care of him.

27

At the disco that night he didn't see her. He sat and waited while the crowd stridulated. Finally her friend, the photographer's girl, came to the table. She was slick with sweat; she must have been dancing. He asked the English teacher who didn't speak English to ask her where his girl was. They saw him frequently in the disco, and he would try to translate for them. The man said: She don't come here today. Already they were bringing him another girl. He said not right now, thank you. He tried to find out more, and then there was another girl sitting down by him and he figured he had to buy her a drink so she wouldn't be hurt, and the photographer's girl was biting her lip and stamping her foot, and then his girl came and stood looking on at him and the other girl silently.

28

He pointed to his girl and traced the usual imaginary bracelet around his wrist. (He didn't even know his girl's name. He'd asked the photographer's girl and she said something that sounded like *Pala*. He'd tried calling her Pala and she looked at him without recognition.) Finally the other girl got up, carrying her drink, and began to trudge away. He patted her shoulder to let her know that he was sorry, but that seemed to be the wrong thing to do, too. His girl sat down in her place, and he could feel her anger, steady and flame-white in the darkness, almost impersonal.

29

But that night when he put his closed lips gently on her closed lips, not trying to do anything more because he knew how much Thai and Cambodian women hated kissing, her mouth slowly opened and the tip of her tongue came out.

30

You got her to french you? laughed the photographer, as the two chauvinists lay at ease, discussing their conquests. Oh, *good!* She must have been *really* repulsed.

31

She almost never smiled. Once again that night she traced an invisible bracelet around her wrist, then his. He watched her sleeping. In the middle of the night he pulled her on top of him just to hug her more tightly, and she seemed no heavier than the blanket.

32

In the morning she cracked his finger joints and toe joints for him; she stretched and twisted his arms and legs; she slapped him gently all over. Then she made her rendezvous with the mirror, where she stood painting her eyebrows in slow silence. When she was finished he sat her down with his guidebook, which contained a few dictionary pages. He pointed to all the different words for food, pointed to her and then to him. She just sat there. He made motions to indicate the two of them going off together. She followed soundlessly. He locked the door. She headed downstairs with him, toward the lobby's ocean of staring faces, which surely judged him; he could not smile as usual, and the faces watched him in silence. She was behind him on the stairs, creeping slowly down. They hadn't even traversed the lobby yet. The faces watched and waited. He dropped the key onto the front desk and she was far behind him. He let her catch up to him a little, not too much because she might not want that, and went out, into the street that was filled with even more eyes that watched, and she was farther behind than before. He looked back to make sure that she was there. It must be difficult for her to be seen next to him. So he went half a block to an outdoor restaurant and sat down. They brought him tea and bread. He drank a few sips of the tea and paid. She had not come; she was gone.

33

He felt miserable all day. He didn't want to have sex with her any more, only to straighten things out. He'd find someone in the city who could translate for him.

34

Night having smothered the wasted day at last, he set out for the disco while his dear friend the photographer lurked kindly in the rat-infested shadow of the garbage heap, not wishing to show himself to *his* girl, who'd already latched onto him. As soon as he'd been sucked into the sweaty inner darkness, the photographer's girl came running up, seizing him by the hand, weeping, pleading in a rush of alien sing-song. He shook his head, patted her shoulder (this was becoming his stereotyped Pontius Pilate act), and she stamped away in a rage. Then she was back again, snarling and groveling monstrously (did she need to eat so badly as that? what didn't he understand?), and he wondered whether she only wanted him to buy her out so that she could rush to the hotel in pursuit of the photographer or whether she wanted *him* now; anyhow it was clear that she wasn't Pala's friend (that night she finally took the trouble to tell him that the woman he was falling in love with was not named Pala but Vanna). Did he love the idea of loving Vanna? Or did he love Vanna?

I want Vanna, he said. Excuse me, sir, said a low-level pimp or waiter or enforcer, presenting him with two other girls, each of whom slid pleading hands up his knee. I want Vanna, the journalist repeated. The photographer's girl said something, and the others laughed scornfully. There was no possibility of finding her if she didn't want to be found. She was a taxi girl; it was her profession to find him. If she wanted him she'd come.

At last she arrived from across the dance floor, eyeing him with what he interpreted to be an aloof and hangdog look. A man said to him: *Yes*, my friend! . . . and began to explain something to him at great length, while the journalist nodded solemnly and Vanna stared straight through everything. The journalist offered him a can of cream soda as a prize for the speech. At last the man pointed to Vanna and then to himself, joining two fingers together. Then he said something involving many vowels, concluding with the words *twenty dollah*. Buying a girl out was only ten. The journalist reached into his money pouch and handed the man a twenty-dollar bill. The man rose formally and went behind the bar, speaking to a gaggle of other smooth operators as the journalist took Vanna's hand and tried to get her to rise, but she made a motion for him to wait. The man came back and announced: *twenty-five dollah*. The journalist shook his head. Then he took Vanna's hand. She walked behind him without enthusiasm. Every eye was on them. The photographer's girl made one more attempt, weeping again. He was too exhausted now to feel anything for her. Outside, Vanna shook her hand away from his. He'd already slipped her a stack of riels under the table. She picked out a motorbike and he got on behind her. The hotel was only three blocks away but she didn't like to walk much, it seemed. When they got to the hotel she paid the driver two hundred from her new stack, and they went in. The lobby crowd watched them in silence as they went upstairs.

35

Wait, he said gently, his hand on her shoulder. He left her in the room and went downstairs.

Do either of you speak English? he asked the desk men.

Yes, they both replied in low voices.

Will one of you please come and help me? There is someone I want to talk to, and I cannot speak Khmer.

There is some kind of problem?

No problem. I just want to talk to her.

I cannot go, one clerk said, and the other clerk said nothing. Maybe if my friend comes I go or I send him. What is your room number, please?

36

OK. I go with you, the other clerk finally said.

That's *great*, the journalist said with what he realized was all the enthusiasm of his nationality. I sure appreciate it.

She was standing in the middle of the room, staring into the mirror.

The journalist said: Please tell her I want to talk to her. I want to find out if she is angry with me.

The man in the yellow shirt said something, and she

opened her mouth and began to reply. It was nearly the first time he had heard her speak (but as long as he knew her it always seemed that way when she said something; she talked so seldom). He marveled at the lisping syllables, the clear calm childish incomprehensible voice.

Oh, it is only a misunderstanding, the man laughed. She think you are ashamed of her, because you walk in front of her very fast.

Tell her I thought she was ashamed of being with me, because she walked very slowly.

You walk very fast, she walks very slowly; it is nothing. I told her you seem to be a nice person, a good person; she says she likes you very much.

Please ask her what she expects from me.

Well, you know she does not like to ask you for anything. She never ask. But a small gold chain, for a souvenir of you, that would please her very much. To show your . . . well, it makes her very happy.

Ask her if she has anything to ask me.

She says she wants to do what you want, to make you happy.

Ask her if she can stay with me until tomorrow morning.

She says she can stay until eleven or twelve. She has a job in the morning. She gets paid by the hour to work in the fields for small wage; that is no problem, to miss that; she simply won't get paid. But after that time maybe her uncle comes looking for her. These taxi girls, you know, they do this work to make money for the family. They never tell the family what they do.

37

He'd made up his mind, as I've said. No sex. He just wanted to be with her. When they lay in bed that night he kept his arm around her and she drew him close, drumming playfully on his belly, pinching his nipples; but then she was very still on her back beside him and he could see that she was waiting for him to do what he usually did. He didn't even kiss her or touch her breasts. He just held her very close, and the two of them fell asleep. All night they held each other. In the morning he could see that she was waiting for it again, so he got up and took a shower and started getting dressed. He couldn't tell if she was surprised. She got up, too, and pulled her bra on, while in the other bed the photographer lay grinning.

You mind if I hop her while you're in the shower? he said.

I don't think she'd like that, the journalist said evenly.

That's a good one, the photographer jeered.

The photographer drew an imaginary gold circlet on her wrist, and she nodded.

They went out, and he was about to take her by the hand to go to the market where he'd seen some gold things for sale, but she took *him* by the hand and led him to a motorbike and they got on.

They traveled far across the city. At last they reached a video arcade that was also a jewelry store without any jewelry, without anything in the glass case except for a tiny set of scales on top of a cigar box. The Chinese-looking man in the straw hat opened the cigar box and took out three gold bracelets. Vanna gestured to the journalist to choose. He smiled and signed that it was up to her. She smiled a little at him. Already a new crowd was secreting itself, like the swarm of black bees eating the sugar and flour in the market's open bowls. Two of the bracelets were slender and lacy. The third was quite heavy and had three blocks that said ABC. That one would obviously be the most expensive. She took that one. He took a hundred-dollar bill from his pocket and gave it to her. She looked at it as if she'd never seen one before, which she probably hadn't. The man in the straw hat said something to her; the motorbike driver joined in, and they all began to discuss the alphabet bracelet with its every ramification. There was one chair, and she gestured to him to sit down; he gestured to her to do it, but she shook her head. The man in the straw hat gestured to him to sit down; he gave in. The man in the straw hat got a calculator from somewhere and clicked out the figure 30 and said *dollah*. The journalist nodded. I guess I can give Vanna a lot of change, he thought. They all talked some more. The man in the straw hat clicked out 137. They were all watching him to see what he'd do. When he got out two twenties, everybody but Vanna started to laugh. Were they happy, polite, scornful, or sorry for him? What did it matter?

The man in the straw hat brought out his miniature scales and weighed the alphabet bracelet against a weight. Then he switched the pans and did the same thing again. The journalist nodded. Vanna took the bracelet and draped it over her left wrist. He realized that everyone was waiting for him to fasten it for her. He bent down and did it, taking a while because the catch was very delicate and he was clumsy and nervous with his fat, sweaty fingers. The man in the straw hat came to help him, but he waved him away. When he'd finished, he looked up. An old lady was standing at the edge of the crowd. He smiled at her tentatively, and she stared back stonily.

Then he looked at Vanna. The smile that she gave him was worth everything. And she took his hand in front of them all.

People stared at them and snickered. A woman with her three young children was sitting on a bed frame on the sidewalk, eating rice. When they spied Vanna and the journalist, they forgot their rice. Someone called out: *Does you loves her?* She stared ahead proudly; he hoped that their cruelty did not touch her.

He still didn't really want to fuck her. He just wanted to be naked next to her, holding her for the last ten minutes or two hours or whatever it would be until she went to work. He stripped and took a shower. While she did the same, he looked for his gonorrhea pills. When she came out he got into bed with her. She pointed to her watch. She had to go soon. She snuggled him for a minute, then pointed to the tube of K-Y jelly. He didn't want to confuse or disappoint her any more. If that was what she expected, then he'd better do it. She touched his penis, and he squirted the jelly into her and rolled the rubber on and got ready to mount her, and then something in her face made him start to cry and he went soft

inside her and rolled off. She was not pleased, no two ways
about it. After all, it was their honeymoon. She was rubbing
him; she wanted him to try again. He put more lubricant
inside her and took the rubber off and threw it on the floor.
The doctor had said he wouldn't be contagious any more; sex
was only hurting him, not anyone else. As soon as he was
inside her, he went soft again. He was crying and she smiled,
looking into his face, trying to cheer him up; he was behaving
like a baby. He traced a heart on his chest, pointed from
himself to her, and drew a heart between her breasts. She
nodded very seriously. He made a motion of two hands
joining and she nodded. He said: You, me, go America
together . . . and she shook her head. She drew a square
on his chest, not a heart, then pointed to a heart-shaped chain
of gold that some other man must have given her.

  She got up and took a shower. He started to get dressed,
too, but she gently motioned him back into bed. She dressed
very quickly. She came and sat with him for a moment on the
bed, and he pointed to the number eight on his watch and
signed to her to come to the hotel then and she nodded and he
said: *Ar kun*. Then she stood up to go. She clasped her hands
together goodbye and he was crying and she was waving and
kissing her hands to him and then she was gone.

38

I wonder if she's waiting for me at the disco, the journalist
said. Maybe she misunderstood.

  I'm sure she is, drawled the photographer. Yep, she's just
sitting around waiting for her knight in shining armor.

39

That night he had a dream that he was getting married to
Vanna and everyone was so happy for him; all the street
orphans were there drumming and dancing; reformed Sta-
linists made him fish soup; the cyclo drivers donated their
vehicles to serve as chairs.

When he told the photographer a little more about the dream, the photographer said: She must think you're a real pain in the ass.

40

The chief of protocol received them on a high porch. He was pleased with the journalist's French. He read their dossiers and clapped a hand to his mouth in mirth.

Later, in the car, he pointed out the window and said, Ah, a beautiful girl there – did you remark her?

No, monsieur, said the journalist.

But I believe you do regard them.

Yes, I do regard them, replied the journalist in the most pompous French that he could muster. For me, every girl in Cambodia is beautiful.

The chief of protocol laughed so hard that he had a coughing fit.

Clearly it was his job to amuse the chief of protocol. In Phnom Penh, every girl is a delicious banquet, he said.

Delighted, the chief of protocol embraced him.

What did you tell him? asked the interpreter.

I said that it is very hot today, said the journalist.

The chief of protocol said something to the interpreter, who giggled.

Yes, yes, said the interpreter, and Battambang is famed for its lovely roadside flowers.

41

Riding atop the jolting Soviet tank in the rain, he saluted the staring or laughing girls, kissing his hand to them, waving to the kids, the old men and ladies, tossing ten-riel notes down into the road like bonbons (the photographer and the driver did the same; the driver was dressed in a black uniform today and wore his Russian pistol especially for the occasion); and the interpreter and the chief of protocol and the soldiers with their upraised machine guns watched the journalist, grinning, and the journalist saluted for hours as they rolled back in from the tame battlefield. He was utterly and completely happy. In Cambodia he could never disappear; now at least when people gawked at him they saw someone comic and grand, a man with a private army who gave them money; he felt like God – a loving God, moreover; he loved everyone he saluted; he wanted to love the whole world, which (it now seemed to him) was all he'd ever wanted when he had whores; his balls still felt funny; all he wanted to do with people was hug them and kiss them and give them money. His forehead glowing with sunburn and three beers, he sat against the spare tire, blessing everyone like the pope, nodding to his elders, wishing that his lordliness would never end. Most of the time they waved back. Girls on bicycles giggled to one another. Children saluted back with slow smiles. Skinny grinning men waved back. These gratifying demonstrations almost balanced those other stares they'd given him and Vanna. He ached to hold her. Since he was drunk and only a flightless butterfly, he squeezed the spare tire instead.

42

They were staying in the Hotel Victoire, which just after the liberation they used to call the Hotel Lavatoire. It had running water, electricity, air conditioning, a toilet, and screen windows. No matter that none of these worked. It cost two thousand riels a night for the photographer and journalist's room, five hundred for the driver and interpreter's. Sleeping at the hotel was like sleeping in a sweltering locker room.

So are you going to do one or not? the photographer wanted to know.

Not me. No whores for me. I'm going to wait for Vanna.

Oh, *Jesus*, said the photographer, covering his face in disgust.

Besides, my balls ache.

All right, all right.

So, said the journalist, the long and the short of it is: maybe. After all, I'll never see Vanna again . . .

At these cheerful tidings the photographer brightened markedly. He came out from under the sheet, killed two mosquitoes, played with his flash, and initiated a fabulous conversation. For hours the two of them discussed the differences between Thai and Cambodian women and how many times the photographer or the journalist had been so low, cowardly, perverted, and immoral as to use a rubber. So they whiled away the suffocating hours until it was time to pick up the chief of protocol and head for the Blue River restaurant . . .

Ask this sixteen-year-old if she wants to marry me, said the photographer with a mirthful glance at the journalist.

She says she will bear your children, cook for you, do dishes, but she cannot marry you because she is too far beneath you.

The photographer shrugged. Tell her she is prettier than a flower.

She says a flower that is smelled too many times begins to wilt.

Interesting that the photographer, who wanted to break as many hearts as possible, and the journalist, who wanted to make as many happy as possible, accomplished the same results! Does that prove that the journalist was lying to himself?

43

Please believe me when I say that he did not want to be unfaithful to Vanna. It's just that when anyone asked him for something, he hated to cause disappointment. I honestly think that the journalist was fundamentally good. I believe that the photographer was fundamentally good. No matter how naive it sounds, I suspect even Pol Pot must have meant well.

44

He went to the disco. The photographer did not come because he did not want his girl to know that he was around. The photographer had told him: You know what the difference between us is? There's no difference. We're both assholes. The journalist knew that he was starting trouble for the photographer by going in there but he missed Vanna too much; maybe he loved her; maybe he really did. As always in that hot darkness, he felt that he was doing something stupid and dangerous by being there. He could see nothing. The air was brownish-black like the tree they'd shown him at Choeung Ek, the tree whose bark was ingrown with hardened blood where the Khmer Rouge used to smash babies' skulls. He fumbled his way to a table sticky with spilled beer.

Is Vanna here?

You want one beer?

Vanna. Girl. I want Vanna. Tall girl.

No no you miss *mistake*, my friend.

Vanna.

My friend . . .

I want to take home Vanna. Only Vanna. Vanna and me like this.

No no no!

I want to marry Vanna. I buy her gold ring.

No no no, my friend, no no!

Gripping the journalist's upper arm firmly enough to bruise, the pimp or waiter or bouncer or whatever he was led the journalist outside. He looked back at all the faces watching him in darkness, the fat yellow cat faces.

45

Well, said the photographer, why *should* she come to work? You already got her a gold *bracelet*, for Chrissakes. She probably sold it ten minutes after she got rid of you. *That* money should probably last her a few weeks.

46

I used to not have enough money to spend on whores, the photographer said. Now I don't know what else I would ever spend my money on.

47

No, sir, the boy said (he was yet another of their impromptu interpreters), I'm sorry; she's not here today.

Then she came like a ghost in the darkness, smelling like her sickly-sweet face powder, giving him for a while her triangular face, and he had to concentrate too hard on everything to be happy but he knew that later on when he had time to remember he'd be happy, and she sat beside him and he slipped her ten thousand riels under the table, a middling stack of money that she made vanish.

Can I buy you a beer before I go? said the journalist to the new interpreter.

But, sir, I have not had any supper! the boy whined.

The journalist started to despise the boy then. He'd showed up uninvited at lunchtime; the photographer had yelled: *Fuck off! Screw!* but the journalist had said: All right, if you want to come to lunch you can come to lunch, but you have to pay for yourself. And then the photographer said: Aw, you can't make him pay for his own meal; the kid's probably got no money . . . and so they'd taken him out, handing the waiter rubber-banded blocks of hundred-riel notes that smelled like mildew; it was after lunch that the journalist had gotten him to write a love letter, a commission he'd fulfilled in beautiful script, even folding the sheet of paper as delicately as if he'd studied origami, so the journalist had been grateful, but this request to be bought dinner at a rip-off place was too much, especially with Vanna waiting to be taken home; he told the boy he'd buy him a beer and a dance but that was that. Then he was on his feet, following Vanna off to the hotel.

As soon as he'd closed the door of the room behind them he gave her the love letter, and she sat down to read it. (I have one sure rule for you, one of his friends said to him much later, when he told the friend about her. The rule is this: Whatever you think she's thinking, you're going to be wrong.) It took her half an hour to read the letter. He saw her lips moving three times or more over each word. Then he saw that instead of explaining himself to her and making the situation any easier, he'd only set her another ordeal. But he had to know. He had to know! He gave her pen and paper and waited. She smiled anxiously. She strained over her writing, sounding out every letter in her whisper-sweet, passionless voice. Then she crossed out what she'd written – only a single word – and turned the page. She tried again and again. Finally she had three or four lines for him. It had taken her twenty minutes. The next day he got his government interpreter to translate, and the man laughed and said: But it is all together like nothing, all these words! She does not know how to write! I cannot, I . . . uh, she say, uh, that she watch you very carefully the first time, and she is very happy with your letter, her happiness, uh, beyond compare.

48

He had lain beside her thinking she was already asleep and touched her hand, but at once her fingers closed around his very tightly. He began to play with her but she was still, she kept her legs closed. So he patted her and rolled over to sleep. Suddenly she was smiling and slapping his butt. Pretty soon he was pointing to his crotch and hers and she was nodding and he got out the K-Y jelly . . .

49

Back at the disco the journalist drank a Tiger beer; then he bought the English teacher who didn't speak English a Tiger beer as well . . .

She came again like an apparition, looking at him.

She say she's busy with another guest, the English teacher said. Do you want her to come to your bedroom, sir?

Oh, I dunno, said the journalist despondently. Let me think about it.

Tell her it's OK, the journalist said. Tell her she doesn't have to come. Tell her I'll say goodbye.

Eyes bulging, the English teacher repeated this information in a voice of machine-gun command. Or maybe he said something entirely different. That was the beauty of it.

She said something to the English teacher, who said: She is very happy to have meeting you.

Well, the journalist thought, or tried to think, that's it. *Really, it's just as well . . .*

Then Vanna came to him and gave him something wrapped up neatly in a square of paper, and again he had a sinking feeling, believing that she was returning his letter, and it seemed right and fair but also very sad, and then because she was still standing there he opened it to learn that it was something very different – lines of Khmer written very neatly (possibly professionally) with loops, wide hooks, spirals, heart-shaped squiggles, everything rounded and complicated, flowing on indecipherably.

The English teacher said: She go to get free from customer.

OK, he said.

He was happy and amazed. He sat there and the English teacher sat with him.

She came back and said something to the English teacher, who said: She will go home now to dress. Please wait for her. She return in twenty minutes. She come for you.

He took the English teacher outside and sat him down in the light outside an apartment building. He asked him to translate. The English teacher looked at the letter for a long time. Then he said: I will tell you only the highlights . . .

Please tell me everything. Can you write for me everything? Then I go to the hotel to wait for her.

The English teacher wrote:

Dear my friend:

It's for a long time wich you went to Bat tam bang province by keep me alone. I miss you very much and I worry to you. I think that maybe you was abandoned from Kambodia & not told me.

Why can you write so much better than you can speak?

Yes, the English teacher said.

50

She wouldn't ride in front of him on the motorbike any more. She made them ride separately and pay both drivers. Had people been torturing her too much, or was she just lazy? His driver paralleled hers, so that all the way back to the hotel he could watch her sit sidesaddle on the bike, gripping some handle between her legs, her clown-pale face almost a toy, smiling like a happy mask.

He was desperate to know what her letter said. It was so hard not to be able to talk with her. He wondered if she'd had to pay someone to write the letter for her or whether they'd done it for nothing.

He held her, and when the photographer came in and turned on the light, he saw that she'd fallen asleep smiling at him.

51

The letter said:

Dear my friend:

It's for a long time wich you went to Bat tam bang province by keep me alone. I miss you very much and I worry to you. I think that maybe you was abandoned from Kambodia & not told me.

Since you were promiss to meet you at hotel I couldn't went because I can't listen your language. So you forgive me please. In fact I was still to love you and honestly with you for ever.

After day which I promised with you I had hard sickness, and I solt braslet wich you was bought for me. So you forgive me.

When will you go your country. Will you come here again? And you must come Cambodia don't forget I was still loves you for ever.

In final I wish you to meet the happiness and loves me for ever. I wish you every happiness and loves me for good.

Signature
love VANNA XXX

52

He sat rereading the letter under the rainy awning where the cyclo drivers sat drinking their tea from brown ceramic teapots with bird shapes on them; they recounted their skinny stacks of riels as lovingly as he retold her words to himself; they rubbed their veined skinny brown legs; and he thought: *Am I so far beyond them in soul and fortune that I can spend my time worrying about love, or am I just so far gone?*

After a quarter hour the rain stopped, and the cyclo drivers took the sheets of plastic off their cabs and dumped masses of water out of them. The proprietor of the café brought them their bills. The Khmer Rouge had put his family to work near Battambang. They'd beaten his wife and three children to death with steel bars because they couldn't work quickly enough. He had seen and heard their skulls crunch. They did it to them one by one, to make the terror and agony stretch out a little longer. They'd smashed in the baby's head first; then they deflowered his four-year-old daughter; then it was his seven-year-old son's turn to scream and smash like a pumpkin and spatter his parents with blood and bone. They saved the mother for last so that she could see her children die. The proprietor was a good worker; they had nothing against him. He knew that if he wept, though, they'd consider him a traitor. He had never wept after that. His owl eyes were wide and crazy as he fluttered around the café exchanging bread and tea for money. He was like a mayfly in November. And the journalist thought: *Given that any suffering I might have experienced is as nothing compared to his, does that mean I'm nothing compared to him? Is he greater than I in some very important way? Yes. So is there anything I can do for him or give him to demonstrate my recognition of the terrible greatness he's earned?*

But the only thing that he could think of to help the man or make him happy was death, and the man had refused that.

Then he thought about giving the man money, and then he thought: *Yes, but Vanna is as important as he is. And because she loves me and I love her, she is more important.*

As for tragedies (which were a riel a dozen in Cambodia),
what about the circular white scars on her brown back, put
there forever by the Khmer Rouge when as a child she
couldn't carry earth to the ricefield dykes fast enough? If
he could have gotten into his hands the people who'd done
that to her, he would have killed them.

53

Her face lit up, amazed at the ice-cube tray in the freezer; he
knocked a cube out for her and she crunched it happily
between her teeth. She was finally laughing and smiling and
going *psssst!* . . . She finally trusted him; yes, she loves you,
the English teacher who couldn't speak English had said at
the disco; she trusts you; you can see it in her eyes . . . Now
she lay in bed with him singing Khmer songs in a soft voice
until the photographer, who was very ill, sat up in bed and
started mimicking her in the ugliest way that he possibly
could, and Vanna became silent.

54

The photographer had made a mess of things. His girl lay
next to him weeping because the photographer did not care
whether she stayed or went – preferring, in fact, that she go,
because the photographer knew it was only a matter of time
before he had to puke, and anyway Cambodia wasn't exactly
his country the way Thailand was; the girls here didn't
attract him as much, and everyone seemed so docile and
lazy to him, whereas he only respected people like his next-
door neighbor in San Francisco whom he'd caught pissing in
the hall and the photographer started yelling at him but the
neighbor only swung round his bleary terrible face and
shouted: Next time I'll shit on your head! and then the
photographer had to forgive and admire him; his girl in
Cambodia didn't do that, not quite; and when the time came
to send her away forever because they were leaving for
Thailand early next morning, the girl began to weep and

grovel again, soaking his knees with tears, clinging to him; it was horrible to see her; as affectionately as he could, the journalist kissed her hand goodbye . . .

55

In the morning, very early, there was a tapping at the door, and he got up sick and fat and groggy in his underwear to see who it was. He opened the door and shouted *Vanna!* with glee and thankfulness and she was glowing at him; she'd brought loaves of bread for his journey; he shared one with her. The photographer, who'd passed out puking on the floor, lay feverish in bed; and the journalist opened the refrigerator where the photographer had left his fruit to be abandoned and gave it to her, a gift for a gift, and she smiled and took it so that it became something special. Lying in bed beside him she peeled a fruit somewhat like a giant grape-fruit, each sector of it walled off by a bitter cuticle as thick as a flower petal, the reward inside being a mass of rubbery pale-yellow teardrop-shaped fibers with bittersweet juice; and she put the segments into his mouth, and she said: *I wuff you.*

THAILAND

When they got back to Bangkok, the journalist said to the photographer: Well, that was it. No more whores for me. And he'd start talking about how he was going to marry Vanna, until the photographer said: Aw, you're driving me crazy! The photographer went and got laid. He really wanted the journalist to do it too. He looked out for him. When the journalist's balls had been at their worst, the photographer always got him meals in bed. But the journalist wanted to be good now; he said no. Red-boiled by the sun until he resembled a vulture, staring blearily, grimly ahead, the harsh light of Bangkok illuminating the insides of his ears, the photographer had had a hard time getting through the day-light hours. But now all his grace was back. Can I at least

bring you back something? As ever, the journalist envied him
and wanted to be like him. Oh, that's all right, he said. You
go spread one for me.

He stayed in and washed his underwear in the sink. The
room was bright, cool, and quiet, with hardly any cock-
roaches – this being the world-famous Hotel 38, you see,
which they'd never heard of before. When he'd scrubbed his
underwear, he squeezed them out and left them hanging and
dripping on the bathroom doorknob. (The photographer,
pitying his incompetence in almost every sphere of life,
sometimes rearranged his laundry for him. Don't ever leave
your wife, he always said to the journalist. Without her you'd
really have problems!) He went out and stood on the landing
between the second and third floors, looking across inter-
stellar darkness into the window of a garment factory where
girls in pale uniforms sat sewing; it seemed to him very
strange and bleak; the prostitutes probably had a better life,
in spite of the shame . . . Just after he'd turned the light out
and gotten into bed, the light came on, and he opened his eyes
to see the photographer with someone else in the hot glowing
doorway. A moment later, Joy, the photographer's old Bangkok girl, was on the journalist's bed, holding his hand and
hugging him so naturally like he was her brother while the
photographer laughed. Only one boyfriend me! she said,
pointing to the photographer. I love *him*! You are so sweet,
said the journalist in wonder, meaning every word of it,
wondering how many times he'd meant it . . .

Joy went into the bathroom. Then she and the photographer went to bed. The journalist told them both goodnight.
Soon he heard Joy's soft rhythmic moans, faked or unfaked,
while in the hall a cat in heat went *aaoow, aaoow*.

57

What is she to you? a cyclo driver in Phnom Penh had shouted
from among the crowd that encircled him as the journalist
walked Vanna across the street on his last morning in Cambodia, his fingertips gentle and careful against her back.

She's my friend, he said.

And what *was* she to him? She said she loved him, and he did believe that if he asked her to marry him she would come with him, bring her child (her other husband had kicked her in the face and abandoned her), and he thought that she must love him as she understood love, and he loved her as he understood love; was that enough?

When he drew sketches of the Hotel 38 maids, they kissed him on the lips and asked him to take them out dancing; later that day one said to him very tentatively: I *love* you?

58

The next night the photographer brought some women back for them, a sort of midnight snack; he'd asked again before he went and this time the journalist had said: Go ahead; twist my arm. The photographer had Joy again. The journalist's was a greedy thief smooth-shaven between her legs, and as soon as he'd stuck his tongue in her he knew that it was a mistake. He got up and rinsed his mouth out. Then he put a rubber on. The next day his tongue was coated with white fungus and his throat was so swollen that he could hardly breathe. Over and over a fierce fever grabbed him by the scruff of the neck and lifted him out of his dreams, then let him fall back to sleep exhausted. He remembered Vanna's face. Well, doubtless Vanna wasn't celibate, either. Maybe it was then that he began to get the unbounded confidence and ease that permitted him to cut any pretty girl who caught his fancy right out of the Patpong herd and take her straight back to the hotel, so that weeks later, when he awoke in the middle of the night, jet-lagged, he saw a woman sleeping beside him and at once, not knowing who she was, pulled her underpants briskly down to her ankles and rubbed her fuzz and spread her until she stirred and muttered: *What* . . . ? and he suddenly remembered that this was his wife.

He wanted to say to his wife: Who am I? Only to see her expression when he said it, of course. I'm thinking of leaving my wife and marrying an illiterate prostitute from Cambodia whose language I can't speak a word of, he said to one of his friends. That's very interesting, his friend said. Maybe you should sleep on it. I wouldn't do anything drastic. How much do you think I'd need to support her and her baby? he said. We can run through the numbers together, his friend said. A thousand a month for a two-bedroom place. You'd need that; you'd need a room to work, a room for the kid. That's twelve thousand. Then there's food and health insurance. Transportation. She'd be learning English the first year; there'd be a bill for that. Maybe daycare. Figure twenty-five grand. That's after taxes. So you'd need thirty-five, forty grand. So much? whispered the journalist in dismay.

59

The transvestites, skull-grinning with black cobwebs painted over their sparkling eyes, didn't tempt him, not even the ones with black bridles and nostril slits and double eyebrow-slits cut into their sweating glistening faces leering sheer and sweet out of darkness, but by now he'd begun to understand De Sade's prison scribblings when the sex object no longer mattered; an old man was as good as a young girl; there was always a hole somewhere; but unlike De Sade he didn't want to hurt anyone, really didn't, didn't even want to fuck anyone any more particularly; it was just that he was so lost like a drifting spaceman among the pocked and speckled and gilded and lip-pinked grinning heads that floated in flashing darkness, cratered with deer eyes, holding Japanese-style umbrellas like darkness-gilled mushrooms; he was so lonely among them that he wanted to love any and all of them even though loving any of them would only make him more lonely because loving them wasn't really loving them.

60

I can't take you anywhere! the photographer cried out in anguish. Whenever a girl asks you to buy her a drink, you buy her a goddamned drink! I can stay in a bar for hours and tell 'em all to go screw, but you're such a pushover it just blows my mind. You'd better never leave your wife. You need someone to take *care* of you, man!

I agree a hundred per cent, said the journalist, who like the photographer agreed with everyone on everything; it was so much easier. He was feeling sick again; his balls were aching. He certainly didn't know what he'd done to deserve *that*. They were drinking at the Pink Panther, where the lights reflected through his mixed drink.

Then he felt contrite and said: In the next bar I'll do better. I'll watch my money better.

So in the next bar, just barely out of sight of the Pink Panther, a woman said to him: You buy me drink? and he said no and she said: You buy me drink? and he said: Sure, honey. If it'll make you happy I'll buy you two drinks.

When at last he took all the slips from the wide teak cup and added them up, he saw that he was short by almost five hundred baht. He had to call to the photographer for money.

I don't fucking *believe* it, said the photographer in the most genuine amazement that the journalist had seen in a long time.

61

The two of them went back to Joy and Pukki's to sleep. (Remember Pukki? The journalist hardly did. She'd tried to get him to buy her out that night in Joy's bar when he told her he loved Oy.) They couldn't afford the Hotel 38 any more except on special occasions; it was three hundred baht. They'd given Joy twenty dollars apiece, each without knowing what the other had done. Her room was an oven at night, bright and bleak and reeking of insecticide. Splashing sounds came from the hall, where ladies took turns doing the laundry. In the corner crack, a foot or two below the ceiling, a hairy curled wire protruded. The wire began to vibrate. After a while the photographer got up and pulled it; something squeaked; it was a rat's tail . . .

My place no good, said Joy softly. You no angry me?

62

He had gone alone to the National Museum to enjoy an hour of beauty without love, but he was just like the photographer, who'd shouted on the bus: *I can smell a whore a mile away!* because after a diversionary visit to some bird's-head swords, he found himself sniffing out Khmer art (there was more here than in Phnom Penh! – the Khmer Rouge hadn't forgotten much); raining his fever-sweat down on the courtyard grass, he stood lusting for the Bayon-style Dvarapalas of the early thirteenth century.

The stone head leaned forward and down, not quite smiling, not quite grimacing, the balls of its eyes bulging out like tears. Too familiar, that face; he wished now that the photographer were here, to take a picture of it. Marina? Maybe. Yes, Marina – another one of the whores he had been with in Phnom Penh – plump, blurred, and round. Her mouth was definitely grimacing. He stepped back, stood a little to the left so that her eyes could see him. She looked upon him sadly, without interest or malice; this one was long dead. Her nose was eaten away as if by syphilis, her breasts almost imperceptible swellings on the rock, her navel round and deep, her vulva a tiny slit that may have been vandalized from the same ax that cut off her right hand and left arm. She stood square-toed and weary in the heat.

63

Short time mean we do it two time, one hour, said the Hotel 38 girl. All night mean until twel' o'clock. Then I go home, Papa-san.

He tried to tell her that he was a journalist, just to tell her something, just to reach her, and then he asked her if she understood and she said yes, and then he wondered how many men asked her if she understood and how often she said yes.

He showed her the rubber. You want to use this? Up to you.

Yes, she said. Good for you, good for me.

This girl cost three hundred baht. He'd told the night manager to pick one out for him, whoever wanted to come. Be good to her! the night manager had said. He tipped her two hundred. When he saw the expression on her face, he thought: *Well, at least once in my life I've made another human being completely happy.*

64

You butterfly too much, Joy said to him when she and the photographer came in that night. Too much Thai lady! No good for you, no good for her. She no good, no good heart! She have boyfriend! Not me. I no boyfriend. I love you, I go with you; I no love you, I no go. Before, I have boyfriend. He butterfly too much. He fucking too much! (Joy was shouting.) One day he fucking one, two, three, four. I say to him: OK, you no come here again, we finit. I say: You want marry me, see Mama me, Papa me – why? He crying. He say: I don't know. I say: You don't know? You finit! Finit me!

What did you think of *that*? laughed the photographer. Boy, you looked *scared* for a minute!

He pointed solemnly to the journalist and said to Joy: He butterfly too much!

65

Lying in that absurd round bed at half-past four in the morning, he blew his nose, cleared his throat, coughed, and spat on the floor, listening to the rain outside while the air-conditioners droned and the blue curtains hung dirty, fat, and listless. It was not very dark because the rooms with round beds had windows at the tops of the doors to let hall light in, probably so that the whores wouldn't lose money for the hotel by falling asleep. He coughed. Finally he got up, turned on the light, and sat alone in the middle of the round bed, weary and calm. The shrill shouts of the whores had ceased; he could hear nothing but the rain and the air-conditioner. A big bug scuttered across the floor. (In Pat-pong he'd seen the whores eating bugs roasted on a stick.) The late-night feeling went on and on, and he cleared his throat and spat white fungus.

66

All morning and all afternoon the photographer lay in bed. The journalist wandered in and out with his heart racing for Vanna. At the park gate two men were playing checkers with bottlecaps on a piece of cardboard, and the journalist went and sat beside the mud-brown lake as rain clouds guttered like greasy candles in the sky.

He reread her letter, as he'd done every day . . .

67

Joy had told the photographer that she had to see someone before she came that night, so she'd be late. Probably got to make some money, said the photographer. It's not like I've been giving her much . . .

She came at four or five in the morning, smiling and swaying. I drink too much! she giggled.

Are you happy? asked the journalist quietly.

Yes, me very happy, 'cause I drink too much! I bring something for you. Here your clothes; I wash them for you; your shirt not yet; I no iron.

The photographer lay on the bed, his eyes closed.

You angry me?

No, not angry, Joy, just tired.

Look! I got toy monkey! You see? From lady! She like me too much! You go America Friday, I go her Saturday for holiday. No make love! No make love! Only go with her. You not angry?

Nope, yawned the photographer.

He looked at the monkey on the bed for a while. Then he flung it to her, or at her; what he was doing was never entirely clear. But surely he was only playing with her.

She froze in just the same way that Thais jogging in the park freeze into rigid attention when the national anthem comes on the loudspeaker. Then she whirled on him. *Why* you do that? You angry me?

No. Just tired.

You no like me?

I like you fine, Joy.

Why you angry me?

After that, the photographer's face hardened. The journalist knew that something bad would happen.

Joy stood by the mirror. She had been about to undress. She fingered the topmost button of her Patpong uniform, undoing it and then doing it up again. Then she began to speak in a rapid monotone.

You no like me? You no like me OK I go home sleep. You no like me? You no like me?

The photographer said nothing. He didn't even open his eyes.

OK you no like me I go. I go now. You no like me. OK.

She began to pack very rapidly. The journalist lay watching her in silence, saddened to the bottom of his heart, knowing that there was nothing he could or should do, nothing to do in that long, long time when she stood by the doorway waiting and then she said: OK. I go. And she waited a little longer. Then she turned out the light, opened the door, and shut it behind her. Now she would be walking toward the stairs; the photographer could still have leaped up and caught her; now she was downstairs; now she'd be walking very, very quickly in the rain to find a *tuk-tuk*. Lying in the darkness, he heard the photographer groan.

68

In the morning he decided to set out for Joy's to tell her that he was worried about her and possibly to give her flowers or money. He arrived at Joy's with his heart in his throat and knocked, seeing light under the door. At least they weren't sleeping.

Joy? he said.

Yes, she finally said listlessly.

He went in and said: My friend no angry you. I worried you. You drink too much. No problem. OK?

Pukki's face had lit up when he came in, but now it dimmed. You no come for me?

I have something for you, Pukki, he said, giving her his last twenty dollars.

The girls were not their bar selves. They sat sweating and trying to rub away beer headaches. Two Thai boys (whom they vehemently assured him were not their boyfriends, and he thought: *Why does it have to be my business? Why can't they be your boyfriends? We have no claim on you; we're only sick butterflies*) were lying on the futon. Soon Pukki began to pay the journalist his due attentions. She sent one of the boys out to get lunch. When he came back she spooned the journalist's food onto the plate for him, just right. She peeled the skin off his chicken. She poured his water while the boys ironed his shirt and blue jeans. She had him lie down, and she sat fanning him. You good wife, he teased, and she laughed in delight, snuggling against him. The boys massaged his legs, calling him Papa-san and bumming ten baht off him (he gave them twenty), and he thought: *Well, I could do worse than marry Pukki; Pukki is really a dear, dear girl . . .*

69

Before long, the photographer had made up with Joy, and they had gone to buy her some shoes with bells on them. The journalist closed the shutters finally and sat on the unmade bed. One of the photographer's used rubbers was on the floor. A fresh one waited on the bureau, like a fresh battery pack ready to be plugged in.

The bathroom door, a little ajar, was gripped by claws of humid darkness. The dirty walls, splattered with the blood of squashed bugs, seemed his own walls, his soul's skin and prison. How could he set his butterfly free?

Then he remembered the Benadryl and smiled.

He got up and began to search listlessly through the first-aid kit. He felt neither happy nor sad. For a long time he could not even find the Benadryl, but in the end he saw that he was holding the jar in his hand.

After a while he unscrewed the top and swallowed a capsule dry. It went down fairly easily, and so did the next, but the third one didn't, so he took his first swallow of beer. Eventually the bottle was as empty as his heart. In the next room, someone coughed. He lay down on the bed, feeling a little sick, and stared at the ceiling for a while; then he got up and turned the light out. It was very dark. He undressed down to his underwear and got under the covers.

Later, when the dark figures bent over him and he didn't know whether he was in hell or whether he'd simply flubbed it, he strained with all his force to utter the magic words: More Benadryl, muttered the journalist.

SAN FRANCISCO

Ahem! Benadryl, you know, is only an antihistamine – not one of those *profound* and *omnipotent* benzodiazepines that can stop a man's heart even better than a pretty whore.

No, he didn't really know his drugs, just as he didn't know why all the Cambodian whores had taken Russian trick names; but when he walked down Haight Street one foggy afternoon after he got back, it was all *buds? buds? indica buds? get you anything?* wide-eyed faces wanting to help him get high; he'd never been offered drugs so many times at once his entire life! and he thought: *Has something about my face changed over there? Since I said yes to so many women, is my face somehow more open or positive or special or weak?*

71

Back at the city clinic again because his balls still ached, he listened to the other victims of sexual viruses and bacteria explicating their woes: *That's what happens when you get* bored *. . . Well I tole that bitch I wanna become a personal trend . . .*

and I said please touch my mouth I'm a competitive body builder and she says I wanna hug and I says ya want anything more and I dipped her like this! and then I tole her if a man touch my doll like that I'd kill 'im! . . . He gimme five dollahs an' then he stick it in me an' now I be gettin' these night sweats; well sistah if I was serious I was scared so I can't be serious . . .

You should really take the AIDS test, the doctor said. How many sexual partners did you say you've had in the last month?

Seven, the journalist said. No, eight. No, nine.

Well, now, said the doctor. I think that puts you in our highest-risk group, right in this red area at the top of our AIDS thermometer. Did you know the sexual histories of all your partners?

Oh, I know their histories all right.

Well, that's very good, Mr Doe. Because, you see, if you didn't know their histories you might not be aware if they'd engaged in any *high-risk* behaviors such as unprotected sex, anal intercourse, IV-drug use, prostitution . . . They wouldn't have engaged in any of those behaviors, now, would they, Mr Doe?

I don't *think* they were IV-drug abusers.

Mmm-hmm. Now, Mr Doe, do you always use condoms?

I couldn't go so far as to say that, doctor.

Well (the doctor was still struggling to keep a positive attitude), would you say that you use condoms more than half the time, at least?

I did use a rubber with *one* of 'em once, the journalist grinned. But it was kind of an accident.

Mr Doe, said the doctor, you really should take the AIDS test.

I'd rather not know. How about if you just wrote me a prescription for some Benadryl? I'm fresh out.

72

With all due respect, his wife was saying, maybe even because you're so smart, I don't know – but you've definitely got problems. (The journalist had just told her that maybe, just maybe, they should consider a divorce.) You need analysis, his wife said. You've got something to work out. You always say my family's screwed up – *well*! I'm telling you, *your* family's screwed up. Really screwed up. Actually the rest of them aren't so bad. It's you. Everyone thinks you're a freak. All the neighbors think you're a freak, even if they're too nice to say it directly to me. I'm normal; I'm tired of being married to a freak.

I see that, he said.

All your friends are freaks. Either society's rejected them or else they've rejected society. They're the lowest of the low. You've spent years building up a crew of freaks.

I wouldn't necessarily call them freaks, he said.

Tears were snailing their accustomed way down the furrows in her cheeks that all the other tears had made, so many others, and so many from him – why not be conscientious and say that those creek-bed wrinkles were entirely his fault? They shone now with recognition of his guilt; they overflowed until her whole face, sodden with snot and tears, reminded him of a beach where something flickers pitifully alive in every wet sand bubble when the waves retreat.

And that photographer you hang out with, she said, it doesn't do your character any good to be with someone so irreverent.

Hearing that, no matter how sorry for her he was, he could not prevent a happy brutal smile from worming to his lips, twisting his whole face; he could hardly wait to tell the photographer what she'd said and listen to him laughing . . .

73

He kept waking up in the middle of the night not knowing who this person beside him was. After she started sleeping in the other bedroom, they got along much better. Sometimes he'd see her in the backyard, gardening, the puppy frisking between her legs, and she'd seem so adorable there behind window glass that he ached, but as soon as she came in, whether she stormed at him or tried desperately to please him, he could not feel. *He could not feel!* For years he and his wife had had arguments about the air-conditioner. He'd turn it on and then she'd turn it off and he'd wake up stifling and turn it on again and then she'd start screaming. Sometimes he couldn't sleep. Other times he dreamed of struggling in a blue-green jungle the consistency of moldy velvet; the jungle got hotter and deeper and then he'd find himself in the disco again, no Vanna there any more, only the clay-eyed skulls from the killing fields, white and brown, a tooth here and there; from the Christmas lights hung twisted double loops of electrical wire (the Khmer Rouge, ever thrifty, had used those to handcuff their victims); no girls, no beer; they kept bringing him skulls . . .

SPEAKING PARTS

M. Christian

Pell remembered seeing Arc's eye – like it was the first thing she'd ever seen. Tourmaline and onyx. Silver and gold. A masterpiece watch set in a crystal sphere, the iris a mandala of glowing gold. Her blinks were a camera shutter's, as imagined by the archetypal Victorian engineer, but built by surgical perfection not found anywhere in Pell's knowledge. The woman's left eye was jeweled and precise, clicking softly as the woman looked around the gallery – as if the engineers who'd removed her original wet, gray-lensed ball had orchestrated a kind of music to accompany their marvelous creation: a background tempo of perfect watch movements to accompany whatever she saw through their marvelous, and finely crafted, sight: Click, click, click.

An eye like that should have been in a museum, not mounted in a socket of simple human skin and bone, Pell had thought. It should have been in some other gallery, some better gallery – allowed only to look out at, to see other magnificent creations of skilled hands. Jare's splashes of reds and blues, his shallow paintings were an insult to the real artistry of the woman's eye.

That's what Pell thought, *at first*, seeing Arc – but only seeing Arc's perfect, mechanical eye.

Pell didn't like to remember first seeing her that way – through the technology in her face. But it felt, to her, like it had its own kind of ironic perfection to deny it. So Pell lived with the biting truth that she didn't, at first, see Arc – for her eye.

But later, right after she got momentarily lost in the beauty of Arc's implant, the woman looked at Pell with her real eye, the gray penetrating right one – and Pell forgot about the tourmaline, onyx, silver and gold machine.

She had finally seen Arc, herself – the woman, and not the simple, mechanical part. Next to her, the eye was cheap junk: a collection of metal, old rocks, and wires.

She wasn't Arc at first. First she was the woman with the perfectly created eye. Then she was the beautiful woman. Then she was the woman where she didn't belong. Seeing her eye, then seeing her, Pell lastly saw her as oil, the kind of oil you'd see pooling in the street, that had somehow managed to make its way into a glass of wine. Agreed, it was cheap red wine – something out of a box and not even a bottle, but, still – she was oil: she didn't belong and that was obvious, despite the cheapness of the gallery. You could tell, cataloging her bashed and scuffed boots, noting her threadbare jeans, her torn T-shirt; that, amid clean jeans and washed (and too black) turtlenecks that she was a hum, a discordant tone in the finely meshed posing in Jare's tiny South of Market studio.

The woman was aware of her discrepancy. She wandered the tiny gallery with a very large plastic tumbler of *vin* very *ordinaire*, stopping only once in a while to look at one of Jare's paintings.

Holding her own wine tight enough to gently fracture the cheap plastic with cloudy stress-lines, Pell watched her, stared at the tall – all legs and angles, broad and strong – woman with the artificial eye. She tried not to watch her too closely or too intently, sure that if she let slip her fascination she'd scare her off – or, worse, bring down an indifferent examination of Pell: a sad ballet of a slightly curved lip and a stare that was nothing more than a glance of the eyes. The woman would see Pell but wouldn't – and that would be an icy needle in Pell's heart.

Pell had already taken too many risks that night. She already felt like she'd stepped off the edge and had yet to hit the hard reality of the ground. Traps and tigers: beasts and pitfalls for the unwary loomed all around Pell. She moved through her days with a careful-footstep caution, delicately testing the ice in front of her – wary of almost-invisible, cloudy lines of fault. She knew they were there; she'd felt the sudden falling of knowing that she'd stepped too far, moved too quickly, over something that had proven, by intent or accident, not to be there. Pell didn't push on the surface, didn't put all her weight, or herself, on anything.

But then everything changed – she'd seen Arc and her eye.

The plastic chimed once, then collapsed in on itself. Turning first into a squashed oval, the glass cracked, splintered, then folded – the white seams of stress turning into sharp fissures of breakage. The red, freed of its cheap plastic prison, tumbled, cascaded out and down onto her.

Pell had worn something that she knew wouldn't fit with the rest of the crowd. The official color of San Francisco, she knew, would fill the place with charcoal and soot, midnight and ebony. White, she'd decided, would pull some of their eyes to her, make her stand out – absence of color being alone in a room full of people dressed in all colors, combined.

"Looks good on you."

The shock of the wine on her white blouse tumbled through Pell with a avalanche of warmth to her face. The decision to wear cream had come from a different part of herself – a part that had surprised her. She'd relented – abandoning safety for one night in the risky endeavor of wearing something that the rest of the crowd in the tiny gallery wouldn't. She was furiously chastizing that tiny voice, that fashion terrorist that had chosen the blouse over other, blacker ones, when it decided to have a last say, a last statement.

And so Pell responded, "Not as good as you would" to the tall, leggy, broad-shouldered girl with the artificial eye. Which was beautiful, but not as beautiful as the rest of her.

Pell's reason was Jare. While secretly she could never wrap her perceptions around the gaunt boy's paintings, she still came when he asked. Jare, Pell, Fallon, Rasp and Jest. They weren't close – but then foxhole buddies aren't always. They weren't in combat, but they could be. All it would take would be one computer talking to another – no stable job history, thus conscription.

All it took were two computers, passing pieces of information back and forth. Till that happened, they hid and watched the possibility of a real foxhole death in a hot, sweaty part of Central America fly by.

Foxhole buddies. It was Jare's term – some fleck of trivia that'd hung around him. They didn't have an official name for their tiny society of slowly (and in some cases not too slowly) starving artists, but if they did then Pell was sure that Jare would smile at his trivial term being immortalized among a band of too-mortal kids.

That was Jare. While the rest of them tried to focus on pulling their paintings (Pell, Jare, and Rasp), music (Jest), and sculpture (Fallon) as high as they could, there was something else about Jare – something, like his paintings, that refused to be understood. His techniques were simple enough, broad strokes of brilliant color on soot-black canvas, but his reasons were more convoluted.

Or maybe, Pell had thought earlier that evening – before turning a beige blouse red and seeing the woman with the artificial eye for the first time – they both are simple: like his works, broad, bold statements designed to do nothing but catch attention. He was like his paintings, a grab for any kind of attention – an explanation too simple to be easily seen.

In the tiny bathroom, Pell tried to get the wine out of her blouse. Contradictory old wives' tales: first she tried cold, then hot water. The sink ran pink and so, soon, did her blouse.

The woman with the eye stood outside the door, a surprisingly subtle smile on her large mouth. Every once and a while she'd say something, as if throwing a bantering line to the shy girl inside to keep her from drowning in embarrassment.

"Who's he foolin'? I can do better crap than this with a brush up my ass.

"You should see this chick's dress. Looks like her momma's – and momma didn't know how to dress, either.

"Too many earrings, faggot. What year do you think this is?

"Hey, girl. Get out here with that shirt – better-looking than this fucking stuff on the walls."

Cold water on her hands, wine spiraling down the sink. Distantly, Pell was aware that her nipples were hard and tight – and not from the chill water; that down deep and inside, she was wet. It was a basic kind of primal moisture – one that comes even in the burning heat of humiliation. Finally, the blouse was less red than before. Planning to run to where she'd dropped her old leather coat to hide the stigmata of her clumsiness, her excitement in two hard brown points, she opened the door.

The tall woman smiled down at her, hot and strong. In one quick sweep of her eyes, Pell drank her tall length, strong shoulders, columnar legs. She was trapped, held fast between the hot eyes she knew must have been staring at her, pinning her straight to her embarrassment, and the presence of the woman.

Her eye, *the* eye, clicked a quick chime of precision – as if expanding its limits to encompass the totality of Pell. Pell did not mind her intense examination. It added, with a rush of feelings, to the quaking in her belly, the weakness in her knees.

"Gotta splash. Wait right here."

Of course she waited.

After a few hammering heartbeats, the door opened and she came out – butchly tucking her T-shirt back into her jeans – and Pell was again at the focus of her meticulously designed sight.

"You live anywhere close? I'm tired of this shit. You?"

"Down the block. Just on the corner," Pell said, trying hard not to smile too much.

The woman downed the small sample of red in her glass and, looking for a place to put it down, and not finding any, just dropped it with a sharp plastic clatter on the floor. "Show me. It can't be worse than here. Too many fucking artists."

"Arc. Named myself: didn't like the one the old man stuck me with," she said as they walked out the front door.

Pell wanted to paint her. She refused herself.

Naturally she resisted after Arc had frowned and snorted at the gallery, at Jare's streaks of black on red. But she resisted for other reasons – the same reason that she didn't allow herself to imagine what Arc might look like under flickering candlelight or reflective with a gleam of post- or pre-passion. Pell kept thoughts of her lips on the tall woman or putting her hard beauty, her street wise elegance down on rough sketch paper because she felt the night crystal . . . no, *glass* around her. Fragile magic was whipping around them as they walked the short walk from Jare's too crowded, too noisy, too artistic space to Pell's tiny flat. She doubted Arc could feel it, but for Pell it was a chandelier hovering around her, clear and invisible, but sharp and precarious – one wrong move and it would break and she would be standing on a too busy San Francisco boulevard all by herself.

The apartment was a score. Expensive, yes – too expensive to really live in, but it was still a prize in a city that tried to hide the fact that one out of ten people slept in a doorway or in an abandoned car. A friend of a friend of one of her Foxhole Buddies had scored it – a happenstance of urban mythology: an apartment for rent. The toilet barely worked, the shower didn't (she'd taken to sponging herself in the cold, slightly brown, almost yellow water from the sink) and the only furniture she could afford was old, broken, or too ugly for even the hungry-eyed scavengers: her mattress was on the floor, her dishes were all chipped, her only chair wobbled like it sat on a ship at sea.

Key in lock. The same sticking door frame that forced her to lift and push. Frantic jangling thoughts of whether she'd cleaned recently, just how many dirty dishes were in the sink, and if she'd left her usual panties on the floor.

If the dishes in the sink had grown a brilliant fungus, or a pair of wadded underwear stained weak colors of dirt were underfoot, her guest didn't notice or say. What she did, flopping hard on Pell's bed, was smile an arc of teeth and say, "Hungry?"

Food was not on Pell's mind. Nothing much was, actually. The only thing that seemed to be living between her ears was an ache to pick up a pen, pencil, or brush and trap this woman – hold her on a piece of paper, on something she could frame on her wall.

She nodded absently as the woman reached for Pell's phone, dialed a number. After a moment, she passed the phone over, saying, "Give them your cash number. I'm tapped right now."

The fastfood guy spoke so fast as to be all but unintelligible. The image of zits and splattering grease was strong in Pell's mind as she rattled off her numbers and confirmed the purchase.

When she hung up, Arc was sprawled out on her bed, staring at the ceiling. "What a crock of shit."

Pell didn't know what to say. All thoughts of art left her as she stared at the woman's soft tummy peering out like a pale, toothless smile between jeans and T-shirt.

She wasn't – Pell realized, sitting down in a moment of heart-hammering bravery on the side of the bed next to her – really all that pretty. But then Pell never really found "beauty" to hold up. Beauty, she thought to herself, was fragile and temporary. Like the weather – rain following sun following snow. Arc's forehead was high, her thin brown hair pulled back into a thin severe ponytail – so severe as to make her look as if her skull was simply painted the color of bleached earth. Her face was luckily saved from the shallowness that Pell had seen too many times. Her cheekbones were broad commas under her eyes. She lived on the street – Pell knew that without asking – but she hadn't been run over, run down. She had stolen some of the street, used it to keep herself strong. While it was her left eye that had caught Pell, snapped her attention to its elegantly constructed utility, its artistic function, it was her right eye that kept her staring, looking at the bow-string and hardwood woman. Her right was pure gray, a kind that comes from raw iron behind heated by hard years, then suffused with air – a wind developed from a pure determination not to let the ground, the pavement, streets and sidewalks win. Her left eye was technological brilliance. Her right was steel: hard and reflective.

Her body was long and lean, her legs being her best feature. They had the strength good legs have from walking everywhere. Under her T-shirt her breasts were small and conical, with a kind of gravity-defying shape that instantly had Pell dreaming of their color, the way they moved; her nipples were twin dark points, crinkled areolae visible even through the thick cotton of the T-shirt.

"You know that guy?" Arc said, still on her back, still staring at the ceiling. Like the rest of the tiny apartment, the ceiling was bare, empty save for a thin yellow water stain. Her eye click-click-clicked as she looked up at the ceiling. Pell wondered what she found so fascinating. It took her a while for the woman's words to pass through her mind, layers of puzzling till she knew she'd meant Jare, Jare's show.

"Sort of. He's a painter. Not really a friend of mine, but I help him and he helps me sometimes."

"Cocksucker," Arc said, bringing herself up onto her elbows. "He owes me. Told me to come and just hang out. He said he'd credit me. Not a lot but enough, you know? I can make better for doing a lot more but this sounded easy, so I said 'sure'. Asshole. Didn't pay me up front, then says that he was only going to shell out if he got enough people. Then only if someone bought one of his fucking paintings. Fuck him."

"He's like that," Pell said, seeing a quick montage of Jare

approaching Arc on the street – seeing a chance for her hard presence, her burning will. The shallow people he'd invited to the show might not remember his paintings, his red streaks on soft black, but they might remember her, Arc's style and strength, and thus *him*.

"You like him?" Both the steel and the steel gray eye looked at Pell.

She shook her head. "Not really," Pell said, finally answering her question. Her face had gotten hot under Arc's intense perception. Click-click-click. Cannon barrels of perception. Click-click-click. Pell wondered what she found fascinating in her. Like her apartment, Pell was simple and plain. She knew that and often relished in her plainness – it was a carefully constructed ring around herself, a barrier of mediocrity. She knew her hair was dull and flat, black but spared a kind of style. Her face, she knew, was soft and full – a dull moon. She knew her nose was too small and her eyes too big. Her teeth were good, at least, but they were like a child's – delicate and fine. Her body was sturdy and that's how she used it. Wide hips and fat tits. She also walked everywhere but with Pell the softness stayed, locked her down to her suburban heritage – marked her for what she was: a tourist in the city. She had come to see it, not become a part of it.

"Good," Arc said, leaning back onto the bed again. "Just wanted to make sure."

Pell didn't know what to say, so didn't say anything. Half-formed words and sentences tumbled through her mind but couldn't congeal enough to be spoken. So they sat together – quiet, clumsy – till the food arrived: a big black man wearing Kevlar body armor and carrying a huge foam container marked with the bold red swatches of Chinese characters. The food was food, and they filled the silence with quick eating.

When the food was gone, Arc yawned: "Fuck, I'm tired." She pulled off her shirt, showing breasts pale and white, beautifully shaped sculptures of pale skin. Areolae like rough brown coins, nipples like dark finger-tips. "Shitty day. Good night," she said, crawling into Pell's bed and fumbling for the line switch to her broken lamp.

Pell didn't move. Frozen, she watched her hunt.

"You coming?" the woman said finally and, not smiling, reached out and took her hand. Her eye, her single artificial eye, looked at Pell with more warmth and sincerity than did her gray, real one.

But the hand was there, out and firm. Strong and real. A gesture in more ways than just an invitation to crawl in.

So Pell did, removing her clothes and moving into the small bed with a fluid, natural motion that defied her quaking nervousness. Long arms, still somehow cold from the night out, wrapped around her. Taller, Arc's head was above her, the woman's breath a periodic hot wind through Pell's hair. For the smaller woman, Arc was a strong, corded neck and the slope of a hard chest. A fluttering excitement surged through her, and it was all she could do to resist scooting farther down, to see close up, to have Arc's brown nipples close to her lips.

A rough pat in the top of her head snapped Pell out of her tense anticipation – tilting her head up she looked into one crystal, one gray, eye . . . and a face stone still.

The same part of Pell that wore that dress, that stepped outside her constant fear, moved her face close and kissed Arc on her cool lips.

Click, one real, one not looked hard at her. Arc's gaze was penetrating and distant at the same time – holding for too long. Then she lunged – predatory and quick – returning the kiss, but lip to lip, so hard that Pell pulled back suddenly, fearing bruising. But ever stronger, Arc pushed further, roughly parting Pell's lips and striking with a hard, dry tongue.

A beat, maybe two, of Pell's fast-hammering heart, and her tongue met Arc's in the hot duel. The force was strange to Pell, an oral fistfight when she was used to dancing – but her body welcomed it, even though her mind was chilled by the roughness: her nipples became aching points, so hard as to hurt, and deep between her lips her clit jumped as if shocked and the hidden folds of her cunt grew hot with moisture.

Arc's hand was similarly hard and quick, from somewhere it came between them – grabbing Pell's right breast in a muscular clamp. Gentle caresses, butterfly kisses, stroking touches . . . the shock of the grip, the strength was a hard rush – Pell felt her cunt gush hot moisture, felt a voltage shock in her clit, her nipples. She gasped, breaking their kiss and breathing heavy into Arc's face . . . who laughed, deep and brass. Grabbing the heavier girl in those two strong arms, Arc pushed her further up the bed, flopping Pell's bigger breasts into her firm face. Pell started the scream, the cry, long before Arc's teeth met on her left nipple – but let it continue out in a sharp animal sound. On their own, her arms reached down to push the strong woman away – to force her clamping teeth off her nipple – but there was no strength in them, no real desire to break the agony. Her clit, already throbbing, reached out on its own and clamped her legs together in a thigh-clenching near-masturbation.

Then a hand, now warm, reached down and yanked them apart. A smashing ache snapped up through Pell – the initial throb of a sprain – but, again, she let the pain rock up through her, just another kind of stimulus. Deep down, she was crying – fear quaking her, making her sweat cold, her breathing shallow, but she was also too far into it to care, to ask for it to stop. She was more scared of the pleasure she felt, that she was so wet, that her clit was so damned hard, than what she imagined Arc would do.

Her legs were wider apart than they had ever been before – for no one else she'd opened them, allowed them to be forced apart. She showed her cunt to Arc, buried under the cheap sheets – she spread, hungry, wet and open for her.

Sensation, down among the short, brown curls, the wide, wet lips, the pink finger of her hard clit. At first she didn't recognize it, couldn't place it – a filling, a firm thrust that went deep and long into her. For a moment, puzzlement and near-panic flashed through her, and her yawning legs almost snapped shut: dick? Was there something obvious about Arc that she'd missed?

No, that wasn't it – besides, Pell was too far along to really

care if she was being fucked by the woman. Fingers, yes –
rough, hard, fucking fingers. She didn't know how many . . .
not one, not two, maybe three: she hoped not four. But
fingers, yes, Pell was being finger-fucked, hand-fucked, by
Arc.

She repeated it to herself, a mantra, with the hard-edged
and mean images that came with it: finger-fucked in her hot,
wet cunt. Fucked by a butch's hand. Fucked with her legs
open – images, words, thoughts that would have made her
blush, now just made her cunt drip onto the cheap mattress.

Arc's fingers became a brutal beat into her – one, two,
three, four. A hammering, as fast as she could – or almost as
fast as she could. Cold fear again, the thought of internal
bruising, of warm wet from blood and not just from hot
moisture, having her cunt not just fucked but beaten.

She came – with a wave of shame and fear, thinking of hot
blood, she came. It was a hard, fast ride – a teeth-clenching,
body-rigid come and slammed her soft, spread legs down
around Arc's brutal hand in a tendon-aching lock.

The quakes went on and on and on, rolling down into a
body-quiver, a whole self tick that seemed to follow the
beating of her near-spasming heart. Distantly, she was aware
that Arc was moving up the bed to spoon up next to her.

After a point Pell fell asleep, a dreamless empty, to the soft
clicks of Arc's eye, watching her as she did so.

In the morning, Arc was gone. Though she was never proud
of it, Pell spent most of that morning looking through her
cheap, broken or worthless possessions to see if Arc had
taken anything.

The inventory turned up nothing missing. Nothing was
left, either. No note. No number left conveniently for her to
find. Nothing at all.

Pell spent the rest of the day staring at her pad, frozen in
the middle of her own gesture, her own reach to trap the girl
in pen and ink, paint and charcoal. She stared at it for what
felt like hours, crippled by having her own natural eyes, her
own native perceptions.

After a point she got up and moved around the apartment, putting down things and picking up others, absently cataloging the minutiae of her little life – wondering how the woman would have seen them – either through her click-click-clicking sight or through her gray real one so used to seeing things at a street level.

She was two people, walking around doing nothing. One of her was somewhere else, distant on a plane of excitement, who desperately wanted the woman again, fevered for her hand in her wet cunt, for the pain that had been so much a part of her pleasure. The other Pell, though, was frightened – who didn't want to spread her legs again – even in masturbatory memory of the night previous: who was terrified that she had enjoyed any part of it.

One side won. Without a conscious thought, she found herself in her small bed, the sheets still faintly smelling of herself. Rest, she told herself, tired. But she found herself moving against the firm resilience of the mattress, pushing her pelvis down into it, calmly relishing in the memory, the sensations. After a point, she knew she could not go any further – couldn't escape, so she brought her hand down between her legs, finding herself wetter, her clit harder, than ever she could remember.

At first she started down a very familiar road – one finger gingerly, softly stroking her hard nub . . . but Arc intruded – or rather the hard memory of her. Just one finger wouldn't do; soft thighs pressed together wouldn't work. No, after a single moment of fear and shame, she parted her legs – again – as wide as she could and slipped two of her own fingers (three being too frightening) into the molten wetness of herself.

She imagined a lot of things, under the cool sheets of her small bed. Arc's touch, the sight of her brown nipples, the cool strength of her in the bed, and then she came, she bellowed and roared in a powerful wave . . . thinking of a slight amount, just the tiniest trace, of blood on come-slick fingers as Arc had fucked her the night before.

Sleep again, this one lit by dreams of crystal and gray – of clockwork clicks and a cool presence, burning but also remote, removed. After a long few hours, she awoke to darkness beyond the dirty windows.

Getting up to shower, and prepare something simple and cheap to eat, she noticed the bill, laying forgotten and discarded near the crumpled remains of the night before. The meal had been expensive. Very. And Pell could not help but think, couldn't stop herself from pondering, how much Arc charged for a night, and if that amount was the same as a very expensive meal of Chinese food.

Pell hadn't forgotten her. It was a long time, yes, a week and some days, but Arc's memory was strong in her mind. At first it bothered Pell a lot to have the tall woman's face, mannerisms and voice still lurking around every corner in her mind. But soon it became a background of the city, a rhythm to her existence. Water from the faucet was Arc washing her hands after eating. A window was how she'd seen the woman's face reflected there, caught her watching Pell again with her steel-gray and just plain steel eye. Her dirty underwear on the floor pinged a memory of the fear she'd felt, walking into her place that night. It took her a long time to finally pick them up and add them to her laundry bag – simply because she subtly enjoyed the memory of that rush of panic at seeing them: the first time they'd been together.

Other memories, the first sight of Arc's hard nipples, her teeth setting down onto Pell's own, Arc's fingers slamming into her wet cunt. The ornate mandala of her artificial eye, the clicking of her examination, the music of Arc's sight: How could she ever forget?

No, she hadn't forgotten, but when the buzzer sounded she actually wasn't thinking of her. She was working, having caught sight of a book's partial title in a store window the day before: *The Peacock* . . . The images that'd tumbled through her imagination at seeing those words brought her almost running back to her tiny place and forced her pencil into her hand. *The Peacock Eye* was what she thought she'd read, though she was sure that wasn't the title, and that was what she started to draw. First with smooth sweeps of charcoal and graphite and then with a fine camel-hair brush that'd cost her breakfast, lunch and dinner for three days, she started in.

An hour later, the eye started to look like the image she'd formed from that half-seen book. She was lost and alone, caught up in the storm of sketching. It was a good feeling to be not herself, to be captured by the pursuit of the work. It felt great not to just sit on the edge of her bed and let the room, and everything in it, remind her of Arc and that night.

The medium was paper, ink, charcoal and graphite. The image was the eye on the end of a peacock feather. She'd filled its center with geometries and forms like steel gears, compass points, brass fittings, screws and miniature bolts. The form seemed to stare out at her with a cool logic, an immaculate watchmaker's perception.

Then she heard it, deep inside her mind – shattering the turmoil of creation: Click-click –

– *click*.

Then the buzz of her doorbell. Getting up, numb from the hard revelation that Arc still lived deep within her, she went to the door.

"I need someplace," the tall woman said from the street, looking up at Pell through the heavy iron security gate with one hard, cold mechanical eye, and one red-rimmed with a patina of almost tears.

She wouldn't talk – at least, not much: "Just let me sit over here, OK?" was what she said, coming in and sitting in the left-hand corner of the room, wedged in between Pell's kitchen door and her brick-and-board bookshelf. There, she slumped over so that her head rested on the dog-eared familiarity of Carroll's *The Basketball Diaries*.

Drawing her long legs almost up to her chin, Arc closed both her eyes – bloodshot real and too clear, too crystal, artificial, and gently rocked back and forth.

Pell wanted to touch her, wanted to pull the woman into her arms and mimic that rocking, to take her back to a place where, somewhere, she was small and vulnerable. But she didn't. It wasn't that she wasn't able to – it was as if a cold truth had dropped down onto her shoulders: that this, what she was seeing, was just about all of Arc. If she did go down there, drop down into the pain, then she might be walking through the woman's last shut door, last safe place.

So she didn't, though she wanted to.

Instead, for three hours without moving, she sat on the edge of her mattress and calmly watched Arc. For those three hours, Arc remained as she had been since she walked in: head on the softness of a well-read paperback, knees pressed into her strong skin, eyes closed. The only sounds she made were her rattling breaths, in and out, past lungs that had either cried too much or could break the clouds to start, and her eye -- which, soft, muffled, clicked and gently whirred within her puffy lid.

After three hours Pell had to go piss. After, she made some Darjeeling tea and put it at the woman's feet. Arc didn't stop making her two noises, didn't open her eyes (one fake, one real).

Pell went back to her bed, her mattress, and watched Arc till her eyes grew hot and heavy.

She must've, she realized with some horror, fallen asleep – but the embarrassment and disgust with herself was tempered with silk and a single hot, slow, breath on her eyelids and forehead – faded with the tender sensation of Arc's long, lean body slowly slipping into the bed.

Cool, almost cold, before – Arc was warm, near burning, and her skin seemed . . . real, silken. For a long time, they just held each other – an embrace of soft skin, of breaths mixing on each other's shoulders. Pell remembered Arc's slow, ragged breathing, the way she seemed to suck each breath in on the verge of a shattering moan. Then – after how much time, Pell could never be certain – Arc moved forward and kissed Pell's shoulder – as much as the roughness before, this kiss sent even more current tingling through her. It didn't seem to be Arc behind the kiss as much as the small child within her. It was a hungry kiss, a kiss of reassurance – the same kind of grounding happened when her strong hands reached up and cupped both of Pell's heavy breasts.

It wasn't so much sex, Pell realized afterwards, as something simpler . . . if not love, then just *need*. A need for touch, sensitivity, contact. Even when Arc's lips dropped down to Pell's soft nipples and started to kiss them, then suck, it was more a comfort, more a simple need than a burning passion. Still, lips were lips, and Pell felt her body respond – a growing fire deep in her cunt. Not a throbbing excitement, no, but still an excitement all the while – and, despite the heavy silence in the tiny apartment, she found her throat purring out deep vowels of pleasure.

In the soft, warm darkness, touching Arc's skin was like touching something too hot, too smoldering. Maybe it was because she'd been crying, been holding herself too tight, too much together – but the heat was there, nonetheless. As Pell slowly slid her hands down the tall woman's long form, she mixed new sounds with her bass purr – a kind of hissing excitement, a sensual amazement that one person could be so hot, so burning.

Soon – very soon – a patina of sweat slid under her fingertips, making it easier for her to see Arc's body with her touch. Uniqueness added puzzlement to her amazement. Pell's was soft, full – gentle belly, plump breasts, large nipples, soft ass – but this one, this woman in her arms, allowing her to touch, she was so different, so unique. Soft, yes; her skin was like oil over polished marble – the architecture of her body was quick and sudden . . . no languishing valleys, but rather hip-bone, cords of firm muscles, rib, rib, rib, the even hotter swell of a breast – even more silken, soft – the surprising roughness of a hard nipple skipping across her fingertips, even more heated breath on her shoulder.

Muscles, her body was like a finely honed tool – sharp and hard, but there was something else, lurking just on the edge of her senses: tears, maybe? Arc seemed more open, more real than the tall city warrior Pell had seen those other days, other nights. Her hand slipped down, found iron-firm thighs pressed too tight together, felt a brief scratchy tangle of ill-kept pubic hairs. Gently – because she wasn't altogether familiar – Pell pushed them apart.

Arc could have stopped her. Pell really had no chance of victory in their match: those cords of honed muscle could have easily stayed locked, could easily have resisted even Pell's most frantic of attacks. Maybe tears? Maybe because Arc seemed to be burning up with a tightly-controlled fever of need – supposition, wonder for another day. The fact was, Pell gently pushed and – very slowly – Arc spread her strong legs aside for her.

The smell of her excitement was harsh and rich. Pell found herself, in the dark, sucking it in through her nose – a long nasal tone. It was so unusual, so strange . . . her own cunt, she knew, was almost odorless, tasteless. But Arc's, it seemed, had a hard-edge kind of smell – a deep, natural smell that reminded Pell of locker-rooms, of her own pits after a long walk. It wasn't unpleasant – but then Pell didn't think that anything about Arc could ever have been that.

For some reason, putting her lips to where her fingers slowly explored never crossed her mind. Later – after dawn – she'd regret it, but understand a bit. She was inside more than her lips and tongue ever could be: the strong woman had parted herself, opened herself out of need. Pell was in her deepest parts – to simply stick her face down there and lick . . . like pissing in church.

So it was with her narrow fingers that Pell explored her. First, that tangle that continued from a hard mons down into a even thicker one. It was a complex knot, something that Pell instantly knew may not have been untied by gentle touches for a long time. She hesitated, stroking calmly up and down the hairs for a minute, two, uncertain how much to push. But the heat – the burning fires of Arc, the gentle glide of her body next to her, the smell of sweat, and cunt, finally pushed her into executing a gentle parting.

Wet . . . so wet. Wetter than anything Pell had ever felt – like thick, hot soup. Between them, a kind of steam built –

something that completely obscured reason. Normally, Pell would never have been so bold, but with her finger slowly licking up and down Arc's hot, hot cunt . . . from deep cunt-hole to the hard, hard point of her too erect clit . . . she had to do something with her mouth. Arc's was too far away, a hot bellows on the top of Pell's head, but something else was just as close . . . and just as tasty. In a beat of her heart, Arc's left nipple was in her mouth. Salt. Knotted hardness, the smoothness of the rest of Arc's breast against her cheek, her lips. Pell sucked, filling the early part of her mouth with Arc's nipple. All she could hear was the pounding of her own heart, the heaving breaths of Arc, and the whispering of the sheets as they slid over her body.

Movement . . . Arc twisted her body slightly, shifting herself onto her back. For a moment, her nipple popped free of Pell's hungry lips. A frown whipped across Pell's mouth, but the heat was on her and – beyond reason or thought – she quickly climbed on top of the larger woman, spreading her legs wide to straddle her – lips again seeking the cool wetness of her well-sucked nipple. It took some twisting of her own, but in a moment Pell's hand was once again deep in Arc's hot cunt.

Another slight twist, Arc lifting her body slightly – frightened for a moment that this was some kind of way of trying to get her to stop, Pell released the hot nipple and tried to see Arc's face in the darkness. Nothing. Nothing but a soft sound, the sound Arc had been making all that time – a kittenish moan, a childish groan. The hand was a shock, but one that built the heat right up again – Arc's hand hunting out for Pell's, taking it and pushing it back down into Arc's molten cunt.

Again, Pell started to work her, feeling her own cunt turn fluid, melt in its own hot juice. As her fingers energetically worked Arc's lips, hole, clit and all three quickly, Pell felt something – a glancing touch. For a moment, puzzlement flashed through her – then she realized, the knowledge like a skyrocket bursting through her. So fast, hot and bright that Pell had to put her own free hand down between her own hot thighs, into her own volcanic recesses. So hot, so tight, so good.

Meanwhile, Arc continued to fuck her own asshole with one, then two, then three fingers. The bed softly smelled of earth, shit and hot cunts.

Arc came, a primal female cry – deep and bass. Her body went rigid, a board with tits, a hard body pushed to the limits of hardness. Her breath exploded into Pell's face as she panted, heaved and cried out.

Pell felt her come – felt Arc's hands work her asshole as Pell's worked her cunt. Later, Pell couldn't remember if she'd come as well – the explosion from Arc was so special, so shattering, that it had torn away any memories Pell had had of anything she'd been feeling. That moment was pure Arc – a night in a secret, deep church. She'd been lucky to have witnessed the service, the ecstatic blessing being a witness.

Sleep came like a velvet blanket thrown over Pell. No dreams, again, but the cloudy memory of sometime during the night, a kiss landing on her cheek.

The next morning she awoke to find Arc, again, gone.

Pell saw her again, soon after. Living in the city for as long as she had (was the difference between tourist from the suburbs and resident?), Pell was finally starting to understand the clockwork of its people. A day or so before and the desperate Sad-SACs would be prowling for anything or anyone that could mean bucks till their next Subsistence Allotment Check. A day or so after and the streets would be filled with walking psychotic landmines – having spent their biweekly fortunes on whatever chemicals they preferred.

The fifteenth or so of the month was the best time to go out and get supplies. Anyone who depended on their Subsistence Allotment Checks would be too busy haunting their mail drops or be too happy that they would be coming to bother her. Random crazies were impossible to predict – so you always expected someone or something. Feeling good that she'd taken living in the city to heart enough to anticipate street insanity made Pell feel more like a resident, less like a prisoner.

The day was crisp, edging towards too warm. But since the HotFace^{TM} personal scorcher her father had given her was too big to carry in a pants pocket, she had to wear her leather coat again. Stepping out and quickly locking up her place, Pell knew – with a flash of heat as quick and as sharp as the single small arm's round that echoed from the Minimal Income Housing Facility up the street – that she'd be sweating streams by the time she made it to the market, two blocks away.

The street was vibrant in the unexpected sunlight. The expectation of income made the Sad-SACs giddy and flirtatious, without the cruel desperation which other days – such as when the money started to run out – brought to their eyes. Pell's place was one of a sagging parade of typical San Francisco tattered Victorians. Hers was somewhere between the worst – metal-plate window-shields bolted to rotten wood, the whole bay front sagging from the weight of too much fear – and the best – a lady's paint only five years too old, streamers of older, better paint jobs, peeling from its peaked roof. Hers was simply gray, with boxed edges from a previous owner who had somehow decided to convert 1890s gingerbread to 1950s stucco.

Keeping her hand in the ring-trigger of the HotFace^{TM}, Pell moved among Sad-SACs looking expectant, happy and always hungry, other kids with haunted looks that meant that they, too, were hovering on the edge of conscription, and the usual buzzing fringes either too far gone or too keenly focused to match either population.

Pell guessed that she probably appeared as the latter – her eyes clouded inward with a sudden thought of Arc. A fat, black ball of a man, legs spindly twigs, arms twitching from involuntary palsy rolled by in a homemade electric cart – its donut wheels compressed down by his bulk till they acted more like treads. Pell noticed absently that he was naked, and shined with a contouring mirror of perspiration as he rolled towards and past her. His left eye was a tubular prosthetic, darkly tunneling forward as he rolled.

A Latino boy proudly displayed willingness to drop off the dole and into combat by obviously spending most of his SAC on a pair of intense insect green, surely-as-soft-as-silk pants, and a beautiful purple coat fringed with antique wooden rosaries as he moved with dancing steps from behind her, to next to her, to beyond her. His face was long and thin, with an expertly precise mustache. The fingers on his artificial left hand were a dull matte of industrial design, humming butterflies as he played an invisible guitar, or clicked the trigger of an imaginary weapon.

Like a pool of deep cultural waters, a small knot of black-shrouded Arab women flowed by across the street. It was hard to say their numbers as their hands and eyes (all that was visible) seemed to churn and emerge from one unifying mass of their robes. Watching them but not really looking at them, Pell caught one foot as it emerged from the cloth, it was chrome leading to a finely-machined ankle and, no doubt, ending in an artistically-created leg.

A callow-faced young woman slouched in a doorway, hardness in her downcast eyes. The street had carved years on her cheeks and body with scars – like a prisoner's years sloppily etched on the walls of a cell. She wore a pair of slashed fatigues splashed with white and black urban camouflage, and an ancient T-shirt that might have said something a long time ago. As Pell walked past, she caught a glimpse of the girl's ancient steel-and-tubular arm, bent and broken, hydraulics (of all things) splattering her old uniform with glossy oil. She wrapped her mechanical in her real, covering it – as if its malfunctions were disgusting, to be hidden.

The street rolled by her as she walked. A parade of average people. Keeping her hand on the tiny flame-thrower, she walked past a cross-section of the city. Reaching the corner (halfway there) she was gently surprised that she hadn't thought of Arc – and her eye – as she'd passed those who also opted for the cheaper-than-replacement option. It felt good, a surprising justification for the way she felt about the tall woman.

A reflection caught her eye as she waited for the light to

change, a convoy of squat Army personnel carriers roaring by at a shuddering 50 mph – automatic guns calmly tracking her heat signature, seemingly too eager for their masters to release them to the task they were assembled for. Needing an excuse to escape the high velocity intensity of the tracking guns, she turned.

Something bright lanced into her eye, a splinter of sunlight off something silver and gold. Tourmaline and onyx. A chance of stature, placement and angle of reflection. Arc's eye gleamed at her from across the street as the woman turned, saw her, and smiled – quick, reflex – before frowning and turning to walk away, fast.

It was days later. The few groceries Pell was able to afford were safely in her cabinets and her rattling refrigerator. Jare, who'd vanished since that night at the gallery, had shown up on her doorstep two days before, tears gagging in his throat as he carefully unfolded the conscription notice that'd been slipped under his door. It had taken most of the night for her to calm him down – and, still, even after she'd finally managed to get him to stop crying for more than two minutes and out the door, he seemed ready to break into a pile of pure porcelain at any moment.

She hadn't heard from him since. The Conscription Notice had told him to report to the Treasure Island Induction Center in two weeks. She suspected he was either hiding in his tiny apartment, too petrified to move, or was, in vain, trying to scheme his way out of it.

A sense of calm had visited Pell. She knew it was an eye, that winds were tearing apart everything she knew just outside her door but, still, her heart beat regular and her breathing was clockwork. She knew it was just a matter of time before she got her own notice. She had worked through most of her SAC money already. The dream that she was going to be able to fulfill the government's cold illusion of crawling up the economic ladder with her SAC money was almost over. Wide awake and startlingly calm, she slowly began to clean her apartment.

The door buzzed.

"You going to let me in?" Arc said from the landing, looking up with a pure white smile. Her eyes were hidden behind cheap black sunglasses.

Arc was strong. That was one of the things that reached between the two of them and tugged, hard, at Pell's heart. But it was a kind of strong that was precious and priceless because, for Pell, it had come with tears. The strong only share their tears with you if you're special, trusted.

"New?" Pell said as she tried to make good coffee out of freeze-dried beans and yellowish tap water.

"Nice, isn't it?"

Pell wasn't looking but she knew that Arc was – staring at her own right hand with a connoisseur's squint, daring its perfection to show her a loose screw, a matted sensor dot, a dull gleam to the polished metal. Her concentration was a Geiger-counter series of clicks from her eye.

Arc had tried to show it to Pell without really waving it under her nose – so, instead, the street girl had acted like a child trying to catch the eye of an adult, to have Pell notice, to ask, about the new prosthetic.

"He's a freak – but at least the fucker's got taste."

It was beautiful. There was no denying that. It didn't have the jeweler's magnificence of her eye but, still, it had the clean loveliness of a perfect machine. Minimal extravagances, no filigree or bevels. It was the beauty of a revolver, the sensual streaming of a missile. Pure form has its own form of elegance.

"Japanese tech. All the way. See the chop at the wrist. Danomoko. Grow the whole thing in solution, I hear. Just feed juice to those little robots and they grow the thing. Stronger than fuck. Neurofibre optical hookup to meisomolecular fibres. Feels just like a hand, moves just like one, too – but motherfucking fast and *strong*."

Cool metal glided along Pell's cheek. She shivered, mostly from the coldness of it. Looking down at the hand, she saw the puckered ring of tissue where it mated to Arc's wrist, a rubber gasket. Absently she noted the hand wasn't black at all, as she'd first thought, but a deep kind of blue. Like, she imagined, the blue that the sky gets just before it passes into space. Dark to the point of lightlessness.

"Wasn't expensive, actually," Arc said, stepping back and running it – her hand – up and down the corded muscles in her strong legs. "Not that he told me or anything. I thought about having it taken off, you know? Replace it with a cheaper one and pocket the change but, *hell*, I thought it's a fine hand, right? Besides, gotta keep the freak coming back for more. Wouldn't do to see him with a cheap thing stuck on my wrist."

"That makes sense," Pell said, turning from the cheap microwave with two steaming cups of almost, but not quite, coffee in her hand.

Arc patted the bed with her new hand. Pell sat down next to her and, for some reason, put her head on the taller woman's shoulder.

Arc got quiet and tensely sat up straight. The motion was soft, though – not a twitch and definitely not a pull-away. Just a slight electric shock of the contact. After a few thudding heartbeats, Pell felt Arc's new metal hand reach up and stroke her ugly brown hair.

Neither said anything for a long time. Arc repetitively stroked Pell's hair and Pell did nothing but let her. Finally, Arc moved a bit more than usual, a kind of squirming on Pell's old mattress, and Pell straightened up. Her head felt loose and full of sparkles, like she'd held her breath for too long.

"Hey," Arc said, turning to look at Pell with her one steel and one steel gray eye, "I saw where your friend lived – but it don't look like he's there any more. Get sent?"

Pell nodded. "Month or two ago. Could have probably slipped to Australia but he waited too long."

"Hey, if we're lucky, maybe he'll buy it, ya know? One less artist to worry about . . ."

Arc laughed and so did Pell, even though it wasn't funny. After a point they stopped talking, it got dark, and they snuggled together under Pell's old sheets. Pell expected the new hand to get in the way, to be a burst of shocking cold when Arc touched her: but was surprised when, if she closed her eyes, she could almost not feel the difference.

Almost not feel the warm metal of Arc's hand – grown in a vat of microscopic robots, sold to a mystery, given as a present, or as part of an exchange –

Almost not feel the strength of it – a strength beyond that which Pell loved in Arc. As she touched Pell, it seemed not to be the same contact – to come from the same woman. Arc's touch was gentle, yes, loving . . . if that could be the word. But it was also fast, covering Pell's slightly larger, definitely softer body. Not a slow progression, as before . . . lips, chest, breast, nipple . . . more hurried, rushed: straight to her already swollen nipple, the cooler fingers of the artificial hand gripping tighter than before, much faster.

They had not even completely crawled under the covers before Arc's hand grabbed her. In shock, Pell pulled away, sending a bolt of agony through her body when Arc's hand did not let go. After, Pell thought – believed – that perhaps the mechanism just wasn't responsive enough. She knew it was a lie, but she had to believe it, nonetheless.

Pell turned, eventually freeing herself. Turning, she sat and looked at Arc as the taller woman crawled into the old bed. Her eyes glimmered – the artificial with the click, click, click stare of her perception, the gray with a shimmering concentration. The lights were on this time, neither of them moving to turn them off.

The gunmetal hand reached out and laid itself, warm and cool at the same time, on Pell's inner thigh. Reflexively, Pell started to close it – but Arc pushed with its artificial strength, spreading Pell even wider. To hide the nerves that made her shake like the room was cold (it wasn't), Pell laughed – but it sounded like Arc's new hand: artificial and cool.

"I want to fuck you," Arc said, looking straight into Pell's eyes. Click, click, click and cool gray. There was a strength there – *that* strength: a dramatic firmness, a theatrical burst of power. Pell felt her knees go weak and her cunt start to warm . . . soften, melt.

The hand started to stroke her, slowly, up and down – swell of her ass-cheeks to the tuft of hair at the top of her mons. Up and down, up and down, fine mechanics following the contour of Pell's cunt, fingers sweeping through her tangle of pubic hairs. Back and forth, up and down – then one finger, out a bit more than the others, slipped between her lips. The motion slowed, hesitated – the finely-machined metal was cool, but not cold. She could feel its hardness press up, against the opening to her deep cunt. Arc held it there – held her new hand there – and Pell could feel her own pulse against the cool metal.

"I'm going to fuck you –" brass in those words, a metal as hard as her new hand. Pell, frightened and filled with a chilling excitement for the power in Arc's voice, grabbed a pillow from behind her and positioned it – quickly, feverishly – so she could lean slightly forward, to get a better view.

Click, click, click – Arc's view seemed to synch with hers, the taller woman's gray, artificial sight was between Pell's passionately spread legs, hypnotized by her own actions, by the slow up-and-down, up-and-down of her artificial fingers between Pell's moist cunt-lips.

The hand was smooth, its action more precise, more finely engineered than anything Pell had ever seen. Where she'd expected joints, hinges, sockets, and the like, instead there seemed to be immaculate mechanisms. She couldn't tell exactly how – a combination of every hinge, every joint, or a Japanese paper-folded mentality of design – but the gunmetal flesh of the hand just seemed to move. It was more a study in flesh and blood, executed in machined metals, than an approximation of a hand's actions.

And two, then three, of its blue-steel fingers were deep inside of her.

No fingernails. She'd noticed that. Smallish indentations, yes, but not cosmetic details. Watching the first two fingers of Arc's new artificial hand, her metal prosthesis, slide in and out of her cunt, Pell had a clear view of the thumb – a space, that small bit of sculpture, a bow to the needs of some woman, somewhere, to paint their metal art with some kind of gaudy color. For Arc, though, it remained blue-steel, polished. It was its own art, its own beauty.

Four, and hard steel tapped against Pell's G-spot. The shivering started then, the pressure deep within herself. Like taking a piss, like holding it back. A kind of slow, building force that started somewhere inside her cunt and spread, tightness, firmness, up through her body.

She shivered – just slightly. In and out, in and out, the fingers precisely fucked her. "I'm fucking you," growled Arc, locking a click, click, clicking stare into Pell's quivering eyesight. For a beat, or thousand, of their hearts they locked like that – Pell into gray and machinery, Arc into Pell's softer eyes. Hold, hold, hold – Pell thought she was close, on the lip, looking down to where the real Arc lay, hiding. Then a clicking, hard, blink, and Arc turned her head away, looked to the side, and then down – down to where her false hand was fucking Pell's very real, and very wet cunt.

Four. Pell knew it must have been that number – in concentration and to remove herself from the memory of Arc breaking the stare, she leaned slowly back and closed her eyes, trying to lose herself in the in-out, in-out fist-fucking. It wasn't a hard rhythm, yet, wasn't a hard fuck, yet.

"Now I'm really going to fuck you." Strength touching on anger, firm words from Arc. Four fingers and something else, a new – sharper – kind of pressure.

Pain. Pell screamed – no, cried – no, yelled. She made some kind of noise, a mix and match – her own kind of strange movement to match the elegant watchmaker workmanship of Arc's hand. It was a sound that went all kinds of way at once. Frightened – both from the sound and the tearing pain between her legs – Pell put her hand down – quick – and tried to stop Arc's thrusts . . .

. . . no fingers. A hard steel wrist, a ring of rubber where artificial met natural, a seam of skin. No fingers there – all of them gone, hidden deep within her own cunt.

The reach to stop became a reach to explore. Moving herself carefully up, Pell reached down between her legs and touched, keeping her eyes tightly closed. Arc wasn't fucking her – just wrist, rubber gasket, slick skin, hard metal – suspended in her cunt.

Pell started to breathe hard, fast. The orgasm came, quick and hard, from a direction she didn't expect – the surprise, fear and shame forcing her eyes even more closed. It was a soft come, a jittering come. No screams, no cries, no lip-biting, not even a clamping together of her wide-open legs. It was a body-rush, an electrical charge that went from dull glow to brilliant light.

The shame was a heat on her face, in her cunt. The ghostly image continued to hover, just out of reach, just out of understanding, on the verge of her mind. She didn't want to see it, but also felt its allure was too strong to bury away.

Arc, slowly, started to fuck her harder and harder – wet noises from between her legs, feeling to Pell like somewhere distant, removed. Dimly, she was aware that she was even wetter than before, that her juices were flowing, streaming down onto Arc's brand-new hand. No, not juice – piss, maybe. It felt like something inside herself had just let go, draining out of her. She let it, entranced by the feel of the fluid pouring out of her, and the sense of hot release.

A second orgasm – more familiar and welcome – rocked her, tearing her eyes open, forcing her shaking hand down between her legs, feeling the gasket again, the hot skin again, the cooler metal – again – but this time the fast, then slowing, piston action. As she touched, then gripped – hard – Arc's wrist, the clenching of her cunt around the metal prosthesis slowed, dimmed. It didn't stop, not for a long time.

"Push," Arc finally said, and she did: like birthing or taking a shit – a swelling pressure, a bearing down, and she eased out the metal. Even though her eyes stayed closed, she opened them long enough to catch a sight of glistening metal fingers, flexing and flashing in the dim light, strands of cunt-juice webbing between them, the smile on Arc's face . . . that might – just might – have been as cold as the metal they were made of.

The mattress was soaked from her ejaculate. Wordlessly,

Arc pushed her off – making Pell a little nest of the faded blankets, the pillows, that had escaped the drenching, and neatly flipped it over. Watching her through slit eyes, Pell knew that the stain, the dampness, would linger, but was beyond caring.

Then, carefully so as not to disturb her, Arc moved her back, tucked her in and – just before the silence that came before sleep – squeezed her throbbing ass-cheeks with her new metal hand, and said in a gruff voice: "You are a good fuck."

The last thought Pell had that day, before being drawn down into unknown – forgotten – dreams, was that she'd wished that Arc had really fucked her, really touched her with – hard flash of fear and shame again, the image that had pushed her over into that first come – even the raw skin of her fleshy arm, the cauterized stump of her real self.

They stayed together for most of the next day, rolling to and from Pell's bed stopping only to make bad coffee and sprint through the chill, nipping air of the apartment.

It was a sweet time – as if the hard sunlight that streaked through Pell's windows had somehow pushed aside the shadows of the night before. Arc's kisses were passionate, and several times the thought of bruised, purple lips skated across Pell's mind, but they were gentle in her way – and lingered long enough for a dancing touch of tongues.

One time, reason forgotten, Pell had gotten up – gone to the stained sink and washed her hands. Arc had stepped up behind her, a cat tracking a spot of light on the floor, and grabbed her – first her ass, which made Pell yip like a startled child, and then, when she whipped around, hands still dripping, her tits. Arc had held her there, hands on her tits, fingers (some real, some metal) rubbing casually back and forth across her soft, then hard, nipples. Then Pell had leaned forward, just a little, and closed her eyes. The kiss had felt soft, fleeting, and all too real – a real kiss from the real Arc.

She'd also made Arc laugh. Hard and real. It was a

treasure, a prize. They'd been kissing – just that – lost in the landscape of each other's lips, the sweetness of their breaths, when that other, that loud and rambunctious part of Pell, reached down and tickled the tall street girl under the ribs.

Arc had exploded in a booming, percussive laugh that had rung and bounced around the tiny apartment like a frisky dog. Arc had wiped tears from her face, returned the tickle and told Pell that if she did it again she'd "Break your face."

A short time later, as more and more sunlight slowly started to come in the dirty windows, exhausted, they slipped into the cool, slightly smelly bed. They'd held each other for a long time, spooning together, unintentionally matching their in and out breaths. Slowly, Pell had slipped quietly into a sleep. She'd dreamed of floating, drifting on a lake dotted with the mountain ranges of pure white clouds, like warm, insubstantial icebergs.

When she awoke, Arc was gone.

The next time, it'd been raining. Pell had seen her before, in the rain, but this time Arc's urgency scared her. Pell had been asleep, rolling in and out of half-remembered dreams, worried because the Foxhole Buddies hadn't heard from Jare in over three weeks. She didn't really miss him, her embarrassment and self-hate over that a burning kind of ache behind her eyes, but it was a reminder that his fate could be any of theirs. That day she'd checked her bank account, compared it with the SAC statement of the week before. She'd stared at the flimsy paper strips for long, heart-rapping minutes, trying to perform some kind of mathematical legerdemain on them to make them calm her panic. But no matter how many times she added, subtracted and counted on whatever extra income she could acquire, the verdict was still zero in six months. Ten if she didn't eat. A year and a month if she moved out and lived on the street.

The bed was a safe haven. She'd not washed the sheets, or thoroughly dried the mattress, since Arc had spent the night. The smell of her – of them – was a bath that she floated in, not having to put her head out to face the next day or the one after that.

The buzzer was a scream of reality, one that almost forced her back under the covers. She almost ignored it, leaving the world outside to vanish in the surprisingly hard spring rains. But then someone started banging on the gate – the sharp percussive clangs rattled up and through her apartment, making her teeth ache and her eyes squeeze shut.

Then a voice carried against the clamor, just a few pieces of words – not enough to make any kind of sense. But the tones spoke direct and hot to her.

Wearing only a large T-shirt, Pell stood in the doorway, looking down at Arc. The woman had a large plastic garbage bag over her head and was pounding on the metal gate with her matt black hand. "Are you going to let me in or what?!" she screamed, panic rippling through those tones that had got Pell out of bed.

Inside, Arc threw the bag aside and grabbed a pile of Pell's laundry off the floor and quickly, feverishly, started to dry her right leg.

"Fucking Swiss. They know how to build them but can't weatherproof for shit. Get too much on the joints and the servos hesitate. Bitch for an arm, fucked for a hand, but for a leg it means falling on your fucking face. Shit. It's pouring out there. You got a hair dryer or something?"

Pell didn't, and said so. She slowly closed the door. A pool of water distorted the worn wood floor, slowly bringing it back to a more natural shade of brown.

Finally Arc seemed satisfied she'd dried her leg satisfactorily. Her eye clicked with its finely tuned and expertly manufactured sight as she scanned her new leg for any sign of moisture. Then, wadding up Pell's shirts, underwear and socks into a mottled ball, she tossed them, hard, into a far corner. "I was gonna get it sealed, you know, but couldn't find a place that would do it good enough."

Pell stood, folded her arms, and felt a chill race through her. "New present?"

"Yeah. Everyone's a freak, right? Guess, in his case, he likes to improve on people. Not that I need any improvement or nothin'. Just gets off on it, I guess. Likes the metal, the way it feels. Likes taking a bit and giving a bit. I don't fucking know. He pays for it and that's good enough for me."

Pell sat down on the bed next to her. She wanted to reach out and touch Arc's arm, to feel the corded mnemonic fibres, the brief chill of the ferroceramic framework, the humming current of its circuits, the glistening neuroservos. She wanted to pull herself close to Arc, to hold her and lean against her. Yes, she wanted to lean against someone strong and firm.

The room was cold – brushing her hand against Arc's arm made a shiver dance up her hand. Pell gathered up the blankets and shawled them over her pale shoulders. As Arc tucked herself in, Pell jumped up and pulled her T-shirt over her head. Arc's breasts were hard and small, her nipples tight and dark. Pell had seem them before, of course, but not so erect. They seemed almost cracked from the cold, as if all their heat had been sucked out of them, all the life. A thin shine spotted parts of her body where the rain had managed to slip past the trash bag.

Naked, she jumped down next to Pell and pulled some of the covers over herself. Pell had seen a flash of her, naked and firm – corded muscles, a skeleton ghosting through her pale skin, the puckers of arm and leg where the prosthetics mated with skin – as she moved. She realized as Arc snuggled under the thin blanket that the image burning still in her mind was not her ghostly skin, but the way the metal of her, the alloys of her, had gleamed in the dull rainy-day light. It reminded her of the first time she'd seen Arc – what seemed like eons ago. It had been her eye. The metal and jewels of it. Not the woman.

"It's freaky," said Arc next to her, face and body obscured by the sheets, the blanket. Pell could feel her body warmth and the cool firmness of her artificial elements against her skin. "But it pays, ya know? Gotta keep food in the belly, that shit. Freaky but at least you gotta say that he has taste, right? At least the man pays for quality."

"What does he do with the real parts of you?" Pell said before she realized she'd said it.

"Fuck if I know. Sells them. Jerks off over them. They're

gone, you know? Gone. Still me here, right? Still me – just a little tougher." The last came as a barking laugh, a deep, chesty sound that was as different as her giggling laugh under Pell's tickling fingers as Arc's real skin was to her new elements.

"Still me –" Arc said, worming a real, human arm through the sheets, the blanket to hug Pell clumsily. A sudden touch of cold metal echoed the movement, telling Pell that her other arm was also around her.

It seemed cold in the little room. "Doesn't it disturb you?" Pell was finally able to ask.

"He's a creep – like they all are. Fucker pays – get it? I don't really give a fuck about him – he just gives me the cash, and the toys."

"Tell me about him." Not jealousy, the heated emotion wasn't there. But she wanted to know why – to understand the slow replacement, the methodical mechanical encroachment into Arc's life . . . into Pell's life.

"Fuck, I don't know," Arc said, looking uncomfortable, fixing her real/artificial stare at a point somewhere over Pell's head. "He's a guy, you know. Rich fucker. Lives somewhere up in North Beach. Big place. Art and shit – but classy stuff – not like your jerk-off friend."

"Is he old?" The question was inane, but the only thing that came to mind.

A burst of hard laughter. "Aren't they always? Fuck, I don't know. Like a dad, kinda – he ain't all wrinkles or shit. Latino, I think. Speaks English good enough, though."

"Where does he get the money?" Pell's words went with her hands, gently stroking the real flesh, the real skin of Arc's untouched shoulder.

"Not as expensive as you might think. People will give lots for real meat."

"Then he sells them?"

"I guess . . ." Her clicking sight glanced over Pell's, then dropped down to her plump nipples. Casually, like touching something just to be assured of its texture, Arc stroked warm fingers across, seemingly fascinated by the way Pell's skin responded: areola raising, nipple tightening, lifting from the satin skin. "Doesn't say, don't ask."

"What does he do?"

Arc was quiet for a long time – so long that Pell thought that she'd tripped, fallen into a trap. As guilt rose over her pushing, her strident inquiries, Arc slowly started to speak: "Just lets me in – calls me first, you know. Then lets me in. Big, fancy place. A catalog, magazine, TV kind of place – matching shit, you know. He just sits there, in this big chair. Watches me as I come in –"

A cool chill between Pell's legs – too hard fingers playing with the tangle of her pubic hair. She didn't want to, but two of those fingers – much stronger than flesh – pushed her thighs apart. She couldn't tell if she was wet or not, didn't feel anything except for a slight chilliness across her nipples, but guessed that since it was Arc down there, she must have been.

"I take it off for him, you know. Just take it off. No strip or nothin'. Just take it all over and stand there. He's dressed, you know – fancy suit. Expensive shit. Doesn't jack off or anything, just sits there and watches me. Doesn't even sweat – bastard."

Wet, yes – shockingly, embarrassingly wet, thinking of tall and lean Arc standing in front of her swarthy patron. Was his cock hard? Part of Pell wanted it to be – for him to be visceral and primitive. Throbbing but too corked to take it out, to stroke it and thus show himself for the little monkey he really was. But she also wanted it to be flaccid, a soft dick in silk boxers – the deep and impenetrable sexuality of the fetishist, the elaborate and methodical orchestrations of the truly fixated. Maybe his sexuality was in his touch, the way he ran dark-complexioned fingers across corded, street-strong muscles, or – deeper, darker, and Pell got even more wet – not across skin but across alloys, plastics, servos: the fetish of replacement, a chrome and metal hard-on for rebuilding, remaking.

"He just sits there and looks at me. Sometimes, I don't

know why, I get all wet – like I want him to jack off or something. Other times he's just a john, you know? But he doesn't – jack off I mean. Christ, I don't know if he even gets a boner –"

Wet, yes – Arc's hard fingers sliding up and down her swollen cunt-lips, from hard clit to puckered asshole. A rhythmic stroking. Pell looked down at Arc's own nipples, seeing them hard, hard, hard – and hoped it still wasn't from the cool air.

"He just watches me, you know. Looking at my hands, my legs, my face. Sometimes he moves his hand, you know, like this –"

Glistening with cunt-juice on three fingers, the hand came up, whispering along the stained sheets, to demonstrate: a model showing off this season's line in artificial fingers, hands, wrists, arms.

Then Arc smiled, bent down and kissed Pell again – a sweet kiss, with no bite, no hammering tongue. Just a match of lips – silk to silk. Again, as they kissed, exchanging hot breaths, cool metal between Pell's spread thighs, cool fingers in her too hot cunt.

"When he finds something he likes, something about me, he'll hold his hand up and I'll stop right there and just let him look. Then he'll pay me and send me away."

The hand was cooler than before – almost chilled – and Pell put her legs together. But Arc was stronger, and pushed them apart – hard.

"Then he'll get me back – in a day, sometimes a fuck longer. He'll still be sitting there in that chair, still in a fucking suit. But this time he'll have a box on the table – some Japanese thing, wood and everything, you know. I'll take the box and leave."

Arc was playing with her asshole, ringing it with slick, cool metal fingers, tapping gently at her back door. Fear made Pell's ears ring and she, for a moment, pushed herself further up the bed, with the illusion of going for another sweet kiss – but really to escape the penetration. Arc met flesh with the back of her head, though, bent her down and pushed her –

too hard – towards her tight nipples, and at the same time pushed a single artificial finger inside Pell's asshole.

"He's got this doc, over in Chinatown. Private place. Real fancy. I just show up, right, and he does it. Real classy shit, even a fuckin' mint on my pillow when I wake up. Don't even see the fuckin' knife. Just go in, take a fuckin' pill and wake up – a little more."

Arc's fingers pushed hard, deep into Pell's asshole. There was a feeling like having to shit, a deep pushing sensation that matched Arc's movements into herself.

"I just walk in there and that box is sitting there, waiting, for me. Nurses like fuckin' geishas, pasty-faced and quiet as shit. Give me this little blue thing on a satin pillow."

How many fingers now? Hard to say, hard to focus. Words in Pell's ear, Arc's tight little nipple in her hungry sucking mouth, Arc's cold metal fingers in her burning asshole. The world was tight, complete – none of it, not one element, was the reason for the fire in her: the finger – or fingers – methodically fucking her asshole were cool, strong and persistent in their in-out, in-out pumping; in her mouth, Arc's nipple tasted of hot skin and salt, the roughness of the tight flesh like a delicious treat that she rolled around in her savoring mouth; the words were strange, unusual and frightening – and this fear made it all the more wrong, all the more disturbing, all the more hot.

Arc moaned, a growling sound like something a jungle cat might make. Her flesh-and-blood hand stroked the back of Pell's head, tangling itself in her hair. Sharp pulls as strands broke under her passion were like gentle fireworks in Pell's mind.

"Fuck . . . one time I didn't zap out so quick. So I got up and looked in that box. Fuck –" Growl again. "– it was an arm, that time. Already had the hand. Real pretty thing, all metal and smooth. Like jewelry, you know. Like fucking jewelry. Strong, yeah, and firm – lot better than skin."

Two fingers, yes, Pell could feel them – and the fear of tearing, the fear of blood, made her clench down hard, a shitting clench that stopped Arc's methodical fucking for only a second, till she grabbed Pell's hair and pulled her away from her so-sweet (really salty) priceless nipple. That shock, that cascade of pulling hair, the strain on her neck, released her control and her asshole relaxed. Then three fingers in her asshole – yes, three . . .

Satisfied that Pell wasn't going to clamp, wasn't going to stop, Arc shoved her back towards her chest, her small, hard tits, and – yes – her nipples. Again, Pell hunted with her lips, sought with her hunger, the knotted points and started to suck, lick, nibble and even bite – as if this tit, this nipple was the source of all life, all love . . . all desire.

"Opened it up – and there it was. But I saw something else. Man, it's pretty – don't you think? So strong, so clean – perfect, fuckin' perfect. As perfect as someone can make it – like fuckin' art. Art, jewelry – fuckin' jewelry."

How many fingers? Pell didn't care. The only thing in her world was Arc's fingers, her asshole, Arc's flesh-and-blood fingers on the back of her head, and Arc's tight, hard nipple in her mouth – and her cunt: her hungry, hungry cunt. All it took was a quick shift of her body, a tiny movement to free her hand – then, there, her fingers parted her wet cunt-lips, scooped a bit of the slippery juice and started to work her throbbing clit. The first was a shimmer of power that raced from the pulse in her tiny, hard bead up her spine and to her lips – which started to shake around Arc's nipple.

"There was fucking come on the metal. Sure as shit. Ain't that freaky? Just a little, like someone had missed cleaning it all up. Fucker that jacked off on it, thinking of them cutting my arm off, slicing it away like fuckin' meat and sticking that beautiful thing on me –"

There, right there. Fingers in asshole, finger on clit, mouth on tit, real skin on the back of her head, Pell broke the suction with Arc's nipple and cried as the come tore its way out of her, ripped through her throat in a selfless cry of beautiful release. To burst it further, make it fly faster, Arc fucked her harder – slapping her artificial fingers deep within Pell, pounding her puckered asshole.

It lasted for moments, minutes, longer than anything

before – a rolling, surging peaks-and-valley kind of cascade of orgasms. It put spots before Pell's eyes and clamped her thighs around the machine in her asshole.

When it finally faded, leaving behind the hammering of her heart, it also left her the sight of Arc looking down into her eyes – click, click, click – and smiling, wide, broad, and true. "See, I knew you'd like it," she said. Holding Pell still, they both rolled off into sleep.

Pell tried to remember everything she knew about prostheses – about the mating of flesh and machine. Looking out the window, she counted them. Five in half an hour. Some days there seemed to be more, others she almost never saw any. They were all but invisible through their consistency. How many cars did she see in a day? How many computers? How many security cameras? How many did she not see, but were there anyway? She didn't understand the mechanics behind any of them but she still lived with them daily.

Her only intimate knowledge was her father's bank account. She guessed that she really should have known more about the breakthroughs she'd heard – one item, a "polymonic mycelin-sheath" buzzed through her mind but its context was meaningless – after all, her father had ridden the technological wave. Even though most of his claims and patents hadn't held up in court, he'd still managed to make enough in the boom to give his daughter a little nest in the city. Not enough. But a not a little, either.

Thinking of her father and the money was lead in her belly. Instead she thought about the more physical manifestations of artificial limbs, organs. She knew that they were cheaper than they had been – though the ones that Arc had were more expensive: craftsmanship always cost. She knew that you could sell an arm, a leg, an eye and buy a replacement with a little cash left over. It was common among people her age, SAC money disappearing, to sell something to keep conscription at bay – but between selling and buying, the income wasn't all that great.

By presidential decree, first choice of donor limbs always

went to returning vets. Looking out her window, she realized that some of the people she guessed were all flesh and all blood were more than likely made up of someone else's flesh and blood – eyes, ears, legs, arms, hands – and those that clicked, hummed and glimmered under the unexpected sunlight were veterans of only trying to escape the war.

Get busted and the courts offered you a deal: leave something behind and you can walk free (unless you left your legs to pay your fine).

Turning away from the window, Pell went back to her sketch pad. Charcoal and fine line, she'd indulged herself in filling in some of her preliminary sketches of Arc. She didn't really know when the fear of capturing the woman had gone, but one day it had. Possibly because she expected the woman to reappear. Arc was a part of her life. It felt good.

But there was an ache as well. Something had altered. Like the ground shifting beneath her feet so that left wasn't quite *left* any more – as if the whole world had subtly changed – she saw Arc differently. Strong, yes – but there was something else. An edge that hadn't been there since she'd seen Arc's tears. It was a jagged edge, something that Arc seemed to secretly delight in showing Pell.

Like her "client". Sitting on the edge of Arc's bed, she'd spun a long and detailed tale of him. European. Possibly Spanish. She'd even visited him at work, at one of the posh citadels downtown. NeuroGen, Pell remembered. She described his breath, said it smelled of cloves. His skin was dark and shone as if he sweated – but his skin, Arc said, was never damp. He had a gold tooth, far in the back of his mouth, that you could see when he laughed. It was always done, these detailed stories, without a sense of affection. Pell had the sense that Arc was sharing with her – showing her life to her. The man wasn't anything except a client – but one with an unusual inclination. He liked to give her gifts. What he did with Arc's original parts, he never said, or Arc didn't say.

Arc also took meticulous pride in showing Pell her newest additions, giving her endless details of manufacture, limitations, degree of workmanship.

The sketch pad was bulky so she laid it out on the floor. With the first sketch, she'd tried to capture Arc as she'd first seen her. Not her eye. The woman. The sheet of slightly off-yellow paper in fact was blank, undrawn, around that part of her face. Only her gray eye, and not her steel eye, looked out at Pell from the paper.

Lying with her soft belly on the hardwood floor, Pell flipped through the sketches. She knew that she'd failed to capture Arc as she'd walked back and forth through her life but the memories still stirred by the sketches were strong and thrilling to her. The day they'd gone out for coffee. The night Arc had awakened Pell with a nightmare – Pell had held the woman for hours, it'd seemed, while Arc cried from her real eye and heaved air in panic. The day they'd stayed inside and made love for hours.

The last one. Half a face. A torso hovering on an off-yellow void. Just one eye, a nose, a smile, one ear. That was all that remained of Arc.

Pell stared at the sketch for long minutes, and tried not to think of the next sketch she might make.

Days, weeks. Maybe a month. A blur of time, a cascade of events: Arc standing, naked in front of the dirty windows – long, hard body gleaming with elegant artificiality. As Arc moved like a slow dancer, Pell at first thought the performance for her benefit, and slowly started to rub herself. Then she noticed Arc's eyes tightly shut, the dance just a movement, a testing, of her real, and artificial parts.

Arc and Pell in bed together. Hard darkness outside – deep night. They were masturbating together, sweet kisses – butterfly wings – breasts and nipples grazing each other, tingles of feedback sensuality, hands between their legs, working ecstasy. It was a game with natural rules: don't touch, save for glancing lips, and savor the pleasure of the other. Pell lost, with three fingers deep inside the wet folds of her cunt, with her clit a hard finger nestled among them – with her other hand, she brushed Arc's working fingers, needing to know that she, too, was feeling pleasure.

She encountered stillness. No movement. A coolness, a hardness. Why, she wondered when next Arc left her world for a few days, a week, had she expected her to rub herself with her real, flesh and blood, hand? Two choices: meaty reality, or cold artificiality?

Arc didn't want to talk of her benefactor, but, still, some information leaked out . . . tiny portions of information. Pell found herself storing them, building a picture of Arc's time when she wasn't with her. She imagined details, things she knew she didn't have any knowledge of: his eyes, for instance, were jade green. His breath smelled of cilantro. He had an accent, somewhere with palm trees, white-painted houses and a sea so blue as to appear cinematic.

She never asked, but she wanted to. She wanted to frame the words, even more than the explosive "love", to put them out. To ask to capture her lover live, sitting still and poised for her charcoal, her pencils. She didn't though and, like "love" it was an invisible thing between them. But like she could think of Arc as her lover when the strong girl wasn't there, wasn't really there, she could still sketch from memory.

The next sketch she did make, and the one after: fractions of her, pieces separated by blank, white paper. Lips and one gray eye. One hand. The slight rise of her smooth belly, the swell of her mons. The slope of her breasts – the way they seemed a natural extension of her firmness, her muscles.

But the drawings she wanted to make, craved to make with an energy that scared her, was to fill in those blank areas, those sections of cool metal, state-of-the-art technology. She wanted to sketch out the whole of her – but not what she could see.

She had no reason to be there. She didn't belong there – cars glided past on silent induction motors, the occupants just shadows through bullet-proof glass. The few that walked the streets of the Financial District wore suits that would have kept her off the street, away from Induction, for years. They were uniformly clean, manicured, and poised.

Walking through the cool, shadowy canyons between the black-glassed towers she never once saw a copper eye, a steel hand, a plastic leg. She saw a bald man in a shimmering black suit, his eyes hidden behind a complexity of image-intensifying glasses. One of his hands was flesh and blood but black, a powered matt darkness: his crime hadn't reduced him to mating metal, plastics and "polymonic mycelin-sheaths". Money can bring you anything – even skin and bone.

Pell walked the cold canyons for most of the morning, getting cold, suspicious stares from the men and women she passed. Arc had bragged to her, "that big place – all silver and gold, on the corner of California and Sansome". The office where her benefactor had seen her once. It didn't exist. Arc had told her – it slipped out – that his name was Guerrera and that he was some kind of corporate attorney, working for an office of NeuroGen.

Pell walked in the shadows of more money than she could ever count in her lifetime, money that would drown her if she had to swim in it. She walked past men and women who could buy her, every limb, digit, and organ on a whim. These people didn't have the blade of Central America hanging over their heads, the horrible sucking vacuum of the street. That woman with the sterling silver cortical jacks on the back of her neck, that fat man in the cream-colored suit carrying a tattooed briefcase made of human skin, that young boy in the sailor's suit – their world was easy, malleable. With the right application of money and fear, disease, hunger, vanished. It was a comfortable insulation against the rest of the world – anything painful or frightening.

Pell walked, looking for the silver and gold building on the corner of California and Sansome, looking for the offices of NeuroGen, for Mr Guerrera.

She didn't know why she'd come downtown – no, she *did* know: she was well aware of her reasons, but they weren't realistic. They were a child's reasons, pleads and begs: "Find someone else to buy a piece at a time." She couldn't offer money; she thought about offering her body – but she wasn't Arc. She was young and flesh and blood. If he liked the caress of steel and rubber, then she doubted that Mr Guerrera of NeuroGen would find her interesting.

Pell walked downtown till the sun peered over the tops of the highest buildings, casting a brilliant, long shadow through the heart of this people's territory. She walked and walked but never once found anything close to a silver and gold building on California and Sansome, an office of NeuroGen, or a Mr Guerrera who liked to buy girls one part at a time.

Later, as darkness started to fall, she wandered the rest of what Arc had told her, looking for the house, looking for the Chinese clinic. Looking until there wasn't enough light to really see – or, for the first time, seeing for the first time.

Arc was lying back on her bed, smoking a black cigarette. It smelled: the bite of distantly burning rubber. Her one real eye was dilated, the pupil pushed back till there was barely anything left of her gray iris. It was a bottomless pit that was endless soaking up the details of Pell's ceiling.

There was a company called NeuroGen. It was a big one. Worldwide. They manufactured a tailored virus that strengthened neurons, made them easier to connect to "polymonic mycelin-sheaths". They didn't have an office in San Francisco, or even Los Angeles.

Pell was laying at the foot of the bed, at Arc's feet – head on the cold strength of one of her artificial legs. Turning her head, Pell could see up between Arc's legs: the pinched skin around her upper thighs where technology mated with flesh. The curves where hips turned into ass. The seam of her hairless cunt, her dark folds.

Pell wanted to touch her, to put out a hand and place it, careful, on the architecture of her cunt, to feel the heat of her reality – but was unable to reach far enough past the metal to reach what skin remained. She could see but not touch.

There was no Mr Guerrera employed by NeuroGen. There was no Mr Guerrera listed anywhere in the city that she could find. The building on the corner of California and Sansome was a black glass tower. Had been there for twenty-five years. It was solely owned by a Japanese banking conglomerate. Had been for twenty-five years.

Turning her head, Pell looked down Arc's long body. Steel and copper, electronics she didn't understand. High-impact ceramics, "intelligent" plastics, artificial skin. She looked at Arc and saw materials and machinery. They were beautiful in their design, elegant in their purpose.

Pell looked up at her and saw their purpose.

She didn't know what to do. The future was dead, frozen – the world was just her, her tiny apartment and her sudden understanding of Arc. The paths that she could go were fuzzy, unimportant against the pain, the revelation: she would go back to her father. She would live on the street. She would be conscripted and die – her epitaph like Jare's, an automated email message saying "DEATH NOTIFICA-TION" but meaning a young man's body in the jungle. She would sell some drawings, some paintings, earn enough so she could afford flesh and blood, and not have to settle for steel, iron, copper, plastic. Fuzzy futures, part of someone else's history.

Suddenly, she needed Arc. Needed her complete and whole. Needed to touch her, to make contact.

It had been a long time since that other Pell appeared – the brave ghost that lived somewhere in the young girl. The last time had been blood-red wine on a white dress, a burst against San Francisco black. She had been alone, needing company and love. Then, there, on her bed in her little place, she had the same feeling again.

Getting up, she crawled up Arc's long body. Seeing her coming – click, click, click – the tall woman turned a slightly frightened face her way, looking down her body. Then she sighed, a heavy sound ringing of exhaustion and – maybe – fear. She ground out the smelly cigarette on Pell's battered nightstand, blowing out the last of the smoke with two jets of blue smoke from her narrow nostrils.

Pell kissed her, tasting the reality of the harsh smoke on her breath. She was straddling Arc, her heavy breasts and tight nipples pressed against Arc's smooth chest. She hoped that she was wet, hoped that her cunt was dripping – but honestly didn't care. Spreading her legs, she dropped herself down till her cunt-lips spread over the coolness of Arc's prosthetic left knee.

No, not that. She wanted reality, honesty. She wanted the real person, the real woman, Arc. Moving again, she slid herself against Arc's upthrust leg, breaking their kiss and pushing her breasts against Arc's face. Tender kisses – hesitant but with a restrained hunger, landed on their slopes, skipped across her nipples.

Pell knew what she wanted, knew in an instant – but she didn't have the tools to ask, didn't have the tools to even frame the request.

She wanted one of those metal, plastic, alloy, legs off. She wanted the raw reality of Arc's stump, the chopped-off harshness of her. Real flesh, real blood, real scars. She wanted to make love to that, to take it into herself – through her mouth, through her cunt, through her heart. She wanted it, could see it, taste it, feel it. An abrupt mass of scars, like a tightly closed mouth. The black dots where the electronics emerged to mate with the limb. It wasn't the ugliness of what she knew was between Arc and her limb that had her weak, pulsing with desire; it was the thought of finally making love to Arc, the real one, the painful and raw one.

A hand between her legs, slipping between her thighs. A hand between her legs, slipping between her cunt-lips – finding her clit. A gentle tap, a smooth rhythm, and with it Pell let her mind race, let her mind go where her lips couldn't.

A loosening of the socket, a few minor adjustments to divorce rubber gasket from leg, then the peeling of rubber from raw stump. The smell of it, like old worn clothing, like a well-exercised armpit. Maybe dirt, maybe something like earwax. But real, solid, raw. She'd like to taste it, to bring a bit of Arc into herself. Something like snot, maybe something like cunt-juice when she hadn't washed for a while. Real, though – so real.

She wanted that reality in her. She wanted to lie back, to

spread herself as wide as she could, to swallow that actuality –
to have Arc move herself, position herself to those scars, that
tissue, was pressing harder and harder against her lips. She
wanted Arc inside her, wanted the pure skin, the pure gristle,
the pure essence of Arc inside her cunt, inside her. She
wanted Arc to make love to her – with nothing in the way.

There, right there – the thought of stump pushing aside
lips, of wetness closing around scars, of a bigness beyond any
fist, pushed Pell over. The come wasn't something really
physical, though it did have all the notes, all the tempo: it was
a shaking, an emotional blast through her body. Like a come,
she shook and squirted clear liquid down onto Arc's fingers,
soaking the bed once again. Like a come, she felt faint, felt
her heart hammering in her chest. Like a come, her breath
was short and quick.

Unlike just a come, the feeling lasted, a cool sadness. A
knowledge of futility. Only in her dream, only in her fantasy
– raw reality. Only in her mind, the real Arc, the real flesh,
the real bone.

She wasn't tired, but she crawled up and curled up onto
Arc's body. She knew she must have been heavy, but didn't
care. She felt her sweaty skin slide over Arc's cool body and,
slowly, she positioned herself so that all she touched, all she
made contact with, was nothing but Arc.

Arc left in the morning. If she would come back or not, Pell
didn't know. She cared, of course, but didn't know if Arc did.

She sat by the dirty window for close to an hour, feeling the
revelation, the secret knowledge. At the end of that hour she
wanted Arc all the more, feeling privileged at having touched
as much as she had.

Pell had finally seen Arc, herself. That was the real time
ahead, the real choices: maybe Pell would leave – walk away
from the memories of days with Arc. Maybe she would stay,
and watch her lover barricade herself within an artificial
body – retreat against Pell's caring, her love.

Maybe she'd be back, maybe with more parts, maybe with

THE COMFORT OF WOMEN

Michael Hemmingson

ONE

I'd been celibate for five years. I didn't think I was a bad-looking man – women had found me appealing in the past – but between the ages of twenty-two and twenty-seven, I hadn't touched a woman and a woman hadn't touched me. I'd created my own isolation, going from one dumb job to another, spending my time alone in a studio apartment, writing. My first novel was published in an irregular paperback format by a small press operated by an enthusiastic fellow, reminiscent of those old City Lights Pocketbooks. It fitted easily in my back pocket and not too many people read it, despite all the good reviews. The whole matter was a solitary experience with no one to share it with.

One day, I received a letter from an English professor at the local university, Barry McGinnis. He wrote that he'd gotten my address from the publisher of my book, and how the book was an unknown work of genius, and that he'd like to meet me.

I put the letter aside.

A month later, the professor called on the phone.

"Your publisher is an old buddy of mine, a former student, in fact," McGinnis said. "Hope you don't mind. I got your number from him."

"No," I said. "I meant to call you. I did get your letter."

"Listen, why don't we meet for a beer?"

I met the professor at a pub near the campus, and listened to him talk about how great he thought my work was. He'd not only read my novel – and assigned it to one of his classes – but had seen my work in various and (quite) obscure literary journals and underground publications.

"You go by Nicholas?" McGinnis said. "Or –"

"Nicky."

"Nicky, Nicky Bayless – where'd you go to school?"

"College?"

"Yes."

"Never went."

"No degree? No creative writing program?"

"No."

"Probably a good thing," McGinnis said, nodding his head, his long grayish-black bushy hair bouncing. "But you know, I bet I could get you into the MFA program here."

"With no BA?"

"Hell, your published work will vouch your worthiness," the professor said. "I bet I could get you a nice fellowship, too."

And that's just what Barry McGinnis did.

TWO

I met Alexia in one of the graduate courses Barry McGinnis taught. She had a quirky look to her I found appealing – thick, dark-rimmed glasses; a white streak in her otherwise jet black hair; an odd-assortment of attire, cool in this age of awkwardness; when geekiness, coupled with intelligence, was sexy. She was one of the regulars who hung out at the pub where I first encountered McGinnis – often this crowd was orbiting around him, a charismatic man in his own right. He was at the pub three nights a week, and I soon found myself there as well. Alexia was there. I was sort of the odd-ball, I felt, brought into this circle by McGinnis because of my book and not my academic struggle (and I had a new book, a collection of stories, coming out from another small, obscure publisher).

One night, at the pub, McGinnis wasn't there, and many people departed. I sat drinking beer with Alexia and Bart (a blond surfer poet) and his bombshell blonde girlfriend, Randi. We all decided to go to a different bar and play pool – Alexia was *insistent* on this particular bar, telling us all we'd like it very much.

It was an OK bar. Bart and Randi wanted to play pool, which wasn't my thing. Alexia bought a pitcher of beer and we sat together.

Bart was bending, ready to take a shot at the table, his rear end very close to us. "Get your butt somewhere else," Alexia said, "or I'll take a pool stick and shove it up –"

"*Oh, yeah*," said Randi.

"That's not very nice," I said. "How'd you like it if someone stuck a pool stick in your ass?"

Alexia raised her brows. "I just might like it."

That was the first clue I didn't get – I wasn't paying attention. I'd recall in hindsight, yes, as well as overhearing her talk about how her favorite scene in *Last Tango in Paris* was when Marlon Brando put butter up his young lover's backdoor before sodomizing her.

Bart and Randi left (we'll get back to them in another chapter), and Alexia and myself finished the pitcher of beer.

"What will you do now?" Alexia said.

"I don't know," I said.

"Drink more?"

"I don't know."

She took her glasses off and looked at them. "I live a block away, you know."

"No," I said, "I didn't know."

This was the second clue – and I wasn't paying attention.

"Well," she said.

"Maybe we can go there," I said.

She put her glasses back on. "OK."

We walked up the block to her place, which was a small cottage. It was nice, a little messy. I asked how much she paid for it.

"Nothing," she said. "My parents own the property."

"Nice."

"I don't work," she said. "I go to school. Like you."

"I used to work. I worked too much. Dumb jobs, blah blah blah. Now I have a fellowship."

"What about your book?"

"I don't make any money from that."

"Oh. I have it, your book."

"Really?"

"I didn't read it."

"That's OK."

"Dr McGinnis said I should."

"*Listen* to him."

"I have beer, I think," she said, going to the kitchen.

I sat on the couch in the small living room.

Alexia returned with two Budweisers. "Yes, I have beer."

She sat next to me.

I don't remember what we talked about. On the floor, I noticed an action figure of the Warner Brothers Martian from the Bugs Bunny cartoon. "I always loved that Martian," I said.

"Me, too," she said, going to the floor and picking it up. "Marvin the Martian. 'I'm going to destroy planet Earth!' " I touched her hair. She put her head in my lap. It was nice to touch somebody.

"I, um, I don't know what to do," I said.

"What?"

"I haven't been with anyone in a while."

"I don't believe that."

"It's true."

"It's a line," she said. "Do you like me?"

"Yes," I said.

"I like you." She got on the couch with me and we began to kiss. She had to take her glasses off: they were getting in the way. We kissed for a long time. She pushed me back on the couch, and lay on top of me. I grabbed her ass, put my hands down her skirt.

She pulled her mouth from mine. "*Bad* boy," she said.

I grabbed her head, and we kissed more.

When I tried to touch her cunt, she stopped me.

"No," she said.

"Sorry," I said.

"Don't worry about it," she said, and we kissed.

When I touched her breasts over the fabric of her blouse, she pushed them away. "Now, now," she said.

"Sorry," I said.

She took one of my hands and put it back on her ass. "Play with that."

I did, and we kissed. My hand, and my second hand, were all over her butt.

"Hey," Alexia said, "rub my asshole."

"What?"

"With your finger," she said, and I found her asshole with my finger. "In small circles," she said, "yeah, like that —"

She pulled away from me, and sat. She took the finger I'd been rubbing her with, put it in her mouth, sucked on it. She smiled, and gave my finger back. She put her glasses on.

"What's wrong?" I asked, moving to her, wanting to kiss her more.

"Nothing," she said. "I have to pee."

"Hey." I grabbed her hand as she stood up. "Can I watch?"

"You want to watch me pee?"

"Yes," I said.

"I need a commitment before I go that far," she said.

"We hardly know each other."

"Exactly," she said, and went to the bathroom.

I sat there. I got up, and followed. The door was unlocked,

and I went in. Alexia was sitting on the toilet; she glanced up at me. She smiled and said, "You." I could hear the stream of her urine. I sat on the floor, cross-legged.

"You're bold," she said.

"The door was unlocked."

"There *is* no lock."

"I couldn't resist."

She stood up. "OK, Mr Bold. Clean me."

"With my mouth?"

"*Ab*solutely not."

I would've done it with my mouth, if she'd asked. I took a wad of toilet paper, and wiped her cunt. She pulled her panties up.

"I have to go, too," I said.

"Then I get to watch," she said. "*Quid pro quo.*"

She took my place on the floor; I stood in front of the toilet, took my cock out, and started to go.

Alexia made a weird sound. She moved, snagged my cock, and put her mouth before it, drinking my urine; what she didn't get flowed out of her mouth, down her chin, and into the bowl. I liked the sound this made. I breathed hard; it was an experience in itself watching her drink from me.

She pressed her face to my leg. "Nicky, I'm sorry. I couldn't help myself," she said, softly. "Now you know my fetish. OK, I'm weird. You'll never love me."

"I could love you," I said.

"Do you mean that?"

"Yes."

"Will you kiss me, to prove it?" she asked.

"Yes," I said.

She stood, and we kissed, and I tasted her – and me.

"I want to make love to you," I said.

"No, I can't," she said.

Alexia left the bathroom and sat on the edge of her bed. I sat next to her; we both fell back. It was a nice, big, comfortable bed, the kind of bed I liked; the kind of bed I didn't have.

"It's late," she said, moving away from me. "I'm a little drunk."

"Me, too," I said.

"You can stay here," she said, "if you want."

"I'd like that."

"I'd like it, too," she said, standing. "I'm going to turn the light off."

"OK."

In the dark, I saw her silhouette; she was removing her clothes. I also took my clothes off, and got under the covers. She joined me; we didn't touch. My hand went to her body. She was still wearing her bra and panties. I moved closer to her, kissed her.

"I don't think I want to screw," she said.

"OK," I said.

"I mean, I'm not sure if I can."

"OK."

"I'm not sure if I'm in the right frame of mind."

"OK."

"It's not *OK*," she said. "You don't understand, you don't know."

"I *want* to," I said.

"I know you do."

"Alexia," I said.

"It's nice having you in my bed," she said.

"It's nice to be in a bed with someone." She placed her head on my chest, and then a hand, playing with the hair. We were quiet, touching each other. Her hand moved down, and grasped my cock.

"This is nice," she said.

"Yes," I said, "it is."

"Nice . . ."

I kissed her on the head.

"I know," she said, and, "I'm twenty-eight years old."

"Yeah?"

"I'm still a virgin."

I laughed, after a moment.

"This is true," she said.

"Now *who* is giving *who* a line?"

She let go of my cock. "Nicky, listen. I'm Jewish. I'm not a nice Jewish girl, but I'm Jewish and a virgin. I come from a really hard-ass strict Jewish family, even though, like I said, well, I made up my mind years ago that I would save myself for my husband, because some day I plan to marry a nice Jewish man, I mean my family won't have it any other way. And this man will expect me to be a virgin."

"I see."

"No you don't see," she said. "I don't expect you to understand. Other men haven't. Like I said, I'm twenty-eight. This doesn't mean I'm sexual. *Ob*viously I'm sexual, and I have fetishes. I'm really pretty basic in that matter – I have a pee fetish, and a butt fetish. I mean, I'm a virgin, *vaginally*, but I like having sex in my butt."

Things started to come together for me – the pool stick remark, her living close to the bar she wanted to go to. "You lured me here," I said, "from the bar."

"Of course. I'm terribly attracted to you. I want you. I want you inside me. But I want more than a fuck-buddy. I had a fuck-buddy for a while, for a few months: it was just sex, nothing more. I didn't like it. I mean, it was OK, but it wasn't me. It was a different me."

"He fucked you in the ass?"

"Yes. I don't know if he liked it that much. Some men do, some don't." I'd only had anal sex with a woman once, and I think I was nineteen or twenty.

"I want you to fuck me," Alexia said, "but I'm looking for more than just fucking."

"I'm not a nice Jewish boy."

"I'm not looking for a husband. I'll do that in my thirties, maybe my forties. I'm looking for companionship, closeness, a little love. Devotion, all that."

"Sounds nice," I said.

"Yes. It sounds – it sounds nice." She took her panties off. "I'd like you to fuck me," she said. "I want you to."

"I don't have a condom." I felt stupid.

"I'm not going to get pregnant this way," she said.

Lubricant?" I asked, thinking the last time I'd done this, I had to use a lot of petroleum jelly.

"Spit is fine," Alexia said. She spit into her hand, put her hand between her ass-cheeks. She spit into her hand again, and rubbed the saliva over my cock. "I'm getting impatient," she said.

I moved on top of her, feeling inexpert. Alexia reached back, took my cock, and guided me into her ass – where it slid in just fine, without hesitation or resistance. The warmth of her interior sent a tingle up my body and soul. Alexia whispered, "Oh boy," and pushed her rear up, hard, slamming into my pelvis. I looked down at the streak in her hair, which was scattered about the back of her neck and on the bed with the rest of her hair. I swear she had an orgasm, I wasn't sure, but mine came quickly, and it was a lot; I emptied myself inside her.

We lay next to each other, and Alexia commented on the amount of semen I'd gushed out, that she liked how it felt up her ass, and coming out her ass.

She touched and played with my cock and balls, and soon I was hard again. She got on top of me. "This position is always tricky," she said, sitting down on my cock and sliding it in. She leaned forward to kiss me, and it popped out, covered in semen from that first ejaculation. Alexia giggled, and put my cock back in her. I reached for the light. "What are you doing?" she said.

"I want to see you."

"I like the light off."

"OK."

"Oh, turn it on if you want."

I did. She still wore her bra; her hair was a mess. I reached to unclasp her bra and she pushed my hand away; my cock slipped out of her.

"Let's try it like this," I said, gently pushing her off me and onto her back. I put her legs on my shoulders; I didn't need her help to find my way in. I was deep in her now.

"I like this," she said.

"I can kiss you," I said, and did.

"Kiss me more."

I did.

"Fuck me harder."

I did, and I came inside her again.

"I have to piss," I said to her. "Do you want it?"

She made a noise, reached up and bit my right nipple, hard.

"Ouch," I said.

I took her hand, pulling her from the bed, and took her to the bathroom, where she sat before the toilet as I urinated. She drank just about all of it. Then she sucked and licked at my cock for a while, eyes closed.

We went back to bed, in each other's arms, and fell asleep.

I woke up, the next morning, with Alexia messing around with my ass. She had her face down there – I was lying sideways – licking from my balls to my crack. I'm not sure how long she'd been doing this, but it was a nice thing to wake up to. She pushed me onto to my stomach, spreading my buttocks, a light finger on my sphincter, then a tongue. She licked it a bit, asked me if I liked that. I did, of course – "Yes," I said.

She said, "I like it too," and licked more, harder this time, pushing the tip of her tongue into me like a thirsty animal at a waterhole. I felt saliva roll down onto my balls – a funny, ticklish feeling. She started to suck, making sounds that I can only describe as pleasantly perverse. She did this for the good part of an hour, as I lay there in ecstasy, having discovered a new world. She was still making wicked sucking sounds, and there was a soft hum from the back of her throat.

She turned me over, and sucked on my cock for a bit. "My mouth is getting tired," she said. "Can you fuck me?"

She was on her hands and knees, and I took her from behind. I grabbed her hips, and slammed myself inside and out of her. I wanted to come in her mouth: this image was in my head. I told her this. She turned around and took me in her mouth, and I came.

And that's how I ended my period of celibacy.

★   ★   ★

I didn't see Alexia again for over a week. We played phone tag, then she stopped calling, and she didn't come to class (it was a once-a-week thing). I drove to her place; her car was there, but no one answered the door.

The next morning, she answered her phone.

"Hey," I said.

"Hey."

"Where you been?"

"Nowhere," she said.

"I was worried."

"Were you?"

"Yes."

"You really were?"

"Yes."

"That's sweet," she said.

"What's going on?"

"Nothing really," she said. "I've been depressed."

"Depressed?"

"I get that way sometimes."

"About what?"

"This and that."

"I see."

"Don't you ever get depressed?" she asked.

"Well, yes," I said.

"When I get depressed, I get depressed big," she said.

"But you're OK?"

"Yeah," she said, "I'm OK."

She didn't sound OK.

"I've been thinking about you," I said.

"You have? I've been thinking a lot about you. What've you been thinking about?"

"You," I said, "and your ass; how I'd like to be fucking you, how I'd like to lick your ass like you did mine. I've never done that to anyone before."

"I wonder about this," she said.

"What?"

"You could come over," she said.

"When?"

"Now."

I rushed over.

Alexia was wearing a thick, terry-cloth robe, no glasses. We immediately embraced. Her body felt warm and nice.

"Do you want something to eat?" she asked. "I was going to make grilled cheese sandwiches."

"I love grilled cheese sandwiches."

I sat in her small kitchen and watched her cook. We ate the sandwiches in the living room.

"We should've gotten together again sooner," she said.

"Yes," I said.

"What've you been doing?"

"Writing."

"Anything good?"

"I don't know. Another novel."

"About?"

I smiled. "This and that."

"So be it."

"Essays," I said. "I've been writing essays lately for *The USA Viewpoint*."

"Really. That's a big magazine, isn't it?"

"I think so. They pay well."

"What do you write?"

"Opinions, views – viewpoints!"

"Your look at the nation."

"And the world."

"I should be impressed," she said.

"You're not impressed?"

"I'm impressed," she said. "But I'm more impressed with what you want to do with that mouth and tongue. Did you mean what you said? You want to get nasty with my butt?"

"*Very*," I said.

She took my hand, led me to the bedroom. She removed her robe, was naked underneath. I looked at the dark, thick bush of pubic hair between her legs, something I hadn't noticed the last time. Alexia was on her stomach, spread-eagled. I didn't waste time getting to work on her, finding her puckered asshole and going to work at it with my tongue.

Alexia seemed to enjoy my effort, wiggling her hips back and forth. I reached to touch her cunt, thinking she'd like this, but she told me not to touch it, was very adamant about that. I continued to lick and suck, and then she touched herself, and she came. I moved up, my cock out now, my pants down to my ankles, and entered her.

We fucked for the rest of the night, and I stayed there. I stayed there for several days, engulfed in nothing but nasty sex, fucking her in the ass, pissing in her mouth, her face buried in my crotch and rear.

It was fun.

In between, we slept, ate, drank, and talked. It was the usual talk – the past, our lives, our families. She was very close to her family (as I'd already gathered) and wanted me to meet her mother and father and two brothers, and some aunts and cousins tossed in. I nodded my head, but I was never comfortable meeting my lovers' families, both in the act and the thought. We parted, as people must part – I went back to my life, she did what she did.

She called two days later, a Sunday. I was working on the novel.

"My family is having a big dinner tonight," she said. "Do you want to come over and meet them?"

"Well," I said. "Not tonight, I can't."

"You can't?"

"I'm on a roll."

"You just don't want to meet them," Alexia said, an accusation. I guess she could hear it in my voice.

"I'd feel weird."

"Why?"

"I just would."

"It'd mean a lot to me," she said. "I told my mother about you."

"You did? *What'd* you tell her?"

"Not *that*," she said. "Just that – I'd met this guy. I told her: 'I met this great guy.' "

"Oh." I felt like shit.

"You *are* my boyfriend," she said, "right?"

"Yes," I said. I liked the way it sounded.

"I'd like you to come."

"How about next time?"

"Oh, fuck it," she said, and hung up.

I tried calling her back. She didn't answer.

She didn't come to class the next time, either.

Over beers at the pub, I asked Barry McGinnis about her.

"She's a strange one," Barry said.

"Well," I said.

"Fucking her?"

"You could say that."

"I had a feeling," Barry said. "Well, fucking is a good thing. There are plenty of fuck opportunities around here."

"She's kinky," I said.

Barry had this look on his face. "Really?"

I knew that look. "You didn't fuck her, did you?" I asked.

"Well," Barry said, drinking his beer. "Not exactly. Look. OK. This was last year. It was two a.m., the bar had closed, she was sitting in my car with me. We made out, she was reaching down my pants. Then she stops and says, 'I can't.' 'You can't?' She said, 'I can't.' And that was that. There's always been this strange tension between us since. So," he asked, "how kinky is she?"

I told him.

"Wow," Barry said. "Hey, it's my birthday next week. Big party at my place. Do bring Alexia."

"Don't get any ideas."

"*I* never have ideas."

Alexia called the next day. "I guess you should know something about me."

"You're an alien?"

"Sometimes I think so," she laughed. "No. I mean. I'm manic depressive, I mean."

"Who isn't?"

"I'm serious. I get into these bad funks sometimes. That's why I haven't gone to class."

"It's not me?" I asked.

"A little bit, I suppose," she replied. "It's mostly me. My screwed-up head. Do you want to come over?"

"Of course I do."

"In maybe an hour? I need to straighten up a bit."

"An hour," I said.

An hour later, I was there.

I kissed her; it wasn't a long one – she pulled back.

"Hey," she said.

"Hey," I said.

She had the fridge stocked with beer, and we sat on the couch and had a few. The TV was on, no sound. It was an awkward moment again.

"I need someone," she said. "I'm not sure if now is the right time."

"I'm never sure," I said. "I need someone, too. We all do, right? That's what I'm told."

"I'm twenty-eight and I feel like I haven't done shit with my life. OK, OK, so I'm getting my Master's, but so what? Me and a million people. I have all these things in my head that I want to do. I want to write novels like you. I have novels in my head. I just don't know how to write them. And movies. I have screenplays in my head, whole movies."

"Just sit down at your computer and write them," I said.

"Easy for you to say. Maybe you can do that. I can't. I tried, I mean I really tried. I can't. And that's what drives me crazy. That and a zillion other things. I really do want to make movies. I have a camera. It's hidden away: you haven't seen it. I have a camera, I have ideas, I want to make movies. Write books. Compose songs. Maybe even act, you know? So many things. But I'll never do these things."

"You don't know that."

"That's what the little voice in my head says. The Devil on my shoulder. 'Alexia, stop fooling yourself, you could never do those things.' And my parents, they don't care – they think it's all silly. 'Alexia, an artist? How sweet.' They don't even think much about my getting an MA. 'You already have a Bachelor's, Alexia, why waste your time further?' They just want me to get married. Before I'm thirty. 'You need to get married soon, you know,' my mother says. You know, you know – when I told my mother about you, when I said, 'I met this great guy,' she said, 'Is he husband material?' You know what I said?"

"*He's a pervert, Mom!*"

"I'm the pervert. 'No,' I said, 'he may be for someone else, Mother, but he's not Jewish.' 'Not Jewish,' my Mother said, 'why are you wasting your time, Alexia?' And that's just it, Nicky – *wasting time*. I'm always *wasting* time. I don't mean you. I mean in general, my life in general – I always feel like I'm wasting my time! I should be – *doing* something else, I think. I envy you, in your way, how you're always spending your time writing this and that. This is what makes me so depressed – I feel like I'm getting old and I've done nothing."

"You're not old."

"I feel like it," she said. "And yes, I need to get married, right? Find a nice Jewish man who'll take care of me, and bear his fucking children for him. Lose my virginity, keep my secret desires hidden, for surely he'll be offended. And I won't have to *work*. He'll take *care* of me; I'll stay home and raise the kids. OH FUCK, NICKY, I DON'T WANT THAT KIND OF FUCKING LIFE! THAT'S NOT ME!! BUT WHAT AM I GOING TO DO?!? MY PARENTS EXPECT THIS OF ME! MY WHOLE FAMILY DOES!! 'WHEN IS ALEXIA GOING TO GET HER HEAD STRAIGHT AND MARRY AND START A FAMILY LIKE *NORMAL* PEOPLE DO???' "

I held her. She hit my chest with her fists . . . not hard.

"I'm sorry, I'm sorry," she said, wiping tears.

"It's all right," I said.

"It's *not* all right. You didn't come over for this."

"No, no, it's all right."

"You came here to fuck. So let's fuck."

"You don't seem in the right –"

"No," she said, "I *want* to fuck."

We went to the bed, took some of our clothes off, kissed a little. She wasn't into it, I wasn't into it.

We lay there.

"Barry McGinnis is having a birthday party next week," I said.

"How old's he going to be?"

"Forty-eight, I think," I said.

"I thought he was fifty."

"I'm not sure."

"You know what," she said.

"What?"

"I'm so pissed off at my whole family, everything, all of it," she said. "Fuck my heritage, fuck tradition. I feel like losing my virginity. Do you want to do that? Fuck my pussy? You can if you want."

"I'd like that," I said. "I never deflowered a virgin."

She laughed. "That sounded so silly, 'I never deflowered a virgin.' "

"It's true."

"Anyone ever tell you that you're melodramatic, some-times?"

"No."

"You are," she said. "Deflower on."

I got on top of her.

"Wait," Alexia said.

"What is it?"

"I can't."

"I have condoms in my car," I said.

"It's not that," she said. "I'm scared all of a sudden," she said. "I can't."

"Well," I said, "OK."

I rolled off her.

"Nicky, I'm sorry."

"It's all right."

"It was a wild moment in my head."

"I know."

"I'll suck you off," she said.

I woke up to the sound of shattering – something. Breaking. And cries. Alexia. She was cursing, and sobbing. In the kitchen. I went to her. There were broken plates and glasses all over the floor; Alexia was naked, standing there, her feet bleeding. Her face streaked with tears. She just looked at me. She cried out, and broke the rest of the plates.

I went to her, cautious. "What the hell are you doing?"

"I need help," she whispered.

I held onto her, and took her to the living room. She was trailing blood on the floor. I went to the bedroom, found her robe, brought it to her.

"My medicine," she said.

"What medicine?"

"You need to call my brother," she said. "It's bad."

"What? What?"

"Just call my brother, he'll know what to do."

She gave me a number, and I called. An office. I told the man on the other line I was a friend of Alexia's – "She told me to call –"

"She's at home?"

"Yes," I said.

"I'll be there."

Half an hour later, a man in his early thirties showed up, in a suit. He looked a little like Alexia. Alexia was curled up on the couch. He went to her, and helped her up.

"Come, now," he said. "Everything's OK."

I felt stupid standing there.

"It's OK," her brother told me. "It happens. I can handle it from here."

And they left me there. Alexia and her brother departed in his car, and I was alone in her place, with broken plates and glasses and a bad energy lingering.

I tiptoed through the kitchen, like a mine field, and got myself a beer. I needed a beer. And another. She had vodka, and I had some of that. I waited. Weren't they coming back? It was night. I finished the vodka and beer and I was drunk and went to sleep. I dreamed Alexia's ghost came to visit me. *Hello, Nicky, I'm dead.* I woke, sweating. I went back to sleep. I kept thinking she'd come in any minute, and join me, and we could make love. In the morning, I was still alone. I took a shower, washed up. In the bathroom cabinet, I found a large assortment of pills. I didn't know what they were all for. I knew what Prozac was for.

I remembered her brother's number and called it, told him who I was. "I was just wondering if she's OK," I said. "I'm worried."

"Oh, she's just fine," her brother said. "I took her to the hospital."

"The hospital?"

"Yes. It happens sometimes. They bandaged her feet. She'll be okay. She'll be out in a few days. She has her medication. You're a friend of hers?"

"Yes."

"You're a nice friend."

I locked her place up, and went home.

THREE

I went to Barry's birthday party alone.

Barry's party was well-attended – faculty from the school, students, writers, odd friends here and there. I drank, and I intended to get quite drunk. There were plenty of drugs going around, mostly pot and speed and I heard somewhere that someone had acid, but I couldn't find the acid. I think Barry was on acid – he was acting like it – and he'd done a lot of speed as well.

This is where I connected with Hanna.

Hanna was in the same class with me as Alexia, plus another class, and I'd never really taken note of her. She had tattoos, punk-style short hair dyed red, green, and blue, and wore baggy nondescript clothes. At the party, however, she wore a low-cut, short dress, showing a good portion of her milky white skin and assorted tats. Some time during the party, a good four hours into it, we started talking, and when we weren't talking, she was staring at me from across the party. She was pretty drunk (and on acid, I found out later) and I wondered what the sudden interest was. Well, I didn't care. I found myself sitting on the outside stairs and talking with her, and we got closer, mentioning how we liked each other, and then we were kissing.

"Oh," she said, looking down. "Oh, I'm drunk."

"Me, too."

"Kiss me again, man."

I did.

"This is funny," I said. "I had no idea you liked me."

"Neither did I. I just found out tonight. Maybe it's the acid."

"You have acid?"

"I took acid. You want to fuck me?"

"Yeah."

"We need to find a place to fuck."

We searched out and discovered Barry, who was swaying about, a beer in both hands.

"Barry," I said, "we need a place to fuck."

"Well," Barry said, "you should use the guest room."

We were all hanging onto each other, so we wouldn't fall.

"Thanks," Hanna said, and kissed Barry. He kissed her back. Then they were kissing quite passionately.

I smiled. "Maybe we should have a threesome."

"Hey," Barry said, "I'm there."

"Really?" Hanna said. "God, Dr McGinnis, I've been wanting to fuck you for a long time."

The three of us went to the guest room. It was dark, and we fell to the bed. Barry and I were all over Hanna, undressing her, kissing her, touching her. Hanna kept saying how much she wanted us both. Barry sat up and said, "I can't do this. What am I doing?"

"What?" Hanna said.

"If my wife walked in, she'd kill me," he said. "I'm in enough trouble as it is."

The last I saw his wife, she was lying in the grass, on acid, staring at the stars.

"Damn," Hanna said.

"Some other time," Barry said, and kissed her. He left.

"Come here and fuck me," Hanna said, and I got on top of her. After a minute, she said, "Wait!"

"What is it?"

She got up and ran to the bathroom, closing the door. I listened, heard her throwing up. I left the bedroom and rejoined the party, which was starting to scatter at this point. Barry's wife was still on the grass and Barry was snorting a line of speed in the living room.

"Back so soon?" Barry asked.

"Hanna's sick," I said.

"Ah, ah," he sniffed. "Well, really, look, Nicky, this threesome sounds like fun: we have to do it a different time."

I suddenly realized I didn't think sharing a woman with Barry, as much as I liked him, would be my thing.

I made myself a tequila tonic, and went outside. I sat on the stairs.

Hanna joined me. Her dress was back on. "Sorry 'bout that."

"You OK?"

"I'm OK."

"Sure?"

"It happens. I've puked before."

"Can I have a kiss?"

"I puked."

"That's OK."

We kissed. She didn't taste like anything bad.

"The party seems to be ending," I said.

"Parties end, you go home."

"I'm too drunk to drive."

"I can drive."

"You're on acid."

"I'm coming down," she said. "That puke sobered me up. I can drive, believe me. You want me to drive you home?"

"That'd be nice."

We said our goodbyes, and got into her car, a small two-seater.

"You want to come home with me?" she asked.

"Yes," I said.

She lived in the graduate housing section on campus, a studio apartment, really, which was packed with books, CDs, clothes, a water bed, and a Fender electric guitar – not to mention a single goldfish in a bowl that, Hanna told me, had no name. It was around three in the morning when we got there.

"I feel so weird," Hanna said, "and I feel so good."

We lay on the waterbed, kissed and touched.

"Does my goldfish look weird to you?" she asked.

"Looks like a goldfish."

"I think he may be getting sick," she said. "I've had him all year."

I remembered that it was almost the end of the school year – I'd entered the program in the spring semester. Summer was close. I hadn't felt this since high school – summer, no school, what to do? I wanted Hanna.

"I know this is gonna sound bad, man," she told me, "but I'm not sure if we should fuck."

"Oh, boy," I said.

"What?"

"Nothing."

"I mean I wanna fuck, of course I wanna fuck, but I'm always fucking. I mean, fucking guys I just meet. I have to stop this. I started this two years ago. I was raped. After I was raped, I just fucked any guy who walked by. It messes with my head. I'm sorry."

I was actually tired, and suggested we sleep. Hanna couldn't sleep – the acid was still in her, and she'd done some speed.

We undressed. I liked looking at her tattoos – a dragon on her back, a snake on her left arm, a spider above her right tit, assorted butterflies and black roses on her hip, near her cunt, and on her legs. It was four-thirty in the morning.

I got on top of her.

We woke up early that afternoon, fucked again, dressed, and went onto campus to get something to eat. Slices of thick pizza, ice cold soda. I needed a beer.

"Damn, you know," Hanna said, "I have this paper to write."

"On?"

"Comparison of the poetry of Sharon Olds and Carolyn Forsche."

"I love both their work."

"You know their work?"

"Of course I know their work," I said.

"Not too many guys . . ." She shrugged.

"When's the paper due?"

"Two days."

"Two days?"

"Twelve pages."

"Two days," I said.

"I always wait until the last minute," she said. "And I always get As. I'm an A student: ask Dr McGinnis."

"A as in ass?"

"What?"

"Guess you need to work on that paper today," I said.

"Tomorrow." She finished the last bite of her pizza. "I want to fuck you some more today."

FOUR

Hanna was twenty-two, used to play in a rock band, was now an MA candidate in comparative lit (obviously). She was worried about her goldfish, but the goldfish seemed fine to me, as far as goldfish go. Our sex that day was fun and normal – we kept to several positions, we didn't do anything kinky. I liked being with her, enclosed in her room, the world just the two of us. The world was fucked, and Hanna knew this as well as me. She'd had some bad experiences – the rape, yes, and a short stint as a heroin addict when she was a teenager, and the death of a brother by a drive-by shooting.

"I've seen your novel at the bookstore," she told me, "but I haven't read it. I'd like to."

I gave her a copy.

That evening, I decided I should leave. I needed a change of clothes, a shower; I needed to go home and be alone for a little while, maybe write. Hanna needed to work on her paper.

"Don't worry," she said, hugging me, "I'll get it done on time. I always do."

"Good, good."

"Well."

"Well."

"I always hate this part," she said. "You want to see me again?"

"Yes," I said. "When?"

She shrugged. "Let's just flow."

I went by Barry's office. He was going through his mail.

"Nicky," he said, "this was left on my door."

It was a small envelope, to me from Hanna.

"Look," he said, "I'm not your mail service."

Dear Nicky,

I'm leaving this letter on Dr McGinnis' door because I don't have your number and I don't know how to reach you. We should've exchanged phone numbers! What was I thinking? I need you! God, I can't believe what's going on. All I can think about is you being here, holding me in your arms and making me feel safe. I read your novel and it made me cry. The ending was so sad. I haven't felt so sad in a long time. It is a good kind of sad, the kind of sad that makes you think about love and the world. I wrote my paper and now I just want you here inside me. PLEASE CALL IMMEDIATELY!

Love,
Hanna

She left her number, and I called.

"I knew it'd be you," she said.

"Psychic?"

"Just hope."

"The letter was nice," I said.

"Just get over here," she said.

"I don't know why I didn't notice you before," Hanna said, after sex. "I can't get your face out of my mind now. Even looking at your face, I also see it in my mind."

"So you see two faces."

"Someone else noticed you, I could tell. Alexia."

"I know."

"You slept with her?"

"A few times, yes."

"Are you still?"

"Well, no," I said.

"She's pretty."

"Yes."

"I'd fuck her."

"You're bi?"

"When the time is right," she said. "I was gay, for a year. Before I was raped. I had a girlfriend. We lived together. We were in a band together."

"You loved her?"

"I loved her very much," she squeezed me. "Right now, I'm straight as an arrow, with Nicky Bayless. Tell me what she was like."

"Alexia?"

"Yeah. What happened to her anyway?"

"She's – sorting out her life."

"Aren't we all? What was she like?"

"She's a nice person."

"I mean in bed, man."

I laughed. "You won't believe it."

"I won't?"

I told her everything about Alexia – except the broken plates and glasses.

"I believe that," Hanna said. "I hear women from the Mediterranean are like that, too. Not the golden shower stuff, just – you know. You know what? I've never done anal sex."

"No?"

"Nope. For no reason, really. It just never came up. Huh –
it's weird, I guess."

"Well," I said.

She smiled. "You wanna say, 'Can I deflower you?' "

Too much of Alexia was inside my head, and I tried to
push her out. But she *was* there. "Yeah," I said.

"I don't know," Hanna said.

I pulled her close to me.

She said, "You, you."

I grabbed her short hair and kissed her.

"Tell me," Hanna said, "what you wanna do to me."

"Your ass," I said, like I was delirious. "I want your ass."

"Like Alexia?"

"Like you."

"There's a first time for everything," she said.

I played with her butt, fingers exploring. Hanna's ass was
meatier than Alexia's, an alabaster white. I went down on her
ass, my tongue pressing against her virgin pucker. I asked if
she liked this and she said it felt nice. Next, I slid a finger into
her. She liked this very much. I finger-fucked her for a good
half hour, my other hand at her cunt, and I made her come.

"This is so good," she said.

"Do you feel ready to be fucked in the ass?"

"The finger is nice," she said, "but a whole cock?"

I took my finger out of her, and put it in my mouth.
"You're yummy."

"Let's do it."

"You have Vaseline?"

"Cabinet, bathroom."

I went to the bathroom, got the Vaseline, applied some to
my cock, to her ass, and tried to get in her. Hanna was on her
stomach, butt up. I got the head of my cock in her when she
cried out, "Oh, shit, oh, crap, no! OWW! FUCK! TAKE IT
OUT!"

I removed myself.

She turned around. "It's not me, it's just not me. A
tongue, a finger, sure, but not a fucking dick, man."

"I'm sorry," I said.

"I'm sorry," she said. "You really wanted me that way."
"I'll live."
"I want to please you."
"You do."
"Lie back." A hand pushed my chest.

Hanna took me in her mouth. She deep-throated me, her nose pressed into my pubic hair. I immediately shot into her mouth.

"I usually don't like the taste of come," she told me. "Yours is OK."
"Just OK?"
"Wanna taste?" She moved to kiss me.
"Hey, it is OK."
"I really did cry at the end of your book," she said later.
"So did I," I said. "When I was writing it."
"You've felt pain."
"Sure."
"Pain is sexy."
"Never thought about it like that."
"I don't mean physical pain. I mean here," she touched her head, "and here," touching her chest, "the pain inside. Maybe I mean sadness. Maybe I'm a cerebral masochist."
"I like that: 'cerebral masochist'."
"I love you," she said.
"You do?"
"Is it OK to say that?"
"We hardly know each other."
"I fall in love pretty fast. Don't say 'I love you' back. Because you don't."
I didn't.

FIVE

"Fuck her," Bart said, "I want to watch you fuck the shit out of her."

Lying naked on the bed, Randi smiled. She was on acid and pot and vodka and coke and I don't know what else. I was with them, the both of them, in Bart's apartment, and I wasn't quite sure how I got there. We were at the pub, but it was summer, and there wasn't the usual crowd – there wasn't any Barry McGinnis or Hanna or even Alexia.

Bart found it funny that I was sleeping with Hanna.

"Funny? Why is that so funny?" I asked.

"She doesn't seem your type," he said.

"My type?"

"Or Alexia," he said.

"What's my type?" I asked.

"You tell me. Take Randi, for example."

She was a few feet away, talking to someone, and she couldn't hear us.

"OK," I said.

"She looks good."

"Yes."

"Nice ass."

"Yes."

"Nice tits."

"Yeah."

"She's fuckable," Bart said.

"I imagine so."

"Sucks cock GOOD," Bart said.

"I imagine so."

"Is she your type?"

"She could be my type," I said.

"You want to fuck her?"

"What kind of question is that?"

"Nick," he said, "I like watching guys fuck her. It really turns me on."

Then we were at his place, and Randi got undressed and sat on the bed. We'd dropped acid before leaving the bar, and Randi was doing coke on the way.

"Who would've thought," Bart said, and laughed, and slapped me on the back.

I wasn't sure what he was getting at.

"C'mon, fuck her." Bart pulled up a chair.

Randi looked good. They were both beautiful and blonde and tan. While Bart was an MFA poet, Randi worked as a hostess of some upscale club downtown, and I knew she made good money at it. I could not help but feel aroused, especially looking at the blonde pubes between her legs. Randi saw what I was looking at and opened her legs. Her finger touched her clit, and made a circular motion. "You like what you see, Nicky?" she said. I did. I went down on her, engulfed her, got a mouthful, got a taste, ate her. The acid was hitting me pretty hard at this point. I put my tongue in her as far as I could get it. I was about to turn her over when Randi started pulling at my pants, saying she wanted my cock. Bart was getting a real kick out of this, sitting in the chair, drinking a Heineken. I was on my knees on the bed, and Randi was reaching around, cupping my balls with one hand, squeezing my ass with the other, and sucking me off. Then I had a condom on my cock, and I was fucking her. I fucked her several ways, and came. She peeled the condom off, and emptied my come into her mouth. Some of the semen spilled out the side of her lips, going down her neck and shoulder.

"Right on," Bart said.

Bart got on the bed, and I sat in the chair. I needed a beer. I watched Bart kiss her, my come still on her lips, in her mouth. Bart started fucking her, his ass going up and down. He had a perfect, round, tanned ass. Randi spread his ass with her hands, and said, "Hey, Nicky, would you like some of this?"

"Crazy woman," Bart laughed.

"I like watching men fuck him," she said, "as much as he likes watching men fuck me."

"I don't think Nick swings that way," Bart said.

"Do you or don't you?" she asked me.

I got up, and went to get a beer. Bart continued to fuck her.

Later, I wondered if I shouldn't have fucked Bart after all. I was in the mood for anything.

SIX

I had lunch with Alexia.

"You just vanished," I said.

"I had to," she said. "I don't expect you to understand."

"I want to understand," I said.

She wouldn't explain. Lunch was awkward, but it was good to see her. We went to a bar nearby to have a few drinks.

"Come home with me," I said.

"I can't," she said.

"We can go to your place," I suggested.

"You don't want me," she said. "You just want to fuck me."

"I want you," I told her, "I need you."

"You just want to fuck me," she said. "Fuck my ass, piss on me. You want the dirty world."

"The world *is* dirty," I said.

"I want the nice world," she said, and added, "I'm moving, Nicky."

"Moving?"

"To San Francisco," she said. "Next week."

"That's rather sudden."

"I've been thinking about it for a while."

"What about your Master's?"

"I can transfer to SFSU."

"What's in San Francisco?"

She said, "My family is not there."

I'd been playing around on the Internet more and more, and had discovered on-line chat and all the various channels and rooms. There were some local channels, where a lot of people from the University hung out; women, in particular. Or so they claimed. This is where I met Mo. Mo was her on-line name, and evidently what people called her in real life (short for Maureen, her real name).

My on-line play with Mo was consistent with that of many others: vampirism, sexual descriptions, strange adventures and scatology. It was fun, but for the most part, silly. I soon started to grow tired of it; it was all right when you were bored, but the novelty could only last for so long.

What are you doing right now? Mo typed.

Nothing, I wrote back. *Just sitting here.*

Why don't you come over?
Where do you live?
On campus, she replied, *at the student apartments.*

She gave me her address. I was leery at first, wondering if I was being set up. For all I knew, Mo could be a guy. She did tell me she was Asian, nineteen, and that people said she was pretty. What the hell, I believed her, and went to her place.

She was fortunate to be in the apartments and not the dorms, for an undergraduate, but still shared the apartment with three other young women (whom I had not met yet). Mo greeted me in a long white terry-cloth robe (like most kids at the University, she didn't get out of bed until afternoon). She was an exquisite young woman, and part of my delight was that she was, indeed, a young woman, and real at that. She was Asian, as she said, with dark slanted eyes, brown skin, and long black hair. She was tall and slender and she smiled and said, "Hello," and let me in. "So," she said, "you're WmGibson."

"WmGibson" was the screen name I used on line, a bad one at that, all the cyberpunk connotations laid right out.

"Actually," I said, "my name is Nick."

"You said."

"I did?"

"Yeah."

"Nicky," I said.

"I like 'WmGibson'," Mo said.

The apartment smelled of and looked of young women. I felt awkward, being older than Mo. I knew that many of the graduate students who were TAs slept with their freshmen students – it was all par for the course. But I wasn't a TA, and Mo wasn't one of my students. I was getting ahead of myself anyway – how did I know something of a sexual nature was going to occur between Mo and myself? Maybe she just invited me over to be friendly?

Mo offered me something to drink, and I said milk would be nice. She laughed at that, and said, "Don't you want a beer?"

"Not now," I said.

"I have milk," she said.

She got me a glass of milk and she had a soda. We talked some; it was small talk. Her robe kept opening, giving me a glance of cleavage, but she'd quickly close it. I was falling in lust. Mo never wiped away the sultry grin she maintained, and I couldn't read what was in her small dark eyes, often covered by strands of black hair. I detected something insidious. I didn't know if I should make a move or not.

"Let's get on-line," she suggested, "and tell everyone you're here. That should stir up some gossip."

It didn't sound exciting to me but I said why not. Mo lived to be on-line; she was a true William Gibson character in the flesh – bright, Asian, and Net-savvy. I asked about her heritage, and she said her family had come from Korea.

She took me to her bedroom, one of three in the unit. It was small and cluttered, with a single bed, a desk, and a Macintosh computer. It smelled feminine. There were clothes all over the floor – skirts, jeans, blouses, bras and panties.

She logged into one of the chatrooms we both frequented; sure enough, there were people we knew there, both on-campus and all over the globe.

Guess who is here in my room? Mo typed. *WmGibson!:^)*

Some people said hello to me, some said they didn't believe it.

"Say hello," Mo said to me, getting up from her desk.

I sat at the desk, Mo sat on the edge of her bed, which was very close to the desk.

Hey everyone, I typed. *It is me, WmGibson, aka Nicky Bayless, and I am here with Mo.*

Answers were like so:

No way!

Kiss Mo!

Jerk!

It's Mo fooling again.

I felt silly typing, *No it's really me.*

This is when Mo slipped her foot between my legs. First

she guided her naked foot, with clean, well-clipped nails, up my leg, leaned back on the bed, and got her foot into my crotch. This wasn't an easy thing to do, but I had my torso half-turned in the chair. I turned some more.

She sprung up, and came to me. She sat in my lap. She reached for the keyboard and typed: *Guess what I'm doing? Rubbing WmGibson's cock and balls with my left foot!*

She added: *I'm now trying to stick my big toe up his asshole. His asshole is resistant, but my toe is getting in there.*

I laughed, and she laughed.

As the chatroom clamor went on, I touched Mo – her back, her neck, her breasts. She stood, and we embraced. She ran her fingers through my hair and it felt very nice. I kissed her chest where the robe opened.

"I haven't showered in three days," she told me. "I must be gross."

"No," I said, although I could smell and taste her sweat.

I started to stand, to kiss her. She pushed me back in the chair.

"I don't kiss," she said.

"What?"

"Anyone."

"Why?"

"I hate saliva," she said. "Mouths, tongues: yuck."

We continued to embrace and touch. I pulled at the sash of her robe.

She said, "What do you think you're doing, little boy?"

"I want to see your body," I said. "You won't let me kiss you; let me see your body."

"Only for a second," she said.

She opened her robe, still in my arms, and revealed her young, beautiful frame. Medium-sized breasts with dark nipples, an outie-bellybutton, a very thick patch of black pubic hair. She then closed her robe and smiled and said, "*There*, you've seen it."

"Kiss me."

"No way."

I pulled her to me, my face pressed between her covered

breasts. She continued to run her fingers through my hair.

"Play on the Net," she said. "I'm going to take a shower."

"Now?"

"I *need* a shower."

She left me there, at her desk, and went into the shower. I heard the water run. I logged her account off, and logged into mine, getting back on the same chatroom channel.

Hey, someone named Nexus said, *are you really at Mo's place?*

Yes, I replied.

Cool, Nexus said.

I was getting all the signals wrong. Mo was naked in the shower; I could see the hot water hitting her brown body, the water rolling down it. I logged off, got up, and tried the bathroom door. It was unlocked. I went in.

"Is that you?" Mo said from the shower.

There was a lot of steam. I said, "Yes."

"It's about time," she said. "Get naked and join me."

I got naked and joined her.

We spent a good twenty minutes cleaning one another with a bar of soap, putting shampoo in each other's hair, and touching each other's sex. I took every opportunity I could get to feel her body – her neck, her chest, her breasts, her stomach, her ass, her cunt. She let me finger her clit, but wouldn't let me slide my finger in; each time I tried, she said, "No, not yet." Not yet? And she still would not kiss me on the lips; she allowed me to kiss other parts of her body, but not the lips. She took my very hard cock in her hand, stroked it, and took it in both hands. I made myself not come. We got out of the shower, and dried each other off. Naked, we went back to her bedroom. I pushed her toward the bed.

"I said I will not kiss you," she said.

"I know," I said, and put my mouth on her tits.

I reached for her cunt. She sat up. I laid on the bed, rubbed her back.

"You should know something," she said. "I'm a virgin."

"I've heard that before," I said, and stifled a sad – a very sad – laugh.

"What?" she said, and just when I thought she would tell me I could fuck her in the ass, Mo said, "I swallow."

"What's that?"

"I can suck like a crazy machine," she said.

"Show me," I said.

"I want to show you," she said, and did. She went down on my cock. She wasted no time, and had the whole thing in her mouth. She cupped my balls in her hand, squeezing just a little too hard. After the whole shower bit, I was ready to explode, and explode I did, several huge spurts of semen, which she swallowed completely.

"Yum," she said. "Reminds me, I'm hungry. You want to go get something to eat?"

"I want to eat you," I said.

"Not now, later," she said. She stood, and went to her closet. "I need food. I don't want to eat on campus."

"There's plenty of places to go," I said.

"OK," she said. "Don't watch me dress."

"I just like looking at you."

"I *don't* like people watching me dress. Go get your clothes on."

I went to the bathroom and retrieved my clothes, like a good boy.

We went to get pizza a few miles off campus. She ordered a beer and wasn't carded.

"So," said Mo, leaning back. "Tell me about Nicky Bayless, aka WmGibson."

"What's to tell?"

She leaned forward, voice low. "I can still taste your come in my mouth. The back of my mouth, really. You just pumped your come in my mouth and I don't know anything about you. Don't you think that's kinda weird, on my part?"

"I'm getting hard again."

"Good. I like guys who're always hard."

"Tell me about you," I said.

"I like sucking dick," she said. "I like to swallow. I could swallow all day."

"I'm twenty-eight," I said.

"Nice."

"Graduate student."

"Nice."

"I write things."

"Nice."

"But you know all this."

"Yes."

"So what do you want to know?"

"Do you have a girlfriend?"

"No."

"Do you want me to be your girlfriend?"

"Yes."

"Will you marry me?"

"I don't know you."

"Will you *marry* me?"

"Yes," I said.

"Tonight?"

"We could drive to Vegas."

"Mo Bayless. Sounds funny."

"Let's do it," I said.

"I'd give up my virginity for the man who'd marry me."

"We can be in Vegas before midnight," I said.

She said, "Many guys wanna marry me."

"I bet."

"I have a lot of boyfriends."

"I bet," I said, and asked, "Do you swallow them all?"

She said, "Yes."

"Oh."

"I bet you have girlfriends."

"Women come and go in my life," I said. "Dark entries."

"And I'm just another," she said.

"Tell me about Maureen."

"Mo."

"Oh?"

"I hate 'Maureen'."

"Mo."

"Mo has nowhere to go," she said, softly.

"What?"

She eyed me. "My parents would never approve of you."

"I'm too old."

"Too white."

"I see."

"I have to marry a nice Korean man –"

"I could fake it," I said.

"– some day."

"But not today?"

"Today," she said, "I'd marry you."

"Let's do it."

"You just want my pussy."

"I want you."

"Are you still hard?"

"Very."

"I want to swallow you again," she said. "Maybe for dessert?"

"Let's eat fast."

"Behavioral science," Mo said.

"What?"

"My major. For now."

"How am I behaving?"

"Too nice," she said.

"What should I do, to not be so nice?"

"Grab me by the hair. Force me to suck your dick."

"Here?"

"Sure."

When we were done, and in my car, I grabbed her hair, hard. I tried to kiss her.

"Don't kiss me," she said, a hand on my chest.

"Dammit," I said.

"Make me suck your dick. I have these elaborate rape fantasies that I'll tell you about someday."

I took my cock out, grabbed her head, and pushed her down. I closed my eyes, enjoying the sensation of her blowjob. I came in her mouth the second time that night.

I took Mo home, and there I met her two roommates, both of whom had short hair and were nineteen or twenty, young.

"Just another guy," I said to Mo, referring to her roommates' looks.

"Do you care?"

"No," I said.

"Do you want your dick sucked more?"

"Yes," I said.

We undressed, in the dark, and lay on the bed, where she took my cock back in her mouth. I wanted her, too; I told her this.

Mo said, "I'd like your face in my pussy."

I was quick to get between her legs. Now I had her cunt before me, the fresh smell of it, and I licked it. I spread it open. I couldn't admire, in the dark, what I knew must have been the beauty of a virgin twat (perhaps quite unlike Alexia's), but I could taste it, and it was the sweetest cunt I've ever had on my tongue, my lips, my mouth. Mo squirmed with delight, and made enough loud sounds that I knew her roommates were getting an earful. I moved a finger to her opening, and was surprised she let me do this. I slid the finger in. Mo's body tensed all over, and began to shake. "That's it, Nicky," she said, "finger-fuck that kitty," and I did, sliding it in and out, my tongue pressed and lapping against her clit the whole time. Mo's shaking became almost frightening, but intriguing and fun at the same time; and she came with such a shrilling cry I'm sure it echoed all across the campus.

I kissed her belly-button, my lips wet with her sex. I moved up to kiss her, but she looked away. I moved up more, so that my cock was at her mouth. She took it. My hands were against the wall by the bed, balancing my body, so that I was able to move my cock in and out of her mouth with the motion of my hips, fucking her pretty Asian face. Looking down, all I could see was the silhouette of her hair, and a slight whiteness of her eyes, as she was looking up at me. Mo's hands grabbed my ass, pulling me, making me fuck her mouth deeper. She squeezed and rubbed my ass, and one

finger moved to touch my asshole. I was a piston, going in
and out of her mouth, and I too let out a loud groan (maybe
too loud, wanting her roommates to hear) and came in Mo's
mouth a third time that night.

I came in her mouth a fourth time a few hours later, waking
up to her sucking me off. It took me a good while to get there
this fourth time, but she didn't seem to mind, and I enjoyed
every minute, every second.

It was awkward sleeping in that single bed with her; we
were close and entwined. Sleeping with someone else, I
usually like room. It was also very nice. Her smell, her body,
her hair, her flesh was always on me. I felt her pubes against
my leg. She slept well, but I didn't. I never sleep well in a
new environment. I looked at her in the night, and pondered
on her beauty, and basked in the comfort of being so near her.

In the morning, we sixty-nined, she on top of me; I licked
her from cunt to asshole as she kept my cock deep into her
mouth. She didn't come, but I did.

She had to get ready to go to class, and I had to go home. I
had nothing to do at home. I tried talking her into skipping
class.

"Kiss me goodbye," she said.

I kissed her, gently, on the lips.

"That's no kiss," Mo said.

"You said you hated kissing."

"I say that to all strangers."

"I'm not a stranger?" I asked.

"After last night?" she said.

We kissed for a good five minutes; then I left.

I was soon to learn I was in a long line of lovers Mo had,
mostly younger men. A few days later, I went to her place,
and she took me inside, wearing shorts and a halter. There
was a guy sitting on her floor. He wore glasses, baggy jeans,
was perhaps twenty. He stared at me.

"Steve," she said, "time to go."

Still looking at me, he got up, and left.

"Someone?" I asked.

"I was blowing him most of the afternoon," Mo said.

"How many times did he come?"

"Twice."

"Your mouth must be tired," I said.

"No." She smiled. "I can suck you for a few hours."

And she did, and I came in her mouth twice.

"Just how many cocks do you suck?" I asked her.

"A *lot*," Mo said. "I'm a suck-machine, you know."

She wasn't kidding. But I was going to Bosnia in a few days, and I really didn't care.

Still, the idea of her sucking cock non-stop rows of dick was a delightful image.

SEVEN

Randi's ass was high in the air, moving back and forth. "Yeah," Bart said. The three of us were royally fucked-up.

"Spread your ass," I said to her.

She reached back and spread her cheeks.

"I want to see that asshole," I said.

"She has a nice little bud," Bart said.

"Spread that asshole," I said.

"You wanna fuck her in the ass?" Bart asked me.

"Deeply."

"I like watching her taking it in the ass," Bart said, "horny little bitch."

"That's *hot* little bitch," Randi said.

Bart went to the store to get more alcohol. Randi and I were kissing on the bed, still naked.

She stopped me.

"I don't like all this as much as you think," she said.

"This?"

"It's Bart's thing," she said. "It's what turns him on."

"Maybe I should go."

"No."

"Now I feel weird."

"Don't. This is fine," she said.

I didn't feel like kissing.

"I shouldn't talk," she said.

"It's all right," I said.

When Bart came back, Randi started sucking on my flaccid cock.

I got hard.

EIGHT

I went to San Francisco to do a reading.

I called Alexia. She lived in this city now, and I had her number.

"Alexia," I said, "it's me."

"Where are you?" she said.

"The City."

"No, you're not."

"Really, I am. I'm doing a reading."

"Now?"

"Yes."

"How weird," she said. "I didn't hear about any reading. How *weird*."

"Why weird?"

"I can't say."

"Why?"

"It's a secret," she said.

"I like secrets," I said.

"I know," she said. "Then you write about other people's secrets. You make the lives around you into stories."

"Well, I'm here and I'd like to see you," I said. "Would you like to see me?"

"Of course," she said, "but I'm sick. Don't I sound sick to you? I must sound sick."

"How sick?" I asked.

"Sick in bed," she said.

I thought she said *sick in the head.*

She said: "I haven't gotten out of bed all day. That's why I'm not at work. You know I got a job – finally. And not in the film biz. I've been sick for a few days but I'm getting over it – the flu, I had the flu, I still have the flu. A little bit."

"Oh, I see," I said. "Well, the reading's tonight," I said. "Where?"

"This bookstore on Valencia, I don't know where: it's called Sucking the Zeitgeist Books."

"If I feel better later on," Alexia said, "I'll go."

"Please go," I said, "I'll feel so rejected and sad if you don't."

"Oh, you're good, Nicky! You know what a guilt sponge I am! You're manipulating me!" She was laughing.

"I work at it," I said.

"OK," she said, "I'll be there."

It was good to see her. She did look a little sick and she kept wiping her nose with a tissue. She wore her dark-rimmed glasses and a short black dress; her long black hair was in a ponytail. I ran my fingers through her hair like I used to when we were together, those brief moments, and she smiled and made a sexy sound and said, "I like you touching my hair." It all seemed so strange. We were sitting in Sucking the Zeitgeist Bookstore, which was also a coffee shop, with my publisher and another writer whose novel was out from this same publisher – his name was Luke and he was a professor from Utah and he also knew Barry McGinnis, they were colleagues of some sort, had edited a few special issues of journals together. Also with us was Karl, one of those – what I say – wannabe hangers-on; he published a magazine with a small circulation (had even published me) and all he liked to talk about were other writers, which was usually something bad; he also liked to talk about the novel he was writing, the novel that one day would blow all our minds. I'd met a lot of Karls since I'd been publishing my work. I was more drawn to his girlfriend, Lori, a tall thin woman who was quite pierced.

Alexia leaned over and told me she had to pee and did I know where the bathroom was? I didn't. I grabbed a glass from a table and put it by her knees and said, "Pee in here."

"I don't know if my aim is that good," she said. She got up and searched for the bathroom.

I looked at the glass.

"So where do you know her from?" Karl asked me.

"Back home," I said. "She was a McGinnis student."

"She's cute," Lori said.

"Yeah," my publisher said, smoking a cigarette, "she's cute."

The reading was somewhat well attended, fifty or so people. They didn't know who I was – no one knew who I was. I was obscure as any writer. I read, signed a few books. Luke read from his novel, Karl read some of his poetry.

I hate readings. But my publisher had talked me into this.

There was an open reading after. I figured that's why most of these people were here: they wanted to read their own stuff, that constant search for an audience. I didn't listen.

We all went outside and talked about where we'd go. My publisher suggested this bar down the street. I wanted Alexia to go; she didn't seem to be into it. She was huddling with Lori; the two girls were talking. Lori oozed sex, in her tight jeans, her cut-off top, exposing her pierced belly-button. Her nose and lips and eyebrows were also pierced.

"Come along," I said to Alexia.

"She's sick," Lori said. "She has to go home."

"Lori is my doctor," Alexia said; she smiled at Lori like they were old friends.

"How far away do you live?" Lori asked her.

"I'll take the Muni," Alexia said.

"I'll walk you," I said.

"You don't have to walk me," she said.

"It's dark," I said.

"It was dark when I came here."

"But if something happened to you, I'd feel guilty for the rest of my life."

She took my hand and said, "How sweet."

It was weird walking hand-in-hand with her.

"This is weird," she said.

"I know," I said.

"I feel weird," she said.

"I don't," I lied.

"I haven't seen you in *months*."

"Months, weeks, years: it's all the same to me."

"What have you been doing with yourself? Other than going off to bad places? You know, I had a dream you were going to come here soon, a dream during my fever. *That's* what's so weird."

"Oh."

We were standing at the Muni tracks. "What train are you getting?"

"The N Judah," she said.

I didn't know what that was. She took her hand from mine. A train was coming and I was disappointed. "Is that yours?" I asked.

"That's the J Church," Alexia said. "I want the N Judah."

I felt better and said, "I like San Francisco – I need to come here more often."

"Be sure to always call me when you do."

I pulled her close to me.

"Oh, now," she said.

"The last time we were together," I said, "before you moved here, remember what you told me –"

"Yes."

"– that when I came up here, your bed was open to me, that you wanted me to stay with you . . ."

"I had a feeling you'd remember that," she said.

"I don't want to go to that bar."

"They'll wonder what happened to you. They'll get worried."

"I'll call," I said. "I'd rather go home with you."

She put her face into my chest.

"Alexia," I said, touching her.

"It's not that I don't want you to," she said, "but I'm sick and you'll get sick, too. I'd love to take you home and fuck you all night and deep down I really want to do that, I want to fuck you: but you'll just get sick."

"So I'll get sick."

"I don't feel very sexual, right now," she said. "I'm too sick to have you in my bed. I wouldn't mind having you there but I'm really very tired and it wouldn't be good for both of us. My ass doesn't feel like fucking. I just, I just . . ."

Another train started to come our way.

"N Judah?" I said.

"Yes."

I wanted a kiss but she turned. She said, "You'll get my flu and you don't want that."

I kissed her cheek.

"You're here for a few days?" she said.

I nodded.

"If I feel better tomorrow night, I want you to come stay with me."

I stood there and watched N Judah go away and then headed back to the location of the bar my colleagues had gone to. I hoped I'd gotten the directions right. This wasn't a good neighborhood, but I'd been in worse. There were a lot of dealers and whores mixed with club-goers – and some pretty tough-looking bars that appeared interesting. A woman was screaming from the third floor of a hotel; she threw a bottle down which shattered not too far from me. She kept scream- ing. I could've took a cab, but I liked what I was seeing. I felt in the zero and I wanted to be with the zero. I was a rising young writer, wasn't I? Wasn't I supposed to be above all this? I didn't feel like it. Someone tried to sell me crack and it was tempting. There were bodies sleeping in all the alleys.

I found the bar. I didn't like it – too many successful- looking thirtysomethings in suits and evening gowns, with a jazz band playing in the corner. I had a beer. It was too *comfortable* here.

We were joined by a young lady who was doing publicity for my publisher. Her name was Kate.

Outside the bar, we debated whether we should walk or take a cab. We were going back to my publisher's house. My feet already hurt from all the San Francisco trekking.

"We could all fit into two cabs," my publisher said. She

stood on the street corner and said, "It's so cheap to get there and so far to go."

"That'd be a great title for a book," I said.

"Write it," she said.

I was sharing a cab with Karl and Lori. My publisher, Luke, and Kate were in the other cab.

"What's to do at her house?" Karl was saying. "I don't feel like going there. Do you?"

"I'm staying there," I said.

"Why don't you stay with us?" Lori said.

I guess I knew, deep down, that I would get the opportunity to fuck Lori. I didn't think that Karl would have to be around.

I plain just did not like Karl, no matter how much he tried to get buddy-buddy with me. He was a fake, he had that air about him. I'd read his fiction and poetry and it was pure crap. The guy didn't know how to write. He had a beer gut and a dull look to his eyes and I had to wonder what Lori saw in him. They'd been together for three years, I was told. She was a delectable person, and I couldn't wait to have her. They had a spacious and dark apartment with a coffin in the living room, which I was told was a guest bed. I had no intention of sleeping in that. We drank some beer, they smoked pot (I didn't care much for pot); then Karl said, "Hey, I have some XTC."

"Let's do some X," Lori said.

"OK," I said.

Karl went to get the drug. Lori licked her lips. I tried projecting to her that I wanted her – could she read my mind? She had the thickest lips. I wondered how painful it was to pierce them. Karl returned with three capsules of the drug in question.

It was the perfect drug to get into the right mood.

Karl put on some music: gothic, electronic, and eerie. Lori began to dance around the room, her body slinky, slithery. She took her top off; small, pointed breasts. She pulled her jeans down, and danced in black thong underwear. There was a tattoo of a naked woman on her ass, a Celtic band around her ankle. She danced and she danced and the drug started to get to us all; my mind was intent on fucking this dancing body. My cock was hard and it hurt.

Lori peeled her panties off. Her cunt was shaved naked, her clit and her labia both pierced. She touched herself.

"I'm so fucking wet," she said. "Won't you two just fuck me?"

We went to the bedroom. There was a futon on the floor, clothes scattered all over. Karl lit a candle. I was sucking on Lori's tits, falling to the futon, undressing myself. Karl loomed over us and watched. He began to undress. I didn't care to watch him.

I put my cock in Lori's mouth. Her tongue was pierced, and the metal ball against my cock's flesh was a nice sensation, especially on the drug.

Karl was naked, and moved to join us. I saw his dick and was amazed. He had the biggest one I'd ever seen up close. I'd say eleven inches, and very thick and veiny, with a large head. Maybe this is why she liked him, lived with him. Was it really just the cock? I'm an average-sized guy; I didn't feel threatened by Karl's dick, I was just flabbergasted.

Lori positioned herself so that she could suck me, and Karl could fuck her from behind. She took in a deep breath and her body stiffened when he entered her. We did this for a while, then Lori turned around so that she could suck Karl, and I slid myself into her cunt. We switched back again. Then Lori got on top of me, riding me. Karl moved behind her. He spat in his palm, rubbed his saliva on her asshole, his hand grazing my cock as he did so. I couldn't imagine him getting that monster flesh into her butt, but he did, and it wasn't easy for her. "Oh God, oh God, oh God," she cried, digging her nails into my chest. I could feel Karl's member through her septum, and realized I'd never done this before, not even with Bart and Randi. Our bodies were hot with the drug and the physical motion, slicked wet with sweat. Each thrust into her anus, Lori grunted, eyes shut. Karl was enjoying himself. Tears formed at Lori's eyes.

"Let's switch positions," Karl suggested.

He laid down on the bed, and Lori got on top of him. I got behind her. Her asshole was a gaping hole; it was like someone had bored a cavern into her ass, it was so wide. Obviously, I didn't have any trouble putting it in her, and I felt nothing. It took a minute for her sphincter to undilate, and snug around my cock. When it did, it was nice, but now her cunt was being drilled by Karl's monster. I closed my eyes and came into her bowels. Lori reached back for me as I pulled out, took my cock in her mouth, and cleaned it. Karl got up, gently pushing her onto her stomach, so he could get on top of her, and go back into her ass. I stood there and watched his prick violate her ass in a glorious way – he was fucking her hard, she was crying into the sheets, he started laughing, and came himself. He got up, his body covered in sweat, and said, "Look at that."

Lori lay there shaking, her ass once again blown open.

"I love wrecking her rectum," he said.

The woman who'd published my collection of stories, her name was Brianna. She had spiked, dyed blonde hair and a number of piercings and tattoos herself, and was two years younger than me. I didn't have any ideas about her because she was a lesbian, and lived with her lover, Raven. Raven didn't like me, I could tell; Raven had dyed black hair and was goth and had a whole lot of tattoos.

Brianna's publishing my book was a fluke. She had a small company that released industrial bands (mostly San Francisco home grown) on CD, and she published a quarterly magazine with a focus on alternative music and literature. She'd published several of my stories, and soon began accepting so many that one day she sent me an email suggesting she publish all the stories as a book, because she also had a novel by this professor in Utah that she wanted to publish. So now she was a book publisher, her press was unknown – another small press in a sea of many. My books were warehoused in her basement. Like the publisher of my first novel, she was a one-person operation, for the most part, and she was probably going to lose a lot of money putting my words into the world.

"So you went to Karl and Lori's," she said.

Her lover, Raven, wrinkled her nose.

"Yeah," I said.

Brianna grinned, and shook her head.

That evening, Luke and I did another reading, at Small Press Traffik. The attendance was small, but the people were very interested in the work. I signed a few books.

Brianna wasn't completely alone in her venture as a publisher; she had her friend Kate helping her with publicity. Kate was at this reading, and she came back to Brianna's apartment, where we drank tequila and vodka, and Brianna and Raven smoked pot. Kate started smoking, and so did Luke. Then Luke wanted to order pizza, so we ordered pizza.

Luke retired early to the guest room; he had to go back to Utah in the morning. Raven also went to bed. I was going to sleep on the fold-out couch in the living room.

It was me, Brianna, and Kate.

The three of us got drunk. Brianna started dancing around the room, saying, "Why am I so crazy? Why am I so crazy?"

She bumped into a bookcase, a tall bookcase, that almost came crashing down on her.

"Bri!" Kate said, laughing.

"Oooohhh," Brianna went. "I'm fucked up. Maybe I should go to bed."

"I'm too drunk to go home," Kate said, "but here's a pillow!" and she laid her head in my lap. I was sitting on the couch.

I looked down at her.

"Hi," she said.

I touched her round face, and caressed it. I ran my fingers through her thick, dirty blonde hair.

"What a cute sight," my publisher said.

I tried to reach down and kiss Kate. It was hard. She sat up, and we kissed. Brianna watched us, weaving.

"I had a feeling you two would hit it off," Brianna said.

"Go to bed," Kate said.

Brianna stumbled into her bedroom.

"Turn off the lights," Kate said.

I got up, switched the lights off, as Kate folded the couch out into a bed. As she adjusted the sheets, I got undressed. I got on the bed. She also took her clothes off, leaving her bra and panties on. I held out my arms; she came to me, and we held each other and kissed.

Her body was small and plump and warm.

"When I saw your author photo, three months ago," she said, "you know, for the book?"

"Yeah."

"I knew I wanted you. I knew I'd have you."

"Wow," I said.

"What?"

"Nothing."

"Tell me."

"I don't know," I said.

"You're sexy," she said.

"You don't know anything about me," I said.

"You don't know anything about me. Do you know my last name?"

"No."

"See."

"You know mine," I said.

"Yeah. I know a lot of things about you."

"Like what?"

"Your stories are very painful," she said.

"To you?"

"To me, to you, to anyone. You're a sad soul."

"Sometimes I'm sad," I said. "Right now, I'm happy."

"I'm happy, too."

We kissed more. I unclasped her bra, touched her round, large breasts. I reached between her legs.

"I haven't had sex in a year," she told me.

"Oh."

"Since my divorce."

"OK."

"But I'm ready to have sex."

Sex with Kate wasn't wild, bizarre, or kinky. I got on top of her; she wrapped her legs around me. We fucked slowly, and it was very nice. It was very warm. It was like we'd known each other for many years.

We slept in each other's arms.

In the morning, she was gone. I looked at the ceiling. Luke was gone, too. I had a flight back home late in the afternoon.

NINE

I was sitting in the patio of the campus bar, drinking a pitcher of dark beer with Bart. Bart had been drinking since noon; he was pretty gone.

"One of these days," Bart was saying, "you have to share one of your women with me!"

"I don't have any women," I said.

"Yeah, right."

"Nothing real, like a girlfriend," I said.

"But you get some now and then."

"Now and then," I said.

"Did you really used to fuck Alexia? Before she vanished?"

"Yeah. She's in San Francisco."

"You liked her?"

"And Hanna."

"Hanna?"

"You know Hanna."

"Of *course* I know Hanna," Bart said. "I fucked her once. Maybe twice."

"I didn't know that."

"Hanna *fucks*," Bart said.

I nodded.

"OK, I didn't fuck her: I was lying," he said. "But I know some people who have."

"OK."

"Hey, there's Zina," he said.

He started waving.

Zina was a poet in the MFA program, whom I'd met several times in passing. She had light brown skin and dark hair, wide brown eyes and a chiseled, distinct face. I knew she was half-Spanish, half-German, something like that, she'd told me once, at a party, I think. She joined Bart and myself.

"Have a beer, Zina," Bart said.

"I was just on my way home," she said.

"You can have a beer," I said.

"I usually don't like beer," she said. "Maybe I'll have some wine." She got up and went to the bar, returned with a glass of white wine. She was wearing tight, dark slacks and a blue blouse.

The three of us didn't talk about much – some gossip, some b.s. on the nature of poetry. It was starting to get dark out. "I wanted to get home before it got dark," Zina said.

"Where do you live?"

"Two blocks away. I don't like walking in the dark. You think you could walk me home?"

"I could," I said.

"See ya," Bart said.

So I walked with Zina.

"You're a strange character," she told me.

"Why do you say that?"

"No one can figure you out."

"Do people try and figure me out?"

"Some people do."

"Like who?"

"People."

"Maybe you're the strange one."

"I *know* I'm the strange one," she said. "My rabbit is going to be mad at me. I'm late; he's hungry I bet."

"Your what?"

"My rabbit," Zina said. "I have a pet rabbit. He's an albino rabbit."

"You keep him in a cage?"

"Not at all. He roams free. I mean, he does have a cage. He doesn't stay in it much."

"Doesn't he shit all over the place?" I said. "Dingle-berries, or whatever they're called."

"No. He's trained to poop in his cage," Zina said.

"No, he's not. You can't train rabbits to do that."

"I did."

"I thought they weren't in control of where they crapped," I said.

"My rabbit has control."

"Your albino rabbit," I said. "I don't believe you," I said.

"Think I'm making this up?"

"You're pulling my leg."

"Do you want to *see* my albino rabbit who's trained to shit in his cage or what?" Zina asked.

She lived on the second floor of the apartment complex. I went inside with her. Her place was sparse of furniture, heavy on books. A small, albino rabbit (white fur, red eyes) was waiting at the door.

"Moby Dick!" She picked up the rabbit and hugged it. "This is Nick; Nick, this is Moby Dick."

I nodded to the rabbit.

"He looks hungry, doesn't he?" she said.

I nodded.

"He's very hungry," she said. I went with her into the kitchen, where she put the rabbit down, and put some rabbit feed and a carrot stick in the rabbit's wire-mesh cage. "You want something real to drink?" she said. "Besides that god-awful beer."

"What's wrong with beer?"

"There's something basically barbaric about beer," she said.

"What do you have?"

"Let's take a look." She opened a cabinet above the stove. I think, for the first time, I took a good look at her body (and her ass) and admired what I saw. "Rum and vanilla sherry," she said, "it's all I have."

"Coke?"

"Pepsi."

"A rum and Pepsi sounds good."

"Your wish is my command."

We both had rum and Pepsi, sitting at the small table near the kitchen. The kitchen was littered with toys – dolls, army men, action figures, dinosaurs.

"Toys for your rabbit?" I said.

"Toys for me," she said, "I like toys."

She was twenty-nine, had majored in religious studies as an undergrad, at this same university. She'd had an affair with one of her professors. We began to drink sherry.

I'll skip right to the sex. We were both pretty drunk. I'm not sure where it began; yes, I was very drunk and we were talking and getting closer and the next thing I knew we were frantically, almost violently kissing. She was sitting in my lap, the way she would sit many times later, and she opened my shirt up and said she liked my chest, said, "It looks delicious," and she bit into it, bit into my skin, but I didn't care, the pain was OK, like the pain when she bit my lips as we kissed, and how she grabbed my throat and started to choke me, the air leaving me, letting go just at the right time. I opened her blouse, unclasped her bra, her nipples at my fingers, her dark eyes glaring at me, and the circles under those eyes. The circles under her eyes would come to haunt me some day, and I only wish I knew then what I was about to get into.

She had a double bed in her bedroom, and a computer on a metal desk. There was an opened document, what looked like a poem.

I was too drunk to fuck; she said it was OK. We were partly undressed. I took her sex to my mouth – she tried to stop me, once, but didn't the second time – her sex small and salty like the sex of any woman, and then she tried to do the same for me but I stopped her because she was hurting me with her teeth and she said she was very drunk, she never got this drunk, and we lay there holding each other. I couldn't sleep, and I wanted her; I thought she was asleep but she wasn't and we were kissing again and I started to put myself in her, whispering, "It's OK, now," and in the dark I saw her eyes roll up in her head and she grabbed the metal rail of her bed and we finally fucked. An hour later, still drunk but awake, we tried again, she told me she liked *men coming in from behind*, but we were still too drunk to be very amorous and she began to masturbate. She masturbated with a frenzy, lying on her stomach, her hand going at it on her cunt like that hand was possessed. I watched and she said, "I'm sorry, I like doing that. I like getting myself off."

She seemed to sleep well. I couldn't sleep. I kept hugging her warm body next to me. I liked it here with her. I liked her bed, her company, more than any of the others, these past few months – my divorce from celibacy, my entrance back into the world of sex and women.

In the morning we looked at each other, feeling awkward, and when I asked if this would happen again, she said, "That's up to you. You can come over any time."

The next night, we made love and we weren't drunk and we were like two regular people connecting and everything seemed to be just right.

TEN

Zina's alarm went off, and we both jumped. Zina grabbed her alarm clock and threw it against the wall. It stopped. Naked, we looked at each other, and again there was that awkward feeling. This was my third stay at her place.

"Oh," we both said.

"God," she said. "I hate alarm clocks."

"What time is it?"

"Must be eight."

"I, um, Zina," I said.

She touched my lips with her hand. "Don't say anything. You don't need to say anything. Do you need to go any-where? I have an early class. Do you actually attend classes? It's not like I'm prying. I just want to start some kind of conversation in an obviously maladroit situation. Listen to the words I use. So I'm a poet and, uh, you already know it. Huh. Like we look at each other and say: 'What should I say?' Is anything really on both our minds? There must be a lot. I'm really not sure what's on my mind. I have this very small mind, you see. Not that I'm small-minded, just that my brain is small like my body is small because I'm small person. I always wanted to be a tall person: so my mind'd be tall with tall thoughts all the time. Are you married and don't want to tell me and: am I assisting in adultery? You're not married, no, I can tell. Maybe you were once married: don't know. Not that I wouldn't have slept with you if you – were married; but I really don't like to sleep with married men any more. Oh, hell, I don't care. I could just pretend I'm sick; we can stay naked and stay in bed and sleep or make love or watch TV –"

"You don't have a TV."

"Stay in bed, fuck."

"My feelings exactly," I said.

"Could just lie here in bed till noon, afternoon. I used to do that a lot. Worked nights. Maybe I should get another night job. I'm really a night owl – used to come home late and stay up late working on my poems and then sleep till past noon and get up for work and – go to work."

"What'd you do?"

"Delivered pizzas."

"You're kidding me."

"No. Thirty minutes or less! I did this for, what? I did this for two years. Undergrad."

"I can't see you doing that," I said.

"Why not? I wore a uniform and everything. I even made good tips."

"Did any men ever come on to you? Drunk men who ordered pizzas?"

"Not really. Sometimes they'd give me wine coolers as part of my tip. That was always fun."

"I bet."

"I want to close my eyes and go back to sleep."

"Do it."

"No."

"Close your eyes."

"OK."

"They're closed?"

"You can see that."

"How is –?"

"Much better."

My body was next to hers. "Just go back to sleep."

"I don't think I can."

"Yes, you can."

"Nicky," she said, "hold me."

"I am."

"Hold me tighter."

I did.

"You're being a bad influence on –"

"Me?"

"Me," she said.

"I know," I said.

ELEVEN

I went to Zina's apartment late in the day, after one of McGinnis' classes. Her front door was unlocked, like she told me it would be, like she said she often left it unlocked. I could hear her in her bedroom, typing away at her computer. I crept in. Moby Dick was at the doorway, and looked at me. I thought better of scaring her. She was sitting at her computer in shorts and a halter, hair pulled up in a messy tail.

"Zina," I said.

She spun around in her chair. "You!"

"Expecting someone else?" I sat on the bed.

"Only you. Only you would be here."

"Maybe you shouldn't leave your door –"

"I was expecting you," she said. "I told you on the phone. I said let yourself –"

"I scared you."

She sat next to me. "A little."

"What are you writing?"

"What does it look like?"

"What's the subject?"

"Flying."

"Oh," I said.

"If I had wings," she said, "I could fly. I could fly here, I could fly there. I'd be rich! Marveling everyone in the world how I can fly."

"*I* can fly." I laid back on the bed.

Zina got on top of me. "Can you now?"

"I'm a superhero, you see. But this is a secret. Well, now you know the secret. When I'm a superhero, I can fly. I'm a superhero – with no name."

"Show me," she said. She kissed my nose. "I want to see you fly."

"Can't," I said. "Not in costume. Right now, I'm a regular person."

"But when you're a superhero –?"

"I can fly."

"Well," Zina said, "not *all* of them fly."

"Superman does."

"Batman doesn't."

"He doesn't have super powers. He's a vigilante."

"Batman is sexy," and she rolled off me, looking at the ceiling. "I've seen those movies. I'm not talking about the goofy Batman on TV. I mean the movies, armor-plated nipples and everything!"

"All superheroes are sexy."

"Does Spiderman fly?"

"No. He swings around the city with his fake webs."

"Who's that guy who runs really fast?"

"Runs?"

"Like lightning."

"The Flash."

"Yeah," she said, "he wears all red."

"The Flash."

She said, "I'd like to be like that, run around all in red, running faster than – faster than I don't know what."

I moved to kiss her, to say, "You're Wonder Woman."

She got up. "No. I'm too short, if you have not noticed. So," she bent down, and grabbed my legs, "when you're a superhero, do you wear one of those tight, sexy spandex outfits?"

"You bet."

"And battle evil foes." Her hands were running up my leg.

"I keep the world safe and clean," I told her.

"Sexy hero," she said, unzipping my pants. She took my cock out, and started sucking on it. She sucked long and slow; I relaxed and allowed myself to enjoy this. I came, but she didn't swallow. She let it go out of her mouth and down my cock. She looked at it. She moved up onto the bed and put her head on my chest. "So where are we going with all this?"

"This?"

"This," she touched my stomach, "and this," touching my wet cock, covered in saliva and semen.

"This." I touched her back, her ass.

"Sing to me," she said.

"What song?"

"Sing to me all night," she said.

"I'll sing to you all week," I said, "all year."

She kissed my neck, nuzzled her face into my neck. "You smell good."

"You smell pretty good yourself."

"You always smell like sex," Zina said. "Is this a good or bad thing?"

"Everything between us is a good thing," I said.

"Will it always be?"

"Don't be a pessimist."

"Everything just seems to be too good."

"Zina," I said.

"We'll end in tragedy," she said.

"Tears?"

"Violence?"

"Pain?"

"Maybe blood," she said.

"You have these thoughts?"

She sat up. "Put your hands here," indicating her neck. She took my hands, and put them there. "There, there. Now choke me."

"Why?"

"I want you to."

"I don't know how."

"Keep your hands there and squeeze."

"Like this?"

"Harder."

"I'll hurt you."

"You won't."

"Well."

"Just do it, you bastard."

I squeezed her neck hard. "You like this?"

"You know what I like?" She broke free from me. She plopped down on her hands and knees, body on top of me; she said, "What I really like is men to fuck me from behind, my ass high in the air, and reach over, here, *here*," taking my hand, "reach over like so and choke me, like so, as they fuck me from behind, like so."

"Is this romantic talk?" I had to laugh.

"Depends on your upbringing," Zina said.

I laid next to her. "Let's not talk."

"Who said we have to talk?"

"Sometimes," I said, "I like the silence."

She kissed me, and put her head on my chest. "Is this getting serious?"

"I don't know what serious is," I said. "I'm just an idiot."

We stopped talking, and started kissing, which led to fucking. I fucked her the way she wanted, my cock in her pussy from behind, and I reached over and choked her. It wasn't an easy thing to do; I thought it'd be easier if she were on her back, so I'd have better access to her neck. "Choke me harder," she pleaded, and I did, and her body spasmed as she came, my hand still at her neck. "Oh boy," she said.

I woke up with a short scream. I stopped myself. I was sweating. It was dark in the room. I was naked.

"What is it?" Zina said. "Superhero, what is it?" She pulled me to her breast.

"Dreaming," I said.

"Hush."

"I was having a bad dream."

"Hush."

"I was dreaming of an angel."

"Angel?"

"A dead angel."

"Angels don't die," she said.

"I thought I saw a dead angel, not too long ago."

"Go back to sleep, Nicky."

We lay there for a while.

"Are you asleep?" she asked.

"No."

"You were dreaming again."

"With eyes open," I said.

"Now I have angels on my mind," she said. "Could I be an angel? I could really fly then. With wings. Do you know what the beauty of angels is?"

"No."

"They have no self-pity."

Zina and I started to make love, in her bed, and she stopped me, a hand on my chest – "Wait."

"What?"

"Why are you here?"

"Why do you ask?"

"Maybe," she said, "I like to ask questions."

"I'm here," I said, "because I want to be here."

"I was hoping for a different answer," she said.

"Like what?"

"Kiss me."

I did.

"That was a peck," she said.

I kissed her again.

"Why are you here?" I said.

"Because this is my apartment and I live here," she said.

"Tell me what's wrong," I said. "Something is wrong."

Zina looked away from me. "Things are getting different. We're seeing more of each other. I'm sorry. I think I forgot all the moves somewhere: how to budge, how to speak, how to make eye contact. Been a while since I've been in a relationship. Maybe I'm afraid of doing the wrong thing. Maybe I don't want to do anything at all. Maybe I don't know what to do."

"Don't do this," I said.

"What?"

She was looking at her lava lamp, next to her computer. "Come here and look at this." She went to the lamp.

"What is it?"

"Come and look."

I joined her.

"That glob in there," she said, pointing to the lamp, "it almost looks like a person. Like a person looking at me."

"Seems just like a glob of lava lamp lava to me," I said.

"I see a person."

"What person?"

"You."

"Me?"

"Don't you see yourself?"

"Well," I said, "no."

"What are you doing in my lava lamp?"

I reached for her – "Trying to get out so I can fuck you."

She pushed me away, hard. I fell on the floor.

"*Get out of my lava lamp,*" Zina said.

"Hey," I said.

She sat on the floor with me. She looked at me. She said, "Can I tell you something, Nicky?"

"Now?"

"Something I want to tell you," she said.

"I'm listening," I said.

"I went crazy, once," she said.

"Crazy?"

"I mean –"

"It happens to us all."

"Nicky –"

"It's a crazy world," I said, "and a dirty one."

"*Listen to me, I'm serious.*"

"OK."

"I wasn't right in the head. This head: you see my head? I don't know what went wrong. Something went wrong with this head. I was really paranoid, like all those conspiracy people who think the United Nations are going to invade America. Well that's an arcane reference. I should shut up. No, I won't. I was convinced everyone was talking about me behind my back – my co-workers, my friends. I had just gotten out of this relationship with an older man –"

"How much older?"

"Older. He was – I told you about him. A professor here. He was divorced."

"OK."

"That's really a different story for a different time. What was I saying?"

"People were talking about you."

"Oh."

"Were they?"

"Thought so. I mean, people do talk about you when you're not around, and I was obsessed. It was driving me crazy. *Crazy.* I – couldn't sleep."

"What were they saying?"

"The usual shit."

"Back-stabbing? The kind of people who smile in your face and stick a huge knife between your shoulder blades every chance they can get? Know the type," I said.

"No. Well, yes, I don't know," she said. "Stop interrupting me," she said. "It was a major problem, especially when the billboard ads starting talking to me."

"Billboard ads?"

"Everywhere I went," Zina told me, "I was convinced billboard ads were delivering subliminal messages *just to me*. Specifically to me, you see. They were telling me things, like what these people were doing, how I was displaced in the universe."

I asked, "Who were sending you these messages?"

She replied, "Spiritual beings, aliens in UFOs, some kind of strange creatures – and then they started to invade my lava lamp and talk to me from there."

"Sounds like a problem."

"Somewhere deep down I kept telling myself this wasn't real. I knew it wasn't real. Finally, I went to get help. I went and saw a hypnotherapist."

"You were hypnotized?" I said.

"Oh, yes. It did me a world of good."

"You were cured?" I said.

"Yeah. I'm not crazy now, am I?"

"No."

"I used to be."

"How long were you . . . ?"

"A few months."

"But you're OK now?"

"Yes," she said.

"Good," I said.

"So," she said.

"So," I said.

"Now that you know I used to be crazy," she said, "do you still want to sleep with me?"

"I'd be crazy not to."

TWELVE

I began to enter Zina's world of pain: her delight.

I was touching, caressing her breasts. I pinched her nipples, which were hard; I pinched lightly.

"Pinch them harder," she said.

I did.

"*Harder*," she said.

I was afraid I'd hurt her.

"I want the pain," she said, "it makes me horny."

She gave an example. She got up, found a pair of clothes-pins in a cabinet in the kitchen, and placed a clothespin on each nipple. With the clamping down on each nipple, she took in a deep breath, almost like a hiss.

"Fuck," she said.

"You like that," I said.

"Yes, yes," she said. "Take them off."

I did, quickly.

"Put them back on."

I did, and this time I took delight, watching the pins squeeze into her flesh.

"Ahh, fuck," she said.

I took one off.

"Now use your fingers."

I took the nipple in question between two fingers.

"*Squeeze*," she said.

I squeezed.

I started to become quite good at choking her while we fucked, whether she was on her belly or on her knees or stomach. Repetition makes you better. I also started to enjoy this activity. I was never quite sure if it was mental or physical for Zina, but as long as it got her off and made her happy, it made me happy.

We started biting one another, soft at first, then harder, sometimes until we drew blood from each other's punctured flesh, fragile as anything in the universe. The biting was not just into the body, but into the soul.

We were in bed, holding each other.

"Are we getting very serious?" Zina said.

"It feels like it," I said.

"Is this OK with you?" she said.

"Yes," I said. "You?"

"Yes," she said. "Very," she said.

"I have something," Zina said, standing naked before me.

"Yeah?"

"Something I want you to use on me," she said.

She went to her closet, and produced a cat o'nine tails. I'd seen such a flogging device in magazines, in movies.

"Where'd you get that?" I asked.

"I've had it a while," Zina said. "I want you to use it on me," she said.

It was black and ominous. She handed it to me. She lay on her stomach, on the bed. "Use it on my back," she told me, "use it on my ass, my legs."

I did so, lightly, uncertain.

"It's OK to start off soft," she said, "but increase your strength. Gradually. I want you to get to a point where you could almost make me bleed."

I did this. I hit her with the cat o'nine tails, just as she said: her back, her ass, her legs. She seemed to like it best on her ass. I started to get into it. I started hitting her harder, the smack of leather against flesh. Harder. She began to cry out with each blow. Tears in her eyes. She wanted more. Welts were beginning to form on her ass, the back of her legs. I concentrated on her back, till welts formed there.

"OK," she said. "*Stop*."

I stopped. I, too, was almost out of breath.

"Now get on me," she said, "fuck me: I can't stand it, fuck me!"

I entered her from behind, I reached over to choke her. We fucked for a bit, then she turned around. She put her legs on my shoulders.

"Slap me," she said.

I raised a hand.

"Slap me."

Fucking her, I slapped her, hard, across the face.

She just looked at me, some blood on her lip. "Not that hard," she said.

"I'm sorry," I said, reaching down and licking the blood away.

"Slap me again," she said.

I did, but not as hard.

Zina bought toys several days a week, usually at thrift stores, sometimes at the toy store. She loved her children's toys, and so did Moby Dick.

She had adult toys hidden under her bed, and it wasn't

until a month after we'd been seeing each other that she brought them all out, and wanted to share them with me.

Anal beads, large double-sided black dildos, a dog collar, other assorted rubber penetrating devices. While Zina liked the beads or my fingers in her ass, she didn't care for anal sex all that much. She wasn't into ass-licking, pissing, or even swallowing my come. She liked pain, she liked to whack her clit off, she liked me to choke her. It was easy to get into what she enjoyed, as I got into any woman's pleasure, however alien it was to me. I adapted well.

"Once," Zina told me, in the dark, in bed, "I was so full of myself, I wanted to colonize my own psyche; I wanted to chase the message owl across fields unfamiliar. I wanted to fly because I was born with wings and I was angry at God for not allowing me to fly."

Being with a poet can sometimes shed new light on pretension.

Zina didn't like to hang out at the bar with McGinnis and his crowd. She didn't think McGinnis cared for her, and she didn't care all that much for him, either. "All those people are from fiction," she said. "I'm from poetry." Only now did I start recognizing the split in the English Department within genres, especially those in comparative literature, rhetoric and writing. All the time I'd been attending this school and only now was I noticing the petty in-fights, jealousies, the mini soap operas. "Do you know what kind of reputation McGinnis has?" Zina said.

"He's well known," I said.

"As a womanizer, as an iconoclast. He's not classical in his approach."

"But his books!"

"They don't make sense."

"He's helped me," I said.

"I know he has," Zina said, taking my face in her hands. "He's your friend."

"I love you," I said.
"I love you," she said.

I'm not sure how it started; it wasn't even talked about. Zina said something like, "It's silly for you to be paying rent on your place when you're always over here." Gradually, my possessions began making their way to her apartment. I gave her money for rent. We bought groceries together. We went to bed at the same time, and got up together. She cooked breakfast and we had breakfast together.

I knew it was over, the night I got really drunk: we had this fight. I don't know what the fight was about. We were fighting more and more, and I was drinking more.

My car was in the downstairs garage. I went into the garage door, got into my car, and floored it, going in reverse. I forgot the main door was down. I smashed right into it. I sat there in the car, in the alley, and thought: shit, I just ruined the garage door.

I laughed. It was like something out of a Raymond Carver story, something Bukowski would've done in a drunken stupor.

"OK," I said, "I gotta write a story about this."

Zina came down, wearing a robe. "What have you done?" she said.

"Oops," I said.

"You better pay for this," she said.

Oh, I would.

After she calmed down about the door, I went to her for comfort. I was shaking. I tried to hug her. She was cold. We went to bed. "Tie me up," she said. I tied her wrists to the metal railing of the bed, and then her ankles to the other railing. I got out the small black whip (a new toy) and went to work on her flesh. I made her bleed. I fucked her from behind. I put it in her ass, much to her seeming protest. I choked her, harder than I've ever choked her. She was coughing at the end, her face red, her body shaking.

"Why haven't you ever fucked me like that before?" she wanted to know.

THIRTEEN

The image I have of her (this image will always stay with me) – and I wanted to tell her this as she sat behind the wheel of her car, driving (I was in her car and she was driving) – was an image of Zina surrounded by her toys, a milieu of toys, the toys she liked to buy and play with: filling the empty spaces of our apartment with.

Zina was driving and we were going to Los Angeles. I was surprised how little traffic there was on Interstate 5; usually there were many cars clogging, the slow march of machines, especially on a summer night, so many people coming or going. We were going, Zina and I, but we were not going to the same place. Places have divisions, spaces that are hard to fill, no matter how many toys you buy from the toy store to make up for some memory or lack thereof.

This is what I knew about her, or this could've been mere assumption – and the image of her that sticks like hot glue to the fingertips of my reverie is Zina as I saw her one night, the night I went to our apartment (when we were going to the same place together and everything was OK and we both seemed happy) and she had bought a bag full of the alphabet ($1 at the thrift store) with magnets on each letter, the colored letters I seem to recall having played with when I was a very small person. "Look! look!" she said: with glee and like a small person, and she said, "Help me with them," an invitation to play. She tore open the plastic bag the colored letters were contained in; they scattered across the floor of her kitchen like stupid human dreams forever lost in a car crash. She went to her knees, told me to come to her: play, help, fight. She started putting the letters on the white refrigerator, where she had a color print of a happy smiley face woman with large eyes and the caption HOME HONEY, I'M HIGH and two postcards, one of a brunette holding a gun and shooting, another of a man with a gun, an image from the movie *Reservoir Dogs*. There was a mixture of delight and anxiety on her face; she looked at me and said, "Won't you help me?"

I got to my knees, picked up several letters, started putting them on the fridge with her. The kitchen was hot (like the rest of the apartment) and I felt very sad. She must've seen something on my face because she said, "You think this is silly. You don't like doing this."

"No," I said, "there's nothing silly about this," and so we were like two children frantically picking up the alphabet from her floor – letters that I thought would any moment now get up and dance – *oh, God, a memory* – sticking them to the door of the fridge. Merriment, yes, a small one's joy on her small triangular face and when I looked at the kitchen table which had a lot of other toys, used and new, I felt sad again; I knew there was something missing. Something was missing from her past (something was missing from mine) and something was missing between us, yet another space to be filled, a vacuous interior needing intestines.

"You buy so many toys," I said. I sat down at the table and played with a dinosaur.

Zina looked at her letters, arranged them in a way she liked better. "Yes, I do," she said.

She sat in my lap, like she always did, arms around my neck and looking down at me with her dark eyes, dark circles under her eyes – my face pressed against her breasts, the smell of her now on me, that smell which was not perfume but some men's cologne I never heard of that mixed well with her skin and gave her the smell I knew I'd forever associate her with, an invasion of my psyche: my memory of Zina.

She kissed me on the lips, she kissed me on the forehead. "Just think," she said, "I keep collecting more and more toys; we'll never have to buy toys for our children."

What the hell was she talking about?

I looked at Zina next to me, Zina's hands on the wheel tonight, going north, going to LA – she to her brother's, me to a reading I didn't really want to do. She wasn't going to come to the reading with me.

I wanted to tell her that I'd hoped this time it would be different, she wouldn't just be another woman to jump into my pool and splash and leave and never come back. I wanted to tell her what was on my mind, what was in my heart. But, in my heart, I knew it was over between us.

My staring at her was making her feel uncomfortable; she looked at me and said, "What?" then looked back at the freeway.

She put her hand to my face. "My hands are cold, do you feel?"

I grabbed her hand at my face, pressed it to my face hard, then pulled it away and kissed it, holding it. "I don't want to fight any more," I said.

She put her hand on my leg and didn't say anything. She continued to drive. We were on the freeway and there was no stopping now –

Now I didn't want to go to LA. I wanted to go south, back south, I wanted to go home, I wanted to hide, I wanted to remember when things were nice and soft and good between us.

"Do you know what I feel like?" Zina said.

"What?"

"French fries! Yummy!"

I was hungry, too. "We have to look for a sign post of some fast food place. Why is it you see them all the time except when you really want to get to one?"

She didn't reply.

"I want that fast food sign," I said, "high on a post for all to see, in neon glow, advertising food, beseeching me to consume, saying –"

"*Eat me!*"

"I was going to say that."

"I know. You're becoming –"

"Predictable?"

"He thinks!" she said. "You got it."

Her hands were tight on the wheel.

There was something rueful inside me; this didn't feel right; we shouldn't be this way; there shouldn't be this distance like aliens coming to earth. ("Right now I need my space," she'd told me, "so this doesn't mean we won't get back together. Just, right now, I have to focus. I can't be in a relationship like this; I have to be like a monk – monastic living, you know what I mean?" Also: "After a while, you get used to being alone, and you even start to like it." I think she said something like: "I've never felt I needed someone else to complete me; I'm complete in myself." I'm a fragment, this I've always known, but knew all the more as we drove, as she drove.)

I looked at her, still feeling the dejection, and she gazed into the rearview, her eyes looking at her own eyes – her reflection – the mirror – playing again "The Whore for Borges" –

– like when she said she was the votive of Borges, the simulacra that never was. "I'm beginning to appear in people's dreams," she told me and, looking at the mirror on the wall of her bedroom, she said, "I am the mirror, but you can never be."

This happens to poets who take courses on critical theory. Perhaps this is where things went wrong, when I did want to be her reflection: I wanted to be inside her, know everything; she started to feel violated, intruded upon.

I went home one evening, the other evening, really, and realized, for the first time, that I did not belong there. I was feeling weak. All day I had this sensation of horror, but all I wanted was to be with her, to hold her, to have her hold me, to play with her toys, to talk, to have her warm body against mine, to make love, to do anything, anything but be away from her, whip her, slap her, beat her, choke her. Our apartment was dark, candles were lit all around, flamenco guitar music playing on the CD. She was in the bathroom, hair pinned up, applying make-up in a way she never did before, looking at herself in the mirror; and when I went into the bathroom, her eyes on me, from the reflection, were eyes of rancor. She seemed angry, like she didn't want me there;

she seemed evil in the candlelight. I tried to kiss her and she pushed me away. Once, she told me she did a lot of symbolic things, some abstruse and some subtle, and I would have to get used to it. "Like this band on my wedding finger," she said, "is to remind me who and what I'm really married to: *myself*, I'm married to myself; and this necklace, these earrings in the shape of hearts, to remind me to always follow my heart."

"Why are you here with me?" she asked after we made love the night before. "I don't understand," she said.

I grabbed her necklace and said, "I'm just following my heart."

In the candle-lit apartment, she told me she was having second thoughts, she wasn't sure if she wanted a partner, someone to tell her to come to bed at four a.m. while she was working on a poem; someone to tell her to eat; someone to even talk to, to be present, to remind herself of herself. "I'm used to being a hermit," she said, "I like being a hermit." I told her I would go but she grabbed me and said no and we held each other and I smelled her and I was all the more confused. Many times I said I would go, I would just leave, and be a hermit myself, like I was for five years; but she would say *no, stay here with me,* and *now* she was saying she didn't like having me around . . .

"I don't see any French fry places," she said, driving.

"Well, it doesn't matter."

"You're hungry."

"It doesn't matter."

"I'm hungry," she said, "but I guess it doesn't matter."

I don't want French fries, I don't want to be here; I wish we were home.

FOURTEEN

Alexia met me at a coffeeshop in San Francisco – it was easy to get there from the airport. I'd made an impromptu flight from LA to The City, calling Alexia on the phone just before I got on the plane. "I'll be there in less than two hours," I said.

She was wearing a black bodysuit and a little hat, and her glasses. She already had a chai tea. The coffeehouse served beer, and I had a beer.

We kissed, lightly. A peck, really, between old friends.

"So where are you reading, this time?" she asked.

"Nowhere."

"You're not here for a reading?"

"No."

"You're just here?"

"I don't know why I'm here," I said. "Maybe I'm here for you," I said.

"I don't believe that," she said.

"Well," I said, "I'm here."

"I'm glad you're here." She reached over for a quick kiss. "I've been wondering about you," she said. "It's been a while. I even missed you. Do you believe me?"

"Yes," I said.

"Do you want to go back to my place?"

"Yes," I said.

I couldn't do it.

We were in bed, we were naked, we were touching, kissing, tasting, all that – a finger in her ass, her hands cupping my balls.

I moved away from her.

"Nicky?"

"I feel like I'm using you," I said.

"I know," she said. "There's something very wrong. But it's OK."

"I think I was in love," I said.

"Love is nice."

"The past five months, I was living with someone. I was actually sharing my life with someone."

"I see."

"We went to LA. In LA, she told me she was staying at her brother's for a week. She said when she got back, she wanted me and my stuff out of her place. She said a week was enough time. Is a week enough time," I said, "to alter one's life?"

"So you came to San Francisco?"

"It was an impulse."

"A good impulse." She put her head against my back, her arm around my waist.

"I called you," I said.

"I was here," she said.

"I feel like a shit," I said.

"*Do* you love her?" she said.

"I don't know," I said. "What the hell do I know?" I said.

"I thought I loved you, once," Alexia said. "But I was using you."

"How?"

"People always use each other," she said, "for one reason or another. It's a selfish world. You know this. You just have to accept it," she said, "and embrace it."

"You loved me?"

"What's love?"

"This is OK?" I said.

"It's very OK," she said.

Alexia told me I could fuck her pussy, if I wanted; she was no longer a virgin.

"What happened?" I asked.

She said, "The whole wait-till-I-get-married thing was bullshit. I was away from my family, and I started to think about it. I said the hell with it."

"Who had the honor?" I couldn't help but think of Mo.

"It was with some guy," Alexia said. "Just this guy. He's living in some stupid place like Arkansas now. I didn't even care for him. A fuck-buddy. I didn't even tell him I was a virgin. I was all prepared for – I don't know what. Pain. Blood. Ecstasy. Angels singing. Bands marching. Motions of love and truth and the face of God. It was no big deal. It was nothing. He put it in and that was that. I was no longer a vagina virgin. And my life was just the same."

I didn't want her cunt. I wanted her like we used to be, a grasp of my past. I fucked her in the ass, very deeply in her ass, and it was good, her ass all over my cock, her ass clamping down on my cock. We went into the bathroom, she opened her mouth, and I peed in her mouth, I peed deeply into her mouth, down her throat, on her tongue and teeth, on her lips and chin. It was good, my urine in her mouth, its taste filling her, warming her. I lay on the bed, she spread my cheeks, and she reamed my anus, deeply tongued my asshole, licking and sucking. It was good, her tongue up my ass.

As I knew it would be good.

It was getting dark, and I held her in my arms. In the bed. In her room. In her home.

I touched her hair.

She touched my hair.

I kissed her.

She kissed me.

Our smell . . .

"This is very nice," Alexia said.

"Yes it is," I said.

THIEF OF NAMES

Lucy Taylor

Afterwards, Nicholas wondered how he could have ever thought the little blonde with the tattoo on her tit could have been worth the risk she posed to his marriage, his self-respect, and – as it turned out – so much more. Yet still, there was that moment of insanity when he actually debated the point, before admitting that nothing could have been worth what the encounter cost him. It was that second's hesitation, though, that gave an indication of how much Nicholas Berringer valued sex – or at least what sex represented to him. Fucking, to him, had always meant freedom and conquest and masculine power. Even when consensual, the act was at heart, forced entry and violent gratification, the plundering of empty space by protuberant member. It was also safety and solace and the warm dark heart of his mother's womb, the sacred place where there was no Nicholas, where nothing was named and there was only One.

Although he would not have put it quite that way. Had he been asked, he would have simply said that fucking made him feel alive, gave him the willingness to make the effort of drawing the next breath. He would have said that, as exclamation points marked memorable sentences, so erections punctuated the climactic points of a man's life.

Now, as he drove well above the speed limit on I–75 in the pouring rain, headed toward the Ambassador Bridge and the US/Canadian border at Detroit-Windsor, he wondered if trying to track down Sonny Valdez wasn't the journey of a masochistic fool, a pathetic attempt to feel like he was taking charge, doing something, for God's sake, to try to save his own life.

I'm going to ask Sonny Valdez for help, he thought, grimacing at the irony of it, for he could scarcely stand to inhabit the same planet as the man. The three best years of his life, of his marriage, had been when he believed that Sonny Valdez was dead, having expired wretchedly in some flophouse in Toronto's commercial sex district. But Valdez, as it turned out, was still very much alive, and now Nicholas needed his help. *Jesus, I am fucked*, he thought bitterly, *I am truly royally fucked*.

"Do you like to fuck?" the cute blonde in the blue satin blouse had asked him.

Her exact words. He'd almost dumped his beer in his lap. She had to be a hooker, of course, but still – talk about coming on strong.

She read his expression and giggled, showing slightly crooked front teeth. "Oh, don't get me wrong. I'm not a working girl. Well, I mean I work, all right. I work on a road construction crew. I'm what they call a flagger, which basically means I'm one of those chicks stands out in the broiling sun on the highway all day holding a sign says *Slow Down* and the good ol' boys goin' by in pick-up trucks holler at us and try to grope our tits out the window."

"I never knew that," he said, quietly bemused.

"I don't usually talk to guys in bars, either, but my boyfriend – ex-boyfriend, that is – he's off with some trailer trash whore he met in a honkytonk. I figure what's sauce for the gander's goose is – I mean, sauce for the goose –" She giggled raucously. "Aww, you know what I mean."

She was drunk, of course, and he reminded himself that he didn't care much for sex with drunken women. They had nasty habits like throwing up on your cock or passing out in the middle of sex. They tended to walk off with your Rolex or look through your wallet when you went to the john.

"So *do* you?" she said.

"Do I what?"

"*You* know."

"What you said?"

"What'sa matter, you scared to say the F-word?"

"I think you've had too much to drink." He turned to the bartender, signaling for his check. He was only in Cincinnati for the one day to look at some lots zoned for residential development. The lots had proved disappointing – people in the market for half-million dollar homes didn't usually want a view, however distant, of an industrial park – and he was scheduled to fly home to Detroit the next morning. Beth was going in late to work so she could meet him at the airport.

Beth – God, what about Beth? If she had been homely or overweight or uninterested in sex, that might have been one thing, but she was lush and lithe and seductive and fucked the way he did – like her life depended on it. Every time he cheated on her, he swore to himself it would be the last time. Afterwards, he would go to church like the good Catholic boy he once was and confess to the priest and vow to be different: yet, sooner or later, it would happen again.

"C'mon, honey, you look like you need to relax." The girl leaned forward, allowing him to look down her blouse and see the tattoo of a bumblebee on the inner swell of one breast. It was done in vivid black and yellow, its stinger pointing downward at her nipple. "I can help you relax real good."

"I'll bet you can." He debated, but only a moment, for his dick had already decided that she was his type. Her slender, sinewy little body was thinner than he would have preferred, but she exuded that slutty decadence that always made him feel like a conqueror on the verge of sacking some foreign city notorious for its depravity. Eau de wench, essence of whore.

Having made the decision, he felt emboldened, eyeing her

up and down with overt and calculating lust, before he said,
"But regarding your question, the answer is, 'Yes. Yes, I
do.' "

Was it his imagination, or did she flinch slightly? Maybe
she'd just been trying to shock him. Maybe this was some
kind of game – somebody had dared her to come on to a man
in a bar, and secretly she'd been hoping he wouldn't take her
up on her offer. For a second, her lower lip quivered, and her
boldness seemed on the verge of disassembling into little-girl
sobs. Then she rallied, took a deep breath, and seemed to pull
herself together from sheer force of will. From the looks of
the effort she exerted, it didn't seem like she had it in her to
do that too many more times.

"My name's Elise." She slid her fingers through his. Her
skin, he noticed, was surprisingly cold, but she managed a
grin as she said, "You got a room?"

"718."

"You got a wife?"

Now it was his turn to grin. "Not tonight."

The rain hammered the windshield of the Volvo with such
force that the wipers couldn't work fast enough to sweep it
away. A semi, lumbering past like a maddened triceratops,
sent up an arc of grey water that inundated the car and forced
Nicholas for a few moments to drive blind. When he saw the
lights of immigration at the Detroit-Windsor border crossing
up ahead, he braked cautiously and pulled up next to a booth,
where an immigration agent, after glancing perfunctorily at
his license plates, waved him on.

Accelerating back into the rain, Nicholas let out his breath
which, until that moment, he didn't realize he'd been holding.

Although his business trips took him to Toronto three or
four times a year, he was always absurdly relieved when it
was done, when no need was seen to run his name through
the computer to check for misdeeds in his past. Even if the
immigration agents pulled his record and realized it was a
convicted felon passing through their country's symbolic

portals, there was nothing they could hold him on, of course. In the years since he got out of prison, he hadn't committed any crime more serious than minor traffic violations. But if they knew about his past, they might be inclined to detain him while they searched him and his car. And this time, for once, there was something for them to find – the 0.9 mm Biretta stashed in the vehicle's console.

By five o'clock that evening, Nicholas was in Toronto, sipping a Scotch and soda in his lakefront room at the Harbor Castle. He debated whether or not to call Beth, but hated having to add to the web of lies he'd already conceived. Supposedly, he was up here at some kind of Home Builders Convention and would be home Sunday night. Should he need more time, he'd have to invent an explanation for the extended stay and hope Beth wouldn't ask too many questions.

Too early to hit any of Sonny Valdez's haunts just yet. He knew he should eat something, but appetite was a memory, these days. His head hurt. He ran cold water over a washcloth and laid it over his eyes as he stretched out on the bed. Outside, the rain was still pounding, grey metallic teeth gnashing against the panes. In the street below, sirens screamed.

When they went up to Nicholas's room at the Cincinnati Sheraton, the girl – Elise – gigglingly chugged two of the little bottles of Scotch out of the minibar while Nicholas unbuttoned her blouse and reveled in the enchanting sounds of her skirt zipper going down and her silk stockings unrolling. Naked, she was even thinner than he expected, and the untanned areas of her skin stood out in pasty contrast to the rest of her body's dark, glossy-looking bronze.

Appraising her, Nicholas reflected that she was certainly no prettier or sexier than Beth; her body hinted at no mysteries to be uncovered or exotic depravities to be unleashed, nor did he get any inkling of a psyche ariot with new and perverse fantasies. Indeed, if anything, there was a certain sad banality to the girl, as though she were somehow grievously miscast in her role as a slut, a tramp, an easy piece of ass.

And yet, for all that, Nicholas could no more *not* fuck her than he could have not fucked the women who had preceded her. Like a compulsive gambler viewing a slot machine or a lottery ticket, for Nicholas, each new sexual encounter seemed to promise the possibility of some as-yet-un-dreamed-of ecstasy. Each pussy was the potential passage to some state of higher bliss that flickered across his mind in dreams and yet always eluded him.

He went over to the bureau and unzipped his shaving kit. She looked up. "What are you doing?"

"Condom," Nicholas said.

She came up behind him, smooshed her tits into his back. "I hate those things. C'mon, you don't have to worry. I'm just a nice girl getting back at her cheating boyfriend. You don't need to wear a rubber."

He turned around to say something sarcastic about what "nice girls" do and don't do, and she dipped to her knees, his dick disappearing into the tight seal of her mouth, his mental processes magically unraveling.

After that, they did all the things Nicholas enjoyed most – with a few other things thrown in for extra. He fucked her standing up, her spine pressed into the wall, while she stood up on her toes and dug her nails into his shoulders, moaning. Then on the bed, driving himself between those ivory tits, until the bumblebee was covered in come that looked like droplets of honey.

When her eyes started to close and she grew sleepy and sated, Nicholas shook her and said, "We're only getting started. You asked me, do I like to fuck? I'll show you just how much."

He flipped her over then and fucked her from the rear, butt raised, head buried in a pillow. For the last half dozen or so thrusts, he put his hands down on her back and leaned his weight into her. Took note that she must be used to rough stuff, because she didn't protest, but took what had to be a painful compression of her ribcage stoically, drawing in tiny gasps of air as best she could.

"*Like* that?" he asked when he was finished for the moment. Recovered from her near-asphyxiation, she snuggled against a pile of pillows and opened up a bourbon from the minibar.

"Christ, you sure can fuck." Her smile was sly and silly, a drunken smile, and yet threaded through with something else, contempt or fear, something dark and ugly that he tried to pretend he didn't see. The cheating boyfriend, he supposed. Her anger at the boyfriend spreading out like the hood of a cobra, directed at any man that came within her line of vision.

Reaching for something to say, he remarked, "You look like you spend a lot of time in the sun. What do you do, flag cars in a bikini and a hardhat?"

"Tanning booths."

"Those are bad for you."

"Yeah, they give you skin cancer." She laughed giddily. "But look who's talking."

She started to unscrew another of the tiny bourbon bottles. He took it from her. "Enough, OK. I don't want you to pass out on me. You won't be any fun to fuck."

"How about your *wife*, Nicholas? Is she any fun to fuck? Or is she fat and frigid or maybe fucking someone else, even as we speak?"

"Don't talk about my wife. You don't know anything about her."

"What is it, she don't satisfy you?" The honey in her voice was laced with venom. "Aww, Nicholas's wife won't fuck him, so he has to cheat."

He grabbed her arm, gripping it tight enough to get her attention, but stopping just short of causing pain. He wanted her to know he was playing, but also to realize he could shortcut play and go straight to something a lot stronger, a lot more serious, real damn fast.

"Yeah, I cheat on her with little blonde sluts who come on to strange men in bars."

"I never do this kind of thing."

"I know, you were a virgin till just now. I could tell the minute I saw you."

She tried to extricate her arm from his grip. He tightened it a fraction, taking pleasure in the hint of fear that crossed her features, then let her go. She rubbed her biceps, glared.

"That *hurt*."

"Sometimes I like to make it hurt."

"Aw, you're no fun."

"I beg to differ. Why don't you pour what's left of the booze you didn't drink over your tits, so I can lick it off?"

He still remembered the rich, dizzyingly sweet taste of the bourbon as it dribbled down her deep cleavage, the scent of her sweat and her floral perfume. He remembered having fleeting thoughts about Beth at home in Detroit and asking himself, "What the hell am I doing? Why am I doing this?" even as he was getting hard again, turning the girl over onto her hands and knees, roughly prying open the cheeks of her buttocks, and ramming himself inside.

And later, although normally he liked to keep some lights on, liked to see a woman looking freshly fucked, he made the room darker as she was getting dressed, because he didn't want to see her eyes. Something in them, the despair and shame that was also tainted with that ugliness he'd noticed earlier – not directed just at Nicholas personally, but at men in general – filled him with a queasy kind of fear.

He watched CNN until a little after ten, then drove away from the waterfront lined with clean, brightly lit luxury hotels to the narrow, congested little lanes where the sex trade thrived. The sleaze end of the sex trade, anyway.

Toronto was a city where you could find anything, and Nicholas, at one time or another, in one capacity or another, had provided or partaken of all. As he drove the depressingly familiar streets, he saw that nothing had changed significantly since his days here – the whores still strutting on stiletto-thin spikes, the prancing drag queens in glitter and fake fur and tiny, tight leather skirts, the hustlers cold-eyed and crotch-heavy, sexy dangerous. *Fuck me, fuck me, buy me, buy me* – the eternal mantra of desire and despair.

The rain had tapered off, leaving a chilly moistness in the late summer air and grey, glassy puddles. Nicholas parked the car under a stoplight and walked up Yonge Street, checking in sex parlors and bookstores and gay clubs as he went. Valdez's name elicited little response in those he queried, other than occasionally, feigned ignorance followed by a sudden, apparently urgent, need to be somewhere else.

"Sonny Valdez? Yeah, I know him. But didn't that fucker croak years ago? Didn't he have heart cancer, dick cancer – or maybe he just *was* a cancer?"

The slant-eyed woman who was speaking was a sodden wreck, breasts like huge jellyfish that swayed beneath her see-through blouse, a pendulous belly, eyes ringed with grey-yellow smudges. She sat at the end of the bar in the *Cha Cha Lounge* and tried to pick up guys, and people moved their seats to get away from her.

"No, Sonny Valdez didn't die," said Nicholas. "He was supposed to die. They let him out of fucking prison so he could go home to die, but then he *didn't* die."

The woman eyed him with bleary, wet-brain eyes. "So you already know that, then why you asking *me*?"

"I need to find him."

"You want sweet pussy, you don't need Sonny for that: you found it right here." She leered and spread her bloated thighs, thumped a hand on her crotch.

Nicholas threw down some money for his drink and headed for the door. The barmaid, a tiny girl with crooked lips and short, raggedy black hair, dashed after him. The expression on her face was so intense he thought that, in his haste to escape, he must have miscalculated his tab.

"You after Sonny?"

"I'm not *after* him. I want to find him, though."

"Wellll . . . maybe . . ."

He pulled out his wallet, counted off a trio of bills.

"Where is he?"

"He's got a suite at the Mayflower Hotel."

"A suite? Last time I saw Sonny, he was holed up in a fleabag hotel without a pot to piss in."

"He was sick, then. Now that he's back on his feet, he's got business deals going again. Entrepreneurial endeavors, he calls them."

Nicholas snorted. "Right. Anything you can snort, shoot, smoke, or fuck, Sonny's got a hand in it. How do you know the son-of-a-bitch, anyway?"

"I do him favors. Bring him his groceries a coupl'a times a week. Hold his hand, suck his dick, listen to him babble."

Nicholas felt a twinge of alarm. "The cancer – it didn't come back?"

"Oh, no, he's healthy," she said, "but he don't like to go outside if he don't have to. His head's fucked up. He's scared of something, scared so bad he don't even want to talk about it."

He's healthy. How those words sang in Nicholas's head. How ironic, given how fervently he'd once wished Sonny Valdez dead.

A few years back, he'd actually gone up to Toronto just to see for himself that what he'd heard was true, that Sonny had been released from prison, where he'd done five years of a twelve-year stretch for drug dealing so he could come home to die. Nicholas had wanted to be sure. He'd told Beth that Sonny was a buddy from his old neighborhood in Chicago, and he was going up to Toronto to pay his respects. Which, in a weird way, he supposed was true.

He'd found Sonny much as he'd imagined he'd be, living in one room of a hotel for the indigent subsidized by the government, looked in on by a sour-faced Filipino hospice worker who barely spoke English. By the time he got there, even to an untrained eye, it was obvious that death was on the verge of crawling into bed with Sonny. He lay staring at a tiny TV set, eyes rheumy, vacant, skin the color and texture of old newspaper. He didn't recognize Nicholas, but kept both hands underneath the dirty sheet, rubbing at himself as though his flaccid dick were an Aladdin's lamp from which a genie or orgasm might yet appear.

Nicholas took a long look, saw what he wanted to see, then muttered under his breath "Rot in hell, Sonny," and turned to leave.

He didn't think that Valdez could even hear him and was shaken when the man said, in a cracked, tortured voice, "Maybe so. But you'll get there before me, motherfucker."

The false bravado of a dying man, Nicholas had thought. The cancer coring out his brain along with his vocal cords.

Although he bought the Toronto paper for a few weeks after that, he never saw any notice of Sonny's death: but then, why should he? How many drug-dealing pimps rate a paragraph in the obituary column anyway?

With Sonny presumably gone, Nicholas had exhaled a three-year long sigh of relief. The scumbag he'd once run drugs for was dead, which meant he didn't have to fear his former colleague's long-term propensity for vileness. Didn't have to worry about Sonny reappearing in his life, exposing parts of his sordid history that not even Beth knew about or trying to blackmail him with the threat of doing so.

It wasn't Sonny who turned up from his past, however, but an ex-con named Danny Sorenson, a guy who'd been a buddy of Nicholas's when they were growing up in Chicago. Sorenson hustled luxury cars, stealing them in Detroit, selling them in Miami or Fort Lauderdale. He was imprudent enough to be driving one such stolen vehicle when, looped on crack, he pulled his first and last bank robbery. When Nicholas went to prison, Danny had just gotten transferred down to Canon City Penitentiary in Colorado, after serving two years of a ten-year stretch in Michigan. He'd known Sonny Valdez there. Had, in fact, been Sonny's little helper in various blackmarket scams.

His first December out of the can, Danny got hold of Nicholas's number and gave him a call. Christmas time and

Danny was lonely and looking for somebody to get shitfaced with.

"No, thanks," said Nicholas, making a mental note to tell Beth they needed an unlisted number. Then, by way of emphasizing his new, domesticated lifestyle, he'd added, "The wife's from Toronto. She and I are driving up there to spend Christmas with her family."

"Hey, that's an idea," said Danny drunkenly. "Maybe I'll head up to Toronto myself, see does old Sonny Valdez know some girls can suck dick like a vacuum cleaner."

"Sonny's dead," said Nicholas. "Cancer. Got let out of prison to die."

"Yeah, well, I guess he's resurrected," Danny said, " 'cause I seen Sonny less'n a month ago. Slidin' out of a taxi on King Street with some Asian cookie on his arm."

Nicholas remembered the wasted wreck of a man he'd visited three years earlier. "Don't bullshit me, Danny. He's dead."

"Man, I *talked* to him. Asked him what the hell was he doin' alive. He said he found the magic cure. His head's fucked up, though. You know what he wanted? He asked me to say his name. Just like that. His name. Over and over, while this Asian chick was rolling her eyes, and I'm saying Sonny Valdez, that's your fucking name, and he's holding onto my arm, saying, *say it, say my name, say it again* . . . And then I mention *you*, and was that a mistake! He goes off on a rant – said you rolled on him, that hadn't'a been for you he'd a never gone to prison."

"Bullshit!"

"Yeah, well, like I said, his head's fucked up."

They talked for a few more minutes, Danny wanting to reminisce about prison days, Nicholas wanting nothing more than to get off the phone. Later on, he tried to convince himself that Danny Sorenson was drunk or drugged when he had his encounter with "Sonny", but it didn't fly. Bizarre as Danny's tale was – because of that very off-the-wall bizarreness – there was a ring of truth to it.

And if Sonny Valdez was still alive, there was the chance

he might just show up at the door one day and introduce Beth to the Nicholas Berringer she *didn't* know – and probably didn't want to.

The Mayflower Arms was one of the small, swank, boutique-hotels located in the Yorkville district, northwest of Bloor Street. As expensive as it was unsubtle, the lobby Nicholas entered was gilded like a Russian Easter egg, appointed with heavy, dark velvet furniture and Rococo lamps whose shades were supported by languidly stretching nymphs and pirouetting ballerinas. Whatever else was going on with Sonny, he wasn't hurting for money any longer.

The artfully made-up woman behind the front desk spoke with a French accent so thick it was almost unintelligible, but the fact that she resembled a young Sophia Loren made asking her to repeat herself a pleasure.

Nicholas gave her his real name and was relieved when she rang Sonny's suite and, evidently, was told to send Nicholas on up. Apparently, Sonny had forgotten the image of Nicholas hovering at his death bed a few years earlier, murmuring "rot in hell".

The elevator was of the old-fashioned cage design only large enough to accommodate two people. As Nicholas ascended, he found himself imagining how it would be to fuck a woman in such close quarters and such potentially embarrassing circumstances. He thought about Elise, who had come into his life and shattered it and disappeared into the night again like some kind of succubus and about what he'd like to do to her if she were here. Decided the only thing more satisfying than fucking her would be strangling her at the same time.

"What's this?" Elise had said, looking at the money Nicholas put on the dressing table as though she'd never seen currency before. "I told you, I'm not a hooker."

"Take it," he said. "I'd feel better."

"I hate taking something from somebody when I don't give nothing back," she'd said. An odd comment, he'd thought, coming from a woman he'd just spent the last few hours boinking.

"Don't worry, sweetheart, you gave me plenty."

She cocked her head, pursed her cupie-doll mouth, pinned him to the wall with her blank blue stare. "Well, you know, you may be right, Nicky. Maybe I did."

The elevator groaned open. He didn't need to look for Sonny's door. It was already open, the view within obscured by the portly drug-dealer's squat bulk. He wore white sweat pants, a white sweat shirt and running shoes – an outfit which, considering the fact that he must weigh close to two hundred and fifty pounds now, gave him the air of a thuggish gnome. A highball glass, clinking with ice cubes, was in one hand.

"Nicky-boy, long time, no see." Despite the distinctly unwelcoming tone, he extended a spade-shaped hand. "To what do I owe the honor of this impromptu social call?"

"I heard you were still alive, and I wanted to see for myself."

"Then this *is* a social call?"

"Not exactly. You gonna let me in?"

Sonny's face split into two portions, the grinning mouth below, the eyes, fraught with hate and cunning, above. Guardedly, like someone relishing a private joke, he motioned Nicholas in.

They sat opposite each other, in fat-cushioned chairs with an absurdly fragile-looking glass-topped coffee table between them, hunched over like men closing a questionable deal. Sonny drank gin. Nicholas had a Scotch, which he intended to nurse, but ended up swigging down like soda in an effort to make this encounter less unbearable.

For his part, Sonny chugged his drink like a man facing a firing squad the next morning. He filled his glass again, leaned back, stroked his scruffy beard. "You look good, Nicky-boy. You look – respectable, prosperous. You must be proud of yourself. From a hot-looking young street kid to drug-dealer to hard-timer to – look at you now, what are you, thirty-five? – a well-dressed businessman, probably married to some sweet woman who has no idea about your past. You *are* married, am I right? Her name's Beth, I believe."

"How the hell do you know about her?"

"Oh, I got ways. That fuck-up Danny Sorenson, he needed a job, so I hired him to do a little PI work. He says you made a good life for yourself there in Detroit. You got a lot to be proud of, Nicky-boy. Not many men could make the transition you did. If the streets don't eat them alive, prison does. Hell, I remember when you —"

"I didn't come here to reminisce," said Nicholas. "I came because I want to know why you aren't dead. I want to know what happened, the name of your doctors, what drugs you took, the clinic you went to, if it was one of those places in Mexico that deals in holistic stuff or something experimental or —"

"Hey, hold on, just hold the fuck on," said Sonny. "What are you talking about? Who says I went anywhere or did anything to get cured? Who says I was even sick?"

"I *saw* you, Sonny, remember? I stood by your bedside. You were down to skin and bones. You smelled like a morgue. Plus you were destitute. You didn't have shit, let alone the big bucks to pay for some fancy cure. So don't bullshit me. I want to know why you didn't die, what drugs you took, where you went to get well."

"Who says I took anything? Who says it weren't the grace of God? A miracle?"

"Bullshit."

"What is this, Nicky-boy, you thinkin' about med school? Trying to get published in some medical journal? If *Sixty* fucking *Minutes* shows up wantin' an interview, maybe I'll have somethin' to say, but why the fuck should I talk to you?"

"Because you've got to," Nicholas said. "Because I'm dying."

So he told Sonny about the night with Elise and the blood test a couple of months later, just being on the safe side, and how the test showed that his white count was decimated, that he was about two T-cells away from full-blown fucking AIDS.

When he finished, there was a beat of silence, like stopped

time, while the words hung in the air between them. Then Sonny gave a deep, satisfied sigh, like a man who's just put away a prime cut of filet mignon, and said, "Will you excuse me a minute, Nicky-boy? What you just said, this shocks me a little bit. I need to take it in."

Maybe it was the Scotch that dulled Nicholas's thinking, but he figured Sonny was only going to take a piss or get another drink. Only when Sonny eased himself back into his seat did he recognize the dramatic change in the man's demeanor, the dreamy slackness of his features, for what it was.

"Fuck, what did you *do*?" He grabbed Sonny's wrist and yanked up the sleeve of the sweatshirt – track marks, some old, some very recent.

"China white," said Sonny, answering the unspoken question. "Pure as twelve-year-old pussy."

Nicholas recoiled. "You always said only assholes use their own product."

"Helps me relax," said Sonny. "Some primo smack and a coupl'a whores and it's almost like I'm back the way I was before."

"Before *what*?"

"What you came here to find out about – the secret to my great good health, the miracle cure."

Nicholas realized he had only minutes before Sonny nodded off into that floaty, pink-lined dream state between sleep and wakefulness. Heroin limbo.

"So *talk*, Sonny."

"You say you're dying. That's too bad, Nicky-boy, but you tell me, why the fuck should I give a shit?"

Nicholas had prepared for this. Calmly he pulled the 0.9 mm Biretta out of his jacket and aimed it at Sonny's head. "Because if you don't tell me what I want to know, I kill you. Right here, right now. I got nothing to lose, Sonny. I got AIDS, so I'm dead anyway. Taking you with me will just be a bonus."

Sonny grinned at the gun like it was somebody's index finger and let loose a laugh. "You can't kill me, Nicky-boy.

Wanna know why? 'Cause there ain't no me to kill. There is no me. I never was. I never will be. It was all a dream, a fucking fabrication."

"What the hell are you talking about?"

Sonny moved as if to stand up. Nicholas cocked the gun, said in a whisper that was sibilant with menace, "Sit the fuck down."

"I need a drink."

"You don't need nothing, Sonny."

"Say that again."

"What?"

"What you called me. I like to hear it. Say it again."

He's trying to con me into thinking he's crazy, Nicholas thought, *into putting the gun away. Either that, or he's drugged himself out of his mind.* But he answered anyway. "I called you Sonny. That's your name, isn't it? Sonny Valdez? Scumbag *par excellence.* A consummate shit. How's that?"

"Sonny Valdez, Sonny Valdez." He shut his eyes, swayed slightly and chanted the words like a schoolyard ditty. So enraged was Nicholas by what he assumed had to be a performance that he shifted the gun to his left hand and backhanded Sonny a stunning blow to the side of the head.

Sonny keeled sideways. But for the heft of the chair arm, he would have collapsed to the floor. Instead, he sagged limply for a second, then righted himself with a slow-motion deliberateness that, under other circumstances, Nicholas would have found unspeakably satisfying.

"How'd you get well, Sonny? Just give me the name of your doctor or your guru or your medicine man and I'll be on my way. You can OD in peace. I don't give a fuck."

Sonny's eyelids fluttered open. He grinned and shook his head like he was trying to dislodge a gnat from his ear. His eyes gleamed with dark joy and a perverse, soulless pleasure.

"So you stuck your dick in the wrong hole, huh, Nicky-boy? So did I, only that's not what gave me the cancer. That's what took the cancer away. Took everything away."

"What?"

"I'm talking about a piece of ass. A fucking piece of pussy."

"A woman?"

"You deserve her, Nicky-boy, and everything she'll do to you. One thing, though – I tell you who she is, you find her, I want you to come back to me and tell me where *she is*."

"Why's that, Sonny?"

But the drug-dealer's eyes were easing shut. He sighed and snored and then jerked semi-awake, a tic twitching at the corner of one eye.

Nicholas shook him so hard his head bounced back and forth like a dashboard dog's. "*Why*, Sonny?"

" 'Cause I got unfinished business with the bitch," he whispered slowly. "She stole from me, the fucking cunt. I'm gonna kill her, 'cause she stole my fucking name."

"Fucking crazy smack-shooting, son-of-a-bitch," muttered Nicholas as he left the hotel.

The rain had started again, warm and stinging, driven in spurts by the wind. Nicholas walked with his head down, avoiding the puddles, trying to think.

The Biretta was back in jacket, unfired. His brain was brimming with booze and the Volvo must've been stolen, because he could swear there was some other vehicle in the space where he'd parked it.

At first he thought of going back to his hotel and trying to sleep, then saying screw it, driving back home to Detroit, explaining the whole nasty business to Beth and facing the consequences. At least, he knew that *she* was healthy. Her system couldn't take the Pill so, for years now, they'd been using condoms for birth control.

He couldn't face her, though. Not yet.

Not while Sonny Valdez, for all his demented ravings, had given him a shred of hope.

So he called Beth and made his excuses. Then, for the next week, he stayed in Toronto, taking in the live sex shows, the backroom peepshows, investigating the upscale callgirl ser-vices, the street hustlers and whores. He didn't have sex, paid or otherwise: which was remarkable for Nicholas, since these streets were his old stomping grounds. They reeked of all his old addictions – bought sex and booze and the oblivion brought on by a trio of hot whores, a few grams of coke, and enough Jack to numb out everything but reptile brain lust. *Names*, he thought, remembering Sonny's babbling, *who even wanted a name then? Who needed to know?*

"Myriam, her name's Myriam," he said to the stringy-haired hustler who sidled up to him outside the strip bar where he'd just spent the last hour trying to get information out of girls so stoned or high or just braindead that they made talking to Sonny seem intellectually stimulating.

To Nicholas's surprise, the boy's sallow face lit up; the somber blankness of his eyes gleamed with animation and a hint of fear.

"Myriam?"

"You know where to find her?"

"No, but if you make it worth my while, I know somebody who might. My lover. She saved his life."

No marquee advertised her. No promoter delivered his pitch or handed out fliers outside a dark doorway. There was only a stairway leading down to a basement underneath a boarded-up adult bookstore. When Nicholas took out his wallet, the smokey-skinned East Indian manning the door shook his head. "No more audience tonight. Full up."

Sonny had told him this might happen, so he took a chance. "I'm a friend of Sonny Valdez. He knows Myriam."

The man shrugged. "Don't know no Valdez."

"Fuck it, man, I'm sick. I know what it is that she does. Sonny told me all about her."

The man nodded knowingly. "Maybe you come in anyway," he said, unblocking the door.

The stage was small and furnished only with a mattress covered in yellow satin sheets and a leather swing of the type sold in sex boutiques. Crimson curtains were gathered back on either side. White carpeting and stark white walls, against which the curtains stood out like stigmata.

The audience sat on a semi-circle of tiers facing the stage. Saffron-tinted track lighting rendered their faces bleak, surreal, and jaundiced-looking. Some of the patrons, almost all men, had removed their shoes and sat cross-legged, like yogis, but any resemblance to an ashram ended there. The room reeked of sex. Half a dozen nude and semi-nude women slunk on their hands and knees along the tiers, offering their mouths to the seated men, a few of whom unzipped in the detached, dispassionate way of bored despots exercising *droits de seigneurs*.

Nicholas aimed himself at a seat at the end of the tier farthest away from the stage. He tottered a bit getting up there and plopped down with an unintended grunt, like an old man losing a grip on his walker. Fuck, not only had he let Sonny Valdez send him on this wild goose chase, but he was shit-faced as well. He thought about getting the hell out of there, finding his way back to the hotel, assuming he still could, and decorating those snazzy gold bathroom fixtures and cushy white towels with part of Sonny's frontal lobe, then he looked down and saw the brunette with her round tawny rump in the air and decided maybe that would be hasty.

She was crawling toward him, naked except for the gold armbands on one wrist and biceps and darker bands, tattooed ones, around her neck and ankles. Gazing up at him, she ran her tongue around full lips that, in the weird light at least, looked purple-black.

"You want to fuck?"

The phrase, in its similarity to Elise's opening remark of so many months ago, jolted him. He ran a hand along the sweet, smooth curve of her buttocks and bent down to cup the furry mound between her legs.

"God, you are fucking beautiful," he said.

She cocked her head, shiny black hair swishing against her breasts. "You want my ass, my tits, my cunt?"

"God, yes, I want," he murmured, "but how about a drink first? Or, better yet, a joint?"

"No drinks," she said, "just fuck. No drugs, just fuck. You understand?"

"Right, I got it," said Nicholas, more perplexed than ever.

So Sonny Valdez had sent him to a place where neither drugs nor alcohol were part of the picture. The very bizarreness of such a scenario made him uneasy.

Someone further along the row was requesting the girl's services. She crawled past Nicholas, long hair sweeping the carpet, ass uptilted, the pierced lips of her vulva hanging meatily between her legs.

As Nicholas looked after her longingly, he was aware of a hush and a collective intaking of breath on the part of the men around him. He turned toward the stage, where a voluptuous, big-hipped blonde with enormous, low-swaying breasts had emerged from behind the curtains. She wore red leather, high-heeled boots that laced up the back of her thighs to below the knees. A black leather thong that made a pretense of covering her crotch disappeared into the crack of her ass. She looked yielding and smotheringly soft, like loamy earth from which a man might not emerge without a struggle. To Nicholas, who preferred his women firm and muscular, she would have merited no more than a glance, but the audience appeared entranced, almost mesmerized. As one, they murmured, "Myriam."

She undulated her lush body along the edge of the stage in rapt silence – no catcalls, no whistles, nobody rising to thrust a bill under the thong. Silence – tense, awestruck, respectful – reigned.

She selected an overweight man from the third tier. Haltingly, as though the sex-steamy air must hurt his lungs, he lumbered onto the stage. Began to remove his clothes with trembling fingers.

Nicholas watched, at once fascinated and repulsed. The guy was no sex-show stud, that was obvious. With agonizing self-consciousness, he undressed, then stood naked, hands flopping nervously over a pendulous abdomen. To Nicholas, he looked pathetic and ridiculous. The woman ran her hands along his chest, arms, crotch. He didn't move: nor did his dick, which peaked softly, shyly from beneath the mound of belly. The only rigid thing about him was his spine, the vertebrae of which seemed to have been fused by pure panic.

Without further preliminaries, Myriam lay down on the mattress, legs spread, back arched. The fat man knelt ponderously over her, his body language and facial expression suggesting he was placing his dick onto a guillotine. Even at this distance, Nicholas could see his hands were trembling, his dick so soft it might have been squeezed out of a toothpaste tube.

Nicholas squirmed, finding the guy's public humiliation almost too painful to watch.

Myriam played with the man's penis for a few minutes, using her hands and mouth: but, if anything, the exercise seemed less about an attempt at copulation than a graphic demonstration of his utter inability to get an erection.

Finally, the two reversed positions, with Myriam guiding her partner down onto the mattress while she squatted above him. Slowly, with almost balletic grace, she removed the thong and lowered herself so that her parted lips touched the crown of his penis where it rested slack against his enormous belly. The oiled muscles of her thighs and abdomen flexed powerfully. Six, twelve times in eye-blink fast succession. Then, again. The fat man gave a little cry. Slowly, like a snake being charmed, his dick began to rise. From what Nicholas could see, it looked like the muscles of Myriam's pussy were tugging at it, lifting it erect, then sucking it inside her.

The fat man started to buck and moan. Soaked with sweat, he puffed and grunted. Tears rolled down his cheeks as his cock disappeared inside. She settled herself on his hips, shut her eyes, and rested motionless. The man beneath her began to shake and sob. Finally, Myriam eased herself up and released his cock. It popped back against his belly, majestically erect.

The hush of the room erupted into cheers. Some of the masturbating men rushed to the stage and surrounded Myriam, anointed her with their semen. One came on her face, another spurted onto her breasts; thickly clotted strings of it were in her hair and glistening on her thighs.

Amazed, but also disappointed, Nicholas turned to the scrawny, blemished-faced man next to him. "So *that's* all she does, she cures impotence?" he said.

The man glared at him. "That's what you think the guy's problem was, a limp dick? He had stomach cancer. That's what she was pulling out of him, the cancer."

Afterward, Nicholas waited until Myriam emerged from a bathroom off the hall. Nothing glamorous now – she wore a baggy white shirt over black tights. Blonde hair clipped back from her round face. Her only make-up a smudge of mascara and a dab of fuschia lipstick.

Nicholas blocked her way. "A man named Sonny Valdez claims you cured him of cancer."

"Oh, does he?" Her cool green gaze washed over him. The scent of her, gardenia with undertones of musk, filled his head.

"I have AIDS," Nicholas said. "Can you help me?"

"If you want it badly enough."

"How much money?"

"How much is your life worth to you?"

"Two cents on a good day. Cut the crap, lady, how much do you want?"

"Nothing," said Myriam. "If I heal you, then you make a gift to me. Whatever you think is fair."

"That's a funny way of doing business."

"This isn't a business."

"And I won't do it in front of an audience. It has to be in private. Just you and me."

She smiled. "A lot of people feel that way. But the sexual energy of others is important for the ceremony. It makes the healing faster. If you're shy about –"

"I'm not shy," said Nicholas. "But I'm not performing for a bunch of perverts, either. I already know what that feels like."

"You know so much, then maybe you don't need me." With surprising strength, she put a hand on his chest and shoved past him.

Contrite and frightened, he went after her. "No, wait. I'm sorry. Please. I need your help."

She glared at him a moment, then her features softened and she drew a long, slow breath. "Tomorrow night, then. Not here, though. Never in the same place twice. I hope you have a good memory. I never write anything down."

"It's good enough," said Nicholas, and she told him an address.

"Take your clothes off and lie down with me," said Myriam. They were in a third floor efficiency of a squalid hotel off Dundas Street that catered to transients, addicts, and hookers, who rented the rooms by the hour. It occupied a tiny nook between a take-away Chinese joint and moss-encrusted St Benedict's Cathedral on the corner and, although Nicholas had cruised this area a hundred times, he didn't remember ever noticing the place before.

Now, awkwardly, as though he were stripping for some unpleasant physical exam, Nicholas undressed and crawled into bed next to Myriam. He laid a hand on her breast, but she only continued staring at the ceiling, her expression meditative, pensive.

"Now what?" he said angrily.

"Do you believe in God, Nicholas?"

"No."

"Do you believe that *I'm* God?"

"Of course not."

"That *you're* God?"

"What is this? Is this about getting it on or are we having a fucking prayer meeting?"

She turned onto her side, breasts lolling in great vanilla mounds. "You're here because you believe – even a little bit – that I might have the power to cure you. That isn't rational, Nicholas. And clearly you're a rational man, who doesn't believe in God, who doesn't expect miracles. So maybe you're just here for one last good fuck." She traced a fingernail around his nipple, teasing it erect. "So what are you waiting for, Nicholas? Don't you want to fuck me?"

"Damn right," he said, affecting his old bravado from the past, but unconvincingly so. As her fingers played with the curls of his chest hair, fear did a counterpoint jig on his spine.

"I told you what's wrong with me," he said. "You don't want to use protection?"

Merriment danced in her green eyes, in the creases at the corners of her smile. "I already have protection, Nicholas."

She pulled his face to hers, kissed him long and wetly. Tongue rimming the roof of his mouth, the tender edge of his gums. Licked his eyelids and throat, filled his ear with the heat of her breath. Her meaty body felt heavy and powerful. Her smell enveloped him, old odors and fragrances, scents of passion and longing and loss. He wanted to fuck her and he wanted to weep, and the juxtaposition of those two conflicting sensations brought up his anger, a sense of brute self-preservation.

He rolled her over, got on top and thrust her open. So she didn't need protection from his disease? Fine: maybe she needed it from him. He rammed his way inside her. Their skin squeaked together. He could hear the thumping of their bellies, the slurp and sputter of moist flesh.

But the instant that he entered her, he felt her grasp him almost to the point of pain, her inner muscles pulling him inside. Tugging his penis, but also something else – his essence, his energy, his very Nicholas-ness – for which his dick seemed to be becoming the conduit. The sensation that he was in the process of ejaculating not just his infection, but his very soul, galvanized all his energy into his thrusts. He fucked her desperately, with the savagery of a man trying to dig his way out of prison, and she was the passage to freedom, to hope. Carving her out with his cock, widening her up until her cunt seemed to expand to suck in the whole world. She was wet and dark and hot, and somehow he was not only fucking her, but seeing her from inside as well – she was a black galaxy pulsing with what seemed at first to be stars, but what he realized were sperm, countless millions of seething, glittering sperm aswarm in her hothouse interior.

The energy built toward an orgasm. Not yet, his ego

protested. For some perverse reason, he wanted to impress this woman, this harlot, this hooker, this bitch, he wanted to fuck her like she'd never been fucked. The excitement intensified, not just in his cock, but at the base of his spine. White energy that burned and blazed, stoking the fire that kept his cock hard as he fucked her and fucked her and fucked . . .

Then suddenly, there was no one fucking her at all or getting fucked. Nicholas – the fiction of Nicholas – was drowning in Myriam's depths. What remained was pure silence, a crystalline nothingness marred only by the swelling of his own primitive terror.

The white radiance of sexual energy blazed like a fiery tree from the base of his spine. It consumed him, reduced him to ashes.

There was a swishing noise, like fabric rustling, and the sensation of light entering the room with a rush, but he didn't dare open his eyes.

For a moment, it seemed every question was answered, every terror assuaged, every evil forgiven. There was no separation. Ecstasy thrilled through his body, his soul. His soul – for he knew now that he had one, that it was his soul that was real, nothing else, not the Nicholas shell he'd accepted as his true self all these years.

He cried out as he came, opened his eyes, and then recoiled from the shock of what he saw – rows of naked men and women observing him in all his fear and vulnerability. He was no longer fucking Myriam on a bed in that miserable hotel room, but back in the basement room where he'd first seen her, performing on stage before an audience of aroused and worshipful voyeurs.

Slowly the watchers filed up onto the stage and began the ritual Nicholas had seen the night before, only tonight it no longer disgusted him – their semen streamed into his mouth, his hair, mingled with the come on his own cock, and he didn't object, didn't feel soiled or outraged or betrayed, but threw his head back, opened his mouth, and drank their spillage along with Myriam.

"God," he breathed, "what happened?"

And she smiled up at him exultantly, and said, "Yes. Exactly. God happened."

The day after the experience with Myriam, Nicholas went to two different clinics and had his blood drawn. A week-long wait for the results at the first one, five days at the other. He could have gone back to Detroit, but the idea never even occurred to him. As long as *she* was here, he would be, too.

Am I in love with her? Nicholas thought. *Am I in thrall to her*?

Not to Myriam herself, he decided, but to the experience she'd given him. For the first few hours after their love-making, the wondrous sensation had lingered. His reality shifted. He felt whole, he felt one with all of Creation. Entranced by the feeling, the *knowing*, that he was not defined by his skin or his mind or his name, Nicholas, but that God Himself was playing peekaboo, peering out from behind his eyes looking at God peering back from the eyes of everyone else. Love suffused him. He no longer hated Sonny Valdez, no longer regretted his past or longed for some fantasy future. For the first time in his life, he felt happy and whole.

Then, gradually, the ecstasy faded and Nicholas became just Nicholas again – separate and lonely and flawed, but longing now to return to that place he had briefly visited.

He returned to the boarded-up storefront and banged his fist on the locked basement door. No one answered, and a passing policeman finally stopped by and shooed him away, thinking him tipsy, but harmless. He went back the next night and slept on the stones by the door, but no one came. Nor the night after that or the next one.

Despondent and heartsick, he asked about Myriam, but the few people who admitted to knowing her said only that she moved around. Here a few days, then somewhere else.

On the fourth day of useless searching, furious and frustrated, he picked up a hooker and took her back to his room, where he tried to recreate the experience he was seeking.

When that failed, he found another young woman and did coke with her before they had sex. On coke, Nicholas could stay hard almost indefinitely. But nothing happened, except that both he and the girl were sore the next morning.

His stay at the upscale Harbor Castle was becoming too costly, and he decided to move to a modest, inexpensive hotel near Queen's Park. The phone rang as he was packing his suitcase. He hesitated, then picked it up. Wished that he hadn't. The pain in Beth's voice stabbed his temporal lobe like an icepick. Worse, though, was the fact that he had to jog his mind to recall the face belonging to that distraught voice. He felt as though decades had passed since he'd last seen her. Since he'd lain down with Myriam and everything changed.

"I'm sorry, Beth, but I can't come home yet. There's a deal in the making, some more property that I want to look at –"

"Stop lying to me, Nicholas."

"Beth, listen –"

"I'm sick of excuses. I want you to come home now. Whatever's happened, whatever you've gotten involved with, I can forgive it, but you have to leave now, just leave and come home. Can't you do that?"

He wanted to tell her, *yes, yes, of course, I'll come home*, but what he heard himself say was, "No, I can't do that. This deal is too important. Leaving here now is out of the question."

She gave a long moan that escalated into a wild wail, like an animal lost and wounded. He held the phone away from his ear, but the sound still reverberated chaotically through his body, ripping synapses with its discordant notes of anguish.

"Don't give me that bullshit, Nicholas. Don't treat me like an idiot. What is it? Are you in love with someone else? Is that what it is? Are you leaving me?"

"No, Beth, no, I mean, I don't know what I'm doing. I just know I can't come home yet, I have to stay here a little bit longer. I can't explain. I want to, but I just can't."

Then there was silence, which was scarier somehow than

the grief-stricken wail of a moment before. "This has something to do with that Sonny Valdez character, doesn't it?" she
said finally, her voice flat and jagged, like ice chipped from a
block with an axe. "He's got you involved in something
illegal, some drug scam. Jesus, Nicholas, are you that big a
fool? Do you want to go back to prison?"

"No, no, I don't." Tears started pouring out of his eyes,
heartfelt and wrenching, but responding to her words in a
way completely different from how she meant them. He
didn't want to go back to prison: that was the whole point.
Prison was what his life had been like before, prison was his
separate identity, his separate skin. Prison was his narrow,
rigid identity as Nicholas Berringer. It was the same realiza-
tion, the same awakening, that must have turned Sonny
Valdez into a paranoid recluse. But how could he tell her
that, how could he say it so she didn't think he'd gone back to
drugs, think him insane?

"It's *this*, Beth," he said finally. "I know it sounds crazy,
but I had – how do I put this? – some kind of experience. It
was something spiritual, something so incredible – I can't
just walk away from it now."

She gave a high, raucous hoot. "A spiritual experience?
You, Nicholas? So what are you saying? Did you get Born
Again, join the Moonies, give up your soul to Lord Krish-
na?"

"Please, Beth, I'm serious."

"Then fucking tell me what you're talking about!"

"I can't. I want to explain, but I can't. I do love you. Please
just believe that. Please just be –"

"Are you leaving me, Nicholas?"

"I just can't come home yet, I –"

"Then you know what, Nicholas? Go to hell. Just go to
hell!"

She hung up the phone.

"This isn't enough. I want more – everything you can do to
me," Nicholas said to the dominatrix. "I don't give a damn
about pain. I don't care if you make me bleed. What I want is

to go beyond my normal limits, to be outside myself. Whatever it takes, I want you to do it."

Madame Yvette was gossamer pale, ethereal-looking with
grey eyes like circles cut from glassy envelopes and long hair,
braided down her back, a violent shade of red. Her milky,
finely freckled skin contrasted vividly with the black leather
regalia, the fetish boots and studded wrist bands, the black
lipstick and the riding crop that Nicholas had watched her
wield with delicate precision against the buttocks of the
bound and blindfolded "slave" that he'd just fucked.

"You're not one of my regulars," she said. "I like to move
slowly with a new client. I need to determine your tolerance
for pain and humiliation. I've had clients lose it in the middle
of a scene and try to rip my throat out."

"My tolerance for pain is high," snapped Nicholas. "And
if I were going to 'lose it' in the middle of a sex scene, I'd
have done that long ago. What I want –" he hesitated, groped
for the right words "– is to be transported mentally, to lose
myself so where I end and you begin becomes unclear. Does
that make sense? Can you give me an experience that's so
intense it clouds the mind and yet, at the same time, clears
it?"

"Short of killing you, you mean?" said Madame Yvette.

"Short of killing me."

"You don't mind blood?"

"Not if bleeding gets me to the place I want to be."

Madame Yvette considered this. Finally she said, "I don't
like dealing with crazy and unstable people. They're dangerous to me and to my business. Neither am I interested in
assisting suicide. So tell me, Nicholas: are you one of the
crazy, unstable people?"

"I don't know."

Madame Yvette touched his wrist with her bright, black
nails and left a tiny scratch. "Then perhaps we will find
out."

Her dungeon was considered the priciest and best
equipped in Toronto, where Madame and her girls had
served the masochistic needs of some of the city's wealthiest

and most powerful for many years. Suitably foreboding, it was a pod of individual cells connected to a central hall. Gloomily, it reminded Nicholas of the time he'd spent behind bars, although the prison accommodation he remembered had been vastly more cheerful and definitely better lit.

She ordered Nicholas to strip, which he did, then manacled him to a crossbeam, arms above his head, legs splayed. His first instinct, when the manacles were tightened painfully around his wrists, was to try to free himself and fuck her till she screamed. Submissiveness was not his natural inclination. All the more reason then, he figured, that he should experience it. Maybe that was the key, he reasoned. Maybe subservience and suffering would bring him to that transcendent point where Nicholas ceased to exist and something else filled the void.

And though she whipped and paddled him until he screamed, tortured him with excruciating nippleclamps, choked him till lights blinked on and off in his head and his orgasms were broken up with spaces of unconsciousness, nothing occurred that ever exceeded the realm of the physical, and Nicholas was always Nicholas – more than ever, in fact, when his ego raged at Madame Yvette's humiliations, the sadistic whimsy of the many degradations to which she subjected him and the undeniably sweet suffering inherent in each one.

At last, towards dawn, he left the Madame's establishment – tormented and pleasured to equal degree, physically sated and emotionally drained, but most of all, wretchedly disappointed.

For the third time that evening, Nicholas trudged along Yonge Street, head lowered, oblivious to the sex shop windows full of leather toys, the sibilant whispers of hookers cooing from the darkening doorways. He'd visited every purveyor of erotica that he could think of, questioned anyone who'd talk to him, even tracked down the young hustler who'd originally told him where Myriam could be found.

He got nothing but blank stares and, occasionally, bitter

laughter, as though the mere fact that he searched for Myriam rendered him an object of pity and disdain.

Now the hopelessness of it was settling over him. Of course someone like Myriam wouldn't stay in one place. Or at least wouldn't permit the *illusion* that she remained in one place, he thought, remembering how he had begun making love with Myriam in a hotel room and then found himself back in the basement room where he'd first seen her.

She's gone, he thought despairingly. *I'll never find her again. I'll never experience that feeling again.*

Which is worse, he wondered, to have an experience so life-changing that you'd spend the rest of your life longing for it, dreaming of it, trying fruitlessly to find it again, or never to have had the experience at all? The first seemed a prescription for wretchedness, yet the second seemed an unthinkable choice.

I'm alive, he thought. *I'm cured. The test results came back, and I'm fine. Why isn't that enough? Why do I want more? Why can't I give this up and go back to Beth – if she'll have me, that is? I love her: why isn't she enough?*

He passed a hooker of indeterminate gender thunking along on platform heels, a gaudily costumed creature who licked its lips and swished its silken tongue at Nicholas. There was a flicker of interest on Nicholas's part, but it was replaced almost immediately by discouragement. Since the session with Madame Yvette, almost a week ago, he'd bought the services of half a dozen professional purveyors of sex, including a buxom she-male with a python-like dick, a Vietnamese whore who claimed knowledge of secret Tantric rites, and a submissive who aroused in Nicholas such powerful aggression that he feared equally for her life and for his sanity.

But nothing, in that smorgasbord of guilty pleasures and perverse games of mind and body, did he find anything that resembled even remotely what he'd felt with Myriam, so he shook his head at the lip-smacking whore and trudged on, headed toward Dundas Street.

Since coming to Toronto, Nicholas had walked past St Benedict's Cathedral dozens of times without giving it more than a passing glance, other than to note the irony of its presence here at the end of a block comprised almost entirely of shops devoted to the sex trade. But he'd been raised Catholic and still had some fleeting attachment to Catholicism's rites and rituals. There was a certain comfort in the familiarity of a religion that, for the most part, he'd left behind in boyhood. On a whim, he decided to go inside.

A few people knelt in prayer. At the altar, a priest was preparing to give Mass.

Nicholas found a confessional and slid inside. He confessed to his adulteries, to the myriad indulgences of the past few days – the group sex, the gay sex, sex as dominator and as dominated. But finally, having exhausted that part of his confession, he said, "I met a woman here who worked a miracle for me. Only a few days ago, I had AIDS, and now the results of two blood tests have come back negative. This woman cured me. I don't expect you to understand this, Father, or to believe it, but she cured me by – well, by having sex with me, and now I can't get over that experience. It haunts me. Not the sex itself, but something else I can't put into words . . ." There was a long pause from the other side. Nicholas slammed his fist against the inside of the confessional and said, "Fuck, I don't know why I'm telling you this. You can't possibly know what I mean. You must think I'm crazy. Hell, *I'm* starting to think I'm crazy."

"Don't go." The firmness of the priest's command halted Nicholas as he was rising to leave. "You say you're haunted by what you felt when you were with this woman. If you could see her again, if you could be with her, do you think this time you could hold onto the experience you describe, that you could absorb it into your soul?"

Nicholas, surprised, responded, "I don't know, Father. All I know is I want to try."

"I don't know if I'm damning you to hell or guiding you along the path to heaven, but maybe I can help."

Beth had packed the car in a rage, not knowing where she was going, only that it would be in the opposite direction from

Nicholas. They'd been married five years. She had known it was dicey going into it, that Nicholas had spent time in prison for dealing cocaine, that his youth was a black hole which he described to her only in the vaguest, most general terms or not at all. She knew the power of his erotic appetites, so the idea that he might cheat on her was more dismaying and disappointing than outright shocking – that he would leave her altogether, though, with no more explanation than that he *had* no explanation, beggared all comprehension.

She had decided to drive south, with New Mexico as a vague and dreamily envisioned destination. She knew no one there, had never indicated to her husband any desire to visit. It was a destination where, should Nicholas ever tire of whatever adventure he was on and decide to look for her, he would never find her. And, in the meantime, she had her own fantasies of Marlboro Men with studly bulges and swarthy, muscular Mexicans on the prowl for paler flesh. *I'll show him*, she thought, before reflecting sadly on the futility of inspiring jealousy in someone who didn't give a fuck.

All this was on her mind when she got the letter post-marked Toronto. Given the contents, outwardly, it was strikingly genteel-looking. Expensive Mayflower Hotel stationery addressed in an elegant cursive that resembled the handwriting of her elderly aunt, not a psychotic-looking T-bar or manic-looking flourish to be seen.

The very elegance and neatness of it, however, like an exquisitely gift-wrapped package that contains manure, flagged her attention as much as if the letters of the address had been clipped out of a magazine and taped onto the envelope.

Inside she found a sheet of stationery with a single sentence written in that same overly controlled hand, as though the writer were making a conscious effort to contrast the vile inscription with the fastidious lettering. And along with that, a faded Polaroid of a much younger Nicholas. He wore a tie-dyed body shirt that showed off a ripped and gleaming chest. Long hair stringy around his face, eyes blank and strange.

Nicky-boy, age 19, the best hustler in the business, the caption read.

Naked, Nicholas sat on the tier nearest the stage, breathing the heady, almost nauseatingly sweet scent of incense and sickness and sex. It was the same basement room that he remembered from the first time he'd seen Myriam, but on a different street in a different section of the city.

A girl so thin, her biceps were scarcely bigger than her wrists, lay on the mattress. Her face was turned towards the audience. Her eyes were huge and frighteningly vacant. The tattoos on her stomach and legs had become misshapen squiggles of color as her flesh withered and shrank beneath the designs. The shroud-color of sickness clung to her.

Behind the blue swirl of incense, Myriam moved over the girl. Her heavy, pendulous breasts lolled against the other's flat chest, huge, coffee-colored nipples brushing smooth pink ones. She lifted the girl's head, tongue-kissed her, then lapped her way down the skeletal torso to the straw-colored thatch between her thighs.

The girl didn't move or give indication that she knew what was happening. Nicholas strained to see if she even breathed. Her eyes were unblinking. He wondered if she might have died.

Myriam angled herself between the girl's legs. A thick, purple-crowned phallus lolled between her thighs. Never had Nicholas seen a dildo so life-like; nor could he determine where it had been strapped on. For a disorienting moment, he suffered the illusion that the cock was actually Myriam's, that she had somehow metamorphosed into a male.

As she slid inside the girl, some of the watchers sank into each other's arms and began to couple with great urgency. Matings of the same and opposite sex in positions both conventional and exotically perverse while, as always, there were men who touched no one but themselves, waiting to anoint the fornicators with their gush of semen.

A woman with long black hair threaded with grey slid her legs through Nicholas's. She dipped down and took his cock into her mouth, but not even that distracted him from what was taking place on stage. The girl that Myriam fucked had come to life now. Writhing, bucking, whimpering, her back arching so the outline of her ribs showed clearly beneath the blue-white skin.

Tears streamed down the girl's thin face. Myriam stopped thrusting. The girl calmed. While those in the audience continued their mating, the two on stage lay quietly together, neither of them moving, suspended in that moment of sublime transcendence that, to Nicholas, had seemed to last for hours, that moment which had removed one illness to replace it with another, a kind of hopeless longing akin to homesickness.

He put his hands down on the head of the woman sucking him. His fingers threaded through her hair. He held her still and shut his eyes, forcing himself to remain motionless as he willed the experience he'd had with Myriam to return. It was in vain – nothing was recaptured, only a greater and more enervating sense of futility and loss.

Gently he slid himself free of the woman's warm, willing mouth. Gazed down into her face searching for some remnant of the experience with Myriam – because he felt nothing, did that mean she felt nothing, too?

"Have you been with Myriam?" he asked.

She nodded – but only after a pause, warily, like a child reluctant to confess a minor theft. "I wasn't sick, though. There was just a lump, a tiny one, that went away on its own."

"When you were having sex with her, what did you feel?"

She shrugged. "I don't remember it," and dipped her head again.

"Wait," said Nicholas, lifting her chin. "Do you think about how it felt to be with her? Do you dream of being with her again?"

"I *told* you, I don't remember what it was like," the woman hissed. Fear capered in her eyes. She pulled away, and Nicholas let her go.

On stage, Myriam lifted the girl up, so that they sat facing each other, the girl astride Myriam's cock. Again, they became motionless, staring into each other's eyes.

It's some kind of hypnotism, thought Nicholas, but even as the idea occurred to him, he rejected it. He hadn't been hypnotized when he was making love with Myriam, nor in the grip of some sex-induced trance. What he'd experienced, for that matter, hadn't even been entirely sexual, although perhaps he simply hadn't recognized it as such, wasn't as well versed with the parameters of eroticism as he'd have liked to think. Maybe not everyone who coupled with Myriam felt it. Maybe they were too frightened to admit that they did or, like Sonny, their minds could simply not expand to accommodate the magnitude of the experience.

Around him, the orgy grew more lusty, the cries and grunts and moans converging in a strange, atonal symphony. He felt absent from his own skin, detached from the eager pulsings that stirred his cock to stiffness. He stood up, retrieved his clothing from the pile beside the door, went outside to the men's room in the corridor and got dressed. As he was coming out, a slender woman with a lustrous tangle of frosted blonde hair was hurrying along the corridor. She wore a suede skirt, high heels, a black leather vest over a white turtleneck.

Nicholas considered making some minor witticism about etiquette at an orgy (don't worry, late-comers are well thought of), but then thought better of it. As she breezed past, she half-turned toward him. He glimpsed her face.

"Wait!"

She kept going.

"Elise!"

He could see she tried to pretend the name meant nothing, but there was a slight cringe when he said it, as though he'd lobbed a small stone.

"Wait, I know it's you!"

He grabbed her arm, spun her around. "Why are you running from me? What are you afraid of?"

"Let me go!"

"You *knew* what you were doing to me," he said. "When I

thought back on it, the last thing you said was that you were giving me something, too. You *knew* you were sick. You did it to me on purpose.''

She pulled away, anger in the twisting of her crimson-lined lips, fear in the overbright sheen of her eyes. "Let go of me!"

"Not until you tell me why you wanted to infect me. You didn't even know me. Why?"

She turned away, shoulders slumping in defeat. "I know you won't believe this, but I never in my life purposely set out to hurt somebody like I did you. I've thought about you so much, wondering what happened to you and to your wife. I am truly sorry."

"I don't give a damn about your being sorry. Answer the fucking question. *Why?*"

Sooty tears spread from the corners of her heavily mascara'd eyes and tracked down her cheeks. "I needed money. For doctors' bills, all kinds of things. I needed money, and I had to get it any way I could."

"You mean, somebody paid you to have sex with me, knowing you were infected?"

She nodded.

"Who?"

But the question was already answered in his mind even before she said it for him: "Sonny."

"Jesus God, that vicious bastard."

"He's obsessed with getting revenge on you. Almost as much as he does –" she nodded toward the door behind which Myriam performed "– her."

"But that doesn't make sense."

"He says you rolled on him years back. Set it up so you walked after only a couple years, and he got sentenced to twelve."

"That's not how it went."

"Maybe not, but he thinks it did. That makes it true."

"So he wanted me dead. Then why did he tell me about Myriam? She saved my life."

"Myriam cured Sonny, too, but she couldn't cure him of all the hate he carries around inside him. She also fucked with his mind. Maybe he thought she'd fuck you up, too, and that would be worse than whatever else he could do to you." She looked toward the door and fidgeted with the buttons of her vest. "I need to get in there."

"Go on."

"I'm sorry, Nicholas. Can you forgive me?"

He started to answer with something along the lines of, *no way, you fucking little bitch.* Instead he said, "Are you cured, now?"

She shrugged. "So far, so good. It would appear so."

"Good. I'm glad for you."

"About Sonny – I shouldn't have told you he hired me. You aren't going to do anything, are you?"

"Only what I wish I'd done a long time ago – blow the fucking scumbag's brains out his asshole."

"I know it was you who sent me this. I want to know why."

Sonny Valdez took the photo Beth handed him and stared at it as though seeing it for the first time. "I thought you'd be interested in a side of your husband's past I'm betting he never told you about."

"He worked for you?"

"Worked for me. Serviced me, whatever."

"So you were his pimp?"

"An ugly word, pimp. I don't like it. I'd rather think of myself as a mentor. Nicky-boy was just a kid then, strung out on drugs. He did what he had to do to survive. I showed him the ropes, helped him along the way. Made a man out of him, you might say. Occasionally made a woman out of him, too."

"And later on, he joined you in the drug business, is that it? Which was how you got sent to jail."

"I got sent to *prison*," said Sonny, " 'cause Nicky-boy ratted me out. He rolled on me to shorten his own sentence."

"Why did you send me that photo?"

Sonny shrugged. "Why not? I wanted to."

"That's not what I mean. I mean why would anyone do something so evil?"

"Ah, you mean you're asking me a metaphysical question,

then?" He must have caught the change in her expression, because he said angrily, "What'sa matter, you think an ex-con don't use words like metaphysical? Well, maybe ex-cons like your husband don't, but I do, lady. I read Nietzsche and Plato and Kant. I get my Tarot cards read too and my astrological chart. So you want to know why I'd do such an evil thing? Because I can. Because I like to stir the pot and see what comes crawling out."

"I want to know where my husband is."

"What makes you think I know?"

"Because I know he came here to see you. Something happened – I don't know what – but he's disappeared."

"If he ain't come home, my guess is that he met someone," said Sonny. "Name of Myriam."

"Is she one of your whores?"

"Not mine, but yeah, you could say she's a whore. She does live sex shows. People pay big bucks to watch her fuck."

Beth swallowed. A debate raging inside her head: *Do I want to know any more? Do I go on?*

She said, "Where does this take place?"

Sonny shrugged. "She has different venues, but I can't say where she is. If I knew for certain, I'd be on my way there now."

Beth flinched and bit her lip. "She's that spectacular in bed, you mean? That all men fall under her spell, not just my husband? He can't stay away from her and neither can you?"

"Yeah, but not in the way you think," Sonny said. "I find out where Myriam is, I ain't going there to have sex with her. Having sex with that witch is the last fucking thing on my mind." His eyes shifted to Beth. "Having sex with Myriam, at any rate. But you now, you're different. More my type. Dark and slender and kinda classy-looking."

"Forget it," Beth said, "Short and fat and flatulent doesn't do it for me. Besides, Nicholas would kill you. If you've ever seen him angry, then you know I'm not exaggerating."

"Maybe so, but he ain't here now, is he?" He moved closer, slowly occupying the space between Beth and the door. "See, this is how I see it, Beth. Nicky-boy, he fucked me over. I figure, by rights, anything belongs to Nicky-boy ought to belong to me."

Myriam stared at him with weary eyes. "Show's over, hon. It's time to go home."

Elise and the rest of the audience had all departed. Myriam and Nicholas stood alone on the small, shabby stage. "What's wrong? Didn't you get what you wanted?"

"Yes. The tests all came back negative. My blood's clean. As far as I know, I'm healthy."

"Then what are you here for? I've done all I can do for you. Go home or, if you have no home, then find one."

"I can't," said Nicholas. "When I was with you, something happened. I have to know what it was and how I can find that again. Otherwise, there's no point in your having cured me, because I won't give up searching. I'll pay you anything you ask. I'll get myself reinfected if I have to, if that's what it takes to be with you again."

He realized what he must sound like: either pathetically desperate or dangerously obsessed.

Myriam brushed at a lock of her platinum hair, shook her head. "Forget about what happened. Go back to your family, if you have one. Make up for the time that you've wasted."

"But that's just it. *Everything* in my life feels like a waste, now. It's all a sham, a lie, a smokescreen covering something else that I glimpsed and then lost sight of. When I was inside you, somehow – God only knows how – I *felt* you pull the disease out of me. But more than that – it felt like everything that I was or that I am – my history, individuality, my thought patterns and personality, everything I've always thought makes me *me* – that all fell away and there was still something else left. And what was left, that felt like the *real* Nicholas, the true Nicholas underneath all the fabrication. It felt like there was something underlying everything else, something besides me, or what I used to think of as me, and I touched that for a second. All I'm asking is that you help me find that again."

"You can't," Myriam said softly, and this time there was

real sadness in her eyes. "You must be still and let It find you."

Sonny Valdez leaned against the door, arms folded. Bloody scratches ran diagonally along his cheek. He stared at Beth, whose lip was bloody and starting to swell.

"You really thought that if you took the bait and came here, I'd let you have your say and then just waltz out the door?"

"This is a mistake, Sonny. Let me leave."

"Oh, I'll let you leave, all right. Just not yet. And maybe not in quite the same condition as you come in."

In her mind, Beth had prepared herself for this moment a hundred times, just as she'd also tried to think out what she'd do if she awoke to find the house on fire or found herself caught in undertow or on a plane whose engines suddenly stalled. The trouble was, you couldn't really predict the specifics of such events – least of all whether it was better to try reasoning with a man like Sonny or fighting back or playing dead and letting whatever happened happen.

"I always wondered what kind of woman Nicky-boy would be shacked up with," he said. "Some sexed-up little slut with boobs out to here, I figured. I mean, that boy could *fuck* – anyone, any time, any place, any kind of kink you could imagine. But *you* – you're a little more genteel-looking than what I'd conjured up in my masturbatory fantasies."

"Looks can be deceiving, Sonny. You think I'm not a match for Nicholas in bed? You think that's not partly why I came looking for him? I can find a man anywhere. I can find a great fuck, if I'm lucky. But a great fuck who also happens to be the person I love – that only comes along once, Sonny. For a lot of people, it never comes at all."

"So you're a match for Nicky-boy in bed, huh? Well, you're gonna have to convince me of that, honey. Fortunately, I got plenty of time to be convinced."

He came towards her, and she retreated, bumping into the coffee table, upending it with a crash and a shattering of glass. She picked up a shard to ward off Sonny, but before he could come at her, the phone on top of the TV set bleated, halting them both.

The answering machine clicked on, and a woman's voice, fluttery and nervous, said, "Sonny, it's Elise. I need to talk to you. Sonny, will you please pick up? I just saw Nicholas."

Sonny rushed for the phone, but Beth was a step ahead and got there first. "Who is this?" she shouted. "Where are you?"

"Give me that!" Sonny grabbed the phone out of her hand and pushed her away. So engrossed was he in what the caller was saying that she could have easily escaped, but she couldn't, *wouldn't* leave now.

"You stupid bitch, you told him *what*?" roared Sonny and slammed down the phone. He whirled on Beth. "You want to find your husband? Well, I know where he is. More important, I know where *she* is, too." He reached for her, and she brought the shard of jagged glass down in an arc, narrowly missing his face. He grimaced and jumped back. "You gonna try and carve me up with that or you gonna come with me to find your husband? C'mon, what'll it be, Beth? You scared of me or what?"

She was shaking, but she wasn't scared – not yet. The fear came a moment later, when Sonny was buttoning his coat, and she saw the pistol tucked inside the waistband of his pants.

"You're an unusual man, Nicholas," said Myriam. "After I cure them, a lot of people never want to see me again. They're grateful, but the experience they have with me is too frightening, too disturbing, to ever want to undergo again. Some of them decide I'm some kind of witch or demon. I've had men claim I stole their souls."

"Or their names," said Nicholas.

"For people sufficiently entrenched in ego, it's the same thing. They're so caught up in their mortal identity, that even a few moments outside their own ego feels terrifying and annihilating. Some of them go insane."

"So what does happen, Myriam? How do you cure people?"

"As far as how I cure them, I'm not sure myself – only that when the ego dissolves, even briefly, so dissolves the disease. As for the experience you had, all I can tell you is you aren't the first to search for it. In the nineteenth century, there was a group of occultists who worshipped what they called the 'holy wisdom fire', a fire they believed to be embodied in all women. Certain women had the power to help bring about a soul's spiritual integration through intercourse and awaken in their partner the highest spiritual powers from deep within. These occultists called themselves the Cult of Myriam, which still exists. I studied with the group and took that name for myself."

"So what happened? You initiated me into some kind of cosmic consciousness?"

"I didn't do anything, Nicholas, except offer you a glimpse of what mystics and holy people have been preaching for centuries. You don't have to be Nicholas, you know. You chose to be that person, but that isn't the real you and, deep inside, you know that. That's why you feel compelled to search for that experience again."

"Not just because I'm a crazy bastard obsessed with fucking you?"

He was joking, of course – more or less – but she didn't smile. Instead, she took his hand and they sat together on the mattress. Sitting turned into reclining, which melted into embracing. Nicholas felt such a surge of longing and desire that it was all he could do not to rip off Myriam's clothing and take her then and there, to hell with her consent. "You're thinking you could rape me if you wanted to," said Myriam, "and you're right, but it wouldn't be the experience you're looking for. It would leave you much further from your destination than you are now."

"Then make love with me," said Nicholas, pulling her against him. "You cured me of my disease: now cure me of my ignorance."

Her arms wound around his neck. Her legs parted. "I think you have a lot of good in you, Nicholas," she said. "More good than you realize. I think your soul longs for a kind of wisdom few people ever find, let alone experience."

"I think you're wrong," said Nicholas. "I'm not a good man. Thirty seconds ago, I was debating whether or not to rape you if you didn't want to have sex. And I'm a lot nicer guy now than I used to be, if that puts it in perspective. I haven't lived a good life. I've been a thief and a drug-dealer and, when I was younger, a prostitute. I don't long for any holiness or wisdom. The only thing I long for is to slide my cock inside your body and fuck you forever and never, ever leave."

Her eyes lit up. She laughed gently. "Have you ever considered, Nicholas, that my body might not be the only place you might find what you're searching for? That if you allowed yourself to love someone, *really* love someone enough to transcend your own self-centeredness, that might make all the difference?"

But before Nicholas could answer, they both heard the footsteps approaching. Then the door that opened onto the stairwell was kicked open with a crash that reverberated throughout the room. Nicholas leaped to his feet, galvanized by an appalling and incongruous vision – Sonny Valdez, his wife, and the gun that Sonny was now pointing at him and Myriam.

Someone screamed. Maybe it was Beth or Myriam or even Nicholas himself – maybe all three of them were screaming at once – but he hurled himself in front of Myriam, who was still on the floor, and the gun went off and suddenly the room was filled with a terrible red rain.

In the instant it took Sonny to recock the trigger, Beth grabbed his wrist and twisted it with all the strength in both her arms. The gun fired again – this time into the ceiling – as Sonny shoved her away and aimed at Myriam again, firing into her as she lay in a spreading pool of blood on the mattress. With a cry, Nicholas charged Sonny, wrestled the gun away from him, and then slammed the grip into the man's skull, again and again, like a gong striking the side of a bell, and he didn't stop, but kept on bashing the caved-in head, even when Beth grabbed him and shouted, "It's all right, Nicholas, it's all right! He's dead, he's dead, he's dead!''

After the police got through investigating, when they were convinced Nicholas had been justified in taking Sonny Valdez's life, after Myriam was cremated and her ashes scattered in the churchyard of St Benedict's, Nicholas and Beth went back to Detroit and pretended to be making an effort to resume their lives. A grim joke, thought Nicholas, given everything that had taken place. He'd told Beth the truth about his past, about Elise, and about how Myriam had somehow cleansed his infected blood: everything except the experience he'd had while he and Myriam were making love. That he couldn't put into words and he was afraid she'd misunderstand, think he was describing sexual passion and, while that was a component of what he'd undergone, the experience was really so much more.

Nor could he explain why, week after week, he avoided having sex with Beth – that the encounters he'd had following Myriam had been so frustrating in their departure from what he sought that he didn't want to risk adding Beth to his list of bitter disappointments or, worse, using her as a momentary distraction from what he perceived as an unutterable and never-ending grief.

"Do you want me to leave?" he asked her when they lay in bed one night.

"Is that what you want to do?"

He thought about that, really let the idea sink into him. If he ever wanted to walk out on his marriage, this was the time. If he had lost Myriam and all she represented, he could still go back to the solace of addictive sex and drugs, immerse himself in the quest for debaucheries that would bring only deeper and darker oblivion.

But what he said was, "No, I don't want to leave. Unless you'd rather I did."

She was silent a few moments. Then: "I want you to stay. But at the same time, I love you. And if what you found with that woman Myriam, what you tried to tell me about on the phone that day when I wouldn't listen, if you need to go and look for that, then I'd be wrong to try to stop you. It would be more than wrong, I think it would be evil."

A great swelling of relief passed through Nicholas. Relief and gratitude that seemed to thaw his loins and melt some of the ice from his heart. He was free to leave her if he wanted to, to look for what he'd lost. That meant that he was also free to stay. Desire, faint but hopeful, stirred in him.

He wrapped Beth in his arms and pulled her to him. She felt warm and welcoming and her body shaped itself to his in the old familiar ways, yet even with some trepidation, there was nothing timid or hesitant about his lovemaking. He forced her legs apart and mounted her. She arched her hips and guided him inside.

You're free to go, if that's what you need to do.

He loved her more then than he ever had loved anyone. A sense of lightness and freedom washed over him, a lifting of bonds. He thrust into her and she moaned his name. "Nicholas, Nicholas, Nicholas."

But for the briefest, most ecstatic of instants, he had forgotten who that was.

THE DARKLING BEETLES

Gene Santagada

The door was easy to force. Luckily the fancy inlaid glass didn't break. Although this building appeared deserted, I did not want to chance being overheard by some cleaning lady. One firm shove – the doorjamb cracked – and I was in.

I felt along the wall for the light switch. I flicked it – but nothing! Some joker had taken all the light bulbs.

Big deal, I thought: I see like a bat in the dark. But lights were not the only things missing from this office. The place was stripped clean: no chairs, desks, or filing cabinets. They had even taken the water cooler.

Across the room, before a half open window, I saw a tipped-over wastepaper basket. Garbage can be a case's Rosetta stone, every detective knows that. Before checking it out, I peered through the blinds. Only a few cars were in the parking lot, two stories below. Some looked abandoned; this was typical for the meat-packing district.

Luck was still with me; the basket was stuffed with papers! This could be the break I needed. I unfolded the first crumpled letter by the dim light of the window.

"Samuel Bigglesworth: Private Detective," announced the

letterhead. What kind of a tinsel-ass name was that? I checked the glass on the door. There it was, in big black stencil: this was Bigglesworth's office. I unfolded another letter.

"Dear Mr. Bigglesworth," it read, "enclosed is a check for $15,000 for your services." The next letter said, "As we agreed, here is the $6,000 advance." I found more and more like this, even a couple of canceled checks. One was for eighteen grand!

This Bigglesworth has a sissy name, but he sure rakes in the bucks. I wish I had this guy's clientele! Whoever he was, he had to be the best. But it made no sense for a guy with such cash flow to keep his office buried downtown. I'd be uptown with the big players and corporate guys. He did make mistakes, though. It was not smart to leave records around where someone could find them. And if I ever got a check for eighteen grand, I would have the fucker framed!

Next in the basket was a dog-eared magazine. A nearly naked babe was plastered on the cover. Big deal, so Bigglesworth was into porn. Who isn't? I flipped through the pages, and instead of naked women, I found reams of classified ads. "Thirty-something white male seeks twenty-ish blonde," that sort of thing. Poor baby! Bigglesworth was lonely, I know how that is! Some people included pictures of themselves with the ads.

The more I saw, the more I realized something funny was going on. One picture had a guy dressed up like a baby, with diapers, even a pacifier stuck in his mouth. He had to be fifty years old! Next, I saw a woman holding her stocking clad foot to the camera. Her ad read, "Hi; I am in desperate need of the right person (guy or gal) to worship my feet." I winced when I saw the photo of the guy with all the clothespins pinching his cock. CLOTHESPINS? For Christ's sake!

The more I saw and read, the stranger it got. I never would have figured Bigglesworth for a pervert. But it takes all kinds, doesn't it? The ads at the back of the magazine were for escort agencies, "licensed" masseurs, and "professional" hostesses. A sweet bunch of words that spelled one thing:

prostitution. Just as I was ready to toss the magazine, I noticed an ad on the back was circled by a felt tip pen.

"Visit Mistress Amanda," the ad proclaimed. "Do you need something different?" It went on to say, "Come be a captive in my Dungeon. No posers, beginners, or wimps allowed! Slaves must submit an application to qualify. Accepting positions for male and female submissives." The phone number was the exchange of this neighborhood. The bottom of the ad included a picture of the proprietor. She was wearing some sort of fancy girdle. Even in this low-resolution picture, I could tell she was a beauty. I ripped the ad out and stuffed it in my back pocket.

The basket held one last surprise: an old hat. It was the kind those pot-smoking Rastafarians use to stuff their dreadlocks under. It had rainbow colors, like something out of a time-warp from the hippie days. It was embroidered with little metallic beetles. Who would have dreamed up such a thing?

Something else was strange. As I handled it, my fingers were getting numb. It was as if it contained a hidden chunk of dry ice.

I sniffed at the rim. It was not soaked with perfume, nor did it smell sweet, the way a lady's sweat smells. This smelled acrid, so it must have belonged to a man. But I detected something else, an odor that reminded me of . . .

Nothing breaks your concentration like the flashing lights of a police car. From the window, I saw one racing into the parking lot. It lurched to a halt. Immediately, two uniformed officers jumped out, followed by two suits climbing from the back seats. One suit carried a high-powered rifle slung from his shoulder. The grenade-launcher attached under the barrel of the gun meant this was not standard issue. The other suit must have stepped out of a science fiction movie. He was muscular and big. He was wearing some sort of goggles, like those fancy night vision things, the infrared type.

"We are doing this legal," I heard the cop say, "by the book. No nasty mess-ups like last time." The suit with the rifle chuckled. "I mean it," insisted the cop. "The chief wants this to go smoothly. Get a good clean fix on him before you shoot . . ."

What were these guys after? I was glad they were not looking for me.

Then the craziest sensation hit me. I had no idea what I was doing or who sent me. What case was I on? I started quizzing myself. My unanswerable list grew larger and larger, even when I got to the fundamental questions. My own name was even a mystery. It was as if I just became self-aware moments ago. What was going on? My pockets were empty: no wallet, cards, license, or money. Not even snapshots of the wife and kids. Did I have a wife and kids? Sickness cramped my stomach. I felt dizzy, so I steadied myself against the windowsill.

That was a big mistake.

TING! A hole shot through the window glass. It spider-webbed out and shattered. I dived for the floor. I heard yelling.

"HEY! No shooting!"

"You missed," another informed, "but I got a clear read on him: he's up there."

They missed, all right. I had to get out of there fast! Crouching low, I headed for the door.

The dark hallway smelled of plastic and mildew. At one end glowed an exit sign by the stairwell. At the other end was an elevator. I chose the stairs.

Just inside the stairwell, a barred window provided a view of the parking lot. I decided to have a peek at my friends.

Both cops were dead. One lay sprawled on the hood of the patrol car, his head smashed clean through the windshield. The other was spread-eagled on the ground, face down in a pool of blood. The suits were nowhere in sight. If those two suits caught up with me, they weren't going to read me my Miranda Rights.

A creaking sound echoed up the stairwell. A glance over the handrail confirmed the worst; the searching beam of a rifle laser sight cut the darkness. They were here.

Dashing upstairs would make noise, so I backed out into

the hallway. The only option was the elevator. If the suits had brains, they would separate; one should take the stairs, the other the lift. So I pressed myself flush against the wall, out of sight, and hit the "up" button. Seconds later, the doors opened. It was empty. I got on and pressed the panel for the top floor. If a chance existed for getting out of this alive, I needed some distance between us.

"Third floor," announced the tinny androgynous-sounding speaker above my head.

I wished the drugs, if that's what had deep-sixed my memory, would finally wear off. But as I concentrated, the wooziness returned. I desperately needed a clear head.

I rechecked my pockets. This time I found a thin black plastic card, hidden by the ripped-out ad I stuffed in earlier. It was like a blank credit card, no names or numbers. But I caught sight of a thin magnetic strip painted down one side. As I passed the sixth floor, I made another discovery.

I had a gun! Clipped to my belt was a leather holster. The pistol slipped out easily. It was my Birretta Cougar 45. This little baby came in handy in Hong Kong, when those three bastards decided to have a surprise party for me. But my Cougar was the perfect host; she fed each man one serving before going around the room and delivering seconds. My little baby would not think of letting them skip dessert, so I went around the table and stuck her cute little barrel right into each gurgling mouth and . . .

Now I was remembering! This gun had saved my life more than once. But I had no time to savor this memory.

Muffled voices. Sounds came from underneath me. Somebody was in the elevator shaft. Grenade launcher! Those words flashed through my brain. Clammy panic washed over my skin. My short hairs stood on end.

"Eighth floor," spoke the hardwired voice. I hit the button for the ninth. The elevator eased to a halt. The doors creaked open.

The explosion blasted me forward out of the elevator.

A ball of smoke and fiery orange sparks shot past. The force slammed me face-down. I rolled over to see the now twisted floor of the elevator. It was ruptured open like a tin can. The elevator snapped its cable. It fell half a flight before I heard the safety gears biting into the shaft. I got up, my gun still planted firmly in my hand. I ran to the stairwell and rushed to the top floor.

I stepped out into a barren hallway, carpeted in royal blue. The ceiling and walls were painted warm red. But there were no offices, signs, or doorways. This place was a gaudy dead end. I heard more noise echoing up the stairs; they were on their way up. There was no escape. My gun was no match for their heat, and it was two against one. This was looking bad.

But my eyes paid off again. Buried flush against the wall, I found a hidden doorway. It was so carefully inlaid that anyone could miss it. But how did it open? I felt a pulsing rhythm through the door. I placed my ear against it and, even though my ears still rung from the elevator explosion, I heard music. Somebody was home. I chanced knocking. Nothing. I banged on the door. Still no response. I scratched and felt along the door, in search of a secret buzzer, touch pad, anything! My fingernail caught what I at first thought was just a deep scratch in the door. But right where a doorknob should be was a two-inch long slit. This looked like a card insert, and I had such a card.

I fed the mysterious black thing into the slit. It was sucked into the slot. Then it shot out, tumbling to the floor. As I bent to retrieve it, I heard the blessed sound of releasing dead bolts. The door slid away.

It was a large spartanly furnished room. Once I stepped in, the door automatically closed behind me.

A large teakwood desk dominated the room. It had legs carved as tiger claws. This was something that belonged in a museum, not a piece of office furniture. The drawers were all locked. On top was a computer keyboard; propped next to it, a flat screen monitor. Before the desk was a plain chair. But the chair behind the desk was upholstered in blue velvet, and had a high wooden back carved with all sorts of exotic animals. This was a throne fit for a king, or a queen.

A number of rooms adjoined this one. One was the source

of the music. I figured I better check out the scene before I met the owner of this place.

The room I chose was unlocked. In the center was a medical examination table. It looked like the kind of table doctors use to examine women's glory holes. Attached to the foot of the table were a pair of stirrups. But these stirrups had secure buckles. The mid-section of the table had a leather belt fastened to the sides. At the head of the table was a pair of leather cuffs. Beside the table stood a metal cart, covered with a sheet of blue paper. I pulled the paper free, and was greeted by the most evil-looking medical instruments I had ever seen: clamps, hemostats, needles, probes, and things with hooks. This was a torture chamber! It was even complete with sound-proof tiles to cover the screams. No wonder they didn't hear the elevator explode.

I returned to the main room, following the music. It was something classical. That's when I heard the strangest sound – and somebody screaming.

WOOSH-THWACK, the sound went, then a woman screamed, "Stop! Please!" I heard it again. Woosh-thwack, "Uh," woosh-thwack, "No . . . No more," woosh-thwack . . .

Some poor lady was getting the third degree. It was time to act. I gripped my gun firmly. I turned the doorknob.

The woman standing before me looked like a riding instructor from hell! Fortunately, I was behind her. Her long dark hair was luscious. She wore black satin gloves that reached past her elbows. Her white shirt was stuffed into some sort of girdle that laced up the back and squeezed her tight. She sported brown leather pants, the legs of which were tucked into knee-high leather boots. She was just completing the swing of a multi-tailed whip.

"Whoosh," it cut through the air, "thwack", it smacked the backside of a completely naked woman. The poor girl was bent pretzel-like over a leather-covered hobbyhorse. Her hands were secured to one side. Her legs were bound to a bar that kept them spread about one meter apart. Her cherry-red ass stuck up in the air.

Then I noticed the man. He was naked except for the tiniest set of briefs I ever saw. He was bound spread-eagled to this large wooden cross. A black rubber ball was crammed into his mouth as an effective gag. As he saw me, he started shaking his head and struggling. He must have been relieved to see me.

"OK, lady, drop that!" I yelled.

The torturer glared at me. A thick lock of hair was obscuring half her face, like that old movie actress Veronica Lake. This woman was beautiful.

"YOU," she exclaimed. Of everything she could have said, that was not what I expected.

"Uh, shut up!" I commanded. "Drop that whip and don't move!"

The whip hit the floor. The female victim spoke up.

"What the fuck is going on?" she asked, twisting her neck to see.

"Don't worry," I assured her, "I'll get you out of this mess."

I needed a man's help, so went to the guy on the cross first. He was staring at me strangely. The cord securing the gag was easy to unfasten.

"Who the FUCK are you?" He shot an angry stare at the whip woman. "Mistress Amanda," he went on, "this is not part of our scene!"

"Yeah," the naked woman added, "what the hell is going on? This is totally unprofessional! Oh, shit." She looked at the man. "Are we being robbed?"

"Sam," the whip woman asked, "how did you get in here?"

My name was Sam?

"You have ruined our honeymoon," proclaimed the man on the cross. "I hope you don't think we are going to pay . . ."

"SILENCE!" the whip woman shouted. Her two prisoners shut right up. She turned to me. "Please, Sam, put the gun down." Most people plead when gazing down the barrel of a gun, but she just acted upset and concerned. "Haven't you hurt me enough? We can work this out and . . ."

Stopping mid-sentence, her expression shifted to one of revelation. "You don't recognize me, do you?"

I had no idea what was up with this bitch, but she was right about that.

"The Darkling hat," she proclaimed. "You've been wearing it, haven't you?"

"You mean, this?" I asked, pulling it from my pocket.

She stepped toward me. I raised the gun, asserting my bead on her. I was still on top, and that's where I wanted to be until I figured this mess out.

"Sam, let me explain." She stopped, as if searching for words. Then her dark eyebrows narrowed. "You weren't followed here, were you?"

Pounding at the front door interrupted our chat.

"I think so," I confirmed. Now I had my angle! I would see if this bitch was on the level.

"Do they want me bad enough to kill two cops?" I asked, my finger tightening on the trigger.

All expression bled from her face. "If it's who I think it is," she said quietly, "we are all dead, even if you surrender the hat."

That was a good answer. I lowered the gun.

"OK," I said. "It's your move, uh, Amanda." She gave me a look of contempt. This woman did not take any shit. I liked that.

"Follow me," she snapped, striding out of the room, her boots striking the floor firmly.

"What's going on?" asked the tied-down woman.

"Yeah," added the man.

"Hey," I said, closing the door, "the lady said shut up!"

Amanda went to the big desk. The monitor came on by itself. It displayed an image of the two goons who were after me.

"That's them," I confirmed.

"Shit! Who the hell are they? And one has a visor." She indicated the big man. "Are they armed?"

"Yeah, big-time!"

Working on its own, the image switched to a wide-angle

shot behind our visitors. That grenade-launching rifle was propped to one side against the wall. This babe had the whole place planted with stealth cameras. A rapid flash of images cycled across the screen. The faces of the two men were being referenced against some sort of database. A wire frame graphic of the visor spun in a window, as reams of data scrolled by. The image of one of the goons froze.

"We have a match for the short one," she informed. "He is an ex-fed. I wonder who he works for?"

Even with all this going on, I found myself staring at her body. Her small breasts fitted the boyish frame of her upper body. Her arms were strong, but not over-developed. Her bottom end was rendered hyper-female by the pinching corset. How did she breathe in that thing? Her backside was firm and round, like that of a dancer. Definitely a butt to die for.

"Wait a minute," I added, "you never touched that keyboard once. You have an EOS, an Encephalized Operating System."

This was illegal. Only the military could lawfully maintain an EOS. Whoever this demon woman was, she was playing for keeps.

They pounded on the front door again. Amanda motioned me to keep still.

"Hello," she said. "Who's there?"

"Uh," we heard from an invisible speaker, "this is the police."

"Yes," she called into the air. "I'm busy with clients, how can I help you?"

"There's a dangerous fugitive in the neighborhood. Can we come in and ask some questions?"

One of the locked drawers on the desk sprang open. She pulled out something that looked like a shower cap. She slipped it over her head, pulling a chinstrap down her face.

"Yes, officer," she said, "just give me a minute to dress. Listen," she confided to me, "I must let them in or they will get suspicious."

I agreed.

"This keeps me insulated." She pointed to the rubber cap. "They can ping me all they want, and all they will get is a brain full of reflections."

"What?" I asked.

"Start stripping. I'll explain."

"WHAT?"

"Off with your clothes," she ordered.

I was stripping before a woman I did not even know.

"Officers," she called out, "I'm getting dressed: give me a minute."

"My business thrives on confidentiality," she quietly explained.

I moved fast. I was down to my socks and underwear. My thumbs hesitated at the waistband. She anticipated my question.

"Yes, those too. Imagine a high-ranking congresswoman who gets off by being walked and spat on? Or the Federal judge who wants to be a prisoner of the Nazis and be interrogated by an Amazon SS agent? What would their political enemies do with such knowledge? And just imagine the media frenzy."

I was now naked. I placed my gun and holster on the pile of clothes. A sexy smirk grew on her face again. It was as if she knew something dirty about me.

"They need a court order," she continued, "if they want a crack at my computer, and it's a fucking Federal case if they want to read my mind. So my cap is licensed." She rubbed her sexy fingers over her head. She gave me a suspicious look. "Your thoughts are our weak spot, but this amnesia might play into our hands."

This babe had looks, brains, attitude, and swore! I liked that combination. This is someone I wanted on my side. She was one cool number, this Amanda. I figured I had better play along.

She stuffed my gun and clothes into the drawer and slammed it shut. Then she led me back to the room with her two captives.

"What about your, uh, clients?" I pointed to the trussed-up man and woman. "Won't their minds be readable?"

"We are lucky you brought my hat."

Her hat?

That was when I saw the scar. A pencil-thin line of pink flesh ran down the middle of her right cheekbone to the corner of her lip.

"You remember nothing?" Her eyes locked on me.

"I lost a lot, didn't I?"

Instead of answering, she held the hat open. She brought it to the man first. He began to struggle. She held it on his head. His face formed a painful grimace. But then his expression – his whole body – went limp. Amanda withdrew the hat, then approached the lady. She started thrashing on the horse.

"Those things are illegal," she complained. "I'm reporting you to the Fetish Industry Board and . . . and . . ." Her eyes darted in panic, then a convulsion shot through her body as Amanda slipped the hat on her. "You . . . are . . . are . . . y –" She went rag-doll limp. Amanda turned to me.

"Your turn, my little detective. It hurts at first, but you used to like it, my sick little puppy." She reached toward me and pulled it over my head.

Blackness on blankness. No circuits, wires, chips, wet ware, or LEDs. Only oblivion. Nothingness raised exponentially to infinity, floating in a blissful void. Peacefully empty. Painless, but not lonely. The beetles were coming. Legs outstretched, touching down like planetary space probes. Mandibles sharp and gnashing. They parted the flesh of my forehead. It was so easy for them to bore through bone. They were hungry from their long trip. Swarming over the convolutions of my brain, antennae waving, mandibles snapping. Foraging on the convolutions of my brain. A forest of delicious memories for their feast. There was much for them to gorge on.

I awoke in darkness. I was sitting on a floor, my arms suspended above my head. Something oppressive hugged my face. I stretched my legs, and felt the confines of a small room. A door opened. Cool air swept my skin.

"How are you doing?"

A familiar voice. She was carefully loosening the bindings at my wrists. My arms tingled. She tugged at my face. The leather hood came free. The light temporarily blinded me. Through my squinting eyes, I saw an angel standing before me.

"How are you feeling?"

"Like shit," I replied. "My arms are pins and needles."

"Sorry, that's the blood returning. I kept you in here too long. You never liked isolation, but I had to check up on you – after our friends left."

"What?

Slap! She answered by striking my face with her palm. She did it again.

"Amanda!" I blocked the next one. "For Christ's sake!"

A devilish smirk marked her face.

"Good. You remember." She helped me to my feet, and I stepped from the closet.

"The Darkling hat was on you just seconds but, in your sensitized state, I worried it would bite too deep. At first it only feeds on your most recent memories, especially emotionally intense ones."

"I guess having a grenade shot at you is pretty intense." I glanced around the room, confirming that the couple had left. "What happened to those customers of yours? And those hit men? Just a few minutes ago . . ."

"Ha!" She laughed. "Silly boy, that was over an hour ago. I even showed you off to those to so-called policemen! The hood I had on your face disguised you. I claimed you were a misbehaving slave and you were being punished by sensory deprivation. Yeah, you used to hate it when I put a hood on you."

"Did they try to read my mind?" I interrupted. "Did they 'ping' me?"

"Yes, and all he got was a brain pan full of confusion. I hope the bastard gagged on it."

"Well," I ventured, "can I put my pants on now?"

"But you look best naked! They gave me a line of shit about looking for a terrorist. After they left, I finished the scene with my two customers. Don't worry, they won't remember a thing about you."

Her face grew stern. "I wish I didn't remember you."

"Look," I said, "since you seem to know me so well, please fill me in?"

"Was it so easy to forget?" Her voice shifting cold, she turned away.

That damn nauseous feeling came back.

"Amanda," I said, "you got me, I mean us, out of a tough jam. I appreciate that. But I can't stand this history act."

"Just shut up!" She glared. I guess "history" was a bad choice of words. It was obvious I was more than a notch on this woman's belt.

"I'm sorry," I found myself saying. "I should go and just –"

"Sure!" she cut in, ignoring the tear traveling down the wound channel of her scar. "So where will you go? You would not last a minute out there."

"Cut the crap!" Now I was getting pissed off. "You can't fool me. I am not into this whips and chains stuff. I don't mean to be disrespectful, especially as you just saved my life. But this is not my thing."

"Oh, yeah?" she sarcastically replied, pointing down to my crotch. "That's not how it looks to me." My penis was sticking out, hard.

"While you were unconscious," she continued, "I took the time to do a thorough search on you. I've been reading up on your adventures. Your detective career has really taken off. You are famous now; one post credited you as being a modern-day Sherlock Holmes."

"Well, that's nice, but . . ."

"Hush! You cracked a big case in Hong Kong."

As she explained, I remembered my agency. My cases came alive in me. But it was imperfect, like someone stole pieces of the puzzle. Even my name came back. How did I ever make it through life with a name like Bigglesworth?

"It's good you saved this." Amanda held up the black card. "Some vestigial remnant of you must be hiding out in your brain. You subconsciously stored many of your old files and memories using a Gordian Worm, just in case something like this happened."

"Wait a minute," I chimed in, "that's a deep encryption algorithm, designed by the military. What was I doing with that?"

"Probably something left over from your friends in Hong Kong. But who knows what you've been up to the last couple of years?" She gave me a stern look. "I hoped to never see you again."

"Could I have been that big of a scum-bag?"

"Shhh," she replied. "The wrong people learned you possessed the hat. In a sense, you did me a favor. You took the heat – as you say it – off me." She kept turning the card in her hands, staring at me. "You know," she continued, "the Worm is a tough beast. But I'd like my computer to have a hack at it."

Technical contraband? Illegal software? Government secrets? Leather and whips? What the hell was I involved with?

Her gloved hand touched my shoulder. Muscles relaxed throughout my body. It was as if I was hypnotized. What power did this creature have over me? I had an impulse to lick that gloved hand. But she pulled it away before I could react.

"Sam," she continued, "you can have it all back: who you are, what happened, and why you came back. The EOS and the Darkling hat are based on the same technology. Your memories can be regurgitated and reinstalled. No one knows about this function," she confided. "At least, not anyone alive."

I just stared at the ground. The tip of her boot nestled into my leg, she gave me a nudge.

"Well, Mr Detective? Want the mystery of yourself revealed?"

"God, yes," I found myself saying.

"That's GODDESS, to you," she corrected. "But you may have physically damaged your nervous system. You dissected away some deep and horrible memories; getting them force-fed back might be a rough ride. It might even be fatal. I will have to monitor you closely."

"Amanda," I finally interrupted, "I know one thing: we are in great danger. Whoever I am, he can help us escape. Let's stop fucking around and get on with it!"

Amanda recuffed my hands to the wall. She left the room for a moment, then returned with that crazy hat.

"Well, here goes. Some of the memories will seem alien. Your thoughts may come back like snapshots from somebody else's dreamscape . . ."

Her voice faded as she brought the hat to my head.

The man Amanda had trussed up was an enigma. She only saw deep bottoms, masochists who had a high pain threshold. Beginners, amateurs, posers, or people just wanting a quick jerk-off never passed her screening process. But he claimed Anexia had sent him; she would never send a pussy.

During his interview, she could tell he had never been to a dominatrix. Yet he had a high pain threshold, especially for a novice. Whatever his nature, Amanda was confident it would soon be exposed. Her dungeon was better – and quicker – than any psychiatrist's couch.

Amanda was wearing a black latex corset. It covered her breasts and sat high on her hips. The front zipper was crossed by a row of seven buckled straps. Her red latex gloves reached to her elbows. A leather thong complemented her fishnet pantyhose. The boots came up to just below the knee; the laces were bright red.

Her customer was naked and bent in an upside-down V over her leather upholstered hobbyhorse. His ass was the highest part of his body. She had started with her riding crop. People curious about bondage, discipline, and sado-masochism – or BDSM, as it was sometimes called – often chose a crop as their first plaything. It was often mistaken for a beginner's implement.

But it could be effective, even dangerous, in the hands of someone like Amanda. And she had just demonstrated her skill on this fellow's backside. His butt was now the nicest shade of red and almost glowing. He could not utter his safe-word – the code word that meant "stop under any circum-stance: I am in trouble" – since a ball gag was stuffed in his mouth. They decided an extended index finger meant the same. So far, he had hardly moaned. But he would, Amanda knew, after she raised a few welts.

At the closet, she inspected her collection of whips. She had over a dozen, in all shapes, sizes, colors, and varieties. The floggers were short, with many tails. Some were longer, like her cherished cat o'nine tails. Others were not whips at all, but flat slappers and paddles. She selected her favorite cat o'nine tails. It was jet black and three feet long, with nine thick leather lashes, each cut to a point to deliver a stinging blow. She could be gentle, prolonging a flogging for what would seem an eternity, or bring someone to their knees with one blow.

Returning to her customer, she spun the whip around her head.

Whoosh . . . Whoosh, she swung it twice above her head, cutting the air, then "snap" as she delivered the blow to his helpless backside. The tips just kissed his skin, but that allowed all the force to be transferred to a small area of his flesh. This was a painful blow. He arched, tugging at his binding.

"Hmmm, you felt that, didn't you?" Good, thought Amanda, I'm getting to him.

Too many blows with the tips would abrade his skin like a cheese grater. She let another swing fly, this time delivering a horizontal stroke, zeroed in on his left cheek. On the return swings, she let the tails fly over her back to strike her. This helped her to gauge her blows. She wanted to take her time with this man.

Then she delivered thirty good strokes, alternating on each of his ever-reddening cheeks. She allowed a greater length of leather to strike his skin. This distributed the force of her blows. She knew he was anticipating each strike, and this helped him to endure and prepare. The red marks begun by the crop were now spreading into a large pattern. If she kept this up too long, his deep tissues would bruise. This would be too much, even for such an eager beginner. She stopped and stood beside her subject, checking his restraints and admiring her handiwork. The restraints were not yet digging into his flesh. A peek between his legs revealed his contracted scrotum. His penis was hard, forced down by the horse.

"Good boy," she said softly. "You did not come." She placed her hand against his ass. He jumped.

"No," she ordered. "Keep still, my victim. If you struggle, it just hurts more. And you don't want to make me angry."

She lovingly ran her hands across his backside. The radiating heat penetrated her latex gloves. His breathing was slow, deep, and steady. A tiny pool of sweat had gathered in the small of his back. She dipped her finger, swirling it in the liquid. She brought her fingertip to her mouth, savoring his bitter saltiness. She now stood next to his head and slowly petted him as if he was a favored dog. The tips of his hair were frosted, making them sparkle. She bent beside him.

"How you doing, Sam?" she whispered in his ear.

". . ."

His eyes were wide and brimming with tears. As she removed the gag, he inhaled a big suck of air. "Oh, is my hour up so soon? I thought, um . . . umph."

Amanda laughed as she pressed the gag back in his mouth. "Ha! Losing track of time, are we? You are mine a bit longer."

Next, she chose the quirt. This stout two-foot whip had a thick handle. The business end was tipped by a bifurcate strip of flat leather – like the tongue of a snake. She gave the air a few swings, to loosen it up. He was now ready for some serious pain.

She put her back into it. The first strike hit both sides of his ass. His back arched. On the next, he bolted against his restraints. The nerves were compressed; she allowed time for them to swell and expand before the next blow. A layer of capillaries under his skin ruptured, stippling his skin with reddish dots. Now she really started in on him, changing the strokes, not allowing him the mercy of anticipation. But his ass was sticking out even more, as if hungry for each swing. Great, she thought, I am going to bring him right to the edge.

His backside took on the patina of a deep-red tattoo. By the fifteenth stroke, his struggles were making the leather horse creak. She paused, checking for the safety sign. He was fine.

She planted the last sting across both cheeks. His body shook. Finally, he let out a muffled moan.

About time, Amanda said to herself. However, he still had not signaled her to stop.

She again went to his side. His breathing was fast and deep. His face had taken on the features of a charging bull. As she pulled the ball-gag free, saliva and a puff of steam came out. He took in a deep breath.

"Oh, man," he said. "That was, that was fantastic!"

"Hush," she replied. "If it was so good, why don't you demonstrate some appreciation?"

She shifted her body to expose her latex-covered ass. He turned, placing a kiss there. He was panting. She moved, offering different areas of her backside to his attention. He reached the border between latex and skin, planting kisses on her fishnet stockings. Amanda felt the soft moistness of his tongue through the material.

"No tongue," she warned. He stopped for a moment, then continued, letting his lips do the work. She pulled away, leaving his last kiss to plant air. She unfastened his hands, then his ankles. He started to rise.

"Careful," she cautioned. "You don't want to hurt your back."

She steadied his arm and helped him up. Rivulets of sweat poured over his naked body as he stood. His nipples were small, tight, and hard. She walked him to the couch.

"Sit slowly," she advised, remaining near. He was looking deep into her eyes. "Those puppy dog eyes are sweet, but did I give you permission to gaze at me?"

Sam looked down. "Uh, can I ask something?"

"Go on."

"I would like something to drink."

Amanda chuckled. "Sure, Sam. Just stay put. I'll be right back."

As she entered her office, her computer came on. There were no messages. She was surprised how worked up she had become during this whipping. Her thong was soaked! She had a full ninety minutes before her next client, a woman with a medical fetish. Amanda needed time to prepare the "Doctor's Office", and get into her nurse's outfit. As she concentrated on her new client, Sam, a live image of him appeared on the screen. He was now standing by her terrarium, peering into its webby darkness. He tapped the glass, then his head snapped back, as if startled. Her pet tarantula never failed to please.

There was something familiar about him. He walked over to the bullwhip she had displayed on one wall. He ran his hands over its eight-foot length. Whenever she left a submissive male unattended after a session, they invariably wasted no time jerking off. Yet there was an unpredictability in this one's nature. Amanda liked a challenge. She drew him a cup of water from the cooler. She again ran his card through her strip reader. Her computer detected no visits to any other known dominatrix. No fetish clothing purchases. His most recent payment had been to a school, and he had just purchased an airline ticket.

She returned to the room. He was still eyeing the bullwhip.

"That's just for show," Amanda commented.

Sam turned; he was lightly massaging his backside. "It looks evil as hell," he said.

"Yes. In the wrong hands, that kind of whip can put someone in the emergency room." She handed him the cup of water. "I no longer use it. I once cut someone by mistake."

He gulped down the drink, thanking her. She pointed to the couch. Sam obediently sat down.

"That spider!" Sam indicated the terrarium. "It's beautiful. I never saw anything like it. Those metallic blue legs!"

"Her scientific name is *Haplopelma lividum*; the common name is the Cobalt Blue Tarantula. But I call her Nagoya."

"Tarantulas are really harmless. Aren't they?"

"Most are not poisonous. But the venom of this species is dangerous."

"I see she is not afraid to use it," laughed Sam.

"Yeah." Amanda smiled. "If anything touches that terrarium, she zooms out of her burrow, fangs erect and dripping with poison. She is one of the aggressive species." Amanda's features shifted to anger. "Enough with this nature lesson – get on your knees and entertain me!"

Sam jumped off the couch. He obediently knelt, facing Amanda. But his hands stayed at his side. He did not know what "entertainment" meant.

She never met a submissive that did not know instinctually.

"Your cock." Amanda stood, pointing.

Sam looked down at his bobbing penis, then back at Amanda.

She almost slapped his face, but instead said, "Masturbate for me. NOW!"

"Oh," he replied, grasping his penis. "Sorry."

"*Silence*," she commanded, "or do we need the ball-gag?"

Sam shook his head.

Amanda sat back on the couch, enjoying his little display. "Rest back on your legs, and spread them wider," she ordered.

After he complied, he started.

"Slow down! You are going too fast," she commented. "And don't even *think* of coming!"

He held his cock gently, moving his hand gracefully over the taut skin. He kept his eyes downcast. After about thirty strokes, his breathing started to quicken. The muscles in his arms tensed. His penis gave a slight pulse, and a drop of pre-come oozed from the tip, slowly dripping to the floor.

"Stop." She patted the seat next to her. "Up here, puppy eyes."

Sam sat beside her. She noticed another clear drop of pre-come dangling at the tip of his penis. He was looking at it as well.

"That is *bad*!" she explained. She reached forward, wrapping her gloved fingers around the shaft of his penis. He froze in answer to her touch. She gave it a gentle pump, milking out another, larger size droplet. "I don't allow pre-come," she explained, "this is B-A-D." She enforced her lesson by giving a harder squeeze. She loved the dramatic impact of saying "no" and "bad" to physical reactions people thought involuntary. Amanda knew that, in time, if he came back, he would learn to control such impulses.

But Amanda's impulses were hers to indulge. She flipped over, straddling Sam's lap, facing him. Her body pressed his hard penis flat against his stomach. The buckles of her corset dug into his skin. His head was buried between her covered breasts. This was too much pleasure for him; she grabbed a fistful of hair at the nape of his neck and pulled his head away. She rocked her hips, thrusting hard onto him. She knew her extra weight was agony to his backside. She felt his hot breath fanning her. She released his hair. He obediently kept in place. His face betrayed the conflicting mix of pleasure and suffering she was causing.

"That's it, my little puppy," she cooed.

It surprised her that he came this soon. She felt his penis pumping between them like a detached entity. His eyes closed; he was panting. When it was over, he gazed up at her. Tears filled his eyes again.

"Oh, that is cute," commented Amanda. "Are you crying from pleasure or pain?" It was careless of him to stare, but she let this indiscretion slide. He was a newbie: he would learn.

"I'm sad because it's over," he said softly.

Good answer, thought Amanda.

She got off him, inspecting the mess that was now on her crotch. Luckily, semen was easy to clean from latex. She smeared her fingers into the milky liquid and touched it to his lips. She painted it across his mouth.

"Lip gloss looks good on you," Amanda said gently. Sam extended his tongue, licked his lips clean.

"Mistress Amanda," he said softly, "that was fantastic. Thank you, thank you."

"Don't expect such kind treatment next time," she interrupted. "I'm just in a generous mood."

She watched him dress. As she did, it struck her why he had such an effect.

"You know, you remind me of an old friend," she said, as he was ready to leave.

"I hope that is a good thing," Sam added, doubt on his face.

"Yes, it is." She walked him back to her desk. "So, I think you should see me soon."

"I would love to see you again. But," he added, "I'm leaving town next week for a five-day seminar." They agreed to another session in two weeks.

"Good, I will see you then." She reclined on her antique chair. "Be prompt!"

"Yes, I will," he said. He turned, the door slid open, and he left the room.

Amanda studied the monitor. She spied on him walking down the hall. He rubbed his backside again as he waited for the elevator. Amanda smiled. She initiated a deeper search on this man, her EOS snapping to attention like a loyal slave. More information was needed on a man who affected her this way. Was it just physical similarities to David? No, it was something else. She was determined to ferret it out.

"Well." Amanda placed the glass of wine down on the table. "Relationships often get complicated for me. People try to change me."

Sam sat across the table, staring at Amanda's plate of fresh oysters. Even though he had been seeing her for six months, he was nervous. After their last session together, he had got up the courage to ask Amanda if she'd like to have dinner one evening. She had immediately agreed, allowing Sam to iron out the details.

He prayed everything would go perfectly. He feared Amanda would feel hiring the limousine was a bit overboard, but she was delighted. She once mentioned her love of seafood; the restaurant he picked was noted for it. Since it was midweek, the place was not crowded. Tonight qualified as a legitimate date, at least in Sam's mind. As far as he could tell, Amanda felt the same way.

"Lemon," she said, staring down at her appetizer.

Sam selected a lemon slice, and squeezed it over one of the shellfish.

"Good boy," Amanda commented, as she raised the shell to her lips, sucking in the raw, glistening creature. Sam's appetizer of smoked salmon and dill sauce had so far remained untouched.

"My pleasure," Sam responded. "I can see how some people would be threatened by your career. I mean, the things you do to people."

"So, honey," she deepened her voice, to imitate a man's, "how was your day?"

"Oh," Sam replied, feminizing himself, "just some cock-and-ball torture, and the toilet training of a sloppy slave." They burst into laughter, drawing the attention of an older couple, who looked to be having dinner with their daughter.

"Female dominance pervades my life," Amanda continued more quietly. "You know that much about me now. On the other hand, I cannot be dominant every moment of the day. I like to cuddle beside the fire with my lover, or go to a movie in regular clothes." She smiled, adding, "Or being taken out to dinner with a nice guy."

Sam smiled back, his nervousness abating.

"For most people, our lifestyle is just a brief fantasy," Sam offered. "It sounds cliché but, for example, say you have a certain type-A executive. All day he bosses his underlings around and acts as if he is carrying the weight of the world on his shoulders. He's married, with kids. A Conservative. But every so often, instead of his usual lunch break, he visits his dominatrix. She bosses him around. Makes him beg."

"Thank goodness for such people," Amanda commented.

"They pay my bills!" She stared down at her plate; only one oyster remained.

"Hot sauce!"

Sam obliged, then continued. "But, after a session, his kinky needs are satisfied. He commutes back to his suburban lifestyle, ashamed of what he needs."

Amanda interrupted, "Hopefully, his dominatrix was skilful enough not to leave any marks."

Sam laughed. "But this part of such people's lives is compartmentalized, isolated from the rest of their lifestyle."

"Yes," agreed Amanda. "But then you have those precious people, rare ones who have this compulsion deep inside them."

Amanda's vision was locked on Sam's hands. He wondered what she was thinking.

"Sometimes," she continued, "you remind me of David. That does not bother you, does it?"

"No," Sam lied. "That's OK."

The spirit of David often wormed its way into Amanda's conversations. He had worked for a tech firm on a secretive government project. The goal was a direct human-to-computer contact. His team's breakthroughs lead to the first operational EOS. But as soon as major progress was made, the government barged in, stopping the project. Just after that, David and most of his colleagues were killed in an airline accident. Amanda and David had been lovers for three years.

"I never told you that the Cobalt Blue Tarantula was a gift of David's. Much research was done with insects and spiders in the early days of the project. The EOS emulates the hive mentality of insects. Some insect colonies are composed of millions of individuals, all subservient to the needs of the whole. How does one end of an ant colony know what the other end is doing? Years ago, it was believed chemical messengers, called pheromones, were the only thing responsible for hive discipline. It is so organized, the hive or colony is sometimes referred to as the 'super-organism': thousands of individuals, codependent, linked together, so intimately joined they act as one living entity. Arachnids were also investigated. Many web spiders build a retreat in which to hide. If you pluck a spider from its web, it instantly runs to its retreat when you return it. It knows the right direction to run to, no matter where you place it in the web. It always knows, even if you blind it. It was discovered that the web is a vast extension of the spider's nervous system. The web is an organ of the spider, as much as our skin is part of us.

"My spider is like a little piece of David, still alive and in my care. I cherish it. Females live much longer than males, you know?" She was smiling broadly, then grew solemn. "The computer he gave me was . . ."

The waitress interrupted them. She was twentyish, with short-cropped hair and dark skin. Her tentative nature betrayed the fact she was new to this job.

"Hello again," she said, giving Sam's untouched food a suspicious look. "Is everything OK?"

"Everything is fine," Sam confirmed.

Amanda gestured for the waitress to come closer. "He knows his place," Amanda confided. "My slaves never touch their food till I'm finished."

"Oh." Her face screwed up. "Your entrées will be out in a few minutes." She hurried to the kitchen.

Amanda stifled a laugh. "Go ahead, eat!"

Sam dug into his appetizer. After a few bites, he asked a question he knew was on her mind.

"You feel David's death was a set-up," he asked, "and the government – or something – had a hand in it?"

"The authorities don't want its citizens to read minds, Sam." Amanda stared into the distance. Sam glanced around to make sure no one was listening.

"But the Darkling hat of yours was just a peripheral," he commented. Amanda had shown him the mysterious device, the other day. "From what little I know," he continued, "it was intended as a tool for the treatment of mental illness."

"Mine was the prototype," Amanda explained. "David gave it to me for safe-keeping when he got suspicious the project was going to be terminated. The psychic powers of the EOS were discovered by accident. Some graduate student kept the files of her PhD thesis on the super-computer where the EOS resided. She was told to remove her work from the drives. That night, she logged on and erased them. Later, they found her wandering the halls, babbling incoherently. Somehow, all memories of her college career had been purged from her mind."

"Jesus!" Sam exclaimed. "How is that possible?"

"I don't know. Nobody does. Except maybe David. But it gets weirder. Luckily, she kept back-ups of her work. David and the others copied the back-ups to the EOS, and her memories were restored!"

Sam listened, his mouth open.

"Another bizarre surprise was that people logged into an EOS network could read each other's thoughts. If the different mechanisms of all this could be isolated –"

"Mind reading," Sam interrupted. "To have your memories excised, it would be like being reborn." He shook his head.

Amanda agreed. "I guess the myths and magic of the past become realities through science." She broke off the conversation and leaned toward Sam. "I have been holding off asking this . . ." Her voice drifted off. He did not need a psychic computer to anticipate her question.

"You want me to investigate David's death, to find out what really happened."

Her eyes brightened; she leaned even closer. "Can you? I mean, his parents did not care at all. They did not even allow me to come to his, to his –" Amanda's eyes welled with tears. "Shit." She stopped herself. "This has nothing to do with you. It's wrong of me . . ."

"Amanda," Sam cut in. He reached across the table, gently placing his hand over hers. Her fingers were cold. "No, it's fine. In a few months, I will have my license, and that will allow me access to so much information, I . . ."

"Why am I telling you all this?"

"You have lived with this too long," Sam encouraged.

"I'm happy you trust me." He needed to deflect the conversation; Amanda's depression was showing on her face. "Well, this is a switch," he added with a wry expression. "The dominatrix confessing to the slave!"

"Oh, yeah?" She pulled her hands away and sat back in the chair. "Take your penis out."

"Excuse me?"

"Correction: take *my* penis out!" Amanda clarified.

The people across the restaurant were looking again.

"You can do it!" she whispered. "Just keep yourself covered with the tablecloth."

Sam reached under the table to undo his pants. He fished out his penis, checking to see that no one was watching. Fortunately, the tablecloth concealed his lap. Amanda shifted in her seat. Sam jumped when he felt her boot press against his flesh. He chanced a glance down, seeing Amanda's boots under the cloth.

"Spread!" Amanda said.

"What?"

"Are you going deaf on me? Your legs! They are too close together. How do you expect me to get comfortable?" She wore the smirk that drove him wild.

Sam parted his legs wider. Now both of her feet were situated on the end of his chair.

Sam's penis was held vice-like between her leather boots. She started to pump her legs gently back and forth, pulling and stretching his rapidly hardening penis in a slow masturbation.

"What would happen to our privacy," Amanda went on, "if people could read minds? In the wrong hands, David's work could mean the end of individuality. But David's team had mental therapy in mind. It would be used like surgically precise shock therapy, excising traumatic memories. But screw the therapy aspect!" She hit her fist on the table. "Don't exorcize my demons: they are the best part of me."

Sam had heard her say that before, but now he was paying little attention.

"Can I take your plates?"

The waitress! She was standing right next to Sam. Amanda showed indifference. But then he saw Amanda slowly, purposely, pushing her fork closer and closer to the edge of the table. It tumbled to the floor.

"Oh, I'll get it," chimed the waitress.

"NO!" Sam shouted. "Ah, that's OK, I'll get it."

Sam contorted himself, leaning forward to successfully retrieve the piece of silverware. Amanda kept his cock in a vice-like grip, the whole time.

"Your entrées will be coming right out." The waitress cleared the table and sped back to the kitchen.

Amanda only partially succeeded in suppressing her laughter. Sam joined in.

"I hope we don't get kicked out of here!" Sam cautioned.

They were still laughing as the waitress returned. She set a huge platter of crab legs in front of Amanda. The Cajun-blackened bluefish was for Sam.

"Our food looks great!" Amanda commented.

Sam begged with his eyes.

"Go ahead, silly. Eat!"

Throughout the meal, Amanda occasionally asserted herself by tugging on Sam's imprisoned cock.

"Hot sauce!" Amanda said, near the end of their dinner. She was listlessly pushing around the spiny shell of the crustacean she just ate. Sam picked up the bottle, but he was unsure what to shake it on.

"I think you could use some lubrication," Amanda suggested.

"What?"

Amanda pointed underneath the table. "Down there!"

"You don't mean . . ."

"Do I have to explain everything?" There was a dismissive edge in her voice. "You were doing so well up to now."

"You mean, you want me, I have to . . ."

Amanda unlocked Sam's penis from the trap of her boots. She acted as if she was going to leave.

"Yes," he quickly assured her. "I mean, yes, mistress."

He pushed the tablecloth back to just reveal his lap. He

inverted the bottle, sprinkling a liberal dose of the condiment over his penis. His skin welcomed the cool wetness. He carefully avoided getting it on the tip of his penis; he did not want to learn the effects of pepper sauce on it.

Amanda eased her feet back together. Now the leather easily glided over his skin. Her movements took on an accommodating, slow tempo. His skin eagerly welcomed the marvelous combination of leather and liquid.

"Mm," he moaned, then under his breath said, "Amanda, that feels nice."

"Just wait." She shot him an evil grin. "You know why it's called the Darkling hat?" Amanda asked.

"Yes," Sam replied, as he began to feel a tingling in his foreskin.

"You do?"

Sam nodded. "It – it's about the beetles embroidered on the hat."

The spice was just now working its way into the nerve-endings of his skin. A tingly warmth was developing. The movement of Amanda's boots remained slow and steady. She moved her foot to place the sole flat against his penis, forcing it up against the confines of his zipper and pants. She nestled the spike heel underneath his scrotum.

"Go on," Amanda encouraged.

Sam cleared his throat.

"Yes, the Darkling Beetles belong to a family called the Tenebrionidae."

Sam closed his eyes. His crotch felt very warm. Amanda pressed her foot harder into him, the arch of her boot spreading his testicles. It was as if she were trying to force her spiked heel into his anus.

"Tell me more!" She asserted her command by giving him a sharp thrust.

"Ooh!" Sam yelped. "Darkling means things done in darkness."

She withdrew her foot. His penis was free. But the burning increased. Next, she forced his penis down, trapping it between her sole and the top of her other boot.

"Now, those other dark beetles you told me about, the Skin beetles, the Dermestids."

Each of her movements pushed more and more of the hot sauce into his skin. Suddenly the tip of his penis felt as if it was on fire. The evil liquid had found an opening. He started to sweat. Sam offered her a pleading expression, but Amanda just smiled.

"Skeleton preparation. Dead animals are stripped by hand of their skins and soft tissues . . ."

Amanda continued to play with him, squeezing, rubbing, changing her movements.

"When it is just bones, cartilage, connective tissue, and bits of muscle, the body dries out." Sam closed his eyes. The burning was growing unbearable.

Amanda finished the explanation for him. "Then the carcass is placed in a big vat of Dermestids," she said, "and the beetles swarm over it, gnawing on the dried bits of flesh. After a time, the skeleton is picked clean and white."

Sam did not hear her words. Beneath the cauldron, a new threat was asserting itself. It promised a moment of relief from the fire. A source of pleasure was rising fast. The table creaked as he hugged it, digging his nails in. Any second now, his orgasm would be joining them for dinner.

A voice cut into his conscience. He willed his eyes open. "How was your meal?"

It was the waitress. She was standing beside them.

Amanda was glaring at Sam. "Our charming waitress asked a question!"

It was as if a huge gripping fist were releasing his body. His back stiffened. He gave in to his orgasm. Amanda held him firm, as surge after surge of his jetting semen poured over her boots.

At the last contraction, he spoke. "Uh, I –" clearing his throat "– it was very good, thank you." Now please just get the fuck out of here, Sam screamed inside.

"Well, would you like any dessert?"

"No, thank you," he heard Amanda say. Sam covered his

forehead and eyes, as if he had a headache. "Just bring our check."

"Sure," the waitress answered.

Sam was still panting. Amanda had the hot sauce in her hands. She poured a little out onto her fingers and brought it to her lips. She painted it there in lip-gloss fashion, like the time she painted his lips with his semen the first time they met.

"Yum," Amanda commented.

The burning was now overpowering; it felt as if his skin was bubbling off.

"Uh, uh," he mouthed.

Amanda perked up. "Yes?" she asked, cocking an eyebrow.

"Please, Amanda," he begged. "I have to use the bathroom."

Amanda chuckled. "Fine; you're excused."

Sam gingerly returned his penis to his pants. As if by some miracle, only a little of the sauce had stained the outside of his pants. The restaurant was dark; he guessed no one would see.

He bolted to the men's room. Fortunately, it appeared vacant. Standing before one of the sinks, Sam undid his pants and pulled them halfway down. He threw open both taps. Water shot out, splashing in the sink. He cradled his penis and scrotum, draping them over the cool porcelain. He frantically splashed handful after handful of water over his inflamed genitals.

"Ooh, ooh," he moaned, as the water bathed and refreshed his skin. He leaned against the sink, adjusting the taps, keeping the stream cool. A mixed droplet of semen and hot sauce oozed from his penis.

Sam heard a flushing toilet. Someone was in there! The door of one of the stalls opened. Out came an older man, one of the people who had been staring. Sam wished he were invisible. In the mirror, he watched the man clean up in a sink that was furthest away. The man carefully avoided making eye contact. Just before leaving, he hesitated at the door, turning in Sam's direction.

"I'm treating my daughter to dinner," the man announced in a stern voice. "It's her graduation!" He slammed the door behind him.

"Well, *congratulations*!" Sam shouted to the empty room. He dried himself off and returned his reproductive organs to their rightful home. When he returned to their table, most of the plates were gone.

"How are you doing?" Amanda asked.

"I'm fine."

"Good. Why not pay the bill, and head back to my apartment?"

Sam had never been to the place she lived. "Not the dungeon?" he asked.

"I could use a little cuddling near the fire. How about you?"

Sam smiled broadly. "That sounds fantastic! I'll pay the bill and get our coats." He rose from the table.

Just as they were about to leave, a crashing sound stopped him. Sam spun around. Amanda had one of her legs up on the table. She swung the other leg up, bringing it down with a thud. She pushed back in her chair, pointing an accusing finger at her boots.

"You horrible pig!" Amanda screamed. Sam saw a mix of hot sauce and come painted on her boots.

"You want me to leave here, in a state like this? And you were doing so well, up to now. I am so disappointed."

"No, Amanda," Sam interrupted. His mind raced, then he chose a course of action. Leaning over, he brought his face down to her boots. In front of the sparsely filled dining room, Sam licked her boots clean. He had tasted his semen before, but the smell of her leather and taste of the hot sauce was delicious. He did it as fast as he could.

Amanda reached over, running her fingers through his hair. "Very good, my little puppy."

Back in the limo, Sam fixed two drinks from the well-stocked bar. They had a forty-five-minute ride ahead of them.

"When did you first become interested in bondage and discipline?" Amanda asked.

Sam took a gulp of his drink. "You mean, how long have I been a pervert?"

"Yes," grinned Amanda. "Basically that's what I'm asking."

"My first experience was when I was a young boy," Sam started. "The neighbors had a daughter who was about a year older than I. We were friends. She was a bit of a tomboy. One day, we were playing at her house. For some reason, we started rolling ourselves in the carpets . . ."

"What?" Amanda laughed and sipped her drink. "You mean the rugs? Oh, that's a good one!"

"Well," Sam went on, "I rolled myself up like a sausage in this one little rug. Only my head and feet stuck out. Suddenly, my friend jumped on my stomach. She started bouncing up and down on me, squeezing me with the sides of her legs."

Amanda laughed. She gave Sam's crotch a playful squeeze.

"Ouch!" Sam exclaimed.

"Oh, sorry. Still sore, but nice and hard for me. Please, continue."

"She was pretending I was a horse, her car, a circus ride – that sort of thing. I was loving every second of it. She announced I was her prisoner! She threatened to keep me like that all day. I begged and begged her to let me out, and she finally relented. When I unrolled, she noticed the bulge in my shorts. She asked what it was. I explained it was called an erection, and that sometimes men got them. She was thrilled! She asked if she could see it. Like the obliging little gentleman I was, I dropped my shorts. She was amazed. She pranced around me, looking at every angle, as if my bobbing penis was a new and wonderful toy. Finally said she could see it better if I took all my clothes off. I stripped. She led me to the couch. The strangest feeling was coming over me. This was not the first time I had been aroused, but I sure felt different. She asked me what the erection felt like. 'I don't know,' I responded. 'Do you want to touch it?' I asked. 'Yes,' she shouted. Well, the moment she placed her hand on my little hard-on, in walked her mother!"

"Oh, shit!" Amanda exclaimed.

"Yeah; she was screaming bloody murder. I was crying as I got dressed. Her mother would not shut up. She was slapping her girl's arm. I wanted to make her stop, but did not know what to do. Her mother forbade me from ever coming back to the house, or ever seeing her daughter again. As I walked off the front porch and across their yard, I turned to look back. I saw my little friend watching me from her bedroom window. I imagined she was grounded for life. Her face was red. She was crying. Her hand came up and she slowly waved goodbye. A few years later, my family moved away. I never saw her again."

"Oh, Sam." Amanda slid closer to him. "That is so sad." She stared out the window for a few moments before continuing. "But total body enclosure, female domination, humiliation, all at such an early age!" She burst into laughter.

"So, what about you?" Sam asked.

"I can't claim that early a beginning," she said. "I had my first impulses early in high school. When looking at fashion magazines, I started fantasizing about tying up the models, both the men and the women. But I didn't act out any of it till I got a bit older."

"Ha!" Sam laughed. "You were a late bloomer."

"Yes," she agreed. "I liked to wrestle with my boyfriends. I would strike up a bargain with them: if I was pinned, he could mess around with me. If I won, I got to do whatever I wanted. Unfortunately, the guys always won. Later, I came up with the idea of using ropes. Then, they could have their way if they escaped in five minutes. If they couldn't escape, well, they would have to promise to do whatever I wanted. At that stage, I was not very good at knot tying."

"I wish I'd gone to your high school!" Sam interrupted.

"Anyway," Amanda continued, "I kept my part of the bargain, although I never dated any of them for very long. But one day, I tied up a classmate who could not escape! I made him stay tied up for hours. I kissed and bit him. I pinched and sucked his nipples. I even pulled his pants down, and played with his hard cock. I squeezed his nuts until he almost cried. I sat over him, my crotch only inches from his face. I made him beg to get a taste of me. I threatened to tell his friends what I had done, if he did not consent to be my slave. He pleaded and pleaded, but finally agreed. He promised he would do anything I wanted. It was so fantastic, I finally took pity on him. But, as I went to untie his wrists, I discovered the knots were loose."

"You mean he could have escaped, any time?"

Amanda nodded. "God, that drove me wild! This guy wanted to be my prisoner! I had an incredible orgasm right on the spot. I realized that I had to be in charge. This was what I needed. Finally, I could do what I wanted, take my time if I needed. My desires came first! And all it took was a piece of rope. I had found my first true boyfriend."

Sam finished his drink. "Amanda, that is such a nice story." He shifted in his seat again.

Amanda was digging for something in her pocket book. She pulled out a small gift-wrapped box. She handed it to Sam.

"Wow, for me?" he asked.

Amanda nodded, smiling sweetly.

Sam eagerly unwrapped his gift. The box contained a brass metal collar. It opened with hinges at the back, and in the front, loops for a padlock. The inside was padded with soft fleece. Embroidered on one side, in delicate script, it read: SLAVE SAM – Property of MISTRESS AMANDA.

"Try it on!" Amanda said, smiling broadly.

It was just snug enough for Sam to squeeze two of his fingers under. Amanda produced a little gold padlock. She locked the collar shut on Sam's neck.

"It fits! It fits!" Amanda exclaimed. She took a triumphant sip of her drink.

But Sam's expression grew concerned. "This is beautiful. But do I have to wear it all the time? I'll have a tough time explaining this to the people I work with."

"If I wanted it on you all the time, you would wear it!" She was staring hard into his eyes. "However, no. But I wish you to wear it at all times in my presence. Whatever we do, wherever we go. You can wear a turtleneck or a high-collared shirt, if you wish, while we are in public."

"Thank you, mistress," Sam answered. Amanda hooked her finger around the gift and pulled him close. Her mouth met his. Sam parted his lips, welcoming Amanda's probing tongue. Sam savored her saliva and the attention of her mouth. He wondered if Amanda could taste the hot sauce and his semen.

"Amanda?" Sam asked.

"Yes?"

"So, I guess you enjoyed dinner?"

The hotel we checked into was the most upscale business-class piece of work I had ever seen. It had spacious conference rooms, mini-theaters, even a four-star restaurant.

I had just graduated from detective school. I had passed all my written tests, and completed my courses. In a few weeks, I would be getting my license. As a reward, Amanda was treating me to this little vacation. During my training at the agency, I had access to national police records; many databases were open to me. One thing we were warned against was digging through the pasts of acquaintances. Who could risk the lure of finding the dirty little secrets of a co-worker or friend? I resisted the temptation of doing a background check on Amanda. The fact she always was surprising me was intriguing. But I had promised to work on David's case, so there was no way of avoiding some confidential information on Amanda.

Our room was fantastic. A state-of-the-art entertainment center, equipped with multiple format video machines, and a powerful stereo system. The bathroom was huge. It even included a shower and a whirlpool bath. The furnishings were New England style; Amanda had specifically asked for this room. Now I understood why: the bed was a well-crafted cherrywood four-poster. Was Amanda going to tie me to these posts tonight?

Amanda started unpacking her suitcase, producing a brown paper bag. She set it on the desk. Next, she had a round silver serving tray in her hands. She placed it next to the bag. Then, with one quick motion, she slipped her finger beneath the top of her boot and retrieved a switchblade. She popped its release. The blade glinted in the light. We had been seeing each other for close to a year, yet she still managed to surprise me. I suppose that, in her line of work, she might need that weapon.

"Be a good boy. Make us up a nice platter." She handed me the open switchblade, grabbed a few things from her suitcase, and pranced off to the bathroom. "I'm taking a shower."

The bag contained a light feast: apples, pears, and kiwis, along with a tin of smoked oysters – she loved oysters. A box of gourmet crackers completed the package.

I carefully peeled and sliced the kiwis, then started cutting up the apples and pears. I spread the fruit sections in semicircular fashion along one edge of the tray. Next, I sliced the hard, smoked cheese. I just unwrapped the Brie. I placed the cheeses just off center. I opened the tin of oysters, carefully plucking each one free from its bed of oil, letting it drain, and setting them in a little pile next to the cheese. I broke open the pack of crackers, depositing them in a continuous arch with the fruit, forming a completed circle. I wiped my hands, then gently spun the tray around, admiring it.

Amanda's suitcase was sitting open on the bed. I could not resist peeking at what playthings she had taken along. I found a pair of sneakers, an extra pair of high-heeled shoes, her little black dress, a T-shirt, some toiletries, and plain pantyhose. But these were just items any woman would bring for an overnight stay. Where was the stuff from her dungeon? She never left home without her favorite cat o'nine tails. My exploring fingers found a long metal chain, more the gauge of jewelry than anything confining. Romantic getaways were not her style, unless . . .

"Found what you're looking for?" Amanda was glaring at me from the bathroom doorway. She was wearing a blue silk robe, and holding her bra and panties.

"You were sniffing for my panties, you little pervert! Well, here!"

She threw the items at my feet. I retrieved them from the floor. It crossed my mind to commit the crime she suspected, to cup them in my hands and inhale her scent. But she was still glaring, so I gently set them on the bed. She went over to the tray of food.

"Oh, that looks scrumptious," she complimented. "Now, time for your shower."

"I was going to unpack . . ."

Her expression grew angry again. "Shower, now!"

I stripped, discarding my clothes in a drawer.

The floral scent of Amanda filled the bathroom. The walls were dark green marble, streaked with yellow mineral. The bathtub was glossy black; it could easily hold four people. Recessed lights reflected on the mirrored walls. A simple shower stall sat in one corner. I showered, making sure to scrub every inch of my body three times over. After drying off, I wrapped a towel around my waist and headed back into the main room. Her nightgown was draped over a chair.

She was sitting cross-legged on the bed, the blanket pulled up around her. A towel was wrapped turban-like around her head. Her hands rested on her covered kneecaps, her strong arms framing her pert breasts. I knew that underneath those blankets she was naked. No corsets, bra, boots, or garters. I had seen every intimate recess of her body, but always isolated or presented to me as a reward for suffering some special humiliation or ordeal. Like the time she butt-fucked me with a strap-on. I came without her permission, but she was not angry. Instead, she offered me both her nipples to suck. And the times she demanded to be slowly kissed all over – every inch of her semi-clothed body. It was body-worship, not kissing. So her body held few mysteries. But now the promise of her total nakedness was overpowering. I was in a trance.

"Hey." Amanda was pointing at my waist. "You should be naked!"

I felt paralyzed.

"Have you suddenly gone deaf?" she asked. Then she shouted, "Lose the fucking towel!"

I snatched off the offending article, tossing it blindly across the room. I noticed that the fine chain was wrapped around my suitcase, looped several times through the handle. A small lock secured it. Even my collar was locked away. My half-hard penis started to fully rise.

"You will be kept naked – the way you belong – till I decide otherwise."

We were supposed to be leaving by noon tomorrow. Checkout was sure to be a humiliating experience!

She pulled the covers slightly higher. "Now," she ordered, "serve me."

I set the tray beside her. She pulled the towel from her hair. Her thick black locks fell across her shoulders.

"My hair is still damp. Be a dear and dry it for me."

I ran handful after handful of her hair through my fingers, softly rubbing it dry on the towel. She selected a slice of apple and cheese, and put them on a cracker. She cupped her hand under her chin, catching crumbs as she ate. Next, she speared an oyster with the switchblade. She kept eating as I worked carefully. After about ten minutes, her hair was suitably dry. She was staring up at me. I let the final handful of hair fall free.

"Oh, I'm being rude. This celebration is for you!" She brought her flattened palm up to my face. Obediently I leaned forward, my lips meeting her soft, moist palm. I picked the crumbs away with my lips, cleaning her carefully. I had to use my tongue to get the bits lodged between her fingers. My tongue discovered a droplet of oyster oil, its pungent aroma filling my mouth.

"Mm," she moaned. "Such a nice mouth, but I think you should save it for later."

She withdrew her hand and continued eating. I remained standing next to her, my penis sticking out like an unwanted chaperone. She activated the remote for the media station and started surfing stations.

"Go ahead," she said, sliding the tray toward me, "have some." I picked up the tray and sat on the floor.

"Nice gesture, Sam," she said giggling, "but I want you up here, tonight." She patted her hand on the covers next to her.

I moved so fast, I nearly spilled the food. I sat beside her, cross-legged like her. I ate while she continued through the TV stations. The "pay-for" shit only had the usual dose of Hollywood's pabulum. Even the porno selections were boring.

She stopped at one of the classic movie channels. An old black-and-white movie was playing. I did not recognize it. As I ate, we watched the story unfold.

A small plane crash-landed in the deep Amazon jungle of South America. The crew and passengers had to fend for themselves, repairing their plane, even cutting a runway through the tangled vegetation. One man was a professorial sort; he knew about the wildlife and the cannibalistic nature of the locals. Another actor portrayed a member of the mob who was caring for the child of an underworld boss. Among the passengers was a political prisoner who turned out to be helpful and kind. The officer who was supposed to guard the prisoner, on the other hand, turned out to be a creep.

"Basil Rathbone!" Amanda pronounced.

"I don't think so. That's John Carradine."

"Oh, I've never heard of him."

"He was a character actor, usually playing a villain or mad scientist or something. He was in hundreds of films."

I finished eating. I set the tray on the nightstand. Amanda turned off the light, then lowered the volume on the TV. I started to get under the covers with her, but her hand came up to stop me.

"Who said anything about that? Stay on top."

I sat back, resting my head on the pillow. In the ghostly light of the TV, I could see she had her eyes trained on me. What was she dreaming up?

"Slide down a bit," she requested. "Make yourself spread-eagled, please." Her words were soft. The dominatrix tone was gone from her voice. She crawled from under the covers and whispered in my ear.

"You must keep your hands down," she instructed, "and don't move. I trained you well enough now to no longer need restraints." It sent a shiver down my spine whenever she used the word "trained" on me. She sat on her haunches, in the sixty-nine position, above me. Her crotch rose directly above my face.

Like some over-eager fool, I eagerly reached for her waist. "No!" That sharp edge was back in her voice. But she added softly, "Arms down, please."

Her pubic hair was closely cropped. The mound of her outer lips was slick and nearly bare. Her delicate inner lips beckoned like a tempting flower for a nectar-hungry animal. But she held herself above me, out of reach. I impulsively gave the inside of her thigh a prolonged kiss. I parted my lips, allowing my tongue to glide over her skin. I turned my head to face her other thigh, giving it the same affection. I lingered there, spreading a dozen gentle kisses, gliding my mouth over her, never taking my lips away, always finishing with the touch of my tongue.

It startled me when her fingers brushed my cock. She began at the base, gently moving her hand upward. I felt the soft tips of her fingers feeling the head. She slid around it, then ran her fingers back to the base. She spread her hand over my scrotum, caressing my testicles. Then she returned to the base. It felt as if she was exploring me. Then she took her hand away.

I resumed kissing, alternately running my tongue on her skin. I kissed behind her knee. She loved to have that area touched, but she was ticklish there, so I had to go slowly. I gently kissed as before, letting my tongue part my lips to meet her skin. She swayed above me. I craned my neck, rising as high as I could bend, but her wonderful treasure was just out of reach.

The slightest hint of her marvelous aroma greeted my senses. Warmth spread through me, then desire took its place. I reached up, stretching my tongue. If only I had the spear tongue of an African chameleon, I would implant my sticky lingus deep within her. I was able to reach halfway up her thigh, so I satisfied myself by nestling my mouth there. Then, as if by some miracle, her sex just brushed my face. She had lowered herself for the briefest second. But now the treasure was gone. Was she measuring my reach? Her crotch was now a centimeter or two beyond me. It might as well have been a mile. I dropped my head in frustration.

Almost imperceptibly, she was tickling the stubby hair at the base of my cock. She kept this up for a time. My senses focused on my crotch, nearly making me forget the goal above me. She next ran her nails over the head of my penis, then again along the shaft. She clamped her fingers around the base, giving me a firm squeeze.

For a moment, her hips floated higher, and she released my penis. But she was only shifting, lowering herself onto me, placing her hips across my chest – but still out of reach. She settled on my side, lying half on my body. A pillow was placed between my knee and her head. One leg remained draped close to my head. The other lay across my chest. She was just getting comfortable. My ordeal was going to be a long one. I moaned.

As if to silence my plea, her foot came up to my face. I kissed along the sole, letting my mouth savor her skin. I slowly took her big toe in my mouth. I cocooned it with my prehensile tongue. I started on her other toes, tasting, sucking, licking. She playfully plucked at my pubic hair, grabbing a few in her fingers, then pulling just hard enough to make me suspect she would yank some out. This had no effect on my worship of her foot; I just moved along the outstep, until I got to her ankle. She replied by moving her leg to make my reach more comfortable. A shiver coursed through her as I licked her ankle. Had I found a new ticklish area? I was delighted! I did not want to overextend my welcome, so I started to kiss up her leg. A mild saltiness was on her skin. Was she sweating?

She shifted, her foot retreating. More of her weight bore down. This must be how a pinned insect feels. Her hands again were at the base of my cock. Fingers ran up the length; I felt a globule of pre-come ooze free. She repeated the lazy milking of my penis. Another run of pre-come trickled down the shaft.

Now I shivered, a mini-orgasm coursing through my body. I got these sometimes, when very excited. Her hips came down slightly. My prize was in reach! Just as I got my tongue on her lips, she pulled away. I moaned again. She giggled. Again she lowered, giving my tongue its next opportunity. I received the briefest touch, then she retreated. I was in agony, and she knew it.

Her hands cupped my scrotum again. She gave me the lightest squeeze, dancing me on the edge of pain. Her grip relaxed, and then she allowed me the briefest facial contact. My tongue led my lips to her. Her clitoris was swollen free of its hood – I cradled it on my tongue. She pulled back. My desperation found release in her thighs once more.

"Oh!" I yelled, as her cruel teeth caught the head of my penis.

She let up; I felt the hot moisture of her breath. She was going down on me, but keeping her mouth open wide, only granting me the barest touch of her interior. I tingled at even the slightest attention. I bucked slightly, trying to acquire firmer contact with her blessed mouth. I touched the back of her throat. She bore down on the base, anchoring me in place. She raised and lowered her head in a mock blowjob. Her hair danced about the inside of my thighs. She was determined and graceful. It would be an eternity before I came. Another mini-orgasm shot through me. I started moaning. She took her mouth away.

"Yeah, I love it when you moan."

Suddenly her hips withdrew. I lost control. My arms shot up. I was desperate and grabbed her around the waist.

"No," I begged. "Please don't stop."

She answered by grabbing my cock painfully, twisting and pulling like she was harvesting some root vegetable. The pain was too much.

"Ouch!" I called out. "Please!"

"Do that again," she explained, "and you will never get a taste of me!"

My arms were slow to do my bidding. I was hyperventilating, losing control. I took deep breaths. Knowing she was aware of my frustration added to my ordeal. She was relishing every second. She returned to her original position, her crotch dancing above me.

She started rhythmically dipping her hips. I craned my neck upward, tongue extended. For a second, I managed her outer lips. On the next leap, I again felt her swollen clitoris. The smell and the taste of her slippery wetness added to my fever. Her body grew tense for a few seconds. A shudder coursed through her, her movements transmitting into my trapped body.

Suddenly she smashed hard against me. Her vulva was pressed flush against my mouth. I sucked at her like a starving leech, feeding and growing by siphoning her juices. Another shudder moved her body. She drifted out of range again. Her gentlest motion was magnified. Our sweat became uniting glue. I wished to remain fixed to her forever, as if I were an ectoparasite. I wanted to be there always, till I extended umbilical blood ducts through my mouth into her. I would grow from her nourishment. Amanda would unwind the coils of my DNA and unzip the double-helix. I needed to fuse with her, to become a triploid entity that had never existed.

She started on my penis again. I was mindless to what she was doing, surrendering freely to her torment. But now I wished desperately to come. The teasing point of no return kept just out of reach, shifting, moving. Moving against her was futile. My jailer knew all my motivations. She had had ample prisoners before me, so she could easily anticipate any move. I struggled to intensify stimulation, nudging the sponge of smooth muscle tissue deep inside me toward the inevitable barrage of contraction. She adapted, reducing friction, evolving to prevent my deserved ascent. My hips thrust on their own, as if some vestigial ganglion in my spine had swollen to become a prehistoric brain. What was I enduring? This was so much more than everything.

To test me, she dug her nails into the flesh of my cock. I

was trapped in a cage of her fingers. But my thrusting was reflexive. Her nails dragged over my skin, her fingers becoming a toothy trap, insisting I suffer more. Pre-come was defeating her, making me slippery, helping her nails to glide over my skin. A spark lit the darkness in me, spreading electrically, crossing the gaps of my nerves. I was suspended in a warm glow for the briefest time. Then it dissipated.

"Please," I heard myself begging. "I want to taste you."

"What?"

"Amanda, please, I need to, to taste you."

"Hm?" she responded.

"I'm begging: please let me have it. I just can't stand it. Let me have, have . . ."

"Have what?"

"You!" I shouted. "Let me, let me stick my tongue in you. I must . . ."

She just pumped another stream of pre-come from her plaything.

"Well," she replied, "begging is good. I love to have you begging. Why did you hold out so long?"

She answered her question by rubbing herself against my mouth. My tongue dived in, lapping every fluid-filled pool within her. Her moisture filled my nose; her glorious taste overwhelmed my senses. She glided slightly away, but not so far as to deny me my prize.

"Now think carefully," she said, as she released my penis. "What do you wish for more? Coming? Or having me sit on your face?"

That was easy.

I frantically grabbed her in a bearhug, not caring of the consequence. I pulled her to my mouth with all my might. I drilled my tongue deeper than possible, consuming all of her.

The gift of pleasure washed over my penis. The soft wet flesh of her mouth closed about me. Her tongue snaked over the head, probing the tip, nosing the rim.

Her clit was perched between my teeth. I held it carefully, sucking gently. It had swollen to the size of a tiny penis. I sucked on it, mirroring her movements.

Like an obsessive lover, my orgasm was stalking me. It was going to draw every thread of life from me, in one joyous blast of soul-wrenching surrender. It draw nearer; now there was no escaping its hold on me. It was futile to fight.

"Amanda!" I shouted. "Don't go, don't leave me!"

But she was still on top of me. Always there, not a million miles lost as my feeble senses lied.

It broke me in one long stream. I arched my back, lifting Amanda from the bed. It did not pulse, but burst like a water balloon. The contractions started, the staccato shaking me, depleting me until I was nothing.

Amanda on top of me. She kept me as my spasms died away. She was always there, not blasted away into starlight. I was here.

My arms fell limp. She rose from my panting body. She repositioned herself, rising on me. She was squatting directly on me, my head clutched between her legs.

She was grinding herself, rubbing, sliding. I stuck my tongue out as far as I could. She rocked against it as if it were a soft worm. Between the pitches of her hips, I was able to snatch what breath I needed.

She was shouting something unintelligible. She dived forward, her hands anchoring against my hips. She held me fast, panting, digging her nails into me.

"Ooh." Her sounds turned deep, vocalizing as if an animal suffering in unfathomable pain. She pressed down on me, hard.

Suffocation meant nothing to me now. My world was closing in, a new blackness surrounding me. A glowing ember was before me. Was that Amanda? I wanted to call to it, to her, but my mouth would not respond.

Suddenly, I felt clear cool air. Amanda had slid off by my side.

"Damn!" she exclaimed.

"Oh, yeah," was all I could manage.

Amanda sat up, pushing her hair away from her face. She flicked on the light and turned to me.

"You bastard," she laughed, "you nearly drowned me!" I

saw a heap of come ringing her mouth. Globs of it were dripping to her breasts. I joined her in laughter.

"Well, you told me to save myself up for this! It was either that or you threatened to put that damn chastity belt on me again." I reached for the nightstand and grabbed a handful of tissues. I changed my mind and tossed them over my back. I wiped the smear of semen from her chin with my finger. After I licked it clean, I bent to her breast. Some made it to her flesh there. Her nipple was washed with my tongue. I worked my way up the trail of semen to her mouth. I cupped her chin and slowly lowered her jaw. My tongue explored the inside of her mouth, tasting me, traces of smoked oyster, and her teeth. Her arms came up and wrapped themselves around my head. Our lips parted.

"Nice clean-up job," she commented.

"Amanda," I said, "that was fantastic." She smiled, gently pushing me away. She crawled back beneath the covers.

"Yeah, that was good," she replied. "Many things are good about you. You never disappoint."

"Well, thank you," I said. "Do you think it's too late to order champagne?"

"Oh," she said, picking up the telephone, "that's just what I had in mind!" When she hung up the phone, she pointed to the TV.

"Look!"

"Wow," I said, recognizing the movie instantly. "It's *The Big Sleep*, with Humphrey Bogart."

"Who?"

"Oh, he's a famous actor. In this one he plays Philip Marlowe, a character created by Raymond Chandler. This was the hard-boiled type of mystery fiction."

I explained how the original story contained drug addiction, pornography, homosexuality, and nymphomania, but that had been too much for the Hollywood censors at the time. Amanda hung on every word.

"That's what you are?" She snuggled closer and wrapped her arm over my shoulder. "My little 'hard-boiled' lover!"

The only interruption we had was the arrival of the

champagne. We drank, arm in arm, until the movie concluded.

"Amanda," I asked, "would you like to do it sometime?"

"Penetration, that's what you mean?" A sullen tone hollowed her voice.

"Yes, mistress. That is what I mean."

"Well . . ." her voice trailed off. "I suppose so, if you need it." She eyed me with cold disregard. Then added, "Sam, if that is what you want . . ."

"Amanda," I interrupted. "It's no big deal. But maybe sometime."

"Fine, I don't mean to, to –"

"No, please," I cut in. "If that is uncomfortable for you, I don't need it."

"Listen." She sat more up in bed. "I want it, too. It's just that I have not had, uh, that kind of sex in five years."

Now I was floored. She had been a dominatrix for so long. With all the sexually-charged scenes she had been in, she had not had intercourse in all that time?

"Does this have anything to do with David?" I hazarded.

"No, not at all." She rolled away from me, facing the wall.

"My love." I placed my hand on her shoulder. "Listen to me. You must believe that sticking my penis in you is not so important to me. Making you happy – that is important."

Her hand joined mine. "Thank you," was all she said.

Just then, a low-frequency rumbling startled us. I thought we were experiencing an earthquake. Then I realized what was happening.

I bolted from the bed and threw open the blinds. Gliding above the choking city was a huge red glowing chevron. It was the Trans-World StratoLiner, its underbelly heat-shield still crimson-hot from the friction of reentry. In a few moments it would glide to landing and disgorge its two thousand passengers. Most were from Japan. In an hour it would be refueled, outfitted with a new crew, stuffed with more passengers, and blast itself into low earth orbit for New York. This behemoth circled the earth in ten hours, making stops at the world's giant cities.

I felt Amanda at my side.

"That thing is huge," she commented.

Her fear of penetration still bothered me. I would have my license soon, as well as needed security codes. Before I investigated David's death, I had someone else in mind. Whatever was in her past would not change my feelings toward Amanda, but I needed to know.

"Yes, Amanda," I affirmed. "Someday, maybe, we'll be able to afford a trip on it."

Sam believed people claiming friendships with ex-lovers were liars. His relationships always ended badly. He even considered himself fortunate to have escaped alive from more than a couple of them. But a brush with death was nothing compared to the loss of a cherished friend and lover.

What started as a professional relationship – a submissive man seeking the talents of a professional – grew into friendship. From there they had become closer, finally falling in love.

This was not what he expected, the first time his penis entered her: the biting, clawing, and whipping, until her blood flowed. Sam followed Amanda's orders without question; the more perverted and imaginative, the happier they both were. Yet this was a level of experience he never wanted.

First Amanda stripped. Then Sam bound her wrists together, in front, palm to palm. She knelt before the bed, her hands tied to the posts.

"Your belt," she requested. "Take it off, and beat me with it."

Sam slipped the belt from pants. Holding the buckle, he wound it around his fist, leaving about two and a half feet free. Belts are difficult to control, so he took a practice swing at the bed. It hit with a loud thud. Amanda's eyes went wild at the sound. He took position behind her and let the first swing fly.

"Harder! Use the buckle!" Amanda yelled. "I can't feel shit!"

He rewrapped the belt, letting the buckle swing free. After

a few strokes, welts covered her backside. Sam worked hard to keep aim, but the belt kept missing its mark, hitting back, thighs, and lower back.

An icy stillness possessed her, even as the sharp burr of the buckle cut through her skin.

The art of blood-play was one if Amanda's specialities. One night she dressed as a vampire, with Sam her helpless victim. With a sterile scalpel she opened a slit in Sam's iodine-cleaned wrist. She guided his flowing blood to a shot glass. She painted her lips with his blood. These exclusive ceremonies were always safe, clean, and sanitized. They were not horrible, painful, or brutal, as this scene was fast becoming.

Amanda let loose a scream. She hurled insults and gibberish at Sam, but never their safe-word.

"Harder – harder, you fuck!" Then, "I'll kill you, kill me! kill me . . ." Her legs spread wider, she pushed herself closer. She turned her head.

"Fuck me!"

Sam dropped the belt. He pulled off his pants. Amazingly, he was hard! He reached for her hips and pulled her close. He impaled her fiercely, entering her; his strokes merged with the struggles of her body.

Sam could not concentrate. He had done the background check on her, and he now cursed himself for that. Amanda's rape had happened shortly after David died. He saw police reports, pictures of the crime scene, the lab tests and line-ups, even the trial. Brutal detail after detail, all displayed in the coldness of his computer screen, even a mug-shot of the monster. It was a miracle she had survived. She had endured all of it, alone.

Amanda fell forward, pulling free. She collapsed in a sobbing heap on her arms.

Sam was transfixed by the sight of her backside. Something was flowing out from between her legs. It was his come, but he had experienced no orgasm.

"Untie me."

Sam was obedient, as always, but a violent wave of nausea

hit him. A bolus of vomit caught mid-way up his throat. He
bolted from the room, a fan of puke spraying through the
spaces between his fingers. He collapsed over the toilet bowl,
dumping the contents of his stomach. He fell hard to the
floor, resting his back against the cold tiled wall. He rested.
His hands shook. He grabbed a section of toilet paper and
cleaned off the mucus edging its way over the side of the
bowl. He stood up. An apparition with a blood-smeared
crotch was staring back from the mirror.

The second he returned to the room, Amanda sprang on
him. She went for his eyes.

"No, Amanda!" He snatched her arms. She nearly over-
powered him. She twisted, sinking her teeth into the flesh of
his chest. For a moment, he submitted to this attack. Her
teeth sank too deep. He shouted, pushing her off as her teeth
cut under his nipple. Sam jumped back in panic. Amanda
scrambled away, grabbing a blanket off the bed. She crawled
to the corner and covered herself.

I will not leave you, Sam thought, no matter what you do
to me – I will not let you suffer alone. He was her submissive,
and he loved her. He was thankful for his inhumanly high
pain threshold, for tonight it would be tested. He took a few
deep breaths to help prepare for whatever pain was coming.
Put the pain somewhere else, he said to himself. He sat next
to her. She was sobbing under the blanket.

"Amanda, please let me help."

"Go. Get the hell out of here – now!"

He had no protection from that level of pain.

Sam did not call her the next day. A week crept by, but still
he kept away. Finally he broke down and left a message with
her service. She did not call back.

One night, he found himself parked in the familiar lot next
to the abandoned cars. It was chilly and well into fall. Even
the weed trees, *Ailanthus altissima*, the "Tree of Heaven",
had lost leaves of their crown-of-thorns branches. Most
businesses had moved from this building, and closing time
had passed for the remaining ones. But, at the top floor, light

was peeking through the shades. It was her office, the
dungeons. It crossed his mind to jump on the elevator, to
go to the twelfth floor, and just walk in. But he successfully
fought the impulse.

Back at his apartment, he found a message waiting. An
hour later, they were speaking on the telephone. Amanda's
voice came halting and stilted. They agreed to meet the next
day, at a diner by the university.

Sam found her seated in a back booth. Her coat rested on
the seat. She wore a synthetic black alligator-skin dress, one
he had never seen. It was short, clinging tight to her body,
coming up around her neck, leaving her strong arms bare.
Mirrored sunglasses hid any emotion Sam might glean from
her eyes. After uncomfortable pleasantries, they ordered
coffee.

"Sam, you don't really know me," Amanda started. Sam
was speechless as she began to talk about her rape. She
recounted every detail. He wished she would stop. But he
was frozen. When finally through, she asked if they could be
"just friends" for a while.

"So that's it, Amanda?" Sam said, rising from table.
"Crush us like a couple of bugs!"

"What?" Amanda asked, looking up in surprise.

Sam stood from the table, and stormed from the restaurant.

"Great, another relationship down the tubes," Amanda
taunted herself.

Sam had only taken a few sips of his coffee. She turned the
cup around, running her thumb over the part that had
touched his lips. She paid the bill and left the restaurant.

She hesitated outside the diner, fiddling with her clothes.
It was getting cold. She pulled her coat tightly. From
the corner of her eye, she saw Sam. He was lurking in
shadows off the alley. She stopped, keeping her back toward
him.

Please, please, say something, Sam, she begged to herself.
Just come back and tell me I'm wrong: call me inhuman, an

asshole, a cunt. She shouted this in her head, as if she were ordering around some buggy software in her EOS.

His footsteps trailed off. He would never see the tears sneaking under her sunglasses, down her face and bouncing off the exoskeleton of her dress. Amanda's walk was now faster; the breeze caused her hair to dance behind.

She hadn't planned to bring up the rape. Her therapist had claimed she had gotten over it the best she could. But, somehow, Sam could see through her, even more than David ever could.

She started speaking aloud to the head wind.

"So, to break up with Sam, I had to stab him with the truth."

She started up the block for the post office. The movie she had ordered for him had arrived. It was a film called *Five Came Back*. It was that B-movie about the people stranded in the jungle, the one they had watched in the hotel. She would send it back, keep it, or give it to someone else.

The wind would not let up. She hurried; the cold was catching up to her.

I'm harder, now, she understood. At least it will be easier next time.

Amanda hated being late.

The meeting with the Japanese businessmen had run long. Their offer was solid, but not solid enough to be set up for life. They were eager to get their hands on the Darkling hat. She knew their scientists would backward-engineer the device and, in a few years, the technology would be copied. She believed no one government should have control of it. David would have approved.

She did not know why she agreed to a session with Sam. But he went on and on about how good she was and that he could find no one as talented. That was true. Amanda knew she was the best. It had been months since she had seen him, and she was curious to see how his investigative career was going. Yet this scene was going to be strictly business. Sam had one hour, then he was out the door.

But he was nowhere in sight. There were no messages. If he cancelled, it gave her the night off. Amanda pulled the Darkling hat out of her bag and placed it on the table.

"Well, if Sam skips out," she told herself, "I can't blame him."

She went to the whipping room, where she kept a change of clothes. The second she entered the room, something moved behind her.

CRACK.

The left side of her face exploded in a spray of blood. She screamed, covering her head.

It was Sam. He had the bullwhip!

She dropped to the floor. The whip again sliced the air.

CRACK.

This time it missed, slicing the air in a supersonic backlash just above her head.

"No, Sam," Amanda pleaded. "Please, stop!"

Blood was pouring through her fingers as she covered her eye. She could barely see. Through the red fog, she could see Sam drop the whip.

"Amanda, I . . ." He bent over, looking as if he was getting sick.

"Why, Sam?" Amanda asked, with inexplicable calm. He answered by running from the room.

Blasting pain and adrenaline crashed the EOS; it could not call for help. Amanda fought a wave of dizziness while struggling to her office. She grabbed the phone. The dispatcher promised an ambulance in three minutes. She slumped into her beautiful regal chair. Blood ran down her face, leaking through her hands, dripping on her breasts. She pressed the wound, trying to stop the flow of blood. Then she thought of the hat. She had to hide it.

The front door was open. Sam was gone – and so was the Darkling hat.

Sam was in darkness. His eyes were open, but he could not see. The ground was moist, like mud under his fingers. The air was hot and stunk of ammonia. He was in a deep cavern.

He crawled forward, his fingers squishing the gook under him. He heard a sound in the distance.

A shimmer of bioluminescent fungus delineated the cave in relief. The ceiling was low. Something was crawling over his skin. The floor was alive with countless larval insects. The mud pulsed and moved. Things were crawling all over him.

Fur brushed his face. Something flew by. He heard a squeak. The cave was filled with bats. He was crawling through guano.

Feeling along in the darkness, his hand touched something hard. His dark-adapting eyes revealed its identity. It was a body: a person, a man. To Sam's horror, he found that the stomach and genitals had been eaten away, as if chewed out by some raging carnivore.

He found another dead man in the same state of partial consumption. Then another. Now he heard voices.

Was that Amanda?

He came to a tight passageway just big enough to squeeze through. Sam went through head-first. It turned downward. He wound up in a larger part of the cavern. This chamber was filled with the dead bodies. They were stacked all around. The air was oppressive with the smell of rotting flesh. In the gloom, something was moving.

It was a huge beast, quadrupedal and hairless. It was the size of a small cow. It made made chomping sounds. Surrounding it were more bodies. Sam turned, trying to crawl back through the aperture. But the slippery earth had him trapped.

The thing heard him. It spun around. It had the head of a human! Blood was caked on its lips. Strips of flesh hung from its mouth. It had long hair. It lurched toward him, close enough now for Sam to get a good look at its face.

It was his mother.

Sam screamed so hard, he tasted blood. The thing charged. He desperately scrambled up the cave wall, slipping and cutting his fingers. He plied the sides for handholds, but got nothing. It was behind him now. He felt himself sliding toward it. Hot breath enveloped his heels.

A small hand reached through the darkness in front of him. Sam grabbed for it. Whoever it was supported him, helping him upward.

"Come on, silly!" It was a little girl's voice. Sam noticed his own hand: it was child-size, like the one he was holding. He kept moving upward, leaving the snarling beast below.

"What are you, a sissy?" teased his companion.

"Stop calling me that, tomboy!" His own voice now rang high-pitched. He struggled back through the opening, and got to his feet.

"Well, then, come on!" his little friend added, running just out of sight.

Sam was standing before a black room. Two people were there. One was a woman, dressed very strangely. The other was a man with no clothes on. He was bent over some funny piece of furniture.

"You-are-a-slow-poke," the little girl added in singsong.

"I am not!"

Sam kept moving. Now he saw two people eating dinner. They were having fun. He could not look for long; his friend kept slipping ahead.

Next he saw two people together in bed. They had no clothes on. The woman was on top of the man. What were they doing? The woman's hand was in the man's lap. She was holding something.

"Ha!" the little girl interrupted. "Thanks to you, I know what that is. It's an erection!"

Now a man appeared before Sam. He had an awful whip in his hands. He looked angry.

"Hey, come here and look at this!" The little girl was at a door. Sam went to her side.

"Sam Bigglesworth," the girl read, pointing to the glass, "Detective Agency."

The girl tugged at Sam's hand.

"I've got to go, now," she said, adding, "I enjoyed playing with you again."

"Me, too," Sam replied. "Maybe we can play . . ." But she vanished into the darkness.

Sam turned the doorknob.

A man was sitting at a desk, a stack of cardboard boxes beside him. Before the man sat two other men, dressed in suits. One was big, the other smaller. The big fellow had on a pair of strange-looking glasses.

"Excuse the appearance of my office, gentlemen," said the man behind the desk. "I am moving downtown, next week . . ."

"That should present no inconvenience," assured the smaller man.

"So, uh," the man behind the desk checked a notebook. "Mr Pierce, you want me to find some lady? I hope you at least have a picture of her."

The big man pulled a magazine from his jacket and slid it across the desk.

"That's her," replied the short man, "on the back cover."

The man behind the desk cocked an eyebrow. He circled the ad with a felt-tip pen. "What is she? Some sort of prostitute?"

"Not exactly. This woman is in possession of top secret computer hardware," explained the short man. "She is trying to smuggle it out of the country."

"Oh," the man behind the desk interrupted, "so you guys work for the Feds. Great, then I can charge double!" He started laughing.

The two others did not join in.

Just then, the men in suits vanished in a puff of glowing blue light. But the man behind the desk remained. His eyes were locked on Sam.

"What the hell are you doing here?"

"Me?" Sam's voice was deeper now. "I should ask you that!"

The man reached into his desk. He pulled out the Darkling hat.

"You know," he said, "I thought I had erased you from my life, you disgusting pervert."

"Oh, yeah?" Sam said, stepping forward. "That is not so easy. And fuck you!"

Sam dived over the desk. His hands locked on the man's throat.

Everything in Sam's mind exploded.

This was not the first time I had woken in a puddle of my own piss. But now semen was mixed in. I raised my head; I was still chained up in the closet. I was looking into the barrel of a gun. It was mine. Pressing the trigger was Amanda.

"No," I found myself saying. "I did not know who they were. They, they –"

My eyes were fixed on Amanda's scar. It now stood out like a curse.

"Oh, God," I found myself saying, "I did this to you, blaming you, blaming all women. But how could I ever hurt you? What, what –"

"Start making sense." Amanda stepped forward. "This is not virtual-reality gaming! I could not see everything you just went through. However, I caught enough to know it was you who led those agents here."

"Yes," I said, feeling calmer. "They hired me to find you. But it was not a set-up. It was just a coincidence. You said I was the new Sherlock Holmes. I can find anybody! You and David kept your relationship hush-hush, and the anonymity of your business made you almost a non-person. You would have been history long ago, had it not been for that. But they knew the Darkling hat was somewhere and, somehow, information on you must have surfaced. The two goons came to me, came to me, with an ad," I broke off in laughter. "I had lost myself, Amanda. Finally I was all gone." I lowered my head. Everything was making sense, but I did not want these revelations.

"Why, Sam?" Amanda persisted, pointing to her maimed face.

"It's not you!" I shouted. "It was my parents. They separated when I was a child. It was messy. Difficult. My dad was a good guy, but my mom was spiteful and vindictive. She had a better lawyer and I wound up in her custody. But it was the men, all the men . . ."

"Neglect? Is that what this is about?" Amanda's voice cut with a dismissive tone.

"This is my nightmare," I calmly explained. "If you're going to kill me, at least let me spit it out." I owed her this. I took a deep breath.

"Neglect, yeah. That is part of it. Promiscuous would be too polite a word for my mother. I was always being dropped off at some baby-sitter's or getting pawned off on neighbors for the night. At best, I was put to bed early. But I could hear them downstairs – from my bedroom, my mom and one of her many friends. I knew she didn't care about me, did not . . ."

"Sam, it's all right,"

"All right? All right to hate women? All of you, especially ones I love? You are my fucked-up mother! Why do you think I paid you to hurt me? And, in time, I knew you would abandon me. You always are abandoning me, betraying me." Sobs started blocking my words.

"I was the catalyst, the focus of your crisis." Amanda acted as if she was talking to herself. "I pushed you too fast. The combination of physical and emotional pain, causing you to snap." Amanda was lowering the gun.

"Why should you care?" I mumbled. "I had a choice. I chose to leave you a bloody mess." I gave my restraints a tug and threw my head back. "Shoot! Get this over with."

Then I felt her closeness. She was standing next to me in the puddle of my juices. She grabbed the back of my head and pulled me forward.

"Look at me," she said firmly.

I couldn't believe what I saw in her face: compassion.

"You think you deserve to die –" she ran her finger down the scar " – for this? A hospital visit and two rounds with a plastic surgeon? Then a few months with a physical therapist and a little acupuncture – I have some nerve damage now; and sometimes it twitches." The side of my face came to rest on her leg. "It would be great," she continued, "if all wounds were so easily healed. Damn, that fucker Freud must be spinning in his grave; you hate me because I remind you of mommy!" She gave me a sharp look. "Who are you?"

"Huh?"

"Are you the smart-mouthed sexist detective or the sensitive, intelligent guy I knew?"

The weirdest feeling came over me.

"Both!" I blurted. "We are both here."

Amanda started unlatching my arms.

"I loved that guy, that man who first came to see me." She helped me to my feet.

God, I stank to high heaven.

"Amanda," I said softly, "he – I mean, we – still love you. The detective is having a hard time with this erotic lifestyle, but for the moment he is under control."

"Sam, we've got to get out of here. I mean, those agents . . ."

"Shut up, sweetie!" I heard myself saying. "If we are going to get out of here alive, we'd better start making with the feet – now!"

We were skipping the country.

I had to hand it to the broad: she moved like lightning. The only things she took from her dungeon were her favorite cat o'nine whip and that damn spider. She scooped it up in an empty yogurt container. Now I had the creepy-crawly in my side pocket; she said it had to be kept warm. Shit, I must really love this bitch. Boy, the customs agents were sure in for a big surprise if they searched me!

We had to stop off at the house she rented. Amanda needed a few things, namely that computer of hers. That thing has some range! It had been networked into the plumbing of Amanda's brain for years. Seems she could just not stand to be without it. And any woman needs a couple of changes of clothes. I hoped she had some clothes for me. I stank like hell!

Hong Kong was our destination. I was still owed big-time favors there. I knew one or two business types who just might like a crack at that Darkling hat. For the right price, that is.

Her home was a little colonial-style deal, way up in the suburbs. It was 3:15 a.m. I had been waiting nearly an hour. She had told me to wait. I always obeyed her. She was the boss. She would punish me if . . .

What the fuck was I thinking? I would just love to get Amanda bent over a stool, and shove my hard cock up her ass. That would show her who was boss! I just, I just . . .

She was taking too long. I turned on the radio, hoping music would calm my nerves.

"Sam Bigglesworth," the reporter snapped in, "is wanted as the suspect in connection with the slaying of the two officers. He was last seen traveling with a woman and –"

Oh, great! Now I'm pegged as a cop-killer. Every cop on the eastern seaboard was now fighting for the honor of blowing my brains out. We needed to be at the dock in two hours. That container ship would not wait, no matter how much I bribed. Finally, the lights blinked off in the house.

After five minutes, there was still no sign of Amanda.

I got out of the car and went to her door. It was half open.

Suddenly, the hair stood up on the back of my neck. What the hell did that mean? As if possessing a mind of its own, my hand gracefully reached inside my jacket, and slipped my gun from its holster.

I pushed the door slowly open and entered Amanda's darkened house. Her stuffed backpack was in the hallway. Just as I was about to call out, I stopped myself. I reached for the light switch, but a little voice went off in my head, saying, "What, are you crazy?"

My feet guided me out of the hallway and into the living room. The carpet quieted my steps. I was standing before the fireplace. A blast of memories raced through me. I could almost see us cuddled there after our late-night dinner in a quiet restaurant. I crouched down, touching the area where we once lay. I scanned the room.

"Sam – watch out!"

Someone slugged me – hard. I lost my balance and fell to

the floor. My gun was kicked free and bounced out of reach. Lights blazed on.

That big goon with the visor was standing above me. How could such a big guy move so fast? That grenade-launching rifle of his was now pointed right at me. Amanda was on the floor, face down. The goon's partner – the shorter guy – was holding her. He kept her arm pinned behind her, and his knee pressed into the small of her back. He had a pistol, too.

"Well," he announced, "you finally join us."

I had my eye on the big guy. Although his face was partly covered by those spaced-out goggles, I was a quick study. Something was puzzling him. His rifle kept swinging, as if he could not get a fix on me.

"So, Mr Bigglesworth," the little guy said softly. "You had us fooled for a while. But you know what we are after."

"No, Sam!" Amanda cut in, then, "Ouch!"

The goon twisted her arm.

"You see, Mr Bigglesworth," he explained, "the mind of your charming friend was easy for my partner to scan. And, I might add, what a naughty mind it is!"

"Cut to the chase, Mr Pierce," I interrupted. I slowly got to my feet.

The big goon grunted.

"Her mind told us you have the hat," he continued. "But scanning you is problematic, it seems. My partner thought two people were waiting in the car."

"OK," I said, "you got us. If I give you the hat, you'll let us go?"

"Sam," Amanda cut in, "don't. They'll kill us."

"Shut up, Amanda. What else can we do?" I reached in my pocket and wrapped my hands around the container.

"As I was saying," the man with Amanda continued, "you are a bit of an enigma. Interesting phenomenon, isn't it?"

"Here!" I snapped the lid of the container open. "Catch!"

The wiggling spider sailed through the air, landing smack on the big goon's face.

I dived to the floor, expecting gun shots.

"Ahhh – you bitch," shouted the little guy. Protruding

from his knee was Amanda's switchblade, buried to the handle. She spun from under him, knocking him off balance. He fired a blind round.

The big guy screamed. He dropped the rifle, covering his face with his hands. The spider was taking care of business, planting both fangs into his nose. I dived for my gun.

I was luckier with my shot. It hit the little guy. A voice went off in my head: "Share the wealth," it said.

My next bullet struck the big, bellowing guy. He hit the wall.

I spun, taking aim at shortie. The splat of blood and bits of brain painting the wall indicated another shot was unnecessary. But the big guy still made noise. He rolled over onto his back.

I flinched as two more rounds shot off. It was Amanda! She had shortie's gun. She emptied the clip into the big guy.

"That's for David, you bastard!" she affirmed, dropping the gun.

"Damn, Amanda!" I said, as she pulled the knife out of the little guy's leg. She folded it and returned it to its home in her boot. "We make a good team."

She threw her arms around me and squeezed me tight. Tears were on her face. She kissed me on the cheek.

"Ouch," I complained. She managed to kiss my throbbing cheekbone, right where I had been punched. "That hurt, but not in a good way."

I went to the one who had held Amanda. His pocket revealed a wallet full of ID and cards. Now we would have a better idea who we were dealing with. Amanda stood above the bigger guy. She pulled the goggles from his face.

"Come on, Amanda," I said, grabbing her backpack and rushing for the door. "We have to fly."

"Sam." She turned to me, a look of horror on her face. "You have to see this!"

I went to her side and stared into the face of the big dead goon. It was the most hideous thing I had ever seen.

It was his eyes! They were huge, like the unfeeling eyes of some nocturnal reptile. His eyelids were small, vestigial, useless. His pupils were fixed wide, the sclera parched and dry, ruffled like dried skin. The skin around his eyes, protected by the visor, was pale with a sickly translucence.

Next to this apparition was Naggie, Amanda's poor spider. Its legs were folded under its body. The big goon had crushed it dead.

I gave Amanda the car keys and told her to meet me at the front of the house. I ran to the kitchen and unplugged the electrical power to the self-starting gas oven. I turned up all the jets and grabbed the grenade rifle.

I was already standing in the road when she pulled up. I motioned for her to roll the window down.

"Bid *sayonara* to your old life, Amanda."

"I already did," I heard her say from the darkened car.

The grenade took off like a rocket, passing clear through the open front door. Amanda's house exploded in a brain-shaped cloud of red flame.

Amanda finally fell asleep, but she was restless. She had suggested cunnilingus might help her relax. We were sweaty from our long trip. We were too exhausted to even shower. I did not hesitate to suckle between her legs. She tasted fantastic!

Here we were, in the same hotel room we had rented for my celebration when I had gotten my license. Sure, it was risky. But what a great place to spend the last hours in the States. I was exhausted myself, but could not sleep. I rubbed my lips and Amanda's aroma revived me.

The stolen visor rested on the table. The Darkling hat was squirreled away in Amanda's suitcase. Her little computer would easily pass as business accessory, so Customs would be a piece of cake. And Sam the private dick knew whose palms to grease if we ran into any trouble. I could hardly wait for the bidding war between the Hong Kong triad and the Japanese. Our goal was enough hard cash to do anything, to go anywhere. And those Asiatic business types were sure kinky: their company benefits plans even budgeted for sex! Amanda could set up the best fetish palace in history. With that spooky visor and her computer, I would be the best private eye that ever hit the Pacific Rim. Nobody on the planet could put the drop on us.

But what about other planets? What was that thing we killed back at Amanda's pad? Was he once human, or something else entirely? Was it possible the visor did this?

Amanda kept tossing. I quietly rose from the chair and picked up the mysterious visor. I just had to take a peek through this thing. I stepped toward the balcony and parted the sliding doors. A blast of humid, polluted air bathed my naked body. I put the visor to my eyes.

For a few seconds, everything was black. Then, one by one, stars began to appear. They were all around me. I realized they were minds. I could see them walking the streets forty-seven stories below. Brains even glowed through the tops of cars and through the buildings around me. After a time, the lights of their minds merged. Each human entity was a lighthouse, casting shadows in a sea of thick conscience.

It was pulling me. It tugged at my face. I felt the thoughts would support me. All I had to do was step off the balcony and crowd-surf on the thick chorus of mentality. A new, powerful sense was growing in me.

A distant rumble broke my thoughts. Gazing upward, I saw the outline of the StratoLiner. Its now transparent fuselage trapped a swarm of mental fireflies: I had access to the minds of the passengers. They were dissected before my scrutiny. In a few hours, one of these ships would carry us over the horizon, delivering us across the near-vacuum of low earth orbit to our new lives.

I was getting dizzy. I stumbled back into our room. My gaze fixed on Amanda. A huge, shapeless entity was squatting on her. She was being torn up by a monster. It ripped at her, digging her, stripping her flesh away. It was splitting her in half. She could not get away. All she could do was toss under the covers, trapped in an unending nightmare.

I grabbed the suitcase. I dialed "007" into the lock. The case popped open. The Darkling hat was in my hands.

I went to Amanda's side. As I took off the visor, the apparition vanished. I pulled the covers back. She was asleep, her eyelids darting in REM. I placed my hand on her shoulder. She flinched but did not awake.

She might curse me for what I was about to do, but she said this was the intention of the Darkling hat. I hoped the woman who got up in the morning would be the same wonderful spirit I so madly loved. She once said our demons might be the best part of us.

But I was no longer going to allow this demon to chew my lover to death.

SCRATCH

Nikki Dillon

The Devil is a lot of things to me and my four housemates: he's our boyfriend, our employer, and our master. For the rest of the world, he's a fashion photographer known as Scratch – a middle-aged man with deformed eyes and a few unusual physical abnormalities, which may or may not be the product of plastic surgery. His signature appears on the upper right-hand corner of each of his photos, in lurid red. It's blood, according to Scratch. He develops only thirteen prints of every picture and, supposedly, burns the negatives in an occult ritual involving goats.

We've never seen a goat around here, though there was a Doberman chained up in the basement – with Gregory – for three or four days last February. Gregory never complains about anything, but the dog whined and barked incessantly. Scratch gave it away to one of the production assistants.

Most people assume that the Devil thing's a gimmick. And it works. One of his early photos sold last week in London, at an auction, for half a million bucks. As usual, Scratch will give a chunk of that money to controversial theatre troupes and undiscovered artists. His detractors say he needs the tax break.

Those of us who sleep with him know why he gives away his cash.

Money is what attracts us.

We're his slaves.

Scratch shoots photos for fashion spreads and slick magazine ads. Designer suits. Designer handbags. Designer lingerie. Financial success has ruined his reputation. Last year, before his retrospective at the Whitney, there was an article in the *New York Times* about him. It quoted an anonymous curator who called Scratch "a third-rate photographer turned con-man".

In any case, I believe Scratch is who he claims to be. I've stroked the two stubby hard lumps on his scalp. Covered by his thinning hair, they're located half an inch behind his pointed ears. I've had my neck scratched by his claws and my foot stepped on by one of his cloven hooves. It sure feels real to me.

The five of us live with Scratch here in Milan, Italy, where his photography studio is based. He owns this four-storey building – a squat, ochre-coloured structure on the waterfront by the *navigli*, canals. The neighborhood, once working class, is in vogue with fashion insiders. Gregory thinks it's so hip and romantic. The rest of us are less convinced. I admit I liked the place when I first arrived here last November. The cobblestoned streets were covered in a thick fog, then, and I couldn't see too clearly. Also, I was more or less delirious.

I had an idea that I was going to get rich,

When it comes to money, I am stupid.

Before Scratch took me to Milan, I'd lived in New York City for nine years. There, I'd led the humbling, wretched existence of an aspiring novelist. I'd been marginally employed as a freelance copywriter for a publishing company that specialized in coloring books. My wages were laughable, so low that I took perverse pride in them. I'd cite the figure to well-dressed, overpaid acquaintances. I enjoyed their stunned reaction.

"How do you survive in New York?" they'd gasp, sounding horrified.

"I guess I have a masochistic streak", I'd say, joking. (It seemed funny, then.) By the time I turned thirty, I'd developed the self-deprecating and slightly paranoid personality of an outsider. My career had showed some early promise, as the saying goes, but was failing to materialize. Mysteriously, one by one, my friends had been absorbed by the middle class. They joined up with that amorphous group, Professionals. I could no longer follow their conversation; it was filled with jargon. As far as I was concerned, they did vague things, in conference rooms, that concerned computers, the law, and television. They owned houses and apartments, furniture, and matching plates. They acquired husbands, wives and children. I saw how they eyed my second-hand clothes, and watched me count out dimes from my change purse to pay for drinks. They'd invite me over to their four-bedroom colonial houses in the suburbs to feed me what I thought of as a "pity dinner". In my apartment, I dined on toast and instant soup.

By the time I met Scratch, I'd written two "literary" novels: *Miracle at the 23rd Street Laundromat* and *Odor of the Swamp*.

Needless to say, I couldn't sell them for my life.

Four days after I hooked up with him, Scratch handed my landlady a cheque from a Swiss bank and removed me from my roach-infested, one-room apartment on West 121st Street, where drug dealers convened on one street corner and drunken vagrants on another. He hired three handsome moving men to pack up my belongings and ship them to Milan. They called me "Ms. Bellamy", and they handled my chipped coffee mugs and paperbacks as if they were priceless, wrapping every object, including my sneakers, in a sheet of newspaper, cushioned by shreds of white Styrofoam which they referred to as "the snow".

The day before we left New York, Scratch took me shopping at Barney's, the trendoid department store. It was cold out, so he bought me a red vinyl baseball cap with fleece-lined earflaps. Now I keep it on the windowledge in the studio, in my office alcove, next to the futon mattress which I unfold at night to sleep on. I don't wear it much, and I never wanted it in the first place.

It cost Scratch $248.00.

It's a number I remember, because it was my weekly salary at Dunn and Bradworth Publishing Co.

Fucking price tag. It impressed me.

I work for Scratch eight hours a day, seven days a week. My desk is a card table equipped with a portable computer in an alcove. I'm separated from the photography studio by a wall of rectangular glass bricks. Back in New York, Scratch and I made a deal to produce a book which would wind up on the bestseller list, or even lead to a lucrative Hollywood movie option. In exchange for room, board, a one-way plane ticket and that useless shopping trip to Barney's, Scratch commissioned me to write a book based on his character. I'm supposed to be his first official, authorized biographer, with exclusive access to his correspondence and private papers.

Unfortunately, the book I'm writing sucks.

It's a fictionalized biography, or what Scratch calls "bio-fic". The working title is *I, Satan*. But Scratch refuses to tell me anything about himself. So I have to take wild guesses and tell lies.

When I objected to doing that, Scratch lost his temper. "Don't be an idiot!" he yelled, stamping the floor with the heel of his motorcycle boot. "Make it up. That's what you're here for, stupid girl." It was one of the few times I've seen him lose control. Usually, he keeps his voice low. Scratch often smiles when he's angry.

My relationship with him is fairly twisted.

I expected that, I guess.

"Candles are in", Scratch told the four of us this morning. He looked up from the latest edition of Italian *Vogue*. We were all sitting at the long dining table, eating our usual breakfast of bread and water. Some of us – including me – were allowed to have a cup of instant coffee. Katrina, the Austrian dancer, was feasting on scrambled eggs and a slice of toast with butter. The rest of us, half-starving, were trying not to watch her eat. My mouth was watering, and I knew that, when she performed for Scratch last night, he'd liked her choreography, for a change. Probably, she'd gotten laid in some way which was pleasurable instead of humiliating or painful. That's part of the reward when he approves.

By now, most of us prefer the food.

"Children!" Scratch was saying. We don't *have* any candles, do we?" He was sounding mighty anxious.

None of us looked at him. We all stared down at our plates, like we were fascinated by the geometric pattern on the ceramic pottery, and concentrated on swallowing and chewing.

"Alexandra, dear?" he said,

My heart sinks when he calls my name. I have no idea why he drags me into these discussions. I could care less about what's "hot".

"Yes, sir?" I said, trying to sound interested, instead of scared. I'm scared of Scratch. I wish I weren't. But I am.

"Alex, don't you think we *need* some candles in this house? After all, we're the fashion vanguard. Aren't we?" He looked stricken. The thought of being less than "cutting-edge" terrifies Scratch. At heart, he's a wimp. That doesn't change the power dynamics much.

"Please look at me, Alexandra. I'm tired of the back of your head. That's better, honey. If candles are in a mainstream glossy like *Vogue* . . . what does that say to you?"

"I dunno, sir. Not my area. I'm arts and letters. Remember, sir?" I tried to sneer at him, to show a grain of irreverence. I do that every now and then, as a mark of self-respect. Usually, I'm as subservient as possible. We all are. That's the job.

"Can't it only mean one thing, Alex? Aren't we a step *behind* the trend? Or, even . . . Oh, no! Have we *missed* the trend, my slavegirl? Are candles over, do you think?"

I bit my lip. If I said "Yes", he'd punish Gregory.

But if I said "No", he'd punish me.

I tried to hedge. "*Candles*", I said in a tone that I hoped was deeply contemplative, as if I were mulling over a Zen koan. "Candles."

That's the way we've all learned to talk to Scratch. We repeat whatever he says. He might walk into the studio and announce, "Platform shoes." And we'll all try to seem surprised and look at one another, frowning and nodding like we'd never heard of platform shoes before. Each of us will say "*Platforms*", with as much passion as we can muster. After a minute or so, you just hear this chorus of "Platforms, platforms." Or neck scarves, or slave bracelets, or tattoos, or whatever.

It works, sometimes.

Anyway, all he did this morning was to send Gregory out to Dolce and Gabbana's new housewares shop on Via della Spiga to buy four dozen scented candles. Gregory was delighted. Scratch hadn't let him out of the basement for a month. He's been down there since the Rust Incident.

The studio has a pungent odor at the moment, because Scratch recently bought a year's supply of herbal oils. The house is filled with black ironwork lanterns, floor pillows, pottery and tiles. Scratch redecorates the whole place twice a year.

This season, the key word is "Morocco".

If you're Scratch, Morocco means black ironwork lanterns, floor pillows, pottery, and – on the floors and walls – Moroccan tiles.

If you're Scratch, Morocco means blue, yellow and rust. That's the colour scheme. It's Morocco. Morocco's "in".

The glass inside the lanterns casts splotches of coloured light onto the tiled floors.

That light is blue, yellow and red.

Red glass. *Red*. Not rust.

If you're Scratch, that mistake is very bad.

If you're Gregory, it's a disaster.

"Rust," Scratch told us at breakfast one day last month. It was our first Moroccan morning – right after the Moroccan redecoration project had been completed. We were eating bread served on handmade Moroccan pottery. In a mood of celebration which turned out to be premature, we were sipping tea from handpainted Moroccan mugs.

Scratch turned to each of us and addressed us, mournfully, in turn. "*Rust*, Matthew," he said. "Katrina, slavegirl, *rust*. Rust, Tomas, my dear young slaveboy. Alex. Sweetslave. Rust?"

"Rust," I answered, in my most consoling tone.

"Rust, rust," we all began to murmur.

The only one who didn't say anything was Gregory. He sat there, biting his lips and getting pale.

Gregory has a degree in architecture. Interior decoration is his area.

We tried saying "rust" for a while, but our voices got softer and softer. It wasn't working, and we knew it.

Gregory got up from the table and went down into the basement. Scratch followed. The rest of us trembled and kept quiet.

Gregory screamed all morning long. I couldn't get a word written. There was no place to hide. He could be heard on every floor. By eleven o'clock, we were all in tears. Even the models and the hairdressers, who don't usually give a shit about anyone. We had to put on our headphones and turn the volume on our CD Walkmans up to ten.

At noon, the screaming stopped. Scratch came upstairs and strolled into the studio. His face was flushed. He threw himself down on the yellow leather couch and began to inspect his claws, which are painted blue. He put one in his mouth and chewed on it, sighing contentedly.

We took our CD Walkmans off and got to work.

Gregory cried for hours afterwards. We each took turns sneaking down the back stairs to see him. He had a black eye and his chest and back were covered with blood. A piece of his left nipple was missing. Scratch had torn out his nipple ring. Aside from that, he looked all right. It wasn't half as bad as the time Gregory stuck his nose into the fashion end of things and advised Scratch to shave off his goatee.

I untied Gregory's hands and tried to put some disinfectant on his tit, but he wouldn't let me.

"Don't worry," he reassured me, "I'll be okay."

I handed him a tissue and he blew his nose.

"I wish I hadn't let him down like that", he said. "His approval means a lot to me, Alex. I respect him."

I left him to himself, since I had half a chapter to finish before sunset – and I was still recovering from the night before, when I hadn't met my deadline. We all gave up on Gregory a long time ago. Getting punished can be confusing, but Gregory actually likes *Scratch*. That's what's so pathetic.

Then again, Gregory's under more pressure than some of us. Architecture and design are more important to Scratch than anything in print. I never get more than bruises and bloody welts. Tomas, the Brazilian painter who lives on the ground floor, gets whipped regularly, too. Katrina, the dancer from Vienna, claims she gets a sharpened stick up her ass, but we doubt the veracity of that. Even Scratch has limits.

Matthew, an American sculptor who lives on the top floor, in the penthouse, has had his arms and face cut up with razor blades half a dozen times. Apparently, he was letting people do that to him before he got here. Out of all of us, I'd say Matthew gets along best with Scratch. Not counting the fashion people, obviously. They don't live with us. They're only at the studio during the day, from ten to six.

No one knows what Scratch does to *them*. Whatever it is, it doesn't happen on the premises. The models and the make-up artists, the production assistants and the stylists have all got their own apartments. When it comes to fashion, Scratch makes housecalls.

I was an easy mark for Scratch. Since adolescence, I've had a weakness for melodrama and bad men: guys who everyone knows will be unfaithful, the ones who radiate danger, talk you into selling heroin, or ask you to sleep with their best friends so they can watch.

I got interested in Scratch's grainy old black-and-white photographs long before I ever knew him personally, around the time I moved to New York City from Pittsburgh after college. I loved the crooked camera angles. I loved the sweatstains and the smeared mascara. I loved the hint of perversion and decay. In the old days, Scratch wasn't selling anything. Aside from that, his work's unchanged. What he's best known for now are the magazine ads which, as he puts it, "push the buttons, just so far". Like the series he did for Ferragosto shoes, with the cop, the nun, and a pair of slingback sandals. He won an award for that one.

About Scratch himself, I'd only heard rumours. I'd been told that he was wanted by the FBI for pandering, and that he had Mafia connections. What intrigued me, though, were the reports that he gave money to the arts. Stories floated around about artists and writers who'd had chance encounters with Scratch. They'd described their projects to him. He'd given them money, based on the "concept", in advance.

I met Scratch in SoHo the night after my thirtieth birthday. I was in a crowded bar on Prince Street. I saw him from across the room and didn't recognize him. The newspapers keep running a retouched photo of him, so I didn't know exactly what he looked like. Even though he was wearing dark glasses, and he was wrinkled and balding, some part of me must have understood that it was him. An excited shiver ran through me when I looked in his direction. I walked across the room and stood a few paces away from him, at the bar. He was flanked by a tall, sun-tanned couple, dressed identically in velvet, They were too gorgeous to be considered human.

When I heard the gorgeous woman call the older guy "Scratch", I knew what I had to do. I was ready for it. I took three long strides – as slinkily as possible – in the direction of the Devil.

I undid a couple of my shirt buttons.

No results. He kept on talking to the Gorgeous Creatures. I propped one high-heeled boot on the rung of a bar stool. Still, nothing.

I hiked my skirt up and ran my hand along my thigh. Scratch glanced in my direction.

Suggestively, I ran the tip of my tongue across my upper lip.

Bingo.

A moment later, he moved to the empty bar stool right beside me, making that Darth Vader wheezing sound I'd read about. He huddled over his beer, hunching his shoulders with his head down, so that I couldn't see his face. He searched his pockets, took out a velvet ski cap, and put it on, pulling it down low over his forehead.

He was acting like he didn't want to be recognized. It's the same game Scratch always plays.

"Excuse me, sir," I said, coming up behind him. "May I ask you something?"

He pushed his sunglasses down on his nose.

"Yes, dear?" he said. "Ask."

I looked straight into those eyes, the long-lashed eyes that resemble a cow's – dark brown, without a pupil or an iris. I'd read descriptions of them in *People* magazine.

I leaned forward and whispered in his hairy pointed ear. "Are you Scratch, the fashion photographer?"

"Why do you ask that, darling?" he whispered back, so that I felt his breath on my neck. "If I were, what difference would it make?"

"Well, sir, you'd get a decent blow job out of it, for one thing."

He smiled, wanly. "In that case, my dear, old Scratch would be inclined to answer yes."

I grabbed him by the arm and led him to the men's room. A guy was pissing in there. He nodded "hi" at us. We nodded back while we walked into a stall. I sat down on the lid of the toilet. Scratch undid his pants and pulled out a flaccid dick. I licked its shaft twice, slowly.

Limp.

I gave his head a tongue kiss.

Nothing.

I slurped his whole worm down my throat.

Bingo. An erection.

I proceeded to treat Scratch to a lengthy session of deep-throating. I nearly gagged twice, but both times I kept it to myself, recovered quickly, and bounced right back in there. By the time Scratch started to whimper, tears were running down my face and my chin was full of drool. I slugged back a tablespoonful of cum.

For the record, Scratch's cock is a hammerhead, bulbous at the end, and I'd say about five inches when erect.

"Haven't I seen you on TV?" Scratch asked me, when I stood up. He was zipping up his fly. "You're an actress, aren't you?"

I rolled my eyes at this old line. Scratch didn't notice, luckily. "No, sir, I'm not an *actress*."

"What a shame. You could be one, you know. You belong among the world's young beauties."

What he meant was, he liked the way I sucked his cock.

"Thank you, sir. You're exaggerating."

"No, dear. Beauty has nothing to do with what you look like. It's all lighting and cosmetics."

"*Oh*." Full of flattery, Scratch is. What a guy.

"Are you a dancer, then? A video artist? Let me guess."

"I'm an emerging writer, sir."

"An unknown author," he sighed. "How pitiful. Most unfortunate. Not much money in that these days."

"You said it, sir", I agreed. I unlatched the stall door and walked over to the sink. Scratch stood beside me, while I washed my hands and face. At the urinals across the room, two guys pretended to ignore us.

"Unless, of course, you have a marketable concept." He held the door open for me. "Do you, child? What's your name?"

"Alexandra Bellamy. Call me Alex if you want, sir."

"Do you have a marketable concept, young Alex who sucks off strangers in the men's room?"

"You bet I have a concept. And, sir, I'm anxious to sell it."

"I thought you might be. Shall we go someplace quiet to discuss it?"

"Sure thing, sir. Thanks."

"It's my pleasure." Scratch came to a stop in the middle of the hallway and extended his hand, formally. I shook it, checking to see if his fingers were covered with fur, like I'd read, but he was wearing velvet gloves.

("Velvet! Sad news, young friends. It's history. I'm thinking nylon. Aren't you, my little sweetslaves?")

He looked down at his heavy silver wristwatch. "My club should be open for another hour or two. Shall we?"

We made our way past the tables. I felt totally at ease. It was as if I'd just jumped out of an airplane and discovered I could fly.

I wasn't scared of Scratch. Not yet.

As we approached the exit, I turned towards the bar and saw the tall couple in dark sunglasses watching us, a crestfallen expression on their perfect faces.

"Go to hell, Gorgeous Creatures," I thought. Scratch would rather fuck *me*.

"Hey, old dude. Are you who I think you are?" said a voice when we stepped outside into the crisp November air. Three guys in tattered overcoats were gathered together, looking hopeful.

Scratch narrowed his eyes. "That depends. Who do you think?"

One, who seemed to be their spokesperson, stepped forward. "You're the most innovative cultural force in the Western world," he said. He had bleached blonde hair which fell into his eyes. His face was partially hidden by black beard stubble.

Scratch took off his sunglasses. He gave the supplicant a thorough looking-over. It took him all of two seconds. Then he put his sunglasses back on.

"Dude, my name is Sand Dune", said the doomed young man, hurriedly. A stream of words poured forth as he pitched his concept to the Devil. "I'm a performance artist from LA and I've got a devoted cult following and now I'd like to compromise myself and whatever artistic values I have left. I don't want to shake the establishment up any more because I'm tired and I'm hungry and more importantly I want a car, so I'd rather be fistfucked and eat shit in exchange for money, Hey, dude? You listening? Lemme introduce my company to you. This hunky little dude to my right is Nathan Smoke of the Smoke Brothers acrobatic team. He's got a washboard stomach, see that? The fox on my left is Jimmy Bob, a transvestite clown from Louisiana. He never insults anyone, anymore. Guys n' gals both love him. You'll find the three of us can be very, very entertaining. We're cutting edge, but not offensive. We push the buttons just so far. You read me, old dude? Our act is up your alley. It's a circus act, featuring the simulated crucifixion of audience members. I thought it, uh, it might, um, you know . . ." Here, Sand Dune faltered. Scratch was ignoring him. He'd taken out a portable telephone from his briefcase, and was speaking into the receiver.

"158 Prince Street", he said into the phone.

"Dude, you interested?" finished Sand Dune, unhappily.

"Not today", he said dismissively, as if poor Sand Dune were a street vendor trying to sell him a plastic watch. Scratch put his hand on the small of my back, guiding me to the corner.

A limousine, painted violet and with its windows darkened, pulled up at the curb. An overweight, middle-aged man in violet jeans and a matching jacket got out of the driver's seat and opened the back door. Scratch ushered me in, and I slid gracefully onto violet seats, with a lot of legroom. A violet carpet lined the floor.

("Matthew, Katrina! Oh, Tomas, honey, do come up here, I implore you. Forget that ghastly painting, this is urgent. I need input. Violet? Finished. Yes or no? Answer me, someone! Today, please! Style marches on!")

As the driver closed the door to the limo, Sand Dune and

company rushed towards the car. Sand Dune managed to stuff a Xeroxed flyer in Scratch's gloved hands before the door slammed.

"Please step back from the curb", the driver ordered, gruffly.

Sand Dune had no chance. I didn't know how long I could keep him but, for the moment, Scratch was mine.

I was proud of myself. I'd been servile, and I'd seduced him. I thought I'd beaten out the competition.

I was so naïve in those days.

As if Scratch were *selective*, and didn't choose his slaves by chance.

The door to Scratch's private club, on Tenth Avenue, was unmarked. Inside, it was almost completely dark. A single spotlight was set into the shiny marble floor. Black candles shaped like lilies floated in oval pools of water, set into shiny marble tabletops. In the dim light, I felt invisible: loose, carefree, and ready to take chances.

A waiter in a white jacket led us to a corner table. He wheeled over a tray with an icebucket on it, uncorked a bottle of champagne and filled our long-stemmed glasses.

"So tell me, pet," Scratch said, "what's your proposal?"

"Well, sir. I'd like to write a book that would sell. Non-fiction. A biography. Yours."

As I was talking, it occurred to me that maybe I should have made my proposal first, and offered him a blowjob afterwards. I had never prostituted myself before. I wasn't sure how it worked.

Scratch seemed to sense my insecurity. He covered my hand with his, and patted it reassuringly. He had removed his gloves. Coarse fur, like the hair on a horse's mane, scraped my skin. He began to scratch my forearm, lightly, with one of his thick, hooked claws. He lifted my hand to his mouth, and kissed it. Suddenly, he bit my knuckles, hard.

I winced.

He gripped my hand with both his hairy paws and bore down with his sharp front teeth.

Groaning in protest, I tried to pull my hand away. I stood up, knocking over my champagne glass. It shattered on the floor. Alerted by the sound, a waiter turned towards us. When he saw who it was, he looked away.

"Let go!" I said.

He relaxed his grip.

I pulled my hand back and rubbed it. It was numb and bumpy, covered with his teethmarks.

"Pain", said Scratch. "Alexandra, pain."

"Pain", I repeated.

I understood immediately.

I'm smart about some things. I sat back down.

Scratch studied me a moment. "It's a job requirement. The artists whom I sponsor all know pain. Don't you, Alex?"

I didn't answer.

"And if not, dear," he said tenderly, "would you like to? Alex who shows off her slender thighs in bar rooms? Alex who eats rice and beans? Alex whose telephone has been shut off? Pretty Alex, who is a disappointment to her parents? Talented Alex, who pulls out her grey hairs? Lovely Alex, who – much to her surprise – is over thirty? Cocksucking Alex, who is so charming and such a failure? In some sense, haven't you been seeking pain and degradation all your life?"

I couldn't answer. He knew things about me which I'd never told anyone. It was as if he'd held up a mirror and shown me a reflection of myself. Had he set some kind of trap, devised specially for me? For the first time, I was frightened

"Shit", I said weakly. "Sir. You hit a nerve."

"Does that surprise you?" Scratch turned a cigarette slowly between his shaggy thumb and index finger.

"Well, sir. Yes."

"Scare you?"

"I admit it does, sir."

"You feel manipulated? Humiliated? Exposed?"

"Uh, yeah. I do."

Scratch rubbed his hands together, gleefully. "How nice

for you, darling. And darling, how nice for me! I'm touching nerves and pushing buttons! That's my area, you see."

"But do you know *me*, somehow, sir? Me? Alexandra Bellamy?"

Scratch chuckled. "What a question! Cocksucking Alexandra! I'm ashamed!"

"*Have* we met before? What . . . what's going on? Please tell me, Scratch."

"Have we *met*? Do I know *you*? As if you were different, or original or important! Is there some scrap of dignity left to protect inside the young whore's body, after all?"

"I'm . . . I'm confused."

"I can see that", murmured Scratch. "I find your innocence most arousing." He leaned back in his chair.

"I want to hurt you, Alexandra Bellamy. Think it over."

I sat, smoking, and watching a metal clock above our table as its violet hands moved, in quivering spasms, counting seconds.

At around four o'clock that morning, I had my skirt pulled up and the Devil's well-greased dick inside my ass. He kept pulling it all the way out and shoving it all the way back in me. I'd had a virgin asshole until that morning and, frankly, the first time wasn't fun. I'd spent an abortive twenty minutes screaming "Stop, please stop!" until I got the hang of it.

Ah, pain.

One pleasant aspect about having my anus split in two was that I barely noticed that I was being beaten. Scratch hit me, repeatedly, with a patent leather belt from Donna Karan's spring menswear collection. I didn't give a shit about that, or anything else. All I could think of was my asshole.

That's the trick to pain, really. It helps you break things down into essentials.

"Well?" said Scratch, stretching out on the rumpled velvet quilt in his hotel room and switching the channel to MTV.

I took a deep breath.

"Hello, Alex! Are you with me?" He snapped his fingers.

"Um, sir," I said. I couldn't speak. I couldn't move. I would have liked to call a doctor.

"Are you *with* me? Yes or no? You've had your trial run, whore. Now I need a final answer."

I looked up at the violet ceiling and closed my eyes. "Sir," I said, "I'm in. Do whatever the fuck to me you want."

"That's nice, Alex. I'm so glad you feel that way. That's what I like to hear."

I dragged myself into the bathroom and shut the door. I didn't want Scratch to hear me crying. I wasn't happy. My initiation had been traumatic. I climbed inside the bathtub and, tearfully, examined my rear end.

I turned the tap on.

Water hurt.

I wondered what my ex-girlfriend, Becca, would have thought if she could have seen me that way, with my back covered with red marks, cleaning out my shitsmeared butt-hole. She would have kissed my forehead and made me some herbal tea. Perhaps we would have discussed our three favourite old topics: commitment, intimacy, and communication.

Those were the things which Becca had wanted our relationship to be based on.

What was the basis of my relationship to Scratch?

Submission, sex and money.

Three real words in exchange for three small loads of crap.

The second floor of Scratch's house in Milan serves as his photo studio. With its bright overhead lights and sense of emptiness, it reminds me of a high school gym. It's minimally furnished, with metal desks, a leather couch, a table, and a row of cabinets to hold our "toys" and magazines. Outside the darkroom, rolls of film hang from a clothesline, drying. There are five floor-to-ceiling windows, with thirty square panels of glass inside each one. I tend to count the panels of glass, from one to 150, over and over again while I'm being punished.

Tonight is like every other night. It's six o'clock. The models, the hairdressers, the stylists, the production assistants and the lighting technicians have gone home. We're all alone with Scratch inside his building – it's just me and the four artists. Every night he comes to us, looks over what we did, and gives us his review.

Right now, he's reading the chapter I wrote for him today. He's lying on the yellow couch. He looks morose. I can already tell he doesn't like it. Why should he? It's such bullshit. The book's supposed to be about *him*, but I don't know what I'm talking about. I have no facts, not even basic information like where Scratch was born, or where he went to school, or when he began to use a camera. Aside from "candles", and "platforms", I have nothing.

"Oh, Alex", says Scratch, sadly. He puts down the sheaf of paper on the Moroccan tile floor. His hand dangles languidly off the couch. "Who or what is this about? You've come up with a crude caricature of me. Surely, you don't *see* me like this, do you, pet? As a silly, self-involved, egotistic fashion person? Surely, darling, you've failed to convey the nature of my . . . power." He strokes the pages with his furry fingertips, tracing circles with his blue claws.

"Maybe so, sir", I concede. In fact, my take on Scratch gets more and more vague as time goes on. My opinions, my beliefs – everything is getting weaker. Living with Scratch, I'm disconnected from the outside world. He pays our rent and provides our meals. Usually, they consist of bread and water, but, if you're being rewarded, the spread can be lavish. Four times a year – winter, fall, spring and summer – he gives us each a stack of mail order catalogues. We check off the books and magazines we want to read, the CDs we want to hear, the clothing we want to wear. Deliveries arrive from the United States, six weeks later, in shapeless brown packages which we tear open eagerly, like presents on Christmas morning.

Scratch pushes up the sleeve of his blue and rust striped T-shirt and runs his thumb across his dragon tattoo (a leftover from last spring, when "dragon" was the word). For a moment he's absorbed in thought.

"Honesty!" Scratch pronounces, suddenly. He hands me back the sheaf of pages.

"Sir?"

"Alexandra, honesty."

"Yes, sir. Honesty."

"This wasn't *honest*, Alex. Was it?"

"No, sir. It was not."

"Wicked slavegirl. You're a liar."

Annoyed, I forget myself – and lose my fear. "Fuck it, Scratch," I blurt out, recklessly. "I'm just doing what you told me to. You *said* to make it up! I asked for facts and information and you . . ."

A terrible, angry smile appears on Scratch's time-worn face. My moment of rebellion vanishes.

"Sorry, sir. Forgive me. Can I take that back, sir, please?"

"Impudent, dishonest Alex," he hisses. "You shall regret those words! Undress."

I unzip my shirtjacket. (Shirtjacket, yes? Yes!) and shrug it off. I unsnap my rust bra. I slip out of my yellow panties and my yellow maxiskirt. (Maxiskirt? Indeed!) I pull off my boots of soft, blue suede. (Suede! The Eternal Return!)

Naked, I walk through the empty room. As I pass the window, a group of male models from the agency across the street glances up at me with passing curiosity. They've seen the routine at Scratch's studio, many times.

When I reach the round wooden conference table in the centre of the room, I clamber onto it, using a chair as a footstep, and lie down. I rest my forehead against the smooth surface of polished wood.

"Head up!" Scratch wheezes.

Lifting my chin, I begin to count the 150 glass panels in the windows. One, two, three, four . . . I hear Scratch's motorcycle boots click against the tile floor. He walks to the file cabinet and opens the drawer where we keep our five tubes of lubricant, and our shared instruments of torture.

I hear him riffle through the contents of the drawer. I count faster. Twelve, thirteen, fourteen . . .

He shuts the drawer, crosses the room, and stops behind me. Fifteen, sixteen . . .

"Hands behind back, slave. Must I remind you every time?"

I start to shiver.

"Slavegirl," says Scratch, "have you been dishonest?"

"Yes, sir. Right, sir. Oh, yes, sir. Yes, I have."

"Dishonest Alex! Repeat after me. I, Alexandra Bellamy, am a lazy parasite who contributes nothing to society."

"I, Alexandra Bellamy, am a lazy parasite", I repeat.

Seventeen, eighteen, nineteen . . .

Before he hurts me, Scratch keeps me waiting. I don't know what's going on behind my back. I don't know what he's holding in his hands.

Twenty, twenty-one, twenty-two . . .

I count, to help the time pass more quickly while I'm waiting for my pain.

I need it, now.

We all do.

Our nerves and buttons work the same.

THE EMPEROR OF NIGHT

Marilyn Jaye-Lewis

It happened that in olden times, in a land far, far away, an ancient people looked up lazily toward the approaching evening.

These were such ancient times that the stars were not yet born and the full-bellied moon was the sole celestial body in the nighttime sky. But on this evening, as twilight crept slowly toward the west, the startled people watched in awe as the sun began to rise again. Along the far horizon of the sea, it sprang up boldly and hid behind the full-bellied moon and all the land fell into sudden night.

The Earth was remarkably still, then, for this was a sacred darkness.

On the far side of the moon, under cover of night, the mighty sun caressed the moon's fat belly with his eager fire, emptying his rays into her hidden crevices and filling her with his power until, it is said, she began to glow.

The glowing moon, unable to withstand her fullness, surrendered to the penetrating flames of the mighty sun so completely that his flames burst through her swollen craters, and together, as the frightened people fled in all directions, the sun and moon exploded in a multitude of stars across the vast, unending sky.

The force of this explosion caused the land to shake and rock; it tugged at the swirling waves of the ocean waters, sending them leaping and curling upward, eddying in great swells until, from the depths of the far-off South China Sea, there emerged from the water a land of splendour, covered in a cloud of sea mist, whose centre burned so gloriously that its proud inhabitants took no notice of the sunless sky. They knew that the sun now walked among them as a sacred man of fire.

This man of walking fire, this falling sun from heaven, came to be called affectionately, the Emperor of Night.

The great emperor was loved by all his people. They basked in his bright fire and were nurtured by his light. Though the emperor taught his people the secret of making fire, none among the mere mortal subjects could ever build a fire whose flames outshone the great falling sun from heaven. For in the emperor's heart there burned an eternal flame; a flame of longing; the seed of heaven itself.

In an effort to ease the daily burdens of his people, to give them a time of rest, when the sands ran through the hourglass twelve times, the emperor draped his regal body in a robe of black silk, Covering the essence of heaven, he shielded his land from the eternal burning flame of his heart while his people gently slept. And it was in this way that the emperor created night.

The emperor's grand palace was hidden on three sides by a shimmering, impenetrable cinnamon forest. Its courtyards were still more hidden behind the shade of mountain plum and wild pear trees, whose clustering blossoms the ladies of the palace had adorned with tiny silver chimes that tinkled in the delicate evening breezes and filled the nights with sounds of trembling music.

The palace itself had been intricately carved from mighty teaks and cedars. The sacred room where the emperor slept extended along the length of the grand palace's fourth side, where it was buttressed against the power of the tossing sea by a huge wall of carved granite. A granite so smooth it glistened, it formed a majestic lagoon of fresh seawater for the emperor alone. Here the cranes and herons, the crested kingfishers and loons, nested in the protruding rocks amid the rarest night-blooming orchids and magnolia blossoms.

When the emperor adorned himself in his black silk robe and thus brought on the night, he retreated in a sacred solitude, surrounded by the graceful calm of the nesting birds, visited only occasionally by the harmless sea creatures who might swim under the great stone wall where the lagoon emptied into the waterway of the South China Sea.

The ladies of the palace were numerous and each was as fair and sturdy as the emperor himself. Like him, their supple forms were lean, their delicate faces appointed with fine high cheekbones and dark almond-shaped eyes. In the daylight, they wore their straight black hair in elaborate braids – sometimes adorned with tender peach blossoms, or lilies-of-the-valley. At night, they let their hair hang free, and exchanged their bright red robes for robes of black silk, so that each palace lady resembled the emperor in every respect save for what remained hidden beneath the folds of the austere black robes.

It was his custom that the emperor rarely slept, even though he'd created night, for great was the longing inside the eternal burning of his royal heart. He seldom passed the unending hours alone, though, sending for the various ladies of the palace for companionship in the darkness.

None was to enter the emperor's sacred room, however. Each lady met him instead on the teakwood verandah, opening onto the majestic lagoon. The verandah was gently illuminated by the tiny flickering flames of a hundred burning candles, each candle ensconced in an elaborately carved shade of ivory. The flickering flames produced tiny dancing shadows all along the granite wall: shadows in the shapes of flying dragons, miniature salamanders, or scattering wild geese. It was on this peaceful verandah, opening onto the majestic lagoon, that the emperor shared his pillow and mat with whichever lady he fancied, being mindful, as he lifted her robe and led her through the many royal positions of tenderness and sharing, not to be wanton about the condition of his own robe, lest it loosen to reveal his heart and cause morning to arrive too quickly.

It is said that the emperor's eternal flame could be depleted only through the expulsion of his seed into a woman who was not his bride, and though the burden of his eternally burning heart was great, the emperor was careful to preserve the power of his fire. The ladies of the palace were entrusted with a temper of restraint when arousing the emperor's pleasure. They were well schooled in the art of pleasing him without bringing his royal seed to the point of expulsion.

The rare few among the palace ladies who took him past the brink of danger, who, knowing they could never be the emperor's bride, for the emperor's bride would not be mortal and would come in the form of a treasure offered up from the depths of the sea, who still longed greedily to fill their barren wombs with the emperor's eternal fire; these few were punished swiftly and with severity. Taken by the palace guards to the hillside in the early morning, the offender was stripped bare of her protective robe and staked openly to an elevated cedar plank, her trembling legs forcibly raised and spread.

While the rest of the palace ladies were commanded to bear witness without lowering their eyes, the rare offender was subjected to the terrible Sixth Punishment, the punishment by horse cock, her wrenching screams ignored until the mounting stallion's bulging shaft had rended the offender's canal completely, making her no longer suitable for pleasuring the emperor.

Only then was the offender released and cast out from the palace walls. Only then were the palace ladies permitted to hide their faces in their sleeves.

It is said that on these bitter days, the emperor fasted

alone and did penance in the royal chamber of his inner sanctum.

A great thing happened every twenty-eight nights.

The emperor was permitted to expel his longing in the manner of an ancient ceremonial sacrifice.

Two ladies of the palace would be summoned to the teakwood verandah, where they assumed the Royal Position of the Gobbling Fishes, one lying atop the other in the posture of intercourse, their robes raised for the eyes of the emperor, their naked genitals rubbing together until their aroused labia swelled to resemble the mouths of gobbling fishes.

When they were close to orgasm, the emperor parted his robe and, kneeling between the spread thighs of the palace ladies, separated their swollen vulvas by easing his stiffening member between the engorged netherlips. The head of his royal shaft would pleasure their erect clitorises as it slipped in and out, until he himself was ready to discharge a burst of his eternal fire.

Then the emperor withdrew his member carefully, and discharged himself into a golden chalice, held ready by a third lady of the palace.

This third lady was the most revered. Adorned in a ceremonial robe of luminescent silver, she and the emperor carried the golden chalice into the calm lagoon together, to the spot where the oysters gathered. Here, the emperor would select the most shimmering oysters. He would lovingly stroke his finger along the seam of their glistening shells and, with the tenderest of words, the emperor coaxed the oysters to reveal to him their secret pearls.

One by one, the emperor would pluck the delicate pearls and drop them into the golden chalice that held his royal sperm.

After the pearls were selected and plucked and a ceremonial prayer recited, the golden chalice was emptied faithfully onto a sacred spot of jagged rock protruding from the waters

of the quiet lagoon. For it was believed that in this way, the
sea would be appeased and offer up to the emperor his long-
awaited bride.

And here, at the sacred rock every twenty-eight nights, the
emperor performed the supreme sacrifice: he removed the
robe of luminescent silver from the lady of the palace, and
while the two remaining ladies lay prone on the verandah and
hid their faces obediently in their sleeves, the emperor
prepared to teach his chosen lady the most secret of the
royal positions.

"Soon you will learn the Position of Stealing Fire", the
emperor announced tenderly. "In return, in gratitude for
joining me in this supreme sacrifice, the emperor wishes to
pleasure you."

The palace lady, now naked, her back steadied against the
sacred rock, would assume the favoured Royal Position of the
Standing Heron, expecting to be pleasured by the emperor's
stiff member, but on this ceremonial occasion, the emperor
would kneel in the salty seawater and place his mouth to the
lady's tender netherlips.

A whimper of confusion and bliss would issue from the
lady, as the sight of her emperor kneeling before her in the
water, his royal mouth pleasuring her in an unexpected
manner, was usually very troubling to a delicate lady of
the palace. But the arousing pressure of the emperor's mouth
exploring her tender secrets would cause the lady to surrender, until, within the tiny stiffening hood at the very tip of
her mound, her pleasure peaked and she could endure no
more of the sweetness. Her modesty then returned.

"Now I will teach you the Position of Stealing Fire", the
emperor would instruct her solemnly as he rose from the
water and parted the folds of his robe. "Come, kneel before
me."

The naked lady trembled before her emperor and knelt in
the water, respectfully lowering her eyes as he revealed
himself. Taking her chin in his hand, he pressed his stiff
member to the lady's quivering lips and commanded her
quietly to open her mouth. So strange was the manner in

which the emperor chose to pleasure himself that it was not uncommon for the chosen lady to lose her repose.

"Open your mouth", he would command her again, all the while keeping a mindful eye on the ladies lying prone on the verandah, lest they become too curious and lift their faces from their sleeves.

"You love your emperor, don't you?" he would entreat her. "You don't wish to see me lonely all my days?"

"No, my liege", came her heartfelt answer.

"Then you must help me to appease the sea, or it will never offer up my bride."

Confused but ever faithful, the lady would be persuaded to part her reluctant lips and take the length of her emperor's thick shaft fully into her mouth. Then, as in the act of intercourse, he pleasured himself in her.

It was in this manner that the emperor discharged a second time, willingly sacrificing some of his fire, emptying it deep into the mouth of the chosen lady, a lady who was not his bride. The eagerness with which the emperor surrendered his fire, and the helpless state to which he sank as it issued from his loins, was why this royal position was regarded as the most secret position of all.

It was because this secret was so treasured by the palace, lest it be known among the ladies who would seek to drain the emperor of his power, that the emperor, having sacrificed himself in her, regretfully closed his hands around the chosen lady's throat. As a sacrificial appeasement to the mighty sea, he held her pretty face beneath the salty water until she was thoroughly drowned.

The two remaining palace ladies were permitted then to lift their faces from their sleeves, and they assisted in silent ignorance as the emperor sent the lifeless body of the sacrificed third under the carved granite wall to be carried out to sea.

It was on those nights that the emperor slept and the following morning would dawn late on the land, as was the customary fashion.

★   ★   ★

After nearly twelve thousand days of longing, in the great emperor's thirty-second year, when he ached beyond reason to ease the burden of his burning heart, he donned his black robe and made it night. It was a sacred twenty-eighth night, and he prepared to send for three ladies of the palace who would assume the Position of the Gobbling Fishes and hold the golden chalice ready to receive the royal seed, when suddenly the emperor noticed an eerie glow coming from the sacred spot on the jagged rock protruding from the majestic lagoon.

"At last," the emperor cried, but not too loudly, for he feared that the sound of his own voice might break some precarious spell.

Anxiously, he waded into the lagoon, being careless with the condition of his black silk robe.

"For many years I have been faithful," he exclaimed aloud. "I have spilled my royal seed every twenty-eighth night. I have offered the precious pearls, and selected a palace lady for the supreme sacrifice. I have prayed that the eternal burning in my heart will come to peace. And now I see that the hour for rejoicing has indeed arrived."

The great emperor beheld that the eerie glow on the sacred rock issued from a membranous sac that contained a gestating female form. It was only a question of hours before the salty seawater would yield her, fully formed.

The emperor was so elated, so exalted in his joy that at long last the sea was responding to his tireless yearning and offering him up his bride, that he was tempted to hurry her progress by summoning more semen from within himself; tempted to shower her with pearls; even tempted to loosen his black robe and let the power of his fiery heart shine into her developing face and bring her more rapidly into being. But she was in a fragile stage and patience was of the utmost importance.

The palace ladies, having not received the customary summons, had gathered curiously on the teakwood verandah, watching their emperor in awed silence as he stood waist-deep in the salty lagoon, his black robe soaking and his beautiful black hair blowing free in the gentle breeze.

More and more the sacred spot glowed before their very eyes, slowly transforming the membranous sac into a discernible female form.

"She's come!" he announced at last, turning to address the palace ladies and weeping openly as the quickening wind showered his beautiful hair with falling petals, the clustered blossoms trembling on the trees and filling the air with the delicate music of the tiny silver chimes. "She has eyes!" he continued at last, gaining control of himself. "I've seen them glowing. She's opened her eyes!"

The ladies of the palace gasped and made haste in sending for the court magician to cut the delicate woman from the membranous sac and release her supple form to the Earth's atmosphere.

"It's happening very quickly now!" the emperor shouted, returning his attention to his creature. "She's moving rapidly along. We must begin. Where is my magician?"

The magician came at once in a cloud of jasmine smoke and a burst of iridescent light. Reciting a secret incantation that has long been forgotten by the palace ladies who witnessed the event, the magician set to work on the treasure from the sea. With his terrifyingly long, sharp fingernails, cultivated for just this occasion, he carefully tore the membranous sac free from the female creature.

With a sharp yelp, she cried as she encountered the open air, then slid from the sac into the warm seawater.

It is said that when the emperor, to prevent her from slipping away from him and drifting out to sea, grabbed her in the water by one of her tender ankles and pulled her to him, she glowed all the more. At first, it seemed that his robe had perhaps loosened, but this was not the case. The female creature contained a fire of her own.

The emperor lifted her carefully out of the water and into his arms. She was round-eyed and golden-haired, although covered in a viscous fluid. She was round-bellied, too, and round-bottomed. She was so round and golden that the

ladies of the palace were said to be reminded of the fabled
fat-bellied moon that had existed long ago, the moon that
had waxed full as the mighty sun filled her to bursting,
scattering them forever in a multitude of stars across the
unending sky.

"You there!" the emperor pointed, as he set his treasured
creature on the crowded verandah, "and you: take her to the
sacred chamber and ready her to be my bride. And you," he
added, pointing to a third palace lady, "fetch my high priest
from the inner sanctum and tell him of my great good
fortune."

The ladies who had not been chosen bowed their heads in
disappointment, stealing glances at the strange round-bottomed creature as she was escorted, on unsteady legs, to the
sacred chamber.

"Disperse!" the emperor commanded.

In a flurry of black robes and flying hair, the ladies of the
palace disappeared.

The emperor, masking his sudden royal terror with a
dignified calm, beseeched his court magician, "What becomes of me now?"

"What becomes of you?" the magician roared with
delight as he disappeared in a cloud of jasmine smoke.
"What becomes of you? You administer the royal touch,
you coax her lips to part. If she releases a pearl, she is
indeed your bride. Then she will steal your fire and you
will die."

"Steal it?!" he emperor cried out to the vanishing smoke.
"But I thought we were destined to share my fire, throughout eternity!"

"You will," a voice thundered on the scattering wind, "but
the nature of everlasting love is first to surrender!"

When the high priest was summoned from the inner sanctum
and told of the great good fortune, he cautioned the palace
ladies sternly, announcing that he would not be hurried.

"Preparing the emperor's bride – if she is, indeed, his
bride – is a task that requires diligence and patience."

He entered the sacred room with a ceremonial demeanour. Like the emperor, the high priest was regal. He, too, wore a flowing robe of fine, black silk. His face was appointed with the same high cheekbones, set off by piercing black, almond-shaped eyes.

If he felt at all aroused by the sight of the treasured creature, if his heartbeat quickened, he showed no signs of it. He approached the trembling female, whose watery round eyes blinked painfully in the candle-lit chamber, and said quietly to her: "So you are the long-awaited treasure of semen and pearls, nourished on seawater and fire."

The female creature could not yet respond, though it seemed to those present that she understood his meaning.

"Tonight, my dear," he continued, "you will feel a burning sensation. This is natural, as you're adjusting to the surface of your own skin. Later, if the emperor can coax your lips to open and you release a pearl, then you are indeed his bride and will be forever. If you fail to produce a pearl, then it's simply not your time. You will dissolve once again into the sea and we will resume our vigil. Come," he entreated her. "We will make you ready. We will start with the ceremonial ablution."

As the ladies readied the shallow basin, the high priest from the inner sanctum explained: "We don't want to shock the surface of her skin. We must proceed with precision and care. She has been nurtured on salty seawater until now. She will fight us if we don't introduce her to the purified water in increments."

The creature was helped to stand in the enamelled basin and was held firmly by either arm by the palace ladies.

"I'll begin with your enchanting face," the high priest announced quietly. As he pressed the soaked sea sponge to the creature's delicate cheek, she resisted only slightly, for his touch was light. As he carefully washed the traces of the membranous sac from her unusual face, the high priest studied her thoughtfully. Though he'd never actually seen a round-eyed creature, he'd heard about them in fabled myths and legends, as he'd prepared his whole life for just this moment of readying the emperor's bride.

"That wasn't so bad", he encouraged her as he completed the cleansing of the creature's face and began on her pale shoulders. Her skin was still so new, so delicate, it was verily translucent, like gleaming pearls.

The priest dipped the sea sponge once again into the purified water and rinsed it lightly over the creature's arms. "You see," he directed the attention of the palace ladies, "how her skin is blanketed in golden hairs which weren't perceptible at first? She seems to be undergoing the final completion process right before our eyes."

The palace ladies marvelled at the female with respectful awe.

"You see how the quality of her skin is changing?" he continued excitedly, bathing the beauty's arms. "How it is covered with downy hair? This is a very good sign."

When it seemed the female was steady enough on her feet, one of the palace ladies attended to the creature's hair. It was long and tangled and still slippery with the viscous fluid from the sac. The palace lady lathered the long golden strands with a mild soap normally reserved for bathing infants. Carelessly, however, the palace lady ascended a small stool and poured purified water over the top of the creature's head to rinse away the suds.

"No, no, no!" the high priest cried.

But it was too late. A terrible whimpering ensued that was of such a high pitch it pierced all their hearts and chilled their spines. The creature attempted to flee the basin but the high priest grabbed her and steadied her back in the bowl.

"We'll try to be a little more careful", he assured her, glancing sternly at the palace ladies.

The creature blinked at him, seemingly terrified.

"That was probably the worst of it," he encouraged her again.

The lady culprit, in turn, stepped timidly from her stool and retreated quietly to a chair in the corner.

The high priest continued his steady, meticulous cleansing

of the creature, washing her round breasts and her full, round belly. When he came to that delicate spot between the creature's legs, he carefully washed the membranous residue from her tightly curled golden hairs.

And then, to the surprise of all those present, the creature released her water, sending a stream of it in a great splash down into the basin. It was so sudden, even the dignified high priest couldn't hide his surprise.

The two palace ladies glanced gleefully at each other, while the creature rapidly blinked her round eyes and smiled.

"You're pleased with yourself, is that it?" the high priest sighed.

The creature's eyes shone all the more.

"Well, as reluctant as I am to admit it, that was an extremely good sign. Come," he said, turning to the palace ladies, "we can't let her just stand in it. One of you empty this basin and we'll attend to her feet."

At last the creature was washed and dried, her hair hanging in fluffy golden curls. The ladies helped her into an embroidered robe of crimson and, following the high priest, led her through an intricately carved passageway, deep into the sacred chamber where the great emperor anxiously waited.

No one but the high priest had ever entered this level of the emperor's sacred chamber.

It was ablaze with flickering candles, and the palace ladies gazed in wonder at the splendid secret room, at the vibrant murals that lined its walls, depicting the distant mountains as they shimmered in an endless vista, rising beyond the mystical clouds.

The room itself was alive with flowers and smelled faintly of heaven, as an aroma of dizzying fragrance scented the air.

Along one wall a towering waterfall trickled and splashed lightly over jagged layers of flat stones, adorned on either side by velvety moss and wild ferns. The water, which seemed to the palace ladies to originate somehow from the majestic lagoon, splashed endlessly into a deep but contained pool, where fat goldfish with billowy fins darted among the sunken rocks and underwater greenery.

The emperor himself was seated rather tentatively on a huge carved throne of teakwood in the centre of the chamber, set grandly on a raised platform of graduated marble, each platform carved by hand to form ornate and opulent steps.

Beyond the throne, and mostly hidden from view by carved ivory screens depicting the fable of the sun and moon in their coital embrace in heaven before they burst into the multitude of stars, stood the royal bed. All the ladies could discern from where they stood was that a beautiful lace netting, suspended from a delicate fixture in the ceiling, draped over the royal resting place like a heavenly veil. The palace ladies recognized this exquisite lace as the type made by the ancient ladies of the distant palisades; the cliff-dwelling ancients who lived so high in the peaks that even in the scorching days of mid-summer, they could not be reached without first traversing for many days deep gorges of ice and snow.

When the great emperor realized the palace ladies were too curious for his comfort, he dispersed them. His high priest, though, remained behind.

"Tell me," the emperor beseeched him, "how do I live through this night? If she won't produce a pearl, she will dissolve into salty water and I will die from the pain of losing her. If she does produce a pearl, I am told she will steal my fire. Either way, I will die."

The high priest chose his words carefully. "There is much I do not know. I only know we have prepared for this throughout our entire existences. If the time has not yet come for her to be your bride – and let me add that the signs do not seem to point to this outcome – rest assured she will come again, at a more propitious time, for that is the nature of all that exists; that is the ebb and flow of life, and that is the law of the sea. If, however, her time has come and she is ready to accept your fire, look on it as a release. You will not die, not in the mortal sense; you will transmogrify into something grander, for you are an energy that never ends."

The emperor tried to take comfort in the high priest's words, but he could not overlook the hint of sorrow creeping into the high priest's face.

"I've been lonely far too long", the emperor began. But then he saw that mere words were useless in the face of destiny and so he bid his high priest to take leave of the sacred chamber.

The emperor parted the lace netting and helped his bride onto the conjugal bed. It was a fine, large bed of carved cedar, padded with a thick mat of embroidered silk over a layer of down.

The emperor could not help but marvel at his creature. Her fine limbs and well-appointed face made her seem quite human, but her curling tresses and translucent skin were much softer than anything he'd known.

He propped her tender back against a pile of soft pillows and then climbed onto the bed himself. He knelt next to her and studied the perfect roundness of her form.

Her eyes, in particular, intrigued him and seemed brimming with understanding. She regarded him with a curious, penetrating gaze.

He loosened her crimson robe and examined her more closely. Such full breasts and the roundest belly – like he had never seen. She seemed an odd mixture of virginity and fecundity.

"You look like you're going to have a child", he whispered to her playfully.

Of course she said nothing in reply, as she had not yet learned to speak.

"You look soft enough to sleep on", he continued, then reached out to stroke her belly. He thought increasingly of lying on top of her, of removing his robe completely, to feel, for the first time in his life, what it might be like to couple completely with a naked female form.

The more he imagined himself coupling with her, the more he stroked her fat belly, until he realized she was entranced by his touch and beginning to respond.

Her legs parted to reveal her netherlips, covered in tiny

golden curls. These were the lips that would part completely, and produce the treasured pearl if she was in her season.

The emperor, intrigued but no less afraid, pushed aside her robe completely. Braving what he did not know, he resolved to examine her tender secrets.

"Very human-like", he thought at first. He caressed the tip of her mound to see if she would respond.

Respond, she did. As the emperor had never witnessed.

She moaned sweetly and offered her secret parts to him completely. She knew no modesty. The more he stroked her there, the more aroused she got. Her netherlips became engorged, separating more like the petals of orchids than like any human female sex. And the tip of her mound seemed to please her so thoroughly that the emperor lost himself in caressing her there.

She undulated and moaned so, and her lips grew so enticingly ripe, that he couldn't help but want to pleasure her there completely. He pressed his mouth to her tender flesh and was overwhelmed by his own excitement. Caught up in her cries and whimpers, and the strange rhythms that flowed from her, the emperor was no longer aware of the time, of whether he should make it day or night. Paying no mind to the condition of his robe, he set aside the cares of his people. So entranced was he by her delight, that all his senses focused on pleasuring his creature.

The more fervently his mouth explored her, the more eager were her cries.

The more her cries entranced him, the more fervently he desired to please her, unaware that the strange rhythms swelling in her were setting his destiny in motion.

In ignorance, he licked and sucked at her delicate petals, his tongue caressing every tender fold, until the urges of his pounding manhood overtook him. He knew his moment had arrived; he would lay on top of her, with no fear of dying, and receive the blessings of heaven.

The emperor tossed aside his robe. His creature glowed all the more profoundly in the presence of his fiery heart.

He raised her legs to mount her, to guide his stiff member

into the folds of her tender flower, when he observed, with shock and awe, a tiny perfect pearl push through her sacred opening!

The emperor's consternation was great. "No", he cried, at the same time feeling elated that she was, indeed, his bride – his for eternity – that she would not dissolve into sea water.

Still the sight of the pearl chilled him. "How will you steal my fire?" he demanded. "How is it that I will die?"

But the creature only stared at him, round-eyed, and smiled; pleased with her pearl, delighted with what her aroused body had created for him.

The emperor picked up the pearl and examined it closely. He knew what was expected of him. He was to send for his high priest and offer the pearl to the mighty sea with a prayer of gratitude and thanksgiving.

"And then what?" he said quietly, searching the face of his bride.

The shaken emperor clutched the tiny pearl tightly in his fist, knowing that somehow it was his doom. "If only it could have remained inside!"

He gathered his robe around him and prepared to send for his high priest. "If only it could have remained inside", he repeated morosely.

And it was at this moment, it is said, that the great Emperor of Night resolved to betray the will of heaven.

"Drink this", the emperor urged his bride.

He held the wine chalice to her lips, having placed the sacred pearl on her trusting tongue.

"It's wine from the Azure Mountain. It will help the pearl slide down."

The emperor's bride drank the wine and found it quite pleasing, holding out her empty goblet for more.

"No", the emperor replied. "Now is the time for tenderness and sharing."

Outside the palace walls, the emperor's weary subjects rose, groggy and overly tired, surprised to discover daylight had arrived so quickly. They dragged their heavy ploughs through the fields, milked their startled cows, and poked at the sleeping sheep to herd them out to the meadows. It wasn't long, though, before news of the arrival of the emperor's bride reached even the farthest hamlets. With knowing sighs, the weary people retreated back to their bedchambers for it was, in fact, the middle of the night.

The robe of crimson lay in a gentle heap atop the robe of black silk on the floor of the emperor's sacred chamber.

The fine lace netting draped over the conjugal bed as if it were indeed a veil from heaven, protecting the lovers from the cares of the outside world.

Though the emperor knew many royal positions for tenderness and sharing, he soon found he was most content when merely lying atop his bride. For in this way, he discovered – as many lovers have discovered since the beginning of time – he could lie with his bride filling his strong arms while their secret parts entwined in a coital union. Their mouths could exchange deep kisses while the emperor ran his fingers through her soft, golden hair. But what thrilled the emperor most of all, was that while they assumed this entwining embrace – belly to belly, mouth against mouth, his stiff member penetrating deep into her secret flower as her legs wrapped around his waist – the soft, round breasts of his bride could press full against the emperor's fiery heart. How long had he waited for a night like this to ease his torment? The emperor no longer knew. The years of loneliness, of yearning in his loins, seemed as remote now as if they had never been part of his experience.

Many times the sands slipped through the hourglass that night, and many times the emperor discharged his fiery seed into the flower of his eagerly responsive bride. The more he shared his fire with her, the more his creature seemed to glow. The emperor was delighted with the passion of his manhood, how it never seemed to wane; no sooner would he discharge his royal seed in her than his member would grow thick and he would penetrate her flower again.

So lost in each other's arms were they, so entranced with all their senses, that the emperor did not notice the high priest enter the sacred chamber until he was readily perceived to be standing just beyond the heavenly veil.

Angered by the intrusion, and protective of the modesty of his bride, the emperor displayed a temper previously unknown to the high priest.

"Your Majesty will forgive me, I'm sure," he apologized, "but there's the matter of the sacred pearl –"

The emperor, stricken by a raw sensation of guilt over having induced his innocent bride to betray heaven with him and swallow the sacred pearl, answered haltingly, "What about it?"

"Your Majesty, the sands have slipped through the hourglass twenty-four times; surely she has released a pearl by now."

"Of course she's released a pearl! She's my bride, mine for eternity."

"Yes, Your Majesty, but – "

"But what?!"

"You never sent for me. We must offer the pearl back to the sea as a gesture of gratitude and thanksgiving."

The emperor was more guilt-stricken still. "I've seen to the matter already", he declared.

The high priest tried hard to hide his feelings of alarm.

"I told you, the matter's been seen to!" the emperor insisted. "I saw no reason to part from my bride for even a moment longer than was necessary, so I tossed the pearl into the lagoon myself and gave a prayer of thanks. I assure you, it was heartfelt. No doubt, Your Grace will understand my sense of urgency."

The high priest could not hide his dismay; still, he approached his emperor with caution. "I dare say, that's not the manner in which those things are usually done, but I suppose what matters is that the ritual was carried out, so that heaven and the mighty sea will be appeased."

The emperor replied hotly, "They're appeased."

"I beg Your Majesty to suffer me just a moment longer."

"What is it?!" the emperor shouted.

"It's the matter of your people, Your Majesty. They tire from the constant day. Might you consider donning your robe for a time, if only for the sake of your people?"

"I have lived my whole life for the sake of my people. Surely they can grant me a little patience in this instance!"

And that was all the emperor deigned to offer on the subject.

Finally, it came to pass that the emperor grew tired. He slipped into his robe and lay with his head on a pillow next to his bride and closed his weary eyes. But it seemed his eyes had only been closed a moment when he felt his member stiffen and again become thick.

He opened his eyes in time to see his beautiful bride climb astride him, burying his protruding shaft deep within her hot flower.

And, indeed, it was hot. It was so hot and so deep that the emperor wished to lose himself completely in her warmth, be absorbed into her body and drift to a never-ending sleep. His eyes closed at last, filled with the vision of her nakedness, her full breasts gently sloping down, and her round golden belly undulating enticingly as she pleasured herself on his royal member.

When the emperor awoke, he feared he was dying. He did not know how long he had slept, but he sensed it had been an inordinately lengthy period.

He was chilled to the bone. He reached down to the floor for a coverlet, but it did little to warm him.

His bride was awake and lying cheerfully beside him. A heat came from her radiant glow that beckoned the emperor close. He took her in his arms and kissed her and, without even knowing it, drifted back into a deep sleep.

"Your Majesty will forgive the intrusion."

It was the high priest again, shaking the emperor gently by the sleeve of his black silk robe.

"Your Majesty, wake up."

"Yes, what is it?" The emperor tried to focus on the high pries, but his brain longed for more sleep.

"Your Majesty, we have some sort of crisis. The land has been stuck in what can best be described as a grey half-twilight for many days. The people grow restless and cold. They threaten to chop down the entire forest for fire."

The emperor went to great lengths to understand the high priest's words, but all he really understood was the direness of his tone.

"Surely the blissful sleep after the wedding night has gone on long enough", the high priest entreated him. "The robe, Your Highness. Your people could use some sun."

"Fine," the emperor managed to reply, and with a tremendous physical effort he stripped away his black robe and fell dead asleep.

In a moment, the troubled high priest had returned. "Your Majesty, it didn't help. The grey twilight remains."

The emperor's powerful will aroused him from his deep need for sleep. He pulled his bride to him, as he suffered now from an extreme chill, but she was so fiery hot, he sprang away from her.

"Your Majesty! What is it?" The high priest made no pretence to mask his alarm. "You look so ashen and pale."

"It's her!" he cried, fearing for the wellness of his bride. "She positively burns with fever!"

The emperor's bride lay happily among the royal pillows.

"She seems quite well to me. She's glowing and rounder than ever."

"No", the emperor spluttered wearily. "She's on fire. Touch her."

When the high priest laid his hand on the bride's arm, he pulled it sharply away, as if he had been burned. "You're right! She burns with fever. Yet you are the one who looks ill."

"I've made a grave error in judgment, Your Grace", the emperor struggled to confess. "I tried to prolong my happiness and still I am dying. You see how she steals my fire? Only now she will perish, too; my fire is consuming her."

The high priest urged the emperor to explain.

"The pearl", he managed to say. "I cheated heaven. I made her swallow the sacred pearl. I tried to hide from my fate by making her consume the product of our passion. I fear now that it is burning her alive."

The high priest ran from the chamber to summon the nearest palace ladies. "You must fetch the magician. There's been a tragic accident. The emperor and his bride are quite ill."

Amid great weeping and hysteria, the emperor and his bride were draped in ceremonial robes and gingerly transported to the teakwood verandah, where they were placed on a sacred mat.

The magician was summoned and he arrived in a burst of iridescent light and a cloud of jasmine smoke.

When it was revealed to the magician how the emperor had attempted to betray the will of heaven, he demanded that the court disperse, even the high priest, and gather in the inner sanctum to pray for the emperor's soul.

When the magician was alone with the emperor and his bride, he gently shook the emperor, who had once again drifted into a deep sleep.

"You have been a fool", the magician declared quietly. "You had all that heaven allowed and still you wanted more."

"I know", the emperor confided. "I've seen my mistakes played out behind my eyes in quite vivid and remorseful dreams. I have an unbearable burden in my heart. I no longer mind that I am dying, but I have sealed the fate of my innocent bride, and who will look after my people when I am gone? See how the stars are forever approaching from the East, yet they never arrive? It is not day, it is not night; will my people be forever trapped in this twilight? And my poor bride. She burns with enough fire to light an empire, yet she cannot shine and save my kingdom."

"I know what must be done", the magician replied, seemingly unmoved by the emperor's plight. "How, may I ask, is the condition of your heart? Have you left anything undone? Have you said your prayers for your people?"

The emperor nodded gravely. "But what about my bride? I will never be ready to tell her good-bye."

"Your Majesty," the magician scolded him, "you are such a foolish man! Your destiny has never been anything but that: your destiny. I told you your love was ordained by fate to last throughout eternity, but love requires you first to surrender. Nothing you do can exert your will over the will of heaven. All you've managed to create in the meantime is human misery and delay."

The emperor's eyes edged with tears. He summoned great strength within himself, braved his creature's hot fire, kissed her tender mouth one last time and surrendered to the will of heaven.

He tried to contain his tears as he watched his court magician conjure an incantation over his blissfully ignorant bride. And then, with not even a moment to prepare, a mighty gale of wind swept across the teakwood verandah and the emperor's treasured creature shot up to the sky as a crackling ball of fire.

Day dawned instantly on the land and all that was left behind for the emperor to cling to was his creature's sacred pearl; the treasure their joy had created had withstood the powerful fire.

It is said that in his profound grief the emperor swallowed his creature's pearl. And as the magician disappeared in a cloud of jasmine smoke, and a gentle breeze tinkled the tiny silver chimes in the tender plum blossoms, the emperor wept bitter tears, and did not stop weeping, even after the sands had slipped through the hourglass twelve more times.

And it is further said that so great was the emperor's remorse, as he could no longer provide night for his tired people who toiled in constant daylight, so bitter were his tears, that he finally dissolved into salty water that trickled down into his majestic lagoon and was carried out to sea.

It was then that the mighty waves leaped and swirled and tossed a sacred glowing pearl far into the western sky, at last bringing on the gentle evening. And it was this sacred pearl, which we've come to call our moon, that was loved in ancient times by a tender, tired people, who came to call it, affectionately, the Emperor of Night.